A VERY MAFIA CHRISTMAS

STANDALONE ENEMIES TO LOVERS HOLIDAY ROMANCE

L. STEELE

1

QUESTION: WHEN DOES CHRISTMAS COME BEFORE THANKSGIVING?

(TURN TO THE END OF THE BOOK FOR THE ANSWER)

Christian

I raise my arm and throw the snifter of whiskey against the wall. The glass shatters, and the amber liquid taints the wall; just like Xander's blood had stained the ground when I dragged him from the car, which had caught fire after the car bomb had gone rogue.

My twin's gone. He's really gone, and he's never coming back.

I turn to the bar counter, grab a bottle of Macallan, and fill up another glass. I take a sip and the alcohol blazes a trail of warmth to my belly. He's gone. My twin brother is no longer here to share a drink with me. Fact is, I can't recall the last time we had a drink together. He'd been busy, focused on his painting, and I... I had been consumed by my role as the *Consigliere* for the *Cosa Nostra*.

The last month had been a bitch with my asshole of a father trying his best to destabilize Michael, my oldest brother. Michael had finally managed to kill him and take over as the Don... The person who had been hurt most in the process?

Xander. My twin, my other half... My soulmate from before we were born... We had shared a womb, but we hadn't shared our thoughts with each other since moving to Los Angeles.

What I remember most about that time are the overwhelmingly bright days, the blue skies, not being able to walk anywhere, playing in the backyard with our brothers Massimo, Luca, Seb, and Adrian; while Michael was already at university. I also learned to paint, something I quickly found I had no aptitude for, while Xander? He took to it like it was his life.

We used to ride the school bus back home to eat the leftovers Nonna had left us. Often, she would be off at some meeting or another, while our older brothers already had girlfriends and football games.

We'd eat, and I'd watch Spiderman on TV, while Xander much preferred to sit in the back garden and gaze at the leaves.

Even then, he was already a dreamer, my little brother.

As we grew older, we finally decided to move to different rooms. Or rather, I decided to move to another room, because it felt like... Well, we needed privacy to jerk off, if you must know.

Still, whenever I stayed over in his room, he'd lend me his guitar—I don't have a single musical bone in my body—and to placate him, I'd pick at the strings. His room was always spotless. And mine? I hated picking up after myself. Nonna grew tired of asking me to straighten out my room. Instead, when she couldn't bear it any longer, she'd ask Xander to put my things away, and he'd oblige.

I'd return from baseball practice—yep, that's how American I had become—to find everything back in its place. Then, I'd be unable to find anything and would have to holler at Xan to help me out. Which he would.

That's how good-natured my little brother was.

The diagram of our life was a complete circle. After yet another bout, when he picked up my damn room again, I would reciprocate by making him peanut butter and jelly sandwiches.

We gamed together, shared our love for weird songs; he had started to paint while I had moved on to consuming the kind of online content which is strictly off-limits to a teenager but the kind of stuff a teenage boy thrives on.

It's not that we never fought, but it wasn't often. We were two wild kittens grown into cats who, at first, were consciously caring and kind to each other. Enough that he told me when I wasn't me.

But somewhere along the line, as in the case of many siblings, we had grown apart, and I never realized it. Not until I found out later that he had secrets in his life which he didn't feel like he could share with me. My twin, my soulmate, my brother. We were each other's life partners and also lifesavers… Until we weren't. Until I failed him.

Now he's gone. My twin is gone, and I miss him. On the other hand, it's good the *stronzo* is no longer here. If he were around, no doubt, he would talk me out of the plan I intend to implement.

2

A day later

Aurora

"Open the door!" The banging on the front door reaches me. I stare at the coffee table wedged against it. That and the bolt I had dropped in place is all that's preventing the asshole on the other side from getting through to me.

It'll hold the door, surely, won't it? I glance around the living room space but don't see any means of escaping. Not that I haven't checked every inch of this house in the last few weeks that I have been held here as a prisoner. Every window is barred, and the door to the terrace on the first floor is sealed tight. The only way in or out of this house is through the front door. The door upon which the man who is trying to enter is currently leaning his weight.

"Shit!"

The door creaks as he puts his shoulder to it.

"Open the fucking door, Aurora, or I'm gonna break it down."

"Who"—my voice cracks, and I clear my throat—"who's there?"

"You know who it is. Who else comes to this house, except me?" Christian's lowers his voice to a growl. "When I get through, I'm going to teach you such a lesson you aren't going to be able to sit down for days!"

"Oh?" My stomach trembles. "OH!" I blink as the full meaning of his words sinks in. My heart rate ratchets up, and moisture laces my core. I should not find that so hot. Why do I find that such a turn-on?

"How can I be sure who it is if you don't tell me who you are? Not like I can recognize your voice or anything, you know."

"Is that right?" His tone is almost lazy now.

Like he's realized I'm playing a game and has decided to go along with it. My belly twists. I rub my damp hands on my thighs. Why the hell did I decide to stop him from coming in? I should have known it would be futile, that nothing I say or do will deter him.

The door creaks again and pushes against the coffee table, which moves forward by an inch.

"Oh, hell!" I race toward the coffee table and push against the door to hold it in place. Something slams into the door from the other side again. The doorframe shudders, the bolt across the door shivers, and the coffee table moves forward by another inch. I yelp and take a step back.

"Don't fucking make me wait, Aurora," Christian growls.

I shiver. Even through the heavy wood of the double doors, the menace rolls off of his voice. Goosebumps pop on my skin. My toes curl. Shit, this should not turn me on so much.

That… that mean edge to his tone, the promise of punishment when he finally gets through… I shouldn't want it so much.

"Last chance, Aurora. Open the door or—"

"Or," I call out, "what are you going to do, eh?"

"Do you really want to find out?" He lowers his voice to a hush, but I can still hear him. "Do you, Aurora?"

Yes.

Yes.

"No," I yell back. "I'm tired of being kept a prisoner here. Tired of being held without anyone telling me how long I'm going to be here."

There's silence for a beat, then another.

"It's why I've come here," he retorts, "to tell you what's going to happen next."

"Do you think I'm going to believe you?"

"I hope you're standing clear, Aurora," he says in a low-pitched voice. "I'm coming through."

I straighten and stare at the door. He's joking. He's not really going to batter down that door, is he?

"Get back, Aurora," he growls. "Now!"

I jump and stumble back just as he smashes into the door. The wood creaks and groans. The coffee table I've wedged against the door screeches forward. I yelp and slide back a few more steps. Just in time. For there's another crash.

The entire door whines, and the bolt jumps then falls off right before the middle of the door cracks.

I scream, turn and race toward the bedroom, then close the door and bolt it. I sink down against it, and my shoulders shudder.

Shit, shit, shit. What is wrong with me? Why did I try to shut him out? I should have known I couldn't win, that he'd find a way to come inside. But the truth is, I'm tired of sitting here in this house, trying to figure out what will happen to me next. Tired of not knowing my fate. Tired of being punished for helping out my friend Karma. She wanted to escape her husband, the then Capo —now Don Michael Sovrano—and of course, I couldn't say no to helping her.

I knew how dangerous it was to do so. To go against the leader of the *Cosa Nostra* is to bring death to yourself and to your family... I knew it, and yet, something in me wasn't able to turn her down. I recognized another woman in need, and something in me snapped.

Maybe it's all the time spent as a woman in the heart of the Mafia. Knowing that we are often seen as disposable. Interchangeable. Good only to procreate, as wives, as mistresses, as objects to be lusted after, but never respected as individuals with our own minds, who can control our own destinies.

And you know what? I, sure as hell, am going to control my future... At least, that's what I thought... That's what I had aimed for during all of my years growing up. And while the Capo had paid off my father's debts and paid for me to go to medical school in London, and I had accepted it then because it seemed like the only way to find my way out of the situation that I was born into—I don't owe him anything. Right?

Clearly, he'd done it so he could indenture my family, ensure that he'd bought our loyalty and that of any future generations. Only, I'm not going to submit to my fate.

It's this streak of defiance in me that had urged me to help Karma. I had treated her when she'd been brought into the hospital in Palermo. She'd been faking the illness, of course, as she'd warned me she would. I had examined her, nevertheless, so the situation would appear as genuine as possible, and discovered that she was pregnant.

I hadn't been able to stop myself from revealing that to her husband. We had returned to her room and found her gone... And the Capo would have killed me on the spot except... His brother, Christian, had intervened. He'd saved my life that day, and I suppose I should be grateful for it.

Only, I'm not sure about his intentions toward me. Since that day, he's shadowed me wherever I go. Oh, he hasn't made a move on me or anything like that... I wish he would. That way, I'd know what he wants from me.

No, he simply watches me with that gray-blue gaze of his that seems to peer into my soul. Wonder what he sees, though? Probably my larger-than-normal bust, no doubt. It's the bane of my life. Every time I want to be taken seriously for my work as a doctor, my breasts get in the way. Hell, during my final examinations, where I had to present my paper to a team of supervisors—all men, of course—the assholes couldn't take their gazes off of my tits. I've learned it's best to play them down by wearing high-collared shirts. Not that it helps.

I also have thick hips and thighs that could rival Roger Federer's. No, they aren't hairy. They are simply quite heavy, and it's not due to muscles. And yeah, I think they look better on Federer. On me, they just look large. Overall, I'm told that my figure is a classical hourglass one. Which I hate. Honestly, I'd do anything to have Karma's slender, svelte figure, all gentle curves and planes, not to mention a flatter chest. But I digress.

He's the person who accompanied me when I went to see Karma while she was pregnant.

Subsequently, she'd lost her child in an unfortunate incident when her car had been rigged with a bomb which, luckily for her, had turned out to be defective. Although... It had killed Xander, Christian's twin. Turned out, it was their father who was behind it. The chain of events had entrenched Christian even more firmly in the inner circle of the *Cosa Nostra*. So, the question is, why is this man, who can have any woman in the city—hell, on the continent, even—beating down the door to my bedroom?

"Go away," I yell as I slap my hands over my ears. "Get the hell away from me...you...you asshole!"

"Now, play nice, Flower," Christian drawls. I can hear him from the other side of the bedroom door.

Hell, I can all but feel the heat of his body as it permeates through the wood, which is likely my imagination. But every time I've been near him, it's as if I've stepped past a furnace. The man has so much vitality, he can probably light up an entire Christmas tree by his proximity. I snort.

That's fanciful thinking. Probably because I spent Christmas Day shut up in here, feeling sorry for myself. Hell, even criminals in jails get to celebrate Christmas. I spent it locked up here, and except for the brief time on Christmas Eve when Christian came in to check on me and lent me his phone so I could call Karma, I was alone. At least, I didn't starve. The fridge is always full of food, as is the pantry, so there's more than enough to eat.

Still, it didn't fill the void of being alone, on the one day of the year when every family is together. Well, every family except my own. We have never been big on Christmas. Mostly, my father would be on call due to one emergency or another. I can count on my fingers how many Christmas Eve's he'd actually been home. So, it had been my mother, sister, and me. And then, my mother had died, and while I had tried to make an attempt at arranging festivities, I have to admit, I hadn't been very successful.

Karma had wanted to organize a Christmas gathering, but Xander's death, and then her losing her baby, had put a damper on that. Christian had updated me that she was spending time in London and had even given me his phone to speak with her. A favor I hadn't wanted to accept, but which I didn't turn down, starved of company as I had been.

But everyone has a limit and I have reached mine. No way, am I going to allow myself to be shut up inside here. I want to leave this prison, go see my family, lead a normal life … Or else … I'm willing to die. Yeah, not being dramatic here…

When you live in the heart of the Mafia community, death is as much a part of life as going out to dinner is. And I—like it or not—am one of them.

I grew up surrounded by macho guys who think they own the world. And you know what? I have spent enough time among them to be able to play them at their own game. I'm not going to let one of them scare me, no matter that he happens to be big, brooding, growly, and sexy and … hot … and that he turns me on by just a glance. I'm not going to let my attraction to him get in the way. No. I'm going to tell him exactly where he can shove this awareness he seems to have for me, the one which has him pushing his shoulder into the bedroom door and applying his weight so the entire barrier shakes.

"Open the door, Flower," he rumbles, "or I'm going to break this down and come inside, and then you're going to regret shutting me out."

Is that right? I jump up to my feet and tuck my elbows into my side.

"Last chance," he warns. "Open. The. Door."

I spin around, unlock the bedroom door, and yank it open. Just as he lunges forward.

3

Christian

I dive forward just as she pulls the door open. I careen through the doorway and toward her, managing to swerve at the last minute. Still, I don't avoid her completely, and my shoulder brushes hers. She yells out in surprise, and her body hurtles toward the floor. I grab her and manage to get my body under hers as we hit the floor.

The back of my head hits the floor, and the breath rushes out of me. On the other hand, it may be because of the soft curves that tremble against my chest, her breath that shivers against my throat, or her sweet scent like honeysuckle and crushed rose petals that teases my nostrils and goes straight to my head. The blood rushes to my groin and my cock thickens. She pushes off of me, or at least tries to, for I've thrown my arm around her waist and hold her in place.

"Let me go," she snarls.

"No." I sit up, then wince when the bump on the back of my head protests. I ignore the pain, push myself up to standing, still holding her close.

"What the hell are you doing?" she hisses as I head toward the bed with her in my arms.

"Let me the hell go," she slaps her palm against my chest, "right now."

"Fine." I lower my arms, and she hits the floor on her ass.

"Ow!" She grunts, then stares up at me, a shocked expression on her face.

"You … you dropped me?" she stutters. "Like, honest to God, you allowed me to crash to the floor?"

"You asked me to let you go," I remind her. "I was only obliging you."

"Asshole," she snaps, then pushes up to stand to her full height, which still means she hits somewhere below my breastbone.

Gesù Cristo, but she's tiny and also very angry right now. Her cheeks are flushed, her hair awry about her features.

She pushes a strand away from her face. "You're a dick, you know that?" She scowls.

"Glad you recognize that."

"Argh!" She makes a noise at the back of her throat. "And insufferable, not to mention, you're so full of yourself that if anyone were to prick your skin, you'd take off."

"Take off?"

"Yeah, all that hot air which you carry around would catapult you into the stratosphere, no doubt."

I glare at her, then can't stop the surprised chuckle that rumbles up my chest. "You're funny," I murmur.

"You're annoying."

'You're on my turf."

"You're in my house," she shoots back.

"A house you're living in, thanks to my intervention on your behalf. If not, you'd be dead by now."

Her features flush further. "Should I be grateful to you for that? I bet you have your reasons for stepping in."

"If nothing else, you're smart." I curl my lips. "So, you'll realize that I'm being very serious when I say that I'm going to punish you."

"Whatever." She huffs. "Why are you here anyway?"

"It's my place, remember? I can come and go as I want."

She firms her lips, then spins around and walks out of the room. I follow her into the kitchen. She reaches the espresso maker, tops it up with coffee grounds, and places it on the stove. She grabs two cups and saucers, places them on the counter, then turns to me. "What do you want from me?"

"Marry me."

"What?" Her gaze widens. "What did you say?"

"Marry me." I allow my smile to widen. "Not for real, of course."

"Of course." She nods. "So, you want me to pretend to marry you?"

"For ten days."

"What happens in ten days?"

"I'll be able to convince my older brother and my nonna that we're really serious about each other. After which time, you are free to go your own way."

"Wait? Ten Days? That's too short a time to convince them that we are serious about each other."

I scratch my chin. "You're right."

"I am?" She scowls.

"Thirty days." I cross my arms over my chest.

"What the—!" She gapes. "What do you mean?"

I raise a shoulder. "It's a respectable amount of time and long enough."

"Long enough for what?"

"To convince them that we mistakenly thought that we were in love."

"But we're not in love," she points out.

"Precisely." I nod. "Which is why, when we decide to get the marriage annulled, no one will raise an eyebrow. In fact, given that, by then, we'd have proven to be incompatible, and it will be all too believable that," I peer into her face, "our marriage was a complete mistake."

"And what's the benefit of that?"

"They won't bother me about getting married to anyone else for a long time after that."

She purses her lips. "Somehow, I can't see you being bothered by anyone about being married."

"Have you met my nonna?" I tilt my head. "She's been planning our weddings from the moment each of us were born. And now that Michael's married, and with Xander's passing…" I firm my lips.

"You were saying?" she prompts.

"Nothing." I straighten my spine. "Fake marriage. You and me. That's all you need to know."

"Hmm…" She takes in my features. "What's in it for me?"

I glare at her. "Really?" I snap. "You dare ask me that?"

She pales but doesn't glance away. "Yes," she says in a firm voice, "I need to know what's in it for me."

I take a step toward her and she leans back, only there's nowhere for her to go so she presses back and into the counter. I close the distance between us, plant my hands on the counter, and cage her in.

"You were saying?"

"I was asking a question, actually." She tips up her chin. "What's in it for me, Christian?"

I peer into her features, and her pupils dilate. Her brown eyes lighten until they seem almost golden in this light. I lean in closer until my breath raises the hair on her forehead. I run my finger down the side of her cheek, and she shivers.

"Don't," she murmurs, "don't try to distract me."

"Oh, so I do distract you?"

"Don't change the topic."

I step back, and the breath rushes out of her.

"Your life, Aurora. You get a new lease on life."

"So," she furrows her forehead, "if I pretend to be your wife for thirty days, I'll be free to leave and live as I want?"

I nod slowly. "If you fulfill all of the conditions, and provided you put up enough of a performance that my nonna and brothers are convinced of the veracity of our relationship."

She bites down on her lower lip, and hell, if my gaze isn't drawn to her glistening flesh. Why the hell does this woman affect me so? She's only a convenience, after all. Someone to use and discard. So I can go back to the life I prefer to lead. To be surrounded by enough pussy so I can forget I lost my twin brother. The other half of my soul. The one who's been with me since before we were born.

Xander and I were so different, yet so alike. He was the artist, and I'm the numbers guy. It's why steering the finances of the *Cosa Nostra* fell to me. If there's one thing I'm good at, it's getting the numbers to speak to me. Numbers don't lie. They can't hide. They can't hurt you like our father did.

After Michael left to study in the States, my father had turned his anger on us. Luca, our second oldest brother, had gotten the brunt of it. Massimo, our middle brother, had already grown big and tall enough that our father didn't dare hurt him. But Xander and me? We were still small and young enough that he knew he could hurt us without fear of retaliation.

Perhaps it's because I was older by a few minutes that I felt responsible for both of us. I had tried to protect Xander from being physically beaten up by our father, and I mostly succeeded. I still have the scars to show for it too... I saved him then, but when he was killed by the car bomb that our father had meant for Michael's wife Karma, I wasn't able to go to his rescue. The bomb was faulty, but a piece of metal had embedded in his chest and killed him immediately. Karma had been in the car, and she managed to escape, but she was pregnant and had lost her child. We've all suffered.

But losing Xander... It's a trauma that haunts me, that sticks to me, that accompanies me day and night, like a shadow which refuses to peel away from me. I'll never be the same again, never be able to see myself in the mirror without seeing my twin brother. Never be able to experience life without thinking that he'll never be able to see, smell, and taste life. It should have been me who died in that incident, not him.

Me who was buried under the earth, not him.

I don't deserve any happiness, not when Xander won't get to experience it.

I should turn away from life itself… Except, that's not what Xander would have wanted. It's for him that I will continue living… Doesn't mean I have to let myself feel, though. It's for him that I will support my family and help Michael consolidate his position as the new Don of the *Cosa Nostra*.

Michael killed our father… Too bad I never had the opportunity to do so. I should feel some level of satisfaction, considering it was our father who was behind rigging the car, the reason that Xander had died, but all I feel is a numbness. Like I'm not in my body. Like nothing else matters except trying to get through life. Trying to swallow down the grief that threatens to overwhelm my every waking moment. And her… How dare she try to infiltrate the nothingness that I have surrounded myself with since Xander died? Why is it that thoughts of her occupy my mind when I should have only enough space to mourn Xander?

"And if I don't?" She tips up her chin. "What if I disagree?"

I move so fast that she flinches. I wrap my fingers around her throat and haul her up to her toes. "If you value the life of your family then you'll do as I say." I tighten my grasp, "Besides, I don't recall giving you a choice, Flower."

She swallows, and I feel the movement against my fingers. Such a slender throat. How would it feel to have my cock sliding down it, hmm?

I tighten my grip, and the color fades from her cheeks. A soft sound emerges from her mouth. She parts her lips, and I take in her flushed features, the contours of her pouty lower lip, and my balls throb. Fuck this, why the hell should I deny myself when I'm going to marry her anyway? Only temporarily, of course. Still… Soon, she will be my wife, and I'm going to take full advantage of it. I pull her even closer until her breasts are flush against my chest, then I lower my mouth to hers.

4

———

Aurora

He fits his mouth over mine, and he takes and takes. His kiss is exactly what I'd expect from a macho, chauvinist pig like him. He thrusts his tongue between my lips and swirls it against mine. His fingers around my throat tighten. He grips my hip, fits me in the cradle of his thighs, and his thick, hard cock stabs into my core. My belly trembles, my nipples harden into pebbles, my belly flip-flops, and *What the hell?*

I shouldn't get turned on. Why am I turned on by his rough handling? I don't feel anything for him. I don't want his hands on me, and yet, I can't stop myself from responding to how he expertly swipes his tongue across the seam of my lower lip, over my teeth, how he drinks from me as if he's trying to suck down the very essence of me, consume me, possess me, ravish me—claim me...

"No." I try to pull away, but his grasp on my hip tightens. Surely, I'm going to bruise there? I slap against his shoulder, and he widens his stance. He yanks me even closer to him until it seems like every part of me is pinned to him, connected to him, reliant on him, already. My pussy clenches, and moisture laces my core. Heat flushes my skin, and I know I have to pull away from him. If I don't, I'll lose myself in his dominance, his mastery, his ability to play my body like a musical instrument. A piano whose keys he'll caress, and strike, and hammer at until it plays the tune he wants. And I'm not going to do that. No way.

I bring down my foot on his boot. I'm only wearing wedges, but it must hurt a little, for he grunts. His grip loosens, but before I can pull away, his lips soften. He stares into my eyes, and in the depths of his, I see something flare. Something hot, something needy… Something almost helpless and vulnerable… Vulnerable? Hah! There's nothing weak about this man; not in how he holds me, or in how the powerful columns of his thighs bracket mine, or how he rubs his thumb across my throat in slow circles. Goose bumps pop on my skin. I draw in a shuddering breath, and my breasts push further into the hard planes of his chest. It's as if every sculpted ridge of those unyielding pecs is imprinted into my skin.

He pulls back, still holding my gaze, his mouth so close to mine that we share breath. Untouching. He simply stares into my eyes, his own even darker, somehow blacker, a shiny polished mirror in which I can see myself. The skin across his cheekbones stretches tight, and there's a furrow between his eyebrows, as if he's somehow confused by what just happened. His eyes, somehow, reflect some of the confusion I'm feeling. I reach up to touch his cheek, and he flinches. His lips firm and his jaw tics. He releases me so quickly that I stumble. But he doesn't right me. He puts distance between us, and I manage to steady myself.

My lips throb, and I can't stop myself from taking in his mouth, a mouth that I know now could bring me to dizzying heights of pleasure. Too bad they are attached to a man who is part of an institution I abhor. An organization I plan to break away from as soon as possible. I'll do anything to get my freedom, including pretending to be his wife.

"Fine," I say in a low voice, "I'll do it."

"If all it took was a kiss to get you to agree, then I wonder what else you'll submit to when I have you completely."

"I won't."

"Oh?" Something glints in the depths of his eyes. "You sure about that?"

Oh, hell, the last thing I need is for him to see me as a challenge. Still, I can't stop myself from tipping my chin in defiance. "Absolutely."

"We'll see." He raises a shoulder. "Not that it matters to me either way. There are enough women out there who'll willingly spread their legs for me."

"So why choose me for this…this farce?"

"Because you owe me." He dusts his sleeves as if he's wiping the feel of me off of himself. "Thirty days, Flower. For thirty days, you'll do as I say."

I pivot, switch off the flame under the Bialetti, then scowl at him over my shoulder. "I agreed to be your fake wife, not your slave."

His lips kick up. "Those are my terms, sweetheart. Take it or leave it."

"Jerk." I turn on him. "What else do you expect from me during this time?" I curl my fingers at my sides. "You may as well lay it all out now."

"We'll be married in a proper wedding in church—"

"What?" I stare at him in horror. "No, no, no, no, no. I agreed to pose as your fake wife—"

"The imperative word there is 'wife.'"

"I did not agree to marry you in a church ceremony," I protest.

"The only way for this to work is if the rest of my family buys into the story."

"We'll act as husband and wife; surely, that should be enough."

"Do you think my nonna is going to let us off without a church wedding?"

"If you think I'm going to agree to that, you have another think coming," I snap back.

"Are you saying no?"

Yes.

Yes.

I shake my head. "Anything else you're not telling me about this arrangement?"

To my right, the Bialetti begins to bubble as the steam rises through the funnel. The espresso must be bubbling over and into the carafe. I don't turn away from him to check it, though. Instead, I hold his gaze as he raises a shoulder.

"Maybe, maybe not." He smirks. "My prerogative."

Anger flares through my veins. My heart thuds in my chest. How dare he treat me like this? Damn it, I'm a qualified doctor. I went to London to study and survived the winters there. Hell, I survived years of residency, not to mention a stint in the ER. I have saved the lives of people, and now this … this … ass treats me like I'm worth nothing. All of my senses hone in on him. Only when my palm connects with his face do I realize that I've slapped him. Oh hell. I stare at the fingerprints that bloom on his cheek. Shit, this is not good, not good at all.

Anger thrums off of him. I take a step back, and his gaze intensifies.

"That was a mistake, Flower," he drawls.

"Don't call me that," I hiss back.

"I'll call you what I want, when I want, and you'll answer to it."

"No."

"Yes." He lowers his voice to a hush, "Come here." He crooks a finger.

I shake my head.

He glares at me, and my stomach twists. Jesus, why did I have to antagonize this man? Why couldn't I simply agree to whatever he wants? After all, the path of least resistance is the best in these situations, isn't it? And then… What would set me apart from my mother and the rest of the women married to Mafia men, those who allow them to walk all over them and bear their suffering in silence?

I'm not like them. I am not. It's why I trained to be a doctor, so I could break out of this cycle. So I could ensure that my younger sister could have a better life than as part of a Mafia clan.

And now this … this asshole thinks he can simply order me around? He says he'll set me free if I do what he wants, but what guarantee do I have of that?

"Don't make me wait." He holds my gaze, and I can't stop myself from being drawn into those dark eyes. Bottomless, fathomless, impenetrable. Any signs of vulnerability I thought I'd seen in them are now gone. His eyes are flat, the look in them almost cruel. It's a relief, actually. I don't want to think of this guy as having a heart or emotions of any kind. I need to see him for what he really is. A Mafia guy, someone who likely kills for a living, someone on the wrong side of the law, someone who clearly doesn't have a conscience. If he did, he wouldn't manipulate me in this way. Wouldn't take me for granted and treat me like I'm an object to be possessed.

His gaze narrows on me, and he lowers his voice to a hush, "I won't ask again." A shiver runs down my back.

"Now," he snaps.

My feet hit the floor, and I close the short distance between us. Goddamn it, why do I feel compelled to obey his command? I stand in front of him and tip my chin up. I will not be cowed by him. I will not.

"You will do as I say, understand?"

I scowl.

"You feel me, Flower?"

Whatever. I curl my fingers into fists at my sides so I don't slap him again. I need to play it smart, just until I figure out a way out of here.

He peers into my eyes, and maybe whatever he sees there satisfies him, for he jerks his chin. "I'll send someone to mend the front door, and I'll have my men stand guard outside until then." He turns and stalks out of the kitchen.

"Wait," I call out. "I made enough espresso for both of us."

"You have it," he says without turning around. "You're going to need that and more to see you through the next few weeks."

Jerk. I stick out my tongue at his retreating back, then gasp in surprise when he glances at me over his shoulder. "Also, don't be late tomorrow."

"Tomorrow?"

"The Christmas gathering that Karma is organizing," he glances at me over his shoulder, "it'll be our first official outing as a couple."

I'd rather slit my wrists. The words are on the tip of my tongue, but I swallow it down.

"Seven pm, tomorrow." He looks me up and down, "I'll send you some dresses to try on."

"No thank you; I have my own dresses."
"You mean those rags that you wear."
"They are not rags," I protest.
"They are not fit for the future wife of a Mafia consigliere."
Right.
"And make sure your bags are packed; you'll be moving in with me after."
Turning, he walks away.

5

Aurora

The tomorrow that Christian was talking about turns out to be the delayed Christmas get-together that Karma and Michael are throwing for the clan. With Xander's death, Christmas itself wasn't celebrated. And while in most Italian families, the period of mourning would last almost up to a year, it seems the Sovranos have decided to go ahead with the celebrations, perhaps because they want to commemorate his life instead of mourning his passing? It's a sentiment I whole-heartedly approve of.

I had contemplated making Christian wait when he walked into the house promptly at seven pm. Only, he didn't give me a chance. He walked up the stairs and into my bedroom. When I protested, he told me to get used to it. What a dick!

Now he takes in my reflection, and his mouth falls open. Like, literally, he opens and shuts his mouth, and no words emerge. I turn to face him, place my hand on my hip, and allow him to sweep his gaze from the top of my auburn curls to my Gucci dress to my feet clad in the Ferragamo's he sent me.

Yeah, so they're borrowed feathers, but what the hell? Given what I'm going to put myself through over the next thirty days, it's the least I can do—embrace the designer wear he's so eager to shower on me. Only, he probably paid for the dress in blood, but that's something I can't afford to think of. Not when I need to make sure that I play my role so well that he doesn't suspect I'm looking for a way out.

So, I permit him to look his fill, noting his heavy-lidded gaze, the way his body stills as he sweeps his gaze up my body and back to my face. He stares at my mouth, and stares, and stares. Goose bumps shiver across my skin, and the blood thuds at my temples. A pulse flares to life between my legs, and I want to squeeze my thighs together, but I stop myself. No way am I allowing him to see the effect he has on me. It's bad enough that my nipples have beaded into pinpoints of pain, that my cheeks are flushed, and that I can hear the blood pumping in my ears.

I bite down on my lower lip, and his chest rises and falls. I tip up my chin, and he raises his gaze to mine. The silence stretches for a beat, another. I will not look away. Will not. My nerves stretch until I'm sure they're going to snap.

"Well?" I finally burst out. "What do you think?"

And why does his opinion matter anyway, hmm?

His lips curl, and he looks me up and down once more, his glance more cursory this time. "You'll do," he drawls.

"What the—!" I flush. "How dare you—?"

"Speak the truth?" He smirks, and anger sears my veins. My fingers tingle and hell, if I don't want to slap him and wipe that self-satisfied expression off of his face, but I don't. Instead, I tip up my chin and brush past him, in my six-inches high stilettos.

"Fuck you," I hiss as I flounce past, then gasp when he grips my wrist and tugs. I lose my balance and fall against him. The hard planes of his chest dig into my upper arm.

He yanks my arm behind my back and pulls me into him. "What did you say?" he says in that low mean voice that arrows straight to my belly and coils in my core.

"N-nothing." I swallow.

"Lying, Flower?"

"Always," I manage to choke out, "and especially to you."

He lowers his face to mine, until his mouth is exactly on top of mine. His breath sears my lips, and his scent, like dark coffee laced with brandy, over-whelms me. He's above me, all around me. The force of his dominance crashes into my chest and pins me in place. I can't stop the moan that bleeds from my lips.

"Christian," I whisper.

It seems to break the spell because he releases me. I stare up at him, my breath coming in pants.

He steps back, and cool air rushes over my heated skin.

"Let's go." He brushes past me and heads for the door.

I walk onto the terrace and take in the assembled guests. In one corner, Christian's brother Michael, who recently took over as Don of the *Cosa Nostra*, and his wife Karma are engaged in conversation with Michael and Christian's grandmother. The older woman says something that makes the couple laugh. The breeze blows over us, lifting Karma's lustrous locks and Michael's thick dark hair. They seem so carefree, so happy.

Considering everything they've been through, including the recent loss of their unborn child, they look well. Like the trials that they've been through have brought them together. I, more than anyone, know how deceptive appearances can be.

My mother had always put on a brave front, though she hated being part of the *Cosa Nostra*. Her father and his father before him were part of the Mafia, as was her husband. My mother and father had fought many nights when she begged him to leave, and he'd always refuse. My father was a doctor, who could have found a career outside of the *Cosa Nostra* if he wanted. But he simply didn't want to leave. He was steeped in the Mafia culture himself, felt beholden to the then Don—Michael and Christian's father—who had helped him out when in need. He felt it was his duty to stay and serve them. *"Chi lascia la strada vecchia per la nuova, sa quel che lascia, ma non sa quel che trova,"* so he loved to say.

Those who leave the old road for the new know what they leave behind, but not what they'll find.

It was another reason I couldn't wait to leave for medical college in the UK. In fact, I tried my best to lose my Italian accent while I was there and succeeded enough that I speak English like a true Brit. It's one of the things I'm proud of, that when someone speaks to me, they can't place me as being from Italy. Given the choice, I wouldn't have returned to Sicily, but my father needed help, and when he had asked, I couldn't refuse him.

Also, I felt guilty about leaving my sister behind when I went to England to study, even though I knew it was the right thing to do. If I could break out of the Mafia and find my own way, then Elena would have a chance to do the same. I'd made sure to come as often as possible to see her. And then my father had asked me to return, and I'd agreed.

Also, it fell in with the larger plan. So, I had to come back. It also helps that I felt compelled to help my family. And now, I'm walking into another family. One much more powerful and complicated when it comes to relationships.

Cassandra, Michael's housekeeper and someone who I have grown to know better over the past month, walks toward us with a tray of prosecco flutes. Christian takes one and offers it to me. Cass glances at me, sweeps her gaze over my outfit—a far cry from the simple pants and shirts that I normally favor—and her gaze widens.

She peers into my features. I see the question in them, but don't allow the expression on my face to change. Instead, I toss back the prosecco, emptying the glass in one go. The cool liquid slides down my throat and hits my stomach. The alcohol sets off a low burn in my belly. Tendrils of heat vibrate through my veins. Guess they weren't lying about alcohol helping you face anything, hmm? I place the now empty flute back on the tray that Cass is holding, then reach for a second glass. Christian grabs my wrist; I turn to him with a frown. "Let go of me," I hiss.

He jerks his chin at Cass, who glances between us. She seems like she is about to say something.

Then, his lips kick up in a smirk. "Watch what you say, Flower," he drawls, "my family is watching."

"Like I care?"

"Well, you should. Your life and your family's life depend on it."

I feel the blood drain from my face. "You wouldn't hurt them, would you?" I swallow.

"That's entirely up to you now, isn't it?"

Anger coils in my chest and pours through my veins. "I hate you," I whisper, "I really do."

Karma glances past Michael's nonna. She spots me and her features break into a smile, then she sweeps her gaze down to where Christian holds my wrist. I try to pull away, but of course, the jerk face only tightens his grip on me. Her eyebrows furrow. She narrows her gaze on me, and I glance away. That's when Christian moves toward them. He pulls me with him, so I have no choice but to follow him.

He pauses in front of Michael and Karma. "Don Sovrano," he declares, "meet the woman who has agreed to become my wife."

6

Aurora

"What?" Karma glances between us. "Is that true?"

I hesitate. Should I tell her the truth? More to the point, do I have the courage to say the truth in front of his family? I open my mouth, then close it. I shoot Christian a sideways glance to find him watching me with a curious expression. As if he's almost daring me to say something that would give him the chance to hurt me or my family. Me? I don't care so much. But my family? Damn him, but I'd never let him do anything to harm them.

"Aurora?" Karma prompts. "Are you going to marry him?"

"Yes," I say without looking away from Christian. "Yes," I clear my throat, "I'm going to be his wife."

Something blazes in the depths of his eyes, then he seems to bank it almost at once.

"Christian proposed to me earlier today, and I agreed. In fact..." I move closer to him until the tips of my Ferragamos brush his shoes. "He made me an offer that I couldn't refuse." I say the last few words in a deep voice.

"What was that?" Christian scowls.

"That," I tip up my chin, "was my best Godfather impression. Do you like it?"

His gaze intensifies. "I like everything about you, Flower." He lowers his voice to a hush, and my insides tremble.

"Oh my god," Karma breathes, "I knew it! I knew there was something between the two of you."

He releases my wrist, only to wrap his arm around my waist and draw me close. "Oh, there's something between us all right," he drawls, "something I can no longer deny."

"I'm so happy that we no longer have to hide our feelings for each other." I force my lips to curve. "He's positively head over heels in love with me. Isn't that right, honey-pie?"

He blinks.

Hope you like the nickname, asshole! "In fact, when he proposed, I couldn't believe it, but you know what he told me?"

"What?" Karma cries. "Tell me, please."

"That he couldn't live a minute more without me agreeing to become his wife. That he loves me so much he had to make sure to claim me before anyone else finds me."

His features wear a look of surprise, then his lips kick up in a smile. "You forgot the part where you insisted that we get married right away. "In fact, the ceremony is set for three days from now."

What? My gaze widens.

His lips curl in a smirk. "You couldn't wait to become mine, could you now, honey-pie?"

I try to pull away, but his arm holds me in place. "And you wanted me to announce it today to make sure everyone could make it to the wedding, right?"

I bring down the heel of my six-inch stiletto on his boot; he doesn't even wince.

His grip turns almost punishing. "Isn't that right, darling?"

I bare my teeth. "One-hundred percent, darling."

"Wait, did I hear that correctly?" Nonna's voice interrupts my thoughts. "Christiano, you're getting married, and this is the first I am hearing of it?"

Christian pales a little, and I stare. What the hell? Apparently, his grandmother really is a terror.

He loosens his hold on me. I step back, and he applies pressure on my back so I turn to face his nonna.

The older woman peers into Christian's face. "Well?" She scowls. "What do you have to say for yourself?"

"You are hearing about this now because we only decided to get married this morning."

"Hmph." She firms her lips. "And you are getting married in three days?"

He nods.

"In church?"

He nods.

"It takes a lot longer than that to arrange a church wedding in Italy," I hiss at him under my breath.

He stares at me. I stiffen. Of course, he's a Mafioso, so he probably has special dispensation on some trumped-up basis or another.

Christian presses his palm into the small of my back. The heat from his touch sinks through the fabric of my dress and into my skin. My heart begins to race. My pulse thuds at my temples. My God, if just his touch arouses me to this extent, how am I going to spend the next thirty days in close quarters with him and not allow myself to give into this attraction between us?

"I know how important a church wedding is to you, Nonna," Christian murmurs, "and my bride was very particular that we say our vows with God as our witness."

What the—! This man, he's milking the situation for all it's worth. I'm so going to make him pay for this.

Nonna turns her shrewd gaze on me. "Aurora, is it?" She takes in my features. "You're Doctor Garibaldi's daughter?"

I nod.

Her brow furrows. "Strange that we haven't met before."

Not so strange because I had made sure to stay clear of the Don's family.

"I was away studying medicine in London," I offer.

"Hmm…" Her lips purse. "How long have you known my grandson?"

I blink. Umm… What should I say? That he held me captive, then threatened my family so I'd have no choice but to agree? I open my mouth, but Christian beats me to it.

"Not long, Nonna. It was a *colpo di fulmine*," he murmurs. A bolt of lightning, as Italians refer to love at first sight.

I shoot him a sideways glance to find him wearing an intent expression on his face. "You know how it is, Nonna. I saw her, and I knew it was her. I wasted no time in asking her to marry me."

She surveys his features for a beat, another. Then, whatever she sees there must convince her, for she nods. "And you, Aurora?" She turns to me. "Was it a *colpo di fulmine* for you too?"

More like hate at first sight. I swallow down the words that threaten to tumble out of my mouth. "Yes." I nod. "I saw Christian, and I knew nothing would ever be the same again." Which is true; my life has turned upside down since I met him.

Nonna's gaze intensifies. "And you want to get married in church?"

"I already told you she does," Christian interjects.

"I want to hear it from Aurora," Nonna says in a sharp voice.

Shit, this woman sure is astute. I'm going to have to be on my toes if I want to make sure that she believes that our marriage is for real. "Yes." I tilt up my chin. "I want to marry Christian in church, in front of our families and God."

"It's settled then." Christian pulls me close and brushes his lips over my temple. "The second wedding in the family will take place in three days."

"Christian," Michael speaks for the first time since Christian made his announcement. "It's time you and I had a word, don't you think?"

Christian kisses my forehead. "Behave," he murmurs. I shoot him a glance, and he chuckles. "Or don't." His grin widens before he leans in to whisper in my ear, "In fact, I rather you don't. I'll take great pleasure in punishing you then."

He pivots on his heel and walks off.

7

____

Christian

"You are not fooling me," Michael drawls from his position near the bar.

All through the earlier conversation, when Nonna was quizzing me and Aurora, he didn't utter a word. Until the end. Then, as the reception got underway, he pulled me aside. He wanted to speak to me separately and ushered me into his study.

Now, he pours a healthy measure of the Macallan 18 into a glass and offers it to me. I walk over and take it as he cradles his tumbler.

"I have no idea what you mean." I take a sip of my whiskey and savor the warmth.

"That. What you said outside," he murmurs, "doesn't cut it for me."

"Oh?" I tilt my head. "What I do with my personal life is my issue."

"Until you trespass on mine."

"What's that supposed to mean?"

"Aurora allowed Karma to escape. If I hadn't found her, there's no telling what could have happened to her."

"And yet JJ did get to her, and under your watch."

Michael's fingers tighten around his glass; the skin around his mouth tightens. "Watch what you say, _fratellino_," he warns in a low voice.

"You know it's true," I insist.

"The fuck you trying to tell me, brother?" he growls.

"Just that it's time you forgave Aurora. Especially now that she's going to become family."

"Is that right?" He looks me up and down, "You expect me to believe that you've fallen in love with her and want to marry her in a matter of weeks?"

"Hell, you did the same thing with Karma, didn't you?"

He blows out a breath, "That was different," he rubs the back of his neck. "I kidnapped her—"

"Then held her captive and had her marry you to repay her father's debt."

"Your point being?" He glowers at me.

"You fell in love with Karma the moment you saw her. Why can't you believe that the same holds true for me?"

"Because you are only marrying her to save her life, and perhaps to get Nonna off your back. In fact, I wouldn't be surprised if this entire charade is one elaborate farce just so you can ultimately buy your freedom so none of us bother you about settling down.

"Your point being?" I arch an eyebrow.

"It's too soon after Xander's death. At least, give it a little more time to make sure that you are confident about your feelings."

"I am." I raise a shoulder. "I appreciate your concern, *fratellone*, but you are worrying unnecessarily. Aurora and I love each other. We want to marry, and we'd love your blessings … or not."

He rakes his gaze across my features, then as if satisfied with whatever he sees he nods. "Fine, but I'm going to be watching the two of you."

"Is that brotherly love or you two simply happy to see each other?" Luca's voice sounds from the doorway.

I glance up as he prowls over to the bar to join us. He's closely followed by Massimo, Seb, and Adrian.

"That," I scowl, "was a terrible joke, even for you."

"Just trying to break the tension." He raises a shoulder. "Don't blame me, I don't have much practice. Normally, I'd count on Xander to lighten the atmosphere but"—he stiffens— "shit, didn't mean to bring up his name." He peers into my features. "I swear, Christian, I am sorry."

"I'm not going to break if you talk about him, you know," I say mildly. I curl my fingers around my glass with such force that my knuckles strain.

"It's okay to miss him," Massimo comes up to stand next to him. "Hell, we all do, but it must be particularly hard on you, considering he was your twin."

"Hard?" I laugh. "Why should it be hard? Xander had his own life, and I had mine. He was the one who felt everything deeply. The curse of an artist, I suppose. Likely, if I had been the one who was killed, he would have fallen apart.

But me?" I curl my lips. "I'm made of stronger stuff. Hell, we all know that being in the Mafia it's possible that our lives could come to an end at any time. It just so happens that Xander was the first to bear the brunt of it."

"Is that what you think?" Seb murmurs. "That he was just unlucky enough to be at the wrong place at the wrong time?"

"Or the right place." I survey the contents of my glass. "He was in the prime of his youth, not even thirty yet, and he's gone. Think about it." I glance between their faces. "We'll forever remember him as young and beautiful. The gorgeous golden boy who we all knew was too good to be true. If there had been one person whose heart was genuine, whose spirit was always ready to help others, who felt every emotion so deeply that he had to take it out on his canvas… Hell, he was the man who helped old ladies across the street and rescued kittens. His sense of empathy was so big, his spirit so pure, both men and women were attracted to him. He was simply… Too good to be true. If he had lived longer, he would have probably simply been taken advantage of—"

"Or his goodness would have rubbed off on the rest of us," Adrian interrupts me. "He was the one man who, despite having grown up among us, in the heart of the Mafia, still managed to not be touched by the violence and death that we deal with every day."

"Until the same violence and death came for him." I toss back my drink, then set the glass on the table with a thump. "We couldn't protect him from his fate. I couldn't protect my own twin from the very evil that lurked within our family. Each of us were tainted by our father. The only person he didn't ever touch physically or emotionally was Xander. Every time Xander caught his eye, I managed to distract him. I took the punishment meant for him. I knew if our father ever got to Xander, he'd be hurt in a way that he would never be able to recover from. I thought that once we were grown up our father wouldn't be able to touch us. I was wrong. I should've known that it was too good to be true. I should've never stopped protecting him."

"It's not your fault." Luca grips my shoulder. "We—all of us—should have realized what our father was capable of. We all underestimated him."

"No one is to blame more than me," Michael says in a hard voice. "The buck stops with me. I am the Capo, the Don, the leader of the *Cosa Nostra*. I should have done a better job of protecting my brother, my wife, my unborn child." His jaw tics. "But…" he glances around at the faces of our brothers, "I also know that we can't dwell in the past. We must focus on the now, on what we have. On us." He stares at me. "On your future nuptials."

I arch an eyebrow. "I take it that means you are in favor of my wedding?"

"Doesn't mean that I'm convinced about the veracity of it, but yeah," Michael tilts his head, "it helps align us with what is to come, and for that alone I support it."

"A-n-d that's all it takes to move on. Death. Here one moment, gone the next, and life fucking moves on," I chuckle.

"You know that's not how it is." Luca frowns. "No one here is forgetting about Xander."

"Except we are all moving on."

Seb opens his mouth, and I shake my head. "You know it's true, all of you. Much as we want to remember him, it's with relief that we want to also move forward."

"It's called life," Luca offers. "It thrives, prospers, finds a way to move forward."

"And those who are not here with us are left behind."

"You are distraught." Michael scowls. "You're grieving. You're still not over what happened to Xander, and you're not able to give vent to it either."

"Oh, I know how to give vent to it all right." I place the glass on the counter, then straighten my shoulders. "In fact, I'm on my way to give vent to it right now."

I brush past Seb, who grabs my shoulder. "Don't do it," he warns me.

"You have no idea what I'm going to do."

"Oh, trust me, brother, I have a good idea." He twists his lips. "Xander might have been your twin, but when it comes to your twisted perversions, no-one knows about them better than I do."

"You don't know anything about me." I glare down at where his fingers grip me, then back at his face. He releases me and I brush past him.

"Christian," Michael calls out, "Seb is right. Whatever it is you want to do, think carefully before you act on it."

"Oh, trust me," I glance at him over my shoulder, "I have thought carefully enough about what I'm going to do, all right."

Turning, I leave.

8

Christian

I shove open the door to the safe house with my shoulder and haul her in.

"Let go of me." She huffs.

I tighten my grasp on her wrist as I half-carry, half-drag her toward the bedroom.

"What is wrong with you?" she yells. I ignore her voice. Ignore the hot sensation that stabs at my chest. Ignore the pinpricks of reason that slice through my mind. What are you doing? What are you doing? Yes, you're angry and pissed off, but does that justify what you're about to do right now? Does it warrant leaving the gathering half-way through, then shoving her into the car, not talking on the way here, despite the fact that she'd asked many times what was wrong? Despite the fact that she had narrowed her gaze on you, her own growing more worried by the second.

I stayed focused on the driving and didn't answer her, and she finally lapsed into silence. She firmed her shoulders, as if preparing for what was to come. Only she had no idea... No fucking clue just what I was going to unleash on her. So far, I had behaved myself. So far, I had kept myself in check—partly so she'd agree to the farce I had suggested. Not that she had a choice, but a compliant person is easier to manipulate. Which, again, doesn't explain why I'm yanking her toward her new bedroom and refusing to listen to her protests. I throw open the door to her room and push her inside. She stumbles forward, rights herself, only to turn on me.

"What the hell?" She rages, "What do you think you're doing?"

"Strip," I order.

"Excuse me?"

"You heard me." I look her up and down. "Take off your clothes, or I'll do it for you."

Color flushes her cheeks. "Not sure what game you're playing at, but—"

I take a step forward, close the distance between us, then hook my finger in the neckline of her dress and tug. The delicate fabric rips from neck to hem. She yelps, "What the—!"

I grip both sides of the gaping halves and yank the fabric over her shoulders and down her arms.

Goose bumps crawl over her skin.

I take in her firm, high breasts cupped in her bra, the nipples already pebbled and outlined against the lacey fabric, the curve of her stomach that leads to her panty-clad core, her gorgeously fleshy thighs that lead to strong calves and shapely ankles with the straps that tie her fuck-me stilettos to her feet.

I throw the now torn dress over my shoulder and raise my gaze to hers.

"Asshole," she snaps, "why the hell did you do that?"

"I gave you a chance to strip on your own, but you didn't comply."

"Whatever it is you have in mind, you can forget about it, mister."

"Is that right?" I curl my fingers around the nape of her neck.

She winces, but doesn't back away. Doesn't let me see the nervousness that she must, surely, be feeling. She tips up her chin and firms her lips. "You don't scare me."

"Oh?" I raise my other hand and drag my thumb across her lower lip. "Open," I say in a hard tone, and she sets her jaw.

"No." She scowls at me. "I'm not going to make this easy for you."

"Oh, you're certainly making it more exciting, though." I drag my palm down her throat to cup her breast. A shudder runs down her body, even as she firms her lips. I pinch her nipple between my finger and thumb and squeeze. She swallows. Her nipple seems to grow even more erect, and her breast seems to swell. A tremor grips her shoulders, but she doesn't glance away. She holds my gaze as I draw my fingers down the curve of her hip, over to her belly button. I circle the indentation, and she draws in a breath.

I can't stop the smirk that curls my lips as I graze my fingers against the waistband of her panties.

She swallows, and her chin trembles, even as her gaze grows stormy. "Fuck you," she says in a low voice. "I hate what you do to me."

"That makes two of us." I cup her pussy with my palm and yank her toward me with the grip I have on her neck. I crash my mouth to hers. She presses her lips together as I kiss her.

I plaster my mouth to hers, lick her mouth, and a shiver runs down her body, even as she freezes. Every muscle in her body grows tense as she tries to resist me.

"Open," I growl against her lips, "open and let me in."

She shakes her head. I stare into those amber eyes as I sink my teeth into her lower lip. She draws in a breath and another shudder grips her shoulders as she locks her lips together. I close my fingers around her throat and increase the pressure. Her gaze widens, color smears her cheeks, her pupils dilate, and she shakes her head.

"You want this. Admit it," I murmur. "You want me to thrust my fingers inside your pussy and bring you to orgasm before I bury myself inside your sweet cunt and bring you to climax."

She purses her lips and shoots daggers with her eyes. I laugh, then sink down to my knees in between her legs.

"What the—!" She gasps, "What are you—?"

I close my mouth around the swollen flesh covered by the crotch of her panties, and she yelps. I bite down on the engorged nub of her clit. Her knees seem to buckle from under her. She buries her fingers in my hair and tugs. Goose bumps trickle down my spine. Blood drains to my groin, and my dick lengthens. I slide my finger under the seam of her panties and thrust a finger inside her. Her dripping flesh welcomes me, and it's all I can do to stop myself from throwing her down and mounting her right there. I add a second finger, then a third as I continue to suck on her clit. I glance up to find her squeezing her eyes shut, even as she thrusts her pelvis into my face. I slide the fingers of my other hand under the seat of her panties, up the valley between her ass cheeks. I finger her puckered hole, and her eyelids snap open. Lust, shock, horror—all three are intertwined in her gaze as I curl my fingers in the moist channel of her pussy.

A trembling grips her. She bites down on her lip as she shakes her head; no doubt trying to fight the orgasm that threatens to overwhelm her.

I pull my fingers from her, then stand and haul her up in my arms. She yells out and grabs a hold of my neck as I march toward the bed. I throw her down on the bed, and she bounces once before coming to a stop.

Her hair flows over her face, and she shoves the strands aside. "You jerk! What the hell do you think you're doing?"

I throw myself over her, and she shrinks back into the bed. I plant my knees on either side of her thighs and glare at her. "You will do as I say."

"Fuck you."

"Oh, I intend to, all right." I peer into her face and order, "Turn over."

"Make me!" She firms her lips together, then yelps in surprise when I flip her onto her front.

She wriggles under me, and I slap her butt. She stills, more out of surprise than anything, then turns to stare at me over her shoulder. "How dare you?" she hisses.

I laugh. "Oh, I'm going to do more than that. Each time you disobey me, I'm going to spank your ass."

"You wouldn't."

I raise an eyebrow. "Try me, Flower."

"I hate that stupid nickname," she spits out.

"Tell me something I don't know." I yawn.

Color suffuses her cheeks. "Get off of me."

"Make me." I grin at her, and she pins me with a scowl.

"I'm not going to let you fuck me."

"By the time I'm done with you, you'll be begging me to."

"No way."

"Oh, yes." I grab her ample butt and haul her up so she's balanced on her knees, ass up in the air, her cheek pushed down into the bed.

"Don't you dare," she snarls. "Don't you dare do it."

I grab the waist of her panties and tear them off of her.

She huffs. I bring my palm down on her behind. The crack echoes around the room, and she yells, "What the hell?!" She tries to pull away, but I grab her waist to hold her in place.

I spank her left ass cheek, then the right, then the left again, and the right. I keep alternating the position of the slaps again and again. Each time my palm connects with her backside, her entire body jolts. Each time I feel the silky, smooth skin of her backside, blood thrums in my veins. A pulse flares to life at my temples, at my wrists, even in my fucking balls. My dick begins to leak precum. I bring my palm down to massage the reddened skin of her backside. She groans as I drag my fingers down the valley between her ass cheeks to the flesh between her legs. She jerks, then whines when I draw my fingers down her sodden pussy lips.

"You're soaked," I growl.

"Not by choice," she tosses over her shoulder. "I'm not responsible for the fact that my body responds to you."

"We'll see, shall we?" I part her ass cheeks, then lower my mouth to her weeping slit.

9

Aurora

He's eating me out. Holy shit, he's eating my pussy like it's the choicest Christmas cake and he's starving and hasn't eaten for the entire year. He sweeps his tongue across my pussy lips and heat sluices through my veins. My belly flip-flops, and my nipples harden until I'm sure they're going to pierce through the mattress cover.

He thrusts his tongue inside my soaking channel, and goose bumps pop on my skin. My heart begins to race. My toes curl. I dig my fingers into the mattress and hold on as he plunges his tongue in and out of me. He increases the pressure of his grip on my ass cheeks, and pain slices up my sides. That, combined with the wetness of his tongue as he continues to suck on my pussy, as he opens his mouth around my clit and bites down on it, sends me over the edge. The orgasm snaps out from the base of my spine and extends to my extremities. I squeeze my eyes shut, waiting for that intense rush to end. To see this through, to finally snap through the tension which has gripped me, as he pushes my body toward the impending orgasm. I brace myself, and that's when he releases his hold on my butt and withdraws his tongue from my soaking channel.

The orgasm instantly retreats. I blink as he lands a final smart slap to my behind. Then, he pushes off of the bed and walks toward the doorway. What in the name of the *Santa Madonna* is he up to?

I watch him reach the door and push it open.

"What the fuck?" I yell as I push myself up to sit on my heels. "Where are you going?"

"Didn't you tell me you weren't going to cooperate with me when I fuck you?" He smirks.

"You come back here and finish what you started," I shriek.

He laughs. He steps through the door, then turns to look at me over his shoulder. "Besides, I'm saving myself for marriage."

"No, you're not," I snarl. "You've slept with enough women to … to … warrant Father Christmas keeping a separate book about your misdeeds."

"You mean, I'm on his naughty list?"

"You're certainly not on his nice list."

"You're right."

I blink. "About what?"

"I'm not saving myself for marriage, but you are."

"The hell are you talking about?"

"I'm not going to let you come, not until we're married, and maybe not even then. Not until you ask me nicely."

"Vattene via." Buzz off. I huff.

He points his finger at me. "You won't come until I give you permission, Flower."

Argh! This man. I grab a pillow and throw it at him, but it hits the door that he's closed after him.

How dare he leave me like this? Alone and wanting, and so damn horny. Well, if he won't bring me to orgasm, doesn't mean I can't fulfill myself, does it? I turn on my back and slide my fingers inside my still sensitive pussy. Vibrations of heat tingle from my touch. The flesh is so sensitive that I can't stop the moan that bleeds from my lips. I add a second finger, and a third… And it's still not enough. Damn it. Not that he'd put his cock inside me, but even his fingers filled me up better than my own. I begin to move my fingers in and out of myself, in and out. I curve my fingers inside … and still… Nothing.

Goddamn, he's clearly spoiled me if I'm not even able to masturbate to my satisfaction. And I had done so plenty of times before with the vibrators I'd bought when I was in London. It was easier then, to satisfy myself, when I stayed in a shared apartment. Since returning to Sicily, my sex life has been non-existent. Given I've been living under the same roof as my father and sister, somehow pleasuring myself doesn't seem to be appropriate. So, I stopped…

Until I met Christian. One glance at him was enough to fire up my imagination. I allowed myself to fantasize about him at night, and since he rescued me and brought me here to this safe house, I also started dreaming about him during the day. Unfortunately, nothing compares to actually being in his presence, drawing in his masculine scent, feeling the heat rolling off his big body, the touch of his large palm on my body, his grasp on my hip, his palm flattened to the small of my back, his fingers inside me...

Aargh. I plunge my fingers inside myself again and again. Where's that orgasm? Why the hell can't I bring myself to climax the way he did? The way I've done countless times before? Goddamn it. I thrust my fingers in and out of myself... Still nothing. Fuck! I pull my fingers out and sit up. Can't believe my body is betraying me now, when I need it to obey me the most.

I swing my legs over the side of the bed and march toward the door. I glance down at my torn clothes, the bra I still wear, but without the panties which the beast had torn off of me earlier. No, if I storm out there, I'll still lose to the asshole. I need a plan, some way of beating him at his own game.

I pause, then pivot on my heel and head to the bathroom. A hot shower later, I pull on a fresh pair of undergarments and a dress of my own. At least, he allowed me to pack and bring my own clothes. Not that I owe him anything. Except my life. And the next twenty-nine days.

At this rate, before the week is over, I'll have thrown myself at him and begged him to make me come... No. No way am I going to humiliate myself in this fashion. I definitely need another way out. Another route to get the better of him. But how?

I'm here on my own, at his command. None of his brothers will help me. Karma could, but am I really going to involve her, when she's newly married and recovering from the loss of her child?

No, I need someone else on my side. Someone who is strong enough to take on the might of the Sovrano brothers. Someone they'd have to pay attention to. Someone who'd be willing to help me out ... someone like Nonna perhaps? Which means I need to find a way to meet her ... for which I need to speak to Christian anyway.

I square my shoulders, wipe my damp palms on my dress, then head for the door.

I walk out into the hallway, peek into the living room, but don't find him. I head to the kitchen and find him standing in front of the kettle. His broad back is to me, his shoulders bunching as he reaches into the shelves overhead and pulls out two mugs. His shirt stretches across his back. The planes meld and flow like they're dancing to some tune which I can't hear, but damn, if I don't appreciate the sheer symmetry, the poetry inherent in every move of that gorgeous, massive body of his.

My still sensitive pussy seems to melt further. Shit. If this is how I react to him whenever I'm in the same space as him, then how the hell am I going to find a way to beat him at his own game? I straighten my spine and walk into the room.

"Take a seat," he says without turning around. I pause halfway to the dining table. Damn it, does the man have eyes at the back of his head or what?

This time, he reaches into the cabinet on his right and pulls out a jar of cocoa mix. He scoops a portion of the powder into each cup. The kettle whistles, and he switches off the flame, then pours water into both cups. He mixes the liquid in both cups before placing the spoon in the sink, then turns with a mug in each hand. He arches an eyebrow, and I can't stop the blush that steals over my cheeks. Damn it, I wasn't ogling him; I wasn't. Okay, I totally was. But what the hell, the man is sex on toast… A walking orgasm... A climax on steroids… Ugh, you know what I mean, right?

I flounce over to the dining table and slip into a chair. He takes the one opposite me and pushes one of the mugs in my direction.

I raise the mug and breathe in the spicy scent of chocolate. For a few seconds, we don't speak as we both drink from our mugs.

When I'm done with mine, I place my mug on the table and lick my lips. "That was delicious," I mutter. "Thank you."

"You're welcome." He smirks.

The curl of his lips, that look in his eyes as he lazily draws his gaze across my features… Shit, my toes curl, my pussy whines, and I have to squeeze my thighs together to clamp down on the yawning emptiness in between them.

His smile broadens. I frown at him. "Your phone," I burst out. "Can I use your phone?"

He pulls out his phone, unlocks it, and slides it across the table. I glance at it then back at him. "You're not worried about who I'm going to call?"

He raises a shoulder. "Should I be worried about who you're going to call?"

"Answering a question with a question." I huff. "You know how annoying that is?"

"Do you want to use my phone or—" He leans forward, and I snatch up the device.

He chuckles as I pull up his list of contacts. I find the one I want and click on it. The phone rings once, twice, then, "Pronto!" Hello! a woman's voice answers.

"Nonna," I murmur.

Opposite me, Christian stiffens. I keep my gaze averted and focus on the voice at the other end of the line. "It's me, Aurora," I add.

"Well, of course, it's you," Nonna says in a sharp voice. "Considering it's not Christian, and you are calling from his phone, it would have to be you, I'd assume."

The silence stretches a beat, then another. "Can I come over and visit with you tomorrow?"

Nonna stays quiet. Shit, is she going to refuse me? Does she suspect there's an ulterior motive to my wanting to meet her? Well, of course, she does. She's sharp, that woman, but is she going to turn me down or—

"Three pm, tomorrow, my place. Don't be late."

She clicks off, and I lower the phone to the table. Only then do I raise my gaze to Christian's and flinch. His blue eyes blaze as he glares at me. "I hope you know what you're doing, Flower." He lowers his voice to a hush. "While the Sovrano brothers may be rattlesnakes, our nonna is the eagle who can take any one of us out if she chooses."

I tip my chin, "I only want to get to know her. After all, she is a very important person in your life."

"You expect me to believe that?"

I raise a shoulder. "You can believe whatever the hell you want." I reach for my cup, then remember I've already drained it. "You'll need to drop me off at her place tomorrow by three pm." I grab his phone. "Thanks again, for the chocolate."

Rising to my feet, I walk toward the door. My heart pounds and I'm almost out of the room when he calls out, "Flower, don't expect me to bail you out of this one."

I scowl at him over my shoulder. "Trust me, I can take care of myself."

10

Aurora

Famous last words. I stare at the two-story villa that Christian had dropped me off at. He had refused to come in. He had walked me to the door, knocked on it, then, with a look that told me I was crazy to be walking into the lioness' den voluntarily, he had told me that he'd be back in an hour to collect me—then he had pivoted and left.

I run my sweaty palms down the fabric of my dress. I chose my most conservative outfit—a high-collared, long-sleeved dress which ends somewhere below my knees. It's the dress I wear to church with my family, and as such, it seems appropriate to wear to meet someone who's the equivalent of the Almighty when it comes to the Sovrano family. The seconds stretch by, and I shift my weight from foot to foot. Despite the weather being relatively mild, a bead of sweat slithers down my spine. I close the distance to the door and raise my hand to knock on it again, when it's flung open.

A wizened man, clad in a dark suit, scowls at me. He looks me up and down and sniffs. What the hell? "I'm here to see Nonna." I tip up my chin. "My name is Aurora Garibaldi."

He scowls at me, then steps back and jerks his chin. I brush past him, and he shuts the door behind me before indicating that I should follow him. He walks down the hallway and into a beautiful living room that has furniture that must, surely, be antique. I glance up to find paintings on the ceiling—honest-to-goodness frescoes. I take in the beautiful mirror that takes up most of one wall, the comfortable yet beautiful sofa set that is pushed against the opposite wall, and even more gorgeous paintings on the walls. All, clearly, originals, though I can't really identify who the artists are.

"This way," the butler, or whoever he is, urges me from the doorway that leads into the next room. I follow him into what seems to be the library. Books line the walls, there's a fire burning in the hearth, and opposite it is a coffee table, on either side of which are two armchairs facing each other. Nonna is seated in one. She glances up as the old man approaches her.

"You didn't tell me you were expecting guests," he fumes.

Nonna arches an eyebrow. "I don't have to tell you everything."

"I'm the one who has to cook and serve your meals, so yes, I do need to know when you're expecting someone to visit."

"Uh, if it's that much of a bother, I don't need anything to eat or drink—"

Both Nonna and the old man raise their hands at the same time. "Basta." Enough, they say in unison.

I blink and purse my lips, as the two of them are engaged in some kind of a face off.

"Go on," Nonna points in the direction of the other doorway, "fetch us the coffee, please."

He sniffs, seems like he's going to refuse, then turns and marches away.

"Don't forget my brioche," she calls after him, "and my cannoli."

He raises his fist with the index and little finger extended and makes a jabbing motion with it over his shoulder as he marches away. What the— Did he just do what I think he did? I turn to Nonna, who beckons me over.

I walk over to stand in front of her. "Is that your..."

"Butler, companion, friend, servant." Nonna raises a shoulder. "Gino has been with me for more than fifty years. His father served my father, and Gino joined my household when I was ten-years-old. He came with me to my husband's house after I got married and helped raise my son. He even came with me to LA when I moved there with my grandsons."

"So, you've known each other for a long time then."

"Maybe too long." Nonna blows out a breath. "He's getting cranky in his old age, and clearly, he doesn't have the patience he once had. But," she shrugs, "he's part of my past, and it seems cruel to let go of him when we're both nearing the ends of our journeys."

"You're hardly nearing the end, Nonna," I murmur. "From what I can see, you are very much in charge of your destiny."

"But appearances can be deceptive, can they not?" She tilts her head.

I frown, open my mouth to ask a question, but she nods toward the armchair in front of her. "Sit down, you're giving me a crick in the neck," she commands.

I walk over and sink into the armchair, and place my bag by my side.

"So, you wanted to see me about the Christmas getaway?"

I glance up at her. "Uh, how did you guess?"

"Why else would my future granddaughter-in-law want to see me?"

"Maybe I just wanted to spend time with you?" I blink rapidly.

She snorts. "Not even Gino, here, would want to spend time with me of his own volition. And I count him among my closest friends... Or enemies, as the case may be. There is only a small line dividing friendship from enmity after all, don't you agree?"

"Um..." How the hell do I react to that statement, anyway? Before I can speak, Gino enters with a tray bearing an espresso maker and two tiny espresso cups in their saucers. Whew! Saved by the coffee, as it were. Gino places the tray on the coffee table. On it, there are also two tiny shot glasses filled with a cloudy liquid, a bowl of sugar, a plate of brioches, another of cannoli, and a third filled with what looks like biscotti. "Don't expect me to pour it for you," he snaps.

I gape. Did he just say that? Surely, Nonna will put him in his place now? But she simply points at the doorway. "You may leave now, old man."

"You're no spring chicken yourself." He snorts as he heads out of the room.

"Wow," I breathe, "the two of you sure do keep each other entertained."

She arches an eyebrow at me. "We're both of an age where our shared past outweighs the fact that we actually cannot stand the sight of each other. Overfamiliarity," she thrusts out her chin in a very Italian gesture, "it's the bane of most families, and not even I have been spared from it."

"He's more than just a servant?"

"He's family, I suppose ... but not really. There's still a line that separates us, for he does come from a background that has been devoted to serving the Sovranos for generations. After his wife and my husband died, we became reluctant companions to each other. Now. I tolerate him because, well, it's hard to find good hired help these days."

"So, he's a servant?"

"Sometimes, and sometimes he's my companion, but you're not here to talk about that, are you?"

Nonna pours the espresso.

I reach for my cup and sip from it. "I wanted to talk to you about the upcoming Christmas getaway," I remind her.

"Hmm..." She reaches for her own cup of espresso and takes a sip.

The silence stretches for a minute, then another.

"Well?" she says impatiently. "Out with it, girl; I don't have all day."

"I want to stay with you," I burst out.

"What?"

"I want to stay here with you, so I can ... keep my chastity."

"Keep your chastity?" She stares at me. "You mean to say, you are—"

"Yes," I say hastily, " I am, and we haven't yet ... you know..." Color sears my cheeks, and I glance away, then back at her.

"You mean Christian wants to marry you without even having—"

I nod. "Yes, exactly." I wring my fingers together. "And I want to keep it that way. I mean, we aren't yet married, and I'm a firm believer in consummating my marriage only on the wedding night."

"Does he know that you are going to ask me for this?" She raises her hand. "Don't answer that. Of course, he doesn't. If he did, he wouldn't have brought you here, would he?"

I shake my head. "So, you'll help me?"

"Even if I did agree to your staying here with me, and that's a big if, it's no guarantee that he will stay away from you."

"It will be an effective deterrent."

"Hmph...." She purses her lips together. "You do realize this will make my grandson hate me even more than he does now."

"He doesn't hate you."

"Maybe hate is too strong a word," she agrees, "but none of them have forgiven me for not intervening earlier to take them away from their father. If I had, they may have turned out to be different, not as hurt or broken, not so in touch with the darkness inside of them. They may have turned out to be more normal."

"You're being too harsh on yourself. He was their biological father. You thought it made more sense to keep them with their father."

"Well, I was wrong. I knew I should have put my foot down for how he treated his wife and children, but I was too caught up in convention. I preferred to turn a blind eye to what was happening, and by the time I decided to get involved, it was too late."

"It's never too late—"

"The only person who loved me unconditionally was Xander, and I never did try to understand him fully either. I was too blinded by the fact that he was unconventional in who he tried to love. I didn't try to comprehend why he was so unorthodox in his relationships. And still, Xander forgave me and loved me... Only, I didn't reciprocate his affection. Not really. I took him for granted and now ... now he's gone."

A tear runs down her cheek. She pulls out a handkerchief, pats her cheek, and glances into the distance. The silence stretches as she composes herself. Then she glances back at me. "I'll do it," she declares, "for Xander, I'll do this. I'll help you."

"You will?"

She nods, "I can't guarantee that Christian will follow the rules I set, but hopefully, you'll figure out a solution to whatever is going on between the two of you by then?"

"Hopefully." I purse my lips. Somehow, I don't think whatever is between me and Christian will have been resolved by then, but yeah, I'll take the time it's going to buy me.

11

Christian

"No." I glare between Nonna and my fake fiancée. "No fucking way am I going to agree to this."

I arrived an hour after dropping Aurora off at Nonna's place and was ushered into her living room, where I caught my fake fiancée laughing at something the old woman had said. Nonna had a smile on her normally stern countenance as if she was enjoying Aurora's company. Huh? My grandmother doesn't bestow her smiles freely. But it's clear that she finds Aurora entertaining enough to actually meet her separately for a coffee.

Nonna reaches for a biscotti before admonishing me. "Language," she says in a casual voice before nibbling on the biscotti.

"The swearing is the least you have to worry about," I growl. "She's my fiancée—"

"I don't see a ring on her finger."

"I'm marrying her in two days."

"No, you're not." Nonna firms her lips. "I allowed Michael to get away with his quick wedding; this time we do it my way."

"And that is?"

"You'll marry her a month from now. That gives us just enough time to plan the wedding." She smiles, anticipating victory.

"A month?" Both Aurora and I burst out at the same time.

"Is that a problem?" She glances between us.

"N ... no," Aurora stutters.

"Yes, it is." I fold my arms across my chest. "I'm not waiting a month to marry her."

"If I say you will, then you will." Nonna turns to me. "Besides, a woman only has one big wedding in her lifetime. It needs to be properly planned so it's an event to remember."

"But Michael got away with a wedding which was organized in less than three days."

"No wonder his bride stabbed him on his wedding day." Nonna sniffs.

She's referring to how Karma was so pissed off with Michael for kidnapping her then forcing her to marry him that she used Michael's knife on him. It resulted in a flesh wound, and Michael wasn't hurt by it, but it did make for a few rocky weeks early in their wedding.

"They are very happy now," I point out.

"On the other hand, I think you make a valid point, Nonna." Aurora keeps her head bowed as if deferring to Nonna's seniority. Ha! The woman doesn't have a docile bone in her body.

"See?" Nonna nods in her direction. "Your fiancée-to-be agrees."

"Wife-to-be," I correct her, "and that doesn't mean I need to."

"I don't see a ring on her finger."

"Nevertheless, we are getting married in two days."

"Oh, no, Christian." Nonna glares at me. "You are getting married in a month and—"

"In one week," I say through gritted teeth. "For you, and only you, Nonna, I'll agree to extend my timeline. We'll get married in a week's time."

"Two weeks, and not a day sooner." Nonna's eyes gleam.

What the hell? Did the old woman just play me?

"Meanwhile," I widen my stance, "there's no way am I staying away from her for that duration."

"It's tradition," Nonna says firmly. "You don't sleep with the bride before the wedding. In fact, you don't stay under the same roof as her... Which is why Aurora is moving in with me."

"Che cazzo!" I snap. "That's the most ridiculous thing I've ever heard. Why would my fiancée—" I raise a hand. "Yes, I plan to rectify the ring situation shortly, but why the hell would I be away from her—" I point a finger at Nonna, effectively shutting off her tirade. "No, I'm not going to sleep with her, but why should we spend the time apart?"

"To remove the both of you from the path of temptation." Nonna folds her hands in her lap. "I was young not too long ago too, you know. I know how it can be with raging hormones. It makes sense that the two of you stay apart."

"Fuck that," I widen my stance. "No one tells me what to do."

"I am your nonna." She scowls. "You won't go against my request."

I dig my fingers into my hair and pull. Jesù Cristo, the old woman is pulling out all the stops here.

"Didn't see you come up with the conditions when Michael kidnapped Karma and kept her under his roof before he married her."

"That was different." She waves a hand in the air. "He took her to repay a debt her father owed; she was his captive."

"Aurora is my—" I pause. If I say that Aurora is also my captive, Nonna will never agree to this wedding. As it is, based on the interrogation she subjected both of us to the last time we saw her, it's clear that she doesn't completely believe the story of our falling in love and rushing to get married. Now, if I tell her that Aurora is effectively my prisoner, that will effectively destroy this entire charade before it's even started.

"Aurora is your..." Nonna fixes me with a shrew gaze. "What were you going to say."

"My bride-to-be," I force the words out, "the love of my life."

Aurora stiffens. She stares at me as if she can't quite believe what I'm saying. Hell, I can't believe the crap I'm about to spew, but what-fucking-ever. Apparently, dialogues from Hallmark movies are all the rage at Christmas time, and since my family has decided that Christmas this year will last well into the New Year, I may as well get into the fucking ho-ho-ho spirit here. Not to be confused with the only kind of 'ho' I'm familiar with—a word I dare not utter in Nonna's company. Yes, yes, I know I used the 'F' word earlier, but insulting a woman by calling her 'ho' in front of my grandmother feels wrong, even for me.

Not that Nonna hasn't heard it all. After all, bringing up seven boys means that she is well-accustomed to our rowdy language. Nonna has her faults, but what has never been in doubt is that she loves us. She may have stepped in a little late in yanking us out of the reach of our father and taking us to LA, but it has never been in doubt that she'll do anything for us. She has always prioritized the lot of us. So, why has she decided to take the side of my fake fiancée right now? Unless, she suspects that our engagement is a fake and wants to catch us… But why would she do that? How would it benefit her to expose our plan? No. More likely she is doing it because she truly believes in the concept of staying apart until the wedding night.

"You'll be allowed to visit her, of course." Nonna nods.

No shit.

"In the presence of a chaperone, of course."

"A what?" I glare at her, but the old woman doesn't blink.

"You heard me, Christiano." She pins me with her don't-fuck-with-me look. "We will follow the guidance of our forefathers in this."

"Fuck me," I mutter, "this is going to be the death of me, Nonna. You know that, right?"

"Oh, phst," she waves a hand in the air, "you kids dramatize everything. Now kiss your wife-to-be goodbye."

"What the hell does that mean? Aurora is leaving with me."

"Haven't you heard anything I've said?" Nonna pronounces the words slowly as if I'm an idiot. Well, I must be, considering I am standing here and allowing an eighty-year-old woman to order me around.

"Aurora is coming with me." I scowl between the two of them. "Come on, Flower. You know that you want to be with me."

"No," Aurora tips up her chin, "I don't want to come like that."

"Not what you were saying just a few hours ago..." I cover my mouth with my hand and cough. "I mean, surely, you don't mean that. Wasn't it you who said that you couldn't stand to be away from me for even one second?"

"You must have been dreaming, my dear fiancée-to-be." Her lips curve up in a smile. "Besides, I 'm seeing you at the family getaway very soon."

"Husband-to-be," I growl, "and it's tomorrow." I fold my arms across my chest. "We're leaving on this goddamn outing tomorrow."

"We are?" Nonna scowls. "But we need to make preparations—"

"Basta," I hold up my hand. "Enough, Nonna. I'm allowing her to stay one night with you. That's about all I'm going to be able to offer you right now. Take it or leave it."

Nonna seems like she is going to hesitate, then she nods. "We leave tomorrow. I'll call Michael and tell him now."

"I'll arrange to have Aurora's clothes packed and sent over tonight, so there are no delays," I add.

"Gee, thanks," Aurora scoffs.

"Don't thank me yet." I close the distance between us, then lower my head and brush my lips to her forehead. "If I were you, I'd be careful about what you do next, Flower," I whisper. "After that stunt you pulled, there's a lot I have to punish you for already."

12

Christian

I glance out of the window of the private jet that I boarded with the rest of the family a half-hour ago.

Cortina is a day's drive from Palermo, but why drive when all of us can travel together in comfort?

Below me, the Swiss Alps come into view, their snow-covered peaks seeming so close, it feels like I could reach out and touch them. An illusion, really, as much as my engagement to Aurora is. Considering how fake it is, the fact that she isn't sitting next to me now shouldn't even bother me. I squeeze my fingers together.

Goddamit, how did she pull that on me? She actually colluded with my grandmother and found a way to keep her distance from me. Well, that ends as soon as we reach our destination. I'm going to ensure that she shares a room with me, and if anyone dares stop me, I'm going to... What? It's not like I can pull out a gun and threaten my grandmother. Not that she'd be afraid if I did so. Likely, she'd pull out her own gun on me— Not that I know if she's carrying one, but I wouldn't put it past my nonna.

And Aurora? How the hell did she realize that if she formed a partnership with my nonna, she'd find a way to best me? I can't allow that to happen. No way. She is mine, and she needs to be taught a lesson on what happens when she dares go against me.

"What are you grumbling about, little brother?" Massimo leans forward in the seat opposite me.

"I'm not grumbling," I scowl back at him, "and mind your own business, will ya?"

"Definitely grumbling." Seb walks over and sinks down in the seat next to me. "Ever notice how Christian always pouts when he doesn't get his way?"

"I certainly don't pout," I stick out my lower lip, "and don't you jokers have anything better to do than hover around me?"

"Nope." Luca lowers his bulk into the seat next to Massimo, and all three men stare at me.

"What?" I glower. "What do you assholes want?"

"Knew it," Massimo rumbles, "the man is down for the count."

"Agreed." Adrian walks over to take the last empty seat in between our two rows. "I've never seen him this harried."

"Not even the first time he shot a man." Seb crosses his foot over his knee. "Hell, he never even wavered. It was like he was born to do the deed."

"Now's not the time," I warn Seb. "We are in polite company."

Seb glances around at the faces of my brothers. "What polite company? I don't see any."

Luca laughs. "He means the women." He stabs his thumb over his shoulder. I glance in that direction, knowing I'll see Aurora seated next to my nonna, with Cassandra opposite them. Theresa, Xander's friend, is seated by herself behind them. Nonna insisted that she come along as well. The woman gazes out of her window, an expression of bleakness on her features. I should go over and comfort her. If there's anyone who understands how much it truly hurts to have lost Xander, it's her. But what would I say when I have yet to come to terms with what happened?

Aurora turns, and her gaze collides with mine. I glower at her, and she tilts her head. I scowl, and she curves her lips. *Che cazzo!* Clearly, she thinks that she can get away with this distance that she's put between us. Little does she know, I don't take kindly to being challenged in this fashion.

Cassandra glances up at Adrian. She rakes her gaze over his features, pausing for a few extra seconds. As if sensing her perusal, he turns to glance at her, but she looks away. Well, well, well, isn't that interesting.

"How come she's here with us?" I ask Massimo.

"Who?" He glances toward the women. "If you mean Cassandra, it's because Karma was insistent that she come along with us."

Adrian stiffens at the mention of her name, but doesn't say anything.

"Something up between the two of you?" I turn on him. "Don't think the tension between the two of you has gone unnoticed."

"She's in love with her dead husband." Adrian rolls his shoulders. "I can fight a live man, but not sure if I can compete with a ghost from her past."

"So, you acknowledge there's something between the two of you?"

"Hell yeah," he laughs, "not that I'm going to act on it."

"Didn't take you for a pussy," I murmur.

Adrian's features harden, then he chuckles. "Nice segue there, Christian. I'm not the one getting married, you are, so let's talk about that for a second, shall we?"

"Let's not." I crack my neck. "Don't the rest of you have something more pressing to do than ride my butt?"

"Oh, but it's so much more fun to do that," Seb says with a wide smile. "First Michael, now you, Christian. It seems the Sovranos have finally met their match."

"Speak for yourself." Luca sets his jaw. "I have no plans of settling down anytime soon."

"A-n-d there it is. Famous last words," Seb chortles. "He who protests the most is normally the first to fall."

"Not me." Luca bares his teeth. "I have too many kinks to be satisfied by just one woman."

"You guys done discussing your proclivities?" Michael looms over us. My oldest brother has always been big and brawny. While Massimo is the only one who is taller and broader, Michael holds his own when it comes to presence. He shoves a hand into the pocket of his black jeans as he trains his gaze on me. "Need to talk to you, *fratellino*."

"Thought we'd done enough of that already?" I drawl. "If you're trying to dissuade me from marrying her—"

Michael raises a hand. "Far be it from me to stand in the way of true love." He glances over his shoulder to where Karma walks over to sit next to Cassandra. "I, more than anyone, know that even the most unorthodox of beginnings can have HEAs."

"Did he just use the abbreviation?" Seb blinks.

"He did use the abbreviation," Luca says in a disgusted voice.

"Go on, Chris, you need to join the band of married brothers," Massimo drawls. "Our Don needs to discuss matters of domestic concern with you."

Michael snorts. "If you pussies were any more jealous, I'd see green glowing from the tips of your hairs."

"Jealous? Do I look jealous?" Massimo settles back in his chair. "I plan on taking a nap, since I have no woman to answer to, unlike the two of you."

I glare at him. "You're a fucking joke, you know that?"

"Speak for yourself." Massimo yawns. He folds his massive arms over his chest and shuts his eyes.

Luca and Seb rise to their feet and wander away to the back of the cabin while speaking in low voices.

Adrian ambles over to join Antonio toward the front of the aircraft.

Michael sits down next to me. "Heard your bride-to-be decided to stay the night with Nonna?"

"And I had to arrange to have her clothes packed and brought over to the aircraft, no less."

Michael laughs. "The two of you fight or something?"

"Or something."

He peers into my features. "One thing you need to realize when it comes to matters of the heart."

"First, it's not a matter of the heart, but go on."

Michael stares at me as if he doesn't quite believe what I just said, then he shakes his head. "Grovel," he mutters.

"What?" I scowl. "What the hell do you mean by that?"

"If you've done something to get on her bad side, then the only way to fix it is to grovel."

"First of all, I haven't done anything to her. Period. And fuck, if I'm going to grovel."

Michael's gaze widens, then he throws his head back and laughs. "Good luck with that. You're going to need it with that attitude. If I were you, I'd try to make amends for whatever it is you did."

"Just because you're married doesn't make you an expert on relationships."

"Hey, I'm not the one in the doghouse."

"Doghouse?" I shake my head. "You're the one left holding the cat, as far as I can tell."

A purring sound reaches us as Karma's cat Andy brushes against Michael's leg. Michael bends, scoops up the animal, who's purring only grows louder. He rubs the beast between his eyes, then scratches him under his chin, sending the cat into ecstasy.

"I'd rather be holding my wife's pussy than sitting in the doghouse," he quips before he rises to his feet and walks toward Karma, who holds out her arms. The cat jumps into them, and Karma snuggles the beast, which tucks itself into her chest and closes its eyes. Karma rises to her feet and follows Michael toward the rear of the plane, where they occupy seats next to each other. Bastardo.

I raise my gaze to find Aurora watching me. I hold her gaze a second longer before I crook my finger.

She sets her jaw, then shakes her head.

I glare at her, and she pales.

I jerk my chin. She glances away. Oh, you're going to pay for your impudence, Flower, and you know it.

She turns to glance out of the window as the pilot announces that we are preparing to land.

13

———————

Christian

Forty-five minutes later, we are in the living room of the main chalet in the complex of chalets that we own along with a lodge nearby.

We Sovranos don't do anything in half-measures and this place is a testament to that. A Christmas tree tall enough to almost hit the roof occupies one corner of the room. It's already decorated and the lights twinkle from its branches. Cassandra walks around the room, topping off our Prosecco glasses. As she passes Adrian, they exchange a look that seems to raise the temperature of the room. Clearly, he was mistaken when he said he doesn't stand a chance with her.

The hair on the back of my neck prickles. I turn my head, and my gaze once more clashes with Flower's golden one. She refuses to look away, and I raise my glass in her direction before taking a sip. I lick my lips, and her gaze drops to my mouth. Her chest rises and falls. Even across the distance, I sense the heat that flushes her cheeks and see her nipples outlined against the sweater dress that she's wearing.

Then Michael clinks his knife against his glass. I hold her gaze for a second longer before I turn in his direction.

"Welcome to our first Sovrano Christmas getaway. It's the first time we have all come together for a vacation in..." his forehead crinkles, "well, the first time ever, really." He raises a shoulder. "I have to admit that when Nonna first came up with this idea, I had my reservations." He smirks. "Then my wife seconded the decision, and I knew better than to argue."

A ripple of laughter runs around the gathered crowd.

Michael glances at Karma, and his entire face lights up. "I'd like to propose a toast to my beautiful new bride and to new beginnings."

The rest of us raise our glasses.

Karma places Andy on the floor. The cat saunters over to the cat tree in the corner of the room as Karma walks over to Michael. He wraps his arm around her and pulls her into his side before taking a sip from his glass. "If Xander were here, he'd, no doubt, have something extremely nerdy and witty to say about the proceedings." He chuckles. "I remember the first time I offered him a glass of prosecco; he downed it in one go, then asked me why the apple juice tasted so strange."

I try to smile, but somehow, my facial muscles seem to be frozen. How easy it is for the rest of them to recollect memories of my twin. How difficult it is for me to even think about him. To acknowledge that he'll no longer be able to experience what life has to offer.

Michael chuckles. "I miss you, brother," he murmurs in a low voice, "but wherever you are, I'm sure you are watching us right now and asking why the hell we haven't started the festivities yet. I—"

"You have no idea what you're talking about," I snap. "You think you can raise a toast to Xander then go on with your lives? That you can talk to him as if he is really here and that will make it all right? It's your fault, and yours—" I turn on Luca, "that Xander is not here, and nothing you say or do will ever change that."

"Now that's not fair," Massimo rumbles. "We've been over this. I thought you understood that what happened was no one's fault except our father's, and he's been dealt with for it."

"And if you had spoken out against him," I turn on Nonna, "if you had stopped him when he decided to physically and emotionally abuse us, the day would not have come when he'd take the life of his own son. I hope you regret your actions, for you have as much a part to play in Xander's death as our father."

"Don't talk to Nonna like that." Seb steps toward me, but Nonna raises a hand.

"No, let him speak. This is why we're together—so these unspoken sentiments can finally be aired."

Nonna holds my gaze. "I will always regret not being strong enough to have taken action against my son. And you are right; I am as much to blame for what happened to Xander as your father." She swallows. "It's why I will not repeat the same mistake again."

I frown. "What are you talking about?"

Nonna glances at Aurora, then back at me. "Aurora will be staying in the same chalet as me."

"Not happening. I already told you, Nonna, she got the one night that we spent apart, but that stops now. She's my fiancée—"

"I still don't see a ring."

I slide my hand inside my pocket and pull out a small velvet box.

Cassandra gasps; Karma draws in a breath. But Aurora? She stays silent; not a flicker of an expression crosses her face. I prowl toward her, and she doesn't move. Doesn't take a step back when I pause in front of her. I remove the ring from the box, slide the box back in my pocket, then hold out my left palm.

I hold her gaze as she swallows. The moment stretches a beat, then another. Finally, she places her left hand in mine. I slide the ring onto her finger, and applause sounds from the watching family members. She begins to pull her hand back, but I wrap my fingers around her wrist. I tug, and she stumbles toward me. I hold my arm about her waist and bring her flush against me.

I lower my head, and she tips up her chin. Anger smolders in the depths of her eyes. She firms her lips as I bring my mouth to hers. I stay poised, sharing her breath but not kissing her. Color fires her cheeks, but she doesn't pull away. Her breasts thrust against my chest, and the curve of her waist trembles as I close the distance between our lips. I brush my mouth over hers, then release her so quickly that she blinks. I step back, an arm loosely about her shoulder. "You were saying?" I turn on Nonna. "Now that we're engaged—"

"It's even more important that she stay with me for the duration of our stay."

"What?" I stiffen. "That makes no sense. We live in the twenty-first century, where men and women stay together before they are married."

"We are the Mafia," Nonna retorts, "and you come from one of the oldest families in the country. So, you will heed our traditions and stay apart until you are married."

"No," I snap.

"Yes," Michael drawls.

"Totally, yes," Massimo rumbles.

"I agree," Luca smirks.

"Nonna's right," Seb chuckles. "Time we do things by the book."

Adrian opens his mouth, and I point a finger at him. "Let me guess, you're on board with this sham too."

"It's how things are done in our part of the world," Adrian says gently.

"And you?" I scowl at Karma. "I don't hear you agreeing to this."

"Because I don't," she replies.

"Finally, fuck." I drag my fingers through my hair. "It takes someone who has not grown up in the cradle of the Mafia to see the fault of our ways."

"But I do think you and Aurora should stay apart until you get married," Karma adds.

"What the—!" I growl. "I can't believe you are taking the side of these … these … imbeciles."

"Who are you calling imbeciles?" Michael glowers. "We only have your best interests at heart."

"Oh, yeah?" I growl. "I didn't see you worrying about traditions when you decided to take Karma captive.

"It was an unusual situation, I agree," he murmurs. "And it worked out in the end." He pulls Karma even closer. "But I admit, we had a few hairy situations along the way, something I don't wish on you, or anyone else, hence"—he pins me with his gaze—"I see the wisdom of the old ways now, and I think you and your fiancée will benefit from the distance."

"Che cazzo!" I glare at him. "What is this, some kind of intervention?" I take in the faces of my brothers. "Are the lot of you ganging up on me?"

"We only want what's best for you, *fratellino*," Seb murmurs. "We're looking out for you."

"More like intruding where you're not needed." I turn on Nonna. "This is all your fault. If you hadn't brought up the idea, the rest of these assholes wouldn't be parroting what is, clearly, a foolish idea."

"Is it?" She tilts her head. "It's you who said I should have interfered earlier when your father did what was so clearly wrong."

The blood drains from my face. "I am nothing like my father."

"And I am simply making sure that you and your wife start your new life in the best manner possible."

Anger thrums at my temples. My heartbeat ratchets up. My vision tunnels. I take a step forward, but a soft touch on my chest stops me. I glance down to find Aurora has placed her palm on the skin over my heart.

"Please," she murmurs, "please, Christian, don't fight with your family; they only have your best interests at heart."

I peer into her features, the plea in her eyes, and the anger recedes. My guts churn, a swirling emptiness yawns in my belly, a hot sensation stabs at my chest, and I pull away from her. "You'll pay for this," I say in a low voice.

Then turning, I stalk out of the house.

14

Aurora

"This is all wrong, all wrong." I pace back and forth, back and forth in my room.

After Christian stalked off, the proceedings somewhat lost their color. The brothers peeled off to their different chalets—yeah, there's no concept of just a room for each one of them. There are enough chalets in the complex that each of the brothers have a house to himself.

Michael and Karma were, clearly, relieved that they have their own space. Karma confided to me that this was the main reason Michael agreed to come on this getaway.

The other Sovrano brothers, too, were more than happy to have their own private retreats. Guess that's what happens when you have so many alphas together… They are just too big to share the same space for too long. They need their own territories where they can hold their own.

The more I observe the Sovrano brothers, the more I realize what a feat it must have been for Nonna to actually get them to come away and stay for a few days together like this. A bonding experience may be what she intends, but will these men actually survive this time together without breaking into some kind of a fight, I wonder? And leading the pack may well be my fake fiancé.

I hold up my fingers, and light bounces off the golden yellow stone. It's surrounded by tiny diamonds that accentuate the depth of the piece. It's unlike any stone I have ever seen. More brilliant than a yellow sapphire, more depth than a ruby. And it fits. Gosh, how did he guess my size so accurately? And he managed to come up with it overnight? What does that mean? Not that he was very happy with Nonna insisting that he toe the line she'd drawn, but at least, I've managed to buy myself some breathing space. Though how long that's going to last is anyone's guess.

My phone vibrates. Yes, Nonna had given me my own phone. Shocker! Apparently, the old lady is definitely more in touch with the times than my one-time captor had been.

I glance at the screen.

Blocked number.

The blood drains from my face. My pulse begins to race. The phone vibrates again, and I pick it up.

"He-hello." I gulp.

"I am still waiting for the information," a man's voice drawls.

It's him. OMG, it's him. "How did you get this number?"

"That's not your concern," he informs me. "What about the information?"

"I ... I still need more time." I swallow.

"Remember, it's your family's life at stake."

Like I could ever forget.

"I, uh, found another way to get closer to them. In fact, I am positive that I'll be able to get you what you need," I murmur. "Only—" I hesitate. Say it, do it; it's now or never. I draw in a breath, "I want something in return."

"This is not a negotiation," he says in a flat tone.

"I am aware of that," I swallow. "I also know that you desperately want information related to the Sovranos, which only I can get for you."

The silence stretches a beat, another. My heart begins to race, the pulse pounds at my temples, my stomach ties itself in knots, and I am sure that I am going to be sick. Hell, I played my card and I lost. Now, this man is definitely going to kill me and the rest of my family. What's wrong with me? Why did I have to bring this up, why—

"What is it you want?" He asks.

"Christian Sovrano..." A shudder grips me.

Am I really going to do this? But what other choice do I have? He's threatening my family, unless I do as he says. And I can't do that. I don't want to do that. I left the Mafia behind so I wouldn't have to do anything with them and here he is, dragging me back into their inner circle, and as a mob wife, no less. It may be a pretense, but he's going to make the most of the situation, I have no doubt about it. The chemistry between us speaks to the fact that he'll be fucking me the first chance he gets. He'll seduce me, he'll strip back all of the layers I have carefully built against the world and force me to acknowledge just how much I want him too... and I can't have that. The fact that I am so attracted to him means I'll probably enjoy what he does to me and that... I will not allow. I don't want to feel this powerless, this... completely at his mercy. No, the only way out is to take this guy's help to escape from Christian. That way, I'll have one less problem to contend with.

"You want him dead?" the man asks.

I try to force the words out, but my tongue refuses to cooperate. My fingers tremble and sweat slides down the valley between my breasts.

"Well?" He snaps, "Do you?"

I hesitate.

"I take it that's a yes?" he drawls.

"No," I burst out, "I don't want him dead. Don't hurt him please, just... do something to distract him, long enough for me to get away from him."

I squeeze my eyes shut. I do want to escape from Christian. I do. This is the only way.

"I'll take care of him," the man says in a gruff voice, "you make sure that you deliver the information I need."

I clutch the phone with such force that my fingers hurt.

"If you don't come through on your end of the bargain, your family will suffer."

He disconnects the call. I stare at the blank screen for a few seconds more.

"The view is wonderful, isn't it?"

I scream. The phone slips from my grasp and hits the carpeted floor.

"Hey, you okay?" Cass walks over to me. She bends to pick up the phone at the same time as me, but I reach it first.

I snatch up the phone, then straighten. "Sorry," I laugh, "you scared me."

She looks at me closely. "Are you okay? You seem pale."

"Oh, I'm fine." I wave a hand in the air. "Just, all this excitement around the upcoming wedding, it has me a little on edge."

"It's understandable."

I wrap my arms around myself as I turn back to the window. If she had come in a few seconds earlier she'd have heard me. And then, how would I have explained the conversation I was having? Goddamn it. What have I gotten myself into. I swallow as I stare straight ahead.

"It really is a gorgeous view, isn't it?" She draws abreast of me.

"It seems cold to me."

"It should be"—she laughs—"it's only one of the poshest skiing destinations in the world."

"I suppose." I have heard of Cortina as being a playground for the rich and famous, but I admit, I have never felt curious about it.

"You don't seem very convinced." She chuckles.

"I'm not a snow person." I narrow my gaze against the glare of the sun glinting off of the snow.

"At least, you're dressed for it." She gestures to the large sweater that I had pulled on.

I blow out a breath. "He bought it for me."

"Who, Christian?" Cassandra's gaze widens.

Christian had not only arranged to have my packed clothes delivered, but he also ensured that I had a brand-new winter wardrobe to go with it.

"I wish I didn't have to accept his favors." I had half a mind to return the winter clothes to him, but then I saw the snow and realized that would have been a mistake. I mean, I am stubborn, but not so stupid that I want to be exposed to the elements when I go out there. And while I'm going to put off any adventures in the cold, I have no doubt, at some point, I'll have to venture out.

"So, what's the plan for the next few days, you think?" I turn to Cassandra. "Has Nonna mentioned anything to you yet?"

She purses her lips. "I'm not supposed to say anything."

"Oh, so you know what she has in mind?"

"Other than the meals, which she is very clear that we have to eat together, well…" Cass hesitates. "I really am not allowed to share the program for the next few days."

I scowl. "Aww, come on, Cass," I wheedle, "you can tell me."

"I don't want to get into any trouble with her, you know?"

"You seem almost as wary of her as you are of Michael."

Cass tosses her hair over her shoulder. "Don't underestimate her."

"I know better than that." I grimace. "Still, considering she asked you to help out with the preparations, it means that she trusts you, right?"

"More like she knew I couldn't refuse her and that I'd know how to keep a secret."

"Hmm…" I arch an eyebrow. "Now you definitely have my curiosity piqued; you sure you can't tell me more about what she has planned."

"Trust me, she takes this almost as seriously as the Don takes his Mafia affairs." She firms her lips. "She'd probably have me punished if I so much as breathed a word about it."

"Oh, please," I wave my hand in the air, "surely, you exaggerate."

"Okay, so maybe I won't be killed or tortured, but she'll definitely not be happy with me, and you definitely don't want to be at the receiving end of Nonna's anger."

There's another knock on the door; both of us turn to find Theresa peeking inside. She glances between us, then stares down at the floor. "Okay if I join you?" she asks in a soft voice.

Cassandra and I exchange glances before Cassandra rushes toward her. "Of course, Theresa," she murmurs. "Come in; we were just chatting about the next few days."

Theresa shuffles inside the room. She's wearing an elegant black dress, her hair is coiled in a bun at the base of the neck, and on her feet are wedge-heeled boots, which are stylish but also black. Her face is pale, and there are dark circles under her eyes. She looks like a young woman who is still in mourning. She shifts her weight from foot to foot, then shoots us a glance from under her eyelashes. "Is there anything I can do to help?"

"Oh, no," Cass shakes her head. "The chalets come with their own staff, and this one, the main one where Nonna is staying, has a team to cook and clean and help with the activities being organized, so all you have to do is enjoy the skiing."

"Xander loved to ski. It's one of the activities we loved to do together. Every winter, we came here to ski. He said it was the closest thing to flying..." She swallows, and a tear squeezes out from the corner of her eyes. Her features seem to crumble before she composes herself.

Cassandra pulls out a handkerchief and offers it to her. "I know how tough it must be for you, now that he is gone."

She laughs as she accepts the handkerchief and dabs at her cheeks. "It was tougher when he was alive."

"It was?" I walk over to the settee and motion for her to join me.

Theresa crosses the floor to take a seat. She wraps her arms around herself and lowers her chin to her chest. "He was always conflicted about our relationship. I knew he felt something for me, but he was never honest about it. Every time I thought he'd break down and confess his feelings, he always pulled back. It was like he couldn't quite decide if he wanted me or not."

"Maybe it wasn't you," I say gently. "Maybe he was just trying to decide about what he wanted in life."

"You mean the fact that he was bisexual?"

I blink. "Ah…" I bite the inside of my cheek, "I didn't think—"

"That I knew?" She firms her lips. "Just because I look fragile doesn't mean that I am fragile. I am tired of people underestimating me, you know? I wish they'd stop hiding things from me. Everyone—Xander when he was alive, his brothers, even my own family—feels they need to protect me. But I am tougher than I seem."

"Amen to that, sister." I lean forward in my seat. "And now that you are here, you'll have a little time away from everything, and you can use the space to regroup."

"Except I don't know what to do with myself." She wrings her fingers together. "For so long, my identity was tied with Xander's. I guess I had built up a future for us together. Now I know I was the only one thinking that way." She chuckles in a self-deprecating manner. "Still, for so long, he was my future, and now that he's gone, I don't know what to do with myself."

"I am so sorry." I move closer to her. "Truly, I wish I could do something to make it better."

"You come from a Mafia family; you know how it is." She firms her lips. "From a very young age, you are taught that your self-worth is tied to that of the man you marry. And even though there was never a formal arrangement in place, I always knew that I would marry him. Our families, too, expected it, and then … this happens."

"Maybe it happened for a reason?" Cassandra comes forward to sit on Theresa's other side. "Maybe he wasn't right for you?"

"How do you know that?" Theresa fumes.

"Maybe it's because I thought that I was in love, but later realized that I was fooling myself." Cassandra says in a low voice. "Sometimes we want something to be true so much that our feelings deceive us into creating a reality that doesn't really exist."

Theresa's cheeks flush. "Just because your experience turned out to be far from perfect, doesn't mean the same holds true for me," she snaps.

That's when my phone rings again. I scowl at the name that appears on the screen.

Alphahole calling.

There is only one alphahole I know. And how the hell did he get access to this phone and have his contact details keyed in already?

"Aren't you going to answer it?" Cassandra asks.

"No." I decline the call, switch off the phone for good measure and then drop it on the sofa next to me.

"Hmm…" Cass scowls at me. "Not sure Christian would be happy to hear you say that."

"To hell with Christian." I sniff.

"Was that him?" Theresa scowls. "Is that who you hung up on?"

"Maybe…" I raise a shoulder. "Not that it matters."

She wipes away the moisture on her cheek. "So, are you and he really going to stay separate until your wedding?"

At least, my love life seems to have intercepted what could have been an altercation between the two of them.

"It would seem that way," I reply. "I mean, we are only following tradition, aren't we, by staying apart?"

"You would be the only one who would be doing so." She leans forward in her seat, "Aren't you tempted to, at least, test drive him before the wedding?"

"What?" I frown. "No, of course not. If anything, I am happy Nonna is helping to reinforce this particular convention."

"I don't know of a single couple who hasn't broken this custom," Theresa drawls.

"So you and Xander…?"

Her features crumple, but then she straightens her spine.

"No, we didn't. And not for lack of trying. I mean, I should have known then that he was having second thoughts, but you know, I thought he was only being a gentleman."

"The Sovranos being gentlemanly?" I scoff. "Now I have heard everything."

"Not all of the brothers are so … rough," Cass protests.

"If you are thinking of Adrian," I peer into her features. "Well, of course, you are thinking of Adrian; I have to warn you not to be taken in by a polite facade."

"But he is the most silent of all of them." Cass frowns. "I mean, surely, he can't be worse than your Christian."

"Not my Christian." I huff. "And that's exactly what I mean. The quieter they are, the more lethal their sting is. Still waters and all that."

"Hmm…" She strokes her chin. "I'll keep that in mind. Not that I intend to get to know him better or anything."

"Of course not!" I cough into my hand.

Theresa's gaze bounces between us. "So, the two of you are involved with the Sovrano brothers?"

"No." I scowl.

"Hey," Cass protests, "don't drag me into this." She jerks her chin in my direction. "I'm not the one getting married in a few days."

And I won't be either, if I have my way. "True that," I mumble. I raise my hand to push the hair away from my face, and Theresa's gaze widens. "Wow!" She stares at my fingers. "That's some ring."

"Yeah…" I lower my hand to my lap.

"And that was a very romantic moment the two of you shared earlier when he put the ring on your finger," Cassandra points out.

"He was just making a point," I protest.

"If you mean he was staking his claim, then you are absolutely right." Theresa peers into my face. "How does it feel to be at the receiving end of all that intense obsession?"

I scowl. "He isn't obsessed with me."

"He couldn't take his gaze off of you the entire time we were on the plane," Cassandra offers.

"Right?" Theresa turns to her. "And the way he kept his arm around her while he was trying to get Nonna and his brothers to back down. OMG, that was even more romantic than the kiss."

"Oh, please." I jump up to my feet and begin to pace. "The alphahole has everybody fooled."

"But not you?" Cass retorts.

"No, not me!" I turn on her. "All of this is some elaborate ruse to keep me under his control."

"That's the Sovranos for you," Theresa interjects. "The brothers are alpha, over-the-top, possessive Mafia men, which is why all of us used to swoon over them in school."

"You went to school with them?" I ask.

"Until they left for LA, and they were older than me, but I do recollect them swaggering in and out of class and generally commanding the teachers around."

"That would be them, all right." I huff. "Good thing I wasn't subjected to them."

"You went to a different school, I take it?" Cass interjects.

"And then went to the UK to study medicine."

"Paid for by Michael," Theresa points out.

I deflate a little. "Something I will never live down, especially since it seems like everyone knows it. So, my family owes them. Doesn't mean I need to agree to their every whim and fancy."

"Christian saved your life," Cass points out.

"He did?" Theresa's eyes bug out. "How did he do that?"

"I helped Karma try to escape from Michael, not that it worked out," I blow out a breath, "but when Michael found out, he was livid."

"Of course, he was," Theresa nods, "you tried to turn his wife against him."

"The way he was treating her…" I purse my lips. "It's not for me to judge, but she wasn't happy in the early part of their courtship, and she asked me for help. I did what any woman would do when she finds another of her gender in peril. I helped her."

"And then Christian stepped in to save you from Michael."

"Now I wish he hadn't."

"You don't mean it," Theresa says in a hushed voice. "You don't want to be at the receiving end of a Sovrano's rage."

"They are human, like us." I snort. "And Christian has his failings, like all of us. Let him get angry; see if I care."

The hair on the nape of my neck rises. Goose bumps pop on my skin. I jerk my head in the direction of the doorway.

"Ugh," I wrap my arms around my waist, "what are you doing here?"

15

Christian

"You weren't answering your phone," I growl.

Theresa and Cassandra rise to their feet. They glance from Flower to me, then head toward the door.

"Wait, Cass," Aurora calls out, "we can't meet without a chaperone."

"I don't need a fucking chaperone."

"Nonna's rules"—she sets her jaw—"and we are under her roof."

Something I intend to rectify as soon as possible. I scowl at Cassandra, who stares back at me. Theresa wisely walks out of the room.

"I'll, uh, be standing right outside," Cassandra finally ventures, "and I'll keep the door slightly ajar."

"But, Cass—" Before Aurora can complete the statement, Cassandra walks out of the room, making sure to pull the door closed behind her, but she doesn't shut it completely.

I turn to face Aurora, who draws herself up to her full height; which still means she barely comes up to the level of my chest. I stalk toward her, and she stills. Watches me with a wary expression as I come to a halt in front of her.

"On your knees," I growl.

"What?" Her jaw drops. "The hell are you talking about?"

"Get. On. Your. Knees. Flower."

"And if I say no?"

"Are you saying no?" I smirk. Color flushes her cheek.

"Cass is right outside the room," she hisses.

"I can be quiet"—I bare my teeth—"and your throat will be so stuffed that you won't be able to breathe properly, let alone speak, so I suggest you do as I say.

"Nonna will be here to check on me," she protests.

"I suggest you make it quick, Flower."

She opens her mouth, and I shake my head. I press my hand on her shoulder and apply pressure, and she folds gracefully to drop to her knees. I sink my fingers into the mass of her gorgeous hair, then slide my zipper down the front of my pants. I push down my pants, and my cock springs free—yeah, no underwear, I came prepared to put her in her place. I fist the base of my dick and swipe from root to crown. A drop of precum beads the slit. Instantly, she rises up on her knees. She extends her neck and licks off the moisture from the head of my cock.

A groan rumbles up my chest and I swallow it down. I must have made a noise, for her gaze darts up to my face. She must realize exactly the effect she has on me, for her eyes gleam. She pushes aside my hand and grips the base of my cock. She squeezes down, and I hiss. Her lip curves right before she leans forward and closes her mouth around the already swollen head.

Jesù Cristo! She hoovers down my dick like she was made to swallow my shaft. She licks her tongue around the head, tips her head forward, so my length slides down the column of her throat.

"F-u-c-k," I growl in a low tone as I tighten my hold on her hair. I tug, and she jerks her chin up, never taking her gaze off of mine. Without breaking the connection, she pulls back until my shaft is balanced on the rim of her mouth, then slides forward, so my cock glides down her throat again. She hums, and the vibrations sear through the sensitive skin of my dick and sink into my blood. She begins to suck on me, pulling back and moving forward. And again. My balls swell, and blood drains to my groin. The next time she takes me down her throat, I tighten my grip and hold her there.

"I don't allow anyone to give me blow jobs. I take them, Flower." I yank her head back, so she releases the hold on my cock, then glide her forward again and again. Tears squeeze out from the corners of her eyes; her mascara begins to run. Her gaze turns fierce, and she releases her hold on my dick only to cup my balls.

"Fucking fuck," I swear in a low voice as I pick up speed. I fuck her mouth and feel my length enclosed in the column of her throat as she swallows. She brings her other hand up and cups both of her palms around my balls, and squeezes. Goose bumps pop on my skin. My vision tunnels.

I am not a religious person, I don't believe in God, but right now, with her mouth wrapped around my cock, her small palms clutching my balls, as she runs her finger up the crease between my ass cheeks to toy with my back hole—I swear I have my first out-of-body experience. The blood thuds at my temples, and my heartbeat ratchets up. I feel my pulse flare to life at my wrists, on my eyelids, in my fucking balls, which thicken and draw up.

I tighten my hold on her head as the pressure at the base of my spine explodes out, and I come, shooting my load down her throat. "Take it all," I say in a fierce tone, "every single drop, Flower. You get me?"

She swallows as I continue to pump into her mouth. She sucks down my cum like it's the finest wine. A drop dribbles from the corner of her lips, and I scoop it up. I pull out, then rub my cum-drenched finger across her lips. Pupils blown, she gazes up at me from under heavy-lidded eyes. I haul her up to her feet and crash my mouth to hers.

The taste of my cum, the sweetness of her lips—all of it swirls together creating a potent mixture that explodes on my palate. I tilt my head and deepen the kiss. A moan bleeds from her mouth, and I gulp it down. Her breasts push into my chest, the softness of her curves press against my thighs, and she writhes as she tries to get closer as my dick lengthens, once again, wanting to be inside of her. All of it crashes over me. A hot sensation stabs at my chest. My heart stutters as blood thrums at my temples. I soften the kiss, pulling back until my lips are poised on hers. I brush my mouth on hers once, twice, as I gaze into her bright amber eyes. Her eyelids flutter down, and her entire body seems to melt into mine. I tighten my arm around her, holding her, cradling her, treasuring her... *Che cazzo!* What is she doing to me?

I step back so suddenly that she stumbles, then pushes her hand into my shoulder to right herself. I reach down, tuck myself in, then unable to stop myself, tuck a loose strand of hair behind her ear.

Her gaze widens, and in the depths of her golden eyes, I see hope flare, and something else. An emotion I dare not name.

"Christian, I—"

"Christian, Aurora," Nonna's voice sounds from the doorway.

"Oh, hell," she whispers, "it's your grandmother." She begins to pull away, but I grab her wrist and stop her. Then I wrap an arm around her waist and turn to face the woman who's decided to come between me and my plaything.

16

Aurora

"What are you doing in here?" Nonna strides in, followed by Cassandra, who wrings her hands.

"I … I couldn't stop her," she grimaces.

"Damn right." Nonna fixes her with a stern look. "Don't forget whose employ you are in right now, young lady."

"That's not fair," I begin to protest, and Nonna turns on me.

"I know you young people like to pretend that we're all born equal, but the fact is we are not, and the faster you reconcile yourself to that, the quicker you'll be able to find some measure of happiness."

"Is that what you did?" I frown. "Reconcile?"

"Not a word you like, I take it?" She draws herself up to her full height. "It's not as bad as it sounds. There's a measure of comfort to be found when you acknowledge that things are not always in your hands. The sooner you learn to give in to the inevitable, the better it's going to be for you."

"I'll never do that." I fold my arms around my waist. "I am never going to settle for something that is below my expectations."

"Is that right?" Nonna's lips curve in a smile.

Next to me, Christian stiffens. I sense him shoot me a look, but I don't acknowledge it.

"And you?" Nonna arches an eyebrow at my fake fiancé. "Any words of new-age wisdom that you'd like to add to the conversation?"

"Me?" the rat's ass says with an innocent expression on his features. "You know me, Nonna, I'm a man of simple pleasures. The basic needs of life are what I aim to fulfill, which is why I couldn't stay away from my lovely fiancée."

What the—? I cannot believe he just said that. I try to pull away, but his hold around my waist tightens.

"You don't fool me, either." Nonna scowls at the asshole who just seconds ago had his dick down my throat. Right before he pulled me to my feet and kissed me as if his life depended on it, as if he couldn't go another second without twining his breath with mine and drinking from me. Because that's what it was— him trying to inhale me, trying to claim me, trying to … share some of that grief that lurks inside of him with me? And then, just when I thought that he was going to release me, he softened the kiss. He held his lips to mine, shared my breath, gazed into my eyes as if he was searching for the answer to those secret questions that you ask yourself when you think no one else is listening. When you are on your own, adrift, alone and sure that you'll never find another soul who'll understand you, who'll want to know you, to be with you, the one you'll want to share your life with.

Do I want to share my life with this … this … overbearing, hard, overcome-with-sorrow alphahole? I glance at him sideways and find him training his gaze on his grandmother.

"You wound me, Nonna." He finally releases me and closes the distance to the old woman. "I was simply ensuring that my future wife is comfortable and has everything she needs."

"Hmph." Nonna looks him up and down. "I'm not that old that I don't know when a man and a woman have been going at it."

"Please," I burst out, "will the two of you stop already?"

Both of them turn their gazes on me, and I freeze. "I mean," I raise my hands, "this was just Christian being Christian, and I know I should not have agreed to meet him without a chaperone, but you know how persuasive my fiancé can be, Nonna."

She glances between us, and a sly smile curves her lips. "Are you defending him?"

"Umm," I shuffle my feet, "not really." I hesitate. "Okay, maybe I am. I mean, it's not like I don't appreciate everything you've done for me, Nonna, truly, but he's leaving now. My virtue is still intact"—technically—"so can we just forget about what happened?"

"On one condition."

"Which is?"

"You promise to turn him away the next time he turns up."

"And we both know how impossible it is to say 'no' to him."

"Have you tried to say 'no' to him?"

I hesitate.

"That's what I thought." Nonna smirks. "The fault lies with both of you. After all, you need two hands to clap, don't you?"

"You're really serious about doing this wedding by the book, aren't you?" Christian glares at his Nonna.

"Deadly." Her smile widens. "It's my hope that before I die, at least one of my grandsons will indulge me with a traditional Sicilian wedding where all of the traditions have been met."

"Emotional blackmail doesn't suit you, Nonna," Christian protests.

"Whatever it takes," Nonna raises a shoulder. "And I'm warning you right now—no stabbing your bridegroom in church," she tells me.

"If I do, I'll be sure to cause a lot more damage," I say under my breath.

Christian hears it, though, because he shoots me an amused glance over his shoulder. "I'll be more than happy to stab you back in return; just not with a knife," he says in a voice low enough that only I can hear it.

"Ugh." I grimace. "That's a terrible joke."

"Not a joke; a promise."

"Enough time to make promises when you stand in front of the altar," Nonna admonishes us. Jeez, did she overhear the rest of our X-rated conversation too? Not that it would shock her. Very little seems to pull her out of her comfort zone, at any rate.

"You," she stabs a finger at Christian, "out."

He turns to me, closes the distance between us, then grabs the back of my neck and pulls me close. He kisses me soundly, and by the time he releases me, I am panting. Turning on his feet, he walks over to Nonna. "I'd kiss you on the cheek, but I just French-kissed my bride-to-be, so I'm sure you'll understand if I pass."

"Leave now." Nonna sniffs. "And be sure to clean up before dinner."

Christian ambles over to the doorway. He jerks his chin in Cassandra's direction before he leaves.

"Shut the door and come sit over here," Nonna tells Cassandra before she walks over to sit down in a chair.

Cassandra follows her bidding before she joins me.

Nonna glances between the two of us. "This can't happen again." She shakes her head. "I trusted you, Cassandra, to keep him out. And you..." She scowls at me. "I thought you wanted to follow the conventions leading up to your wedding."

"I do, but—"

"No buts." She taps her fingers together. "I agreed to help you only because I thought you were serious about being away from him before the wedding. If you're not—"

"I am." I hold up a palm. "I promise, the next time he comes in to visit me, I'll … I'll scream."

"Not too loudly. If I'm asleep, I don't want to be woken up."

"Of course, not." I blow out a breath. "Like I said, it's difficult to say 'no' to your grandson when he has his mind set on something."

"Well, he needs to realize that he can't always get what he wants."

"Can't he?" I can't stop the bitter laugh that escapes me.

"You do know you're strong enough to stop him, don't you?" Nonna trains her gaze on me. "Unless, of course, you didn't want to?"

"Nothing like that." I shuffle my feet. "Honestly, I was just swept away in the moment, and he seemed so fierce, so overbearing, and so confident that—"

"You found yourself agreeing to do whatever he wanted?"

"Something like that..." Also, I didn't want to feel like I had a choice. It's much easier to simply follow his lead because I always enjoy the results. Even when he pushed me down on my knees and thrust his cock down my throat, I enjoyed it. The flesh between my legs quivers. I squeeze my thighs together to tamp down on the emptiness that gapes there. Shit, just thinking of how he fucked my mouth is turning me on. And that's crazy. I should be upset about how he had his way with me, but my body seems to have other thoughts. As a doctor, I have seen first-hand how much the heart and mind influence the body. But this time, it seems, despite my wanting to not be attracted to him, my body has already made the decision to be turned on by his proximity.

"If you want my help, then I need to be assured that you are doing your best to resist him," Nonna says in a smooth voice. "Do I have your assurance, Aurora?"

I blink, then nod. "Of course, you do.

"And you?" She turns to Cass. "Can I count on you to stop my grandson the next time he comes around, failing which you need to alert me?"

"Yes, Nonna," Cass folds her fingers together, "you can count on me."

Just then, a loud clanging reaches us.

17

———————

Christian

A clanging sound fills the space. I walk over to the speaker in the wall from which the sound emerges, just as it fades away. "Dinner is served," a voice hollers from it. It's Gino, no doubt. I wince as I depress the button on the panel, cutting off the sound. Silence descends. *Grazie al cazzo! Thank fuck.* If that's how we are going to be summoned for meals, I will have to speak to Nonna about it.

There's a brief knock on the main door of the chalet before it's pushed open. Massimo's frame fills the space before he steps in.

"Dinner is—"

"Served." I grimace. "I know; I heard."

"Doubt anyone missed that." He chuckles.

"Glad you find it funny." I rub the back of my neck.

"You have to admit, it's an effective way of grabbing our attention."

"What-fucking-ever," I growl.

I returned to my chalet after my grandmother almost walked in on me stuffing my cock down my fiancée's throat. Of course, I knew that it would have to be quick when I pushed her down on her knees… What surprised me, though, was the ardor with which she thew herself into the job. She sucked me off, wrung me dry, closed that hot mouth of hers around my swollen cock, and all thought flew from my head. At that moment, I wouldn't have cared if all of my brothers had walked in on us, though that might have been less embarrassing than having my grandmother find us. On the bright side, we were done by the time Nonna walked in, though she still found us kissing. Hopefully, she assumes it was a romantic gesture on my part, or some such shit. No doubt, she thinks that I can't keep my hands off of my fiancée. Which is true. And she's your fake fiancée, remember?

"You seem to be upset about something, *fratellino*."

"Me, upset?" I growl. "What gives you that idea?"

"I don't know; maybe because when I walked in, you were scowling at that speaker like you were going to rip it out of the wall and jump on it."

"Now that you mention it…"

"I was only kidding." Massimo smirks. "But if that helps you get rid of some of the frustration that you are, no doubt, harboring inside, then be my guest."

"Frustration?" I draw myself up to my full height. "You trying to tell me something, amico mio?"

"It's no secret that Nonna has thrown a wrench in your plan."

"And what plan is that?" I ask in a low voice.

"The one where you try to seduce your fianceé before your marriage."

"Like you haven't slept around?"

"I'm not going to marry any of them."

"You mean to say when you choose your bride, you're going to consummate your marriage on the wedding night?"

"You bet; it's how things are done in the Mafia, isn't it?"

"Next, you'll tell me that you're going to marry a virgin."

"Don't tell me you don't expect your fiancée to be a virgin."

"Don't talk about her." I frown.

Massimo blows out a breath. "Look, it was different for Michael—"

"So everyone keeps saying."

"He was out to get revenge for Karma's father selling us out, but you, you're marrying a nice Sicilian girl—"

"Who's spent enough time away to speak like she was born British," I interject.

"Besides the point." Massimo rocks back on his heels. "If you had any sense, you would have eloped with her, but since you didn't…"

"Hold on—what did you say?"

"That you don't have enough sense?"

"After that."

"That you don't have enough sense?" He smirks.

"You said that I should have eloped with her—" I stroke my chin.

"Now, now..." Massimo holds up his hands. "You know Nonna is looking forward to a traditional church wedding."

"Well, Nonna can satisfy that desire with you."

He blanches.

"Come on, Massimo, you just said that you were ready to marry a virgin in an arranged Mafia marriage."

"Because I know the importance of having a good willing woman at home who can bear my babies and keep the house—"

"While you spend your time being a tough Mafioso with a few sidepieces, no doubt?"

"There have to be some benefits of being in this life."

"Didn't think you would be this chauvinistic."

He throws his head back and laughs that full-belly laugh that emerges from the pit of his stomach. "You should speak, brother. You, who all but held your bride-to-be captive and, no doubt, forced her to agree to marry you."

"Only to get Nonna and the rest of you off my back when we finally break up," I murmur under my breath.

"What did you say?"

"Nothing. Fuck." I drag my fingers through my hair. "Why are we talking here, anyway? Shouldn't we be heading out for dinner?"

"I know you're trying to change the subject," Massimo narrows his gaze on my face. "I'll let you get away with it, this time."

There's another knock, and Seb pops his head through the doorway. "You guys coming for dinner?"

I glance across the table to where my fiancée is seated opposite me. Flower wears a soft pink dress that lends a rosy hue to her cheeks. Her thick hair curls about her shoulders, and she pushes away at a strand that falls over her cheek. The yellow sapphire on her finger catches the glow of the light from the candle flame on the table between us.

She throws her head back and laughs at something that Sebastian murmurs to her. The seating at the table was arranged by Nonna. She explained that it would change for every meal so that we'd have a chance to be seated with a different family member and get to know each of them over the next few days. Which also means that she has no intention of ever seating me and Flower together, which is going to be a problem.

"So, you really do have feelings for her, hmm?" Luca's voice cuts through my thoughts.

I raise my glass of wine to my mouth and drink from it. "How much have you had to drink, asshole?" I mutter.

"Not as much as you, clearly." He indicates the almost empty bottle of wine next to me. I had grabbed it from the center of the table and decided to hold onto it. It may be the season of sharing, but I'll be damned if I'm going to miss the opportunity to try to drown out the confusion in my head with alcohol.

I knock back the rest of the wine in the glass, then place it back on the table.

"Probably not a good idea to get drunk either," he cautions.

"Least I can do, considering I have been relegated to trying to sneak in meetings with my own fiancée."

Luca chuckles. "Never thought I'd see the day when you'd be beaten at your own game. And what makes it even worse is she's a woman of eighty."

"Not sure what she is punishing me for or why she is so insistent that everything be done according to tradition. I swear, she's probably just trying to make it as difficult for me as possible to get a good night's sleep."

"You could, of course, come out with us tonight to the nightclub."

I scowl. "Why is this the first I'm hearing about it?"

"Figured you'd want to spend time with your woman like Michael here, but since you do not," he smirks, "might as well cut your losses and come with us, huh?"

Two of the staff clear our dinner plates, then a clinking sound reaches us. Seb and I look up to find Nonna tapping her glass with a knife. "May I have your attention, please?"

The noise dies down and everyone glances at her, "I am so happy to see my family all together for the holidays. I know, it's been a challenge for you boys to get your heads around why I wanted this event to take place, but I'm so pleased that all of you could make it."

"Of course, Nonna," Michael murmurs. "You are the oldest in our family, so your word is law."

Nonna chuckles. "It's generous of you to say so, Don Sovrano," she tilts her head, "but I'll accept the compliment."

"Not just an empty compliment." I raise my glass. "We'll always prioritize your wishes before anything else."

"Why thank you, Christiano." She smiles at me. "I know, at heart, you boys are committed to this family, that you'll prioritize the good of your brothers before anything else. It's what makes our family strong and able to combat any challenge from any outsider." She glances around the table. "I don't know if I'll be here to see another Christmas, so—"

A ripple runs around the table. I open my mouth to protest, and she raises a hand. "I know, I know. God willing, I'll be here for much longer than that, but at my age, you take each day as your last day, so..." She places her glass and knife on the table. "I wanted to make this post-Christmas celebration special."

As if on cue, Cassandra walks in, pushing a trolley laden with gifts. She pauses next to Nonna.

"Thought you said you didn't want us to have any gift-giving this year, Nonna?" Michael interjects.

"I changed my mind." Nonna raises her shoulder, "I think I'm allowed at my age, eh?"

"Bull-fucking-shit," I whisper to Luca. "She planned this all along."

"Of course, she did," Luca says from the corner of his mouth. "But he'll let Nonna get away with it."

Cass walks around the table and places a gift in front of each one of us. Then she pushes the trolley to the side and takes her seat at the table.

Nonna raises her hand. "Open your gifts, please."

I glance down at my gift, then at Aurora, who looks up at me. Our gazes clash. Her champagne eyes sparkle in this light. Her features are flushed; her hair gleams with a healthy shine. She looks relaxed and so damn beautiful. A hot sensation stabs at my chest. She holds my gaze a second longer before turning away. She reaches for her gift, unwraps it, and holds up a bracelet. The light bounces off the simple but elegant design.

"Nonna," she gasps, "it's beautiful."

"And so is this." Karma holds up a chain with a teardrop black diamond as the pendant.

"Both are family heirlooms," Nonna smiles, "and they'll look much better when they are worn than being kept in the family safe."

"Oh, my god," Theresa breathes. She stares at a box with something like reverence. "These are very expensive tulip bulbs." She looks at Nonna with tears in her eyes. "I never thought I'd be able to afford them." She jumps to her feet and runs around to hug Nonna, who looks taken aback. She pats Theresa on her shoulder.

"There, there, use them to grow your florist business."

"I will." Pressing a kiss to Nonna's cheek, Theresa all but skips back to her seat.

"What did you get, Cass?" Aurora turns to where Cass has torn open an envelope and is holding up a sheet of paper.

"It's a one-week all-expenses-paid vacation to a hot springs spa," Cass murmurs.

"Not just any spa; the best spa in all of Europe." Nonna sniffs. "You didn't think I'd let you go anywhere else, did you?"

"Thank you, Nonna." Cass beams. "I am going to enjoy myself."

"You bet you will." Nonna turns to us. "Boys, you haven't opened your gifts yet."

I open the wrapping paper and find a pair of cufflinks. The design is the Sovrano crest, the metal slightly worn with age. I glance around to find each of my brothers have received a similar pair.

"Some of them belonged to your grandfather and others to his father." Nonna's voice softens. "Your grandfather loved wearing them and had them created at different times in his life. I know that, other than Michael and Massimo, the rest of you don't often wear cufflinks, but I hope this will inspire you to remember your family's legacy."

"You didn't give these to our father?" I ask.

Nonna's features shutter. "It didn't seem right." She firms her lips. "Oh, I tried to bring myself to give them to him, but somehow..." She shakes her head. "Somehow I couldn't." She glances around the table. "Now I know why that was so; I was saving them for my grandsons. I know you will all make me proud."

"And now, it's our turn." Michael rises from his seat and walks over to Nonna. He pulls out a package from the inside of his coat pocket and holds it out to her.

"What is this?" Nonna glances up at him.

"This is from all of us."

"Hmph." Nonna frowns. "I did say, no gifts."

"You didn't think we were going to let you gift us all and not get something in return."

"At my age, I do all the giving." She laughs. "But if you insist—"

"I do." Michael's lips curve.

"So do I." I thump the table with my palm.

"And I!" Seb pipes up.

"And I," the others echo our words.

A blush steals over Nonna's face. "You children..." Her throat moves as she swallows. "You shouldn't have." She accepts the package from Michael.

"Go on," I urge her, "open it."

"Yes, open it," Aurora adds. We glance at each other, and once more, our gazes catch and hold. How is it that she fits so easily into my life and with my family? How is it that she seems so right where she is... Well, it would help if she were seated closer, but there's something to be said about being able to look across the table and see her. It puts her just out of reach, and that makes it so much more exciting. As if she's caught the train of my thoughts, Aurora flushes; she looks over to where Nonna unwraps the package.

"Oh," she folds her palms together, "it's beautiful." She laughs. "I can't believe you got this for me."

"Wear it, wear it." Theresa literally jumps up and down on the chair in excitement.

"Should I?" Nonna glances around the table? "Should I really wear it?"

"Yes!" Karma claps her hands together. "You should."

"You absolutely should," Aurora agrees.

Nonna picks the tiara from out of its box and holds it up. The light shines through the gaps between the delicate filigree work. "It's gorgeous," she whispers.

"May I?" Michael takes it from Nonna and places it on her head. "Every queen should have one." He bends and kisses her cheek. "You look magnificent."

Nonna's chin wobbles. "You children are going to make me cry."

"No, don't cry." I raise my glass. "To Nonna."

Michael walks back to his seat and raises his glass of prosecco. "To Nonna."

"To Nonna." The others raise their glasses.

We down our drinks just as Gino bursts into the room with Andy. He all but drops the cat on the floor, and the animal hisses at him before walking toward Karma, who picks him up.

"Someone, please keep that beast away from me," Gino snaps. He turns to leave, then glimpses the tiara on Nonna's head. "Like she didn't already have a big ego." He sniffs, then turns to leave.

There's silence, then we all burst out laughing.

"A-n-d, never let it be said that family can't put you in your place." She chuckles. "Thank you." Her eyes shine. "Thank you, everyone. I will always treasure this tiara and this memory." She takes in everyone's faces as the staff bustle in with the dessert.

"Eat up," Luca turns to me, "so we can get to the nightclub."

18

———————

Aurora

I turn on my side and try to close my eyes, but all I can see are images of the alphahole dancing with someone else. Putting his hands on her waist, pulling her close until her hips are flush with his groin, until she can feel the evidence of his arousal as he leans in close; pushing the hair off the base of her neck, and pressing his nose into the curve of her shoulder. He drags his nose up the side of her neck and bites down on her ear. She groans, throwing her head back against his shoulder. He slides his palm down the flatness of her belly toward the apex of her thighs. He grips her pussy and squeezes. She moans and turns her face toward him. Her features dissolve into mine.

I snap my eyes open. My belly trembles, my core clenches, and heat flushes my skin. I throw my cover off and sit up. "*Santa Rosalia,*" I snarl, "what the hell is wrong with me?" Why can't I get the man out of my head?

The first half of the dinner, he stared at me. Then he turned away and engaged in conversation with Luca. He barely gave me a second glance. When the meal was done, he bid me a polite goodbye and followed his brothers out. I learned later that the brothers had headed out for the nearest nightclub; there was only one in town. Michael had opted to stay back with Karma. I had asked Cass why they hadn't invited us, and she had looked at me like I was crazy.

Apparently, the Sovrano brothers wouldn't stoop to inviting women with them when they go cavorting. Damn it. I should have followed them, stowed away in one of the cars or something. And if I had done that, no doubt, they would have discovered me right away.

I slide out of bed and use the bathroom. I get a drink of water and am about to slip into bed when something taps on the windowpane behind me. I yelp and turn toward the darkened rectangle of the window Did I imagine it? Or did something actually hit the pane? I take a step toward it when the tapping sound reaches me again. I jump, and the hair on the back of my neck rises. Who the hell could it be? I head for the windowpane, then yell when familiar features greet me.

"What the hell are you doing here?" I whisper scream.

Christian grips the windowsill outside and signals to me to open the window. My heart begins to race and my pulse slams against my temples. I grip the latch, lower it, and pull the window open. He instantly throws a leg over the sill, then the other. He straightens, tumbles into me, and we fall toward the floor. He manages to grab me and twist, and somehow, I end up falling on top of him. The breath whooshes out of him as he groans. I begin to pull away, but he grabs the back of my neck and holds me in place.

"Let me go," I hiss.

"No fucking way," he growls, and I wrinkle my nose.

"You've been drinking."

"No shit." He chuckles. "I had to find a way to forget about the fact that you're in the chalet next to me, and yet I wouldn't be able to see you."

"Oh…" Something hot curls in my chest. "Did you miss me?"

"Like I missed a hole in the head."

"A-n-d, there he is," I snap. "Why did you come here anyway? Thought you'd have gone home with whomever you met at the bar."

"The nightclub."

"What-bloody-ever."

"Jealous, Flower?"

"No, and don't call me by that stupid nickname."

"It suits you." He hauls me close and runs his nose up the curve of my neck. Just as I'd imagined earlier in my half-asleep half-awake state, with that other woman.

I turn my head away, then dig my knee into his groin. He hisses in pain. His grasp loosens enough for me to scramble away. I jump to my feet, or try to, because he's already thrown himself at me. He grabs my ankle and tugs.

"Let go." I don't bother to lower my voice. I try to kick out, and he grabs my other leg. He pries them apart, and I pant as I try to pull away. He releases my feet, but before I can scramble forward, he's heaved his bulk up and partially onto me. I collapse to the floor, unable to move.

"What are you doing?" I hiss.

"Feeling up what's mine," he rumbles as he pushes his groin into the curve of my behind. The thick column of his arousal stabs me in the valley between my butt cheeks. My belly flutters, my core clenches, my nipples tighten, and damn him, but if I don't get away, I'm going to push back against him and beg him to take me, and I'll never be able to live with myself after that.

I stop struggling and force my muscles to uncoil. He plants his palms on either side of me, holding most of his weight off of me, except for his hips, which pin me down, ensuring that every inch of his throbbing length is imprinted against my panty-clad bottom. By now, the T-shirt I wore to bed is bunched up under my armpits. Supporting himself on one hand, he slides his hand under the fabric. His fingertips brush my breast, and I shiver. He closes his fingers around my flesh and squeezes. A moan spills from my lips.

"Fuck, the noises you make, Flower, they go straight to my head; you know that?"

He drags his hand down, then slides it under the waistband of my panties. He traces the valley between my butt cheeks and probes at my slippery entrance. The breath rushes out of me.

"Christian," I groan, "don't do this."

"You mean this?" He scoops up some of the moisture from my cunt and drags it up and around my back hole.

I freeze, "Wh-why did you do that?"

"Why do you think?"

"Are you … you don't mean to … do you?"

"Do what?" He probes at my puckered hole, and I huff. "Please, Christian… Please."

"What?"

"Please don't."

He pauses, begins to pull away, and I turn on my back. He rises up to his feet, begins to head for the door, and something inside me seems to crack.

"Christian…"

He keeps going.

"Christian, please stop."

He pauses, "If I stay, I won't be responsible for what I do next."

I swallow.

"You understand what I'm saying, Flower?"

I jerk my chin.

"You sure about this?"

I hesitate.

"If you aren't…" He turns to leave, and this time, I jump up to my feet. I race over to him, throw my arms around his waist, and hold on.

"Don't go, please don't go."

His muscles turn to stone. He lowers his chin, no doubt taking in how I'm clinging to him.

"I know it's stupid. I know I'm the one who asked Nonna to take me under her protection, so I wouldn't be your captive any longer. And I'm still not sure about what you want to do to me, but I don't want you to leave right now."

"You're making this really difficult, you know that?"

"Yeah," I half-laugh half-sob, "tell me about it. When it comes to you, I'm always confused about what I'm supposed to feel for you."

"But you don't want me to leave now?"

"I don't."

"Fine." He turns, then bends his knees and haul me up and over his shoulder.

"What the—" I stutter. "What are you doing? Christian, you—" He slaps his palm across my butt, and the pain shudders up my spine.

"Hey," I protest, "what was that for?"

He stalks over to the bed, then throws me down. I bounce once, then glance up to find him staring down at me. He throws himself down on the bed next to me before sliding up to lay back against the pillow. He taps his chest. "Come here."

"What?"

"Come. Here," he says in that low, hard voice which sends goose bumps rippling up my skin.

I clamber onto my front and crawl over to him. I rise up and am about to throw my leg over his waist, when he holds up a hand. "Stop," he growls. "First, take off your panties."

"What?" I blink.

"Don't have all night, Flower; you in or out?"

You mean, do I want to have an orgasm or two or three and then collapse into slumber? Or do I refuse to do as he says, then toss and turn all night as I try to get myself off? When you put it that way… I slide my panties down my legs. He holds his hand out, and I hand them over.

He stuffs them inside the front pocket of his jeans, then jerks his chin.

I swing my leg up and over his chest. He grips me on either side just below my butt and hauls me up so I'm poised with my pussy bared right over his face.

He stays there, peering up at the most intimate part of me.

Heat flushes my skin, and my belly clenches. "What are you doing?"

"Admiring my pussy; do you mind?" Jesus, did he call it 'my' pussy? He did call it 'my' pussy. And by 'my' pussy, I don't mean mine. I mean his. My belly trembles, and heat flushes my skin.

"As a doctor, I can tell you that my pussy is much like any other. It's functional and fulfills the role of expelling waste matter from the body, not to mention the pivotal role it plays in child-bearing and—" I huff because he's swiped his thick, rough tongue from my back hole to my clit. He licks me again, and heat sears my belly. He wraps that wicked tongue around my clit, and my entire body jolts.

"Christian," I huff. "Please, please, please—"

He thrusts his tongue inside my wet, soaking channel, and I throw my head back. My thighs tremble, and my knees threaten to give way from under me. I throw out my palms and grip the headboard behind him.

He clamps his teeth over my clit and sucks on it, and I swear I see stars. A groan wheezes from me. I try to bring my thighs together, but he thrusts his face up and stabs my channel again and again with his tongue, and a trembling grips me. It sweeps up from my feet, up my legs, my thighs, and slams into my core before it sweeps up my spine.

"I'm going to come, Christian. I'm going to come," I warble, and he pulls back. Jerk face drops his head back on the pillow, then hauls me off of him and to the side. I blink as he wipes the back of his palm across his glistening face.

"You taste sweet, Flower. Too bad I'm not going to settle for cookies when I'd rather be eating Christmas pudding." He swings his legs over and heads for the door.

That's when I jump up on the bed. "Where the hell are you going?" I yell. "You asshole, come back and—"

He holds a finger to his lips. "Don't want to wake up Nonna, do you?" Pushing open the door, he leaves.

19

Aurora

"How … how dare he?" I fold my arms across my waist as I scowl into my coffee.

"Now, what did he do?" Cassandra murmurs from in front of the stove where she's making pancakes.

After Christian left last night, I tried to go back to sleep and failed. After tossing and turning for the rest of the night, I finally fell asleep in the early hours of the morning and woke up with a start to find it was seven am. I stumbled down the stairs to find Cassandra bustling in the kitchen. Even though there was staff to take care of everything she had insisted on making breakfast for us. The woman was a workaholic, honestly! She poured me a cup of coffee and announced that she was making pancakes for breakfast. I asked if I could help, and she shooed me off. She built a tray for Nonna, consisting of coffee, orange juice, and the first batch of the pancakes, and had taken it to her.

By the time she returned, Theresa had also joined us. I refilled my cup of coffee and poured her one as well. We sat sipping our coffees in silence as Cass began to create the next batch of pancakes.

My mind hasn't been able to stop going over the events from last night. How he felt up my back hole, promising, without saying anything overtly, that he intends to own me there. How he put his mouth on my pussy and brought me to the edge, only to pull back as I was on the verge of climax. Damn it! Why the hell did I tell him that I was going to come earlier? After he left, I tried to make myself come after, but of course, each time I thought I was going to climax, I wasn't able to take that final step toward the orgasm. I finally stopped, pulled my fingers out of my pussy, and licked them off, imagining that they were his fingers which had been inside me all this time. That it was his tongue which was licking the cum off my digits, his mouth which had closed around them, his breath that fanned my skin as he sucked off every last drop of evidence of my arousal.

My breath quickens, my palms dampen, and I squeeze my thighs together to try to clamp down on the growing hunger in my core.

"Aurora?" Theresa's soft voice pulls me out of my reverie.

"What?" I scowl at her.

"You were telling us what Christian got up to?"

"Was I?" I pinch my eyebrows together.

"Mmm-hmm." She brings her cup of coffee to her mouth, but not before I've noticed the curve of her lips.

"This is not funny, Theresa," I snap. "This is my … my life we are talking about here."

"Oh, honey." She lowers her cup to the table and reaches over to grasp my hand. "I'm not laughing at you, at all; it's just—"

"Just?"

"Interesting that he has you all tied up in knots."

"It's not very comfortable, I can assure you of that."

"Ever since I've known you—and I admit, until now, I'd only ever seen you from a distance—but what little I've known of you, you've always come across as someone calm and composed, someone who knew what she wanted in life—"

"Which was to be a doctor," I agree. "It's why I took the chance of going to study medicine in England when Michael offered it to me."

"I'm surprised you did, actually." She glances at me with a shrewd look on her face. "I thought you also wanted to get out of the Mafia way of life."

"Was I that transparent?" I wince. "And considering we never really spoke to each other all through our growing years, I'm surprised you gathered so much."

"I guess I am perceptive." She raises a shoulder. "I could tell from a mile off that you hated having to be obligated in any way to the Mafia."

"Given my father was the personal doctor of the Sovranos, there was no escaping them. Don't get me wrong," I shuffle around in my seat, trying to find a more comfortable position, "they helped out my father and my family. You could say that without the Sovranos' help, we couldn't have survived and come this far. But I had always hoped that I'd find a way to leave the Mafia when I was older. Find my own way in the world and be independent, without having their presence looming over me. I had hoped to discover who I am, away from their influence. It's why, when Michael offered me a chance to go study medicine in London, I jumped at the opportunity. Oh, I knew it probably meant that I'd have to come back and pay my dues, but I always thought it would be in the form of offering up my services as a doctor for a while. If I had known it would also mean that his brother would decide to—"

"To—?" Theresa cocks her head. "To marry you?"

"Yeah," I blow out a breath, "marry me. Maybe I would have refused."

"Is that all there is to this situation?" Cass murmurs as she glances at me over her shoulder. "You sure there's nothing else you want to tell us?"

I bite the inside of my cheek. Oh, there's so much more; you have no idea. I shake my head. "No, nothing more to tell. Why?"

She peers at my features, then nods, "Just an instinct, that's all."

"Well, thank you for your concern, but no, I am happily engaged," I raise my left hand so the light from above shines off the ring, "and can't wait to be married; it's only—"

"That you can't wait to physically be with him, hmm?" Theresa leans forward, eyes shining. "There was a time when I was sure that Xander was going to propose to me, you know? He had taken me for a drive to our favorite restaurant with an amazing view. It was outside of Palermo and slightly off the beaten track, where we wouldn't risk running into anyone we knew. I was sure that he was going to tell me that he loved me and propose to me, but instead..." She swallows. "Instead, he told me how he had met someone, a man who he couldn't get out of his mind. Someone who was artistic enough to fascinate him, but also so macho that he made Xander go weak at the knees. Someone who he had fallen head over heels in love with, but who, apparently, didn't reciprocate his feelings."

"So Xander was in love with him?"

"He definitely seemed to have feelings for him." Theresa stares down at the batch of pancakes that Cass has slid in front of her.

"Eat," Cass orders as she places another stack of them in front of me and a third in front of herself. She slides into her chair, then glances around the table. "What do you girls want? Syrup? Butter?"

I reach for the melted butter and pour some of it over my pancakes.

"I ... I'm not hungry," Theresa murmurs.

"You have to eat," Cass says in a soft voice. "I know it feels like the end of the world in some ways, but you have to live through it."

"Doesn't mean I have to thrive." Theresa pokes at the topmost pancake with her fork. "I mean, I'm not even sure why I'm mourning anymore. He was nothing to me; he didn't see me as someone he wanted to share his life with—"

"But you said yourself, you two were best friends. Just because he didn't tell you how he felt, doesn't mean he didn't have feelings for you," I venture.

"Oh, he had feelings all right." She lowers her chin to her chest. "He was just too scared to acknowledge them. I suppose, I can't blame him; he was confused and trying to figure out his sexuality and his preferences. I just wish I hadn't built it all up in my head, you know? I wish..." She swallows. "I wish that I had never met him. I wish that—"

A sound at the door to the kitchen has the three of us turning to glance toward it.

Nonna stands just inside the doorway. She's clad in a silk dressing gown that flows to her feet, and holds her tray with the remnants of her breakfast.

"Oh, Nonna," Cassandra rises to her feet, "you should have called me; I would have cleared your breakfast tray."

"Oh, pffft! I don't expect you to wait on me hand and foot." She walks over to the sink and places her dishes in it. "Besides, I wanted to talk to all three of you." She reaches into the shelves above her, grabs a cup and saucer, and approaches the table. She takes a seat, then pours some of the espresso from the Bialetti into her cup, then glances around the table. "Please, don't let me interrupt your breakfast."

Cass takes her seat again and resumes eating. I follow her example. Theresa pokes at her pancake then cuts a piece for herself.

The silence stretches, broken only by the sound of our eating. When I'm not able to consume more of the pancakes, I place my knife and fork on my plate.

"You wanted to talk to us, Nonna?" I enquire.

She waits until Cass and Theresa too have finished eating, then leans back, railing her cup of espresso.

"A scavenger hunt," she finally proclaims.

"Uh, what?" I frown. "You want to organize a scavenger hunt?"

"The details have been taken care of. I have all the information needed and will be sharing the clues with all of you today."

"So, we're going to have this scavenger hunt today?" Cass blinks at her.

"Did I not just say that?" Nonna says in a sharp voice.

Cass reddens, "Y... yes. I was just surprised; it's not what I was expecting."

"What better way to break down the barriers between all of us and get us to know each other better, hmm?"

"I... I am not sure I want to take part," Theresa ventures. "I'm not a fan of such games."

"Too bad." Nonna trains her gaze on her. "It will do you good to be out in the open and get some fresh air."

"But it's so cold," she whines. "I'd rather be in my room—"

"Where you can mourn my grandson?" Nonna scowls. "Absolutely not; I forbid it."

"Oh." Theresa deflates. "Guess I don't have a choice then?"

"You don't." Nonna turns to me and Cass. "I take it you two have no objection with taking part in the game."

Cass and I glance at each other, then at Nonna.

"I enjoy puzzles, so I think I'll like it," Cass replies.

"Not my favorite pastime, but sure, I'll play," I drain the last of my coffee and place the cup back in its saucer.

"Good." Nonna glances at us over the top of her cup. "Wonder who'll turn out to be the winner?"

20

Christian

"No, absolutely, not!" I glare at Nonna, who is seated in the throne-like armchair in the living room. Hell, she could be the queen, and the rest of us her lowly subjects as she arches an eyebrow at the rest of us assembled in the room.

"Saying no is not a choice, Christian," she informs me. "When you came on this family retreat, you agreed to take part in all the activities."

"I did not agree to take part in a scavenger hunt."

"Not just any scavenger hunt; it's a Christmas-specific murder-mystery scavenger hunt," Theresa pipes up.

"Fuck me," Massimo murmurs under his breath.

"What was that?" Nonna swivels her head in his direction. "I don't believe I heard you correctly."

"I said," Massimo coughs, "that, of course, I'll take part in the, uh, Christmas-specific murder-mystery scavenger hunt, Nonna."

Seb smirks, and Nonna turns her gimlet eye on him next. "Something funny, Sebastian?"

"Nope," Seb straightens, "of course, not; I can't wait to get started on the hunt." He rubs his hands together, as if in anticipation.

Luca chuckles. "Turn it down, compare," he murmurs, "you're laying it on a little too thick."

Of course, Nonna hears him, for she narrows her gaze on him. "Something you want to share with the rest of us, Luca?"

"Just excited, is all, about this chance to, uh ... participate in a scavenger hunt with the rest of the family."

"Don't get so excited that you don't listen to the rules properly," Nonna says dryly.

"Me, not listen when you speak?" Luca thumps his hand over his heart. "That will be the day, Nonna."

"You only have to command us, and we obey," Adrian interjects from where he leans a hip against the wall.

"No need to flatter me." Nonna sniffs. "Just as long as all of you take part in the game and play to the best of your ability."

"We are on board, Nonna." Michael pulls Karma closer into him. If those two were any closer, they'd be joined at the hip. Correction, they are already joined at the hip. My Flower, on the other hand... I glance toward where Aurora stands stiffly in a corner of the room. She's half in shadows as if she's trying to hide from the rest of us. Not that she can ever hide from me. I see you, my Flower. The more you shy away from me, the more I'm going to make sure that you'll never evade me. This ... using Nonna to put distance between us is a temporary reprieve, so make the most of it.

She must sense my perusal, for she turns her head in my direction. Our gazes catch, hold, then she scowls at me before glancing away.

Nonna glances in Cassandra's direction. At her signal, Cassandra picks up an open box filled with what seems to be folded pieces of paper. She walks over to the table in the center of the room and places it there.

"It's time to choose partners for this game."

"Partners?" I scowl. "I don't want to be saddled with any of my loser brothers."

"Then you'd better pick the right one," Nonna snaps. "Go on, boy," she waves a hand in the air, "pick a slip."

What-fucking-ever. Might as well as get this over with. I prowl over to the box, grab a slip, and open it. I can't stop the grin that threatens to split my face in half.

"Well?" Nonna frowns. "Who is it? Share it with us, will you?"

"Don't mind if I show you." I smirk as I cross the room.

Aurora glances at me; her gaze widens as I approach her. By the time I pause in front of her, her features are contorted in an expression that's part horror, part bemusement.

"No," she whispers, "no, no, no."

"Oh, yes, Flower." I lower my head, so my mouth is next to her ear. "I get to partner with you fair and square; now you're mine."

"Fuck that."

She begins to march past me, and I reach for her, but before I can grab her wrist, Nonna calls out, "I have no time for tantrums." She scowls at Aurora. "Can you just partner with him for the duration of this game please?"

Outside, a gust of wind slams into the side of the chalet; Aurora jumps. I wind my arm around her shoulder. "Don't be scared; I'll take care of you."

She grimaces. "That's what I'm afraid of." She tries to pull away, but I tighten my hold on her.

"Relax, you're safe," I murmur. "After all, we are in the presence of so many chaperones; surely, nothing can happen to you here."

"I don't trust you, not one bit," she hisses back.

"Good," I chuckle, "it's good to be wary; you'll last longer in this world if you are."

"I am paired with Karma, of course." Michael tips his chin up at Nonna, who waves a hand in the air.

"Yes, yes, all right."

"What the—!" I scowl. "Doesn't he have to pick a note like all the rest of us."

"He's the Don," she says by way of explanation. "Anyway, you don't have anything to complain about. After all, you are matched with your fiancée."

"No thanks to you." I scowl.

Nonna smiles. "Best make use of the hand you're dealt, boy."

"Oh, I plan to." I glance around the room, taking in how the rest of them have been paired. Massimo with Luca. Seb and Adrian. Theresa and Cass stand next to each other.

"Right." Nonna rubs her hands together. "Gather around, people; I need to hand each of the teams the list of your clues."

"Hold on." Seb scratches his chin, "How does this work, exactly? You give us clues which we are supposed to solve, and if we find the object we are looking for, we bring it back to you?"

"No, dummy." Theresa rolls her eyes. "You need to work your way down the list of clues. As you solve each one, you collect the thing it leads you to. Then, when you have completed the list, you meet back here."

Outside, another gust of wind slams a shutter against the pane. The resounding crack slices through the space. Next to me, Aurora shudders, and I tuck her into my side. "Shh," I whisper, "it's okay."

"I don't need you to take care of me." She digs her elbow into my side, and I wince. My grasp on her loosens, and she pulls away. Just then, the lights overhead flicker and go off, then come on again.

"Guess the weather's getting on board with the game." Nonna cackles. "Speaking of, some safety rules that I hope all of you will take seriously."

She nods toward Cassandra, who glances about the assembled faces. "Don't go too far, but if you do, make sure you keep track of the landmarks. It can be tricky finding your way back to the chalets."

"We're not children." Seb smirks. "Surely, we can find our way home."

"Don't be fooled by the seemingly genteel nature of this place." Nonna gestures to the living room. "The forest in this area is particularly thick and has been known to misguide people. Why, one of my granduncles was lost in a snowstorm, and when they found him—dead, of course—it was less than a mile away, but he had, apparently, been unable to find his way back."

"That was then; this is today." I raise a shoulder. "As long as we have our phones about us, we should be okay, right?"

"Phone reception out here is patchy, at best, so please don't go too far. If you do get lost, you could also try to find your way to the lodge, which is five miles from here, and wait there until someone comes for you," Cassandra reminds us. "Please do keep clear of the pond, which is about three miles from here. It's shallow, and it may seem like the surface is frozen, but it's not safe enough to walk on. Even animals are known to be fooled and caught up in breaks in the ice, so keep a lookout, please. Also," she hesitates, "I know I'm being overly careful, but please do watch out for the wolves."

"W-wolves?" Theresa blinks rapidly. "There are wolves out there?"

"It's a forest, there are animals; deal with it," Nonna huffs. "Now that we have that out of the way," she glances around the assembled faces, "are you all ready for your list of clues?"

"Bring it on." Seb widens his stance. "I'm going to have this game in the bag before the rest of you have even cracked the first clue."

"Don't bet on it," Massimo rumbles. "I'm not one for games, but once I participate, I warn you I can get competitive."

"We're not going to let you win. You know that, right?" Karma calls out.

"Women are better at scavenger hunts than men," Theresa warns the men.

Luca laughs. "We'll see about that, shall we?"

"Everyone, settle down so Nonna can hand out the lists of clues to the various teams," Michael calls out.

The crowd quietens. Nonna pulls out a pair of spectacles, then glances around the room. "Is everyone really ready for this?" The old woman has a very pleased look on her face. One I'm not sure how to interpret.

"Go on, Nonna," Luca calls out. "Hit us with your worst."

"Are all Sovrano men born with big egos?" Aurora grumbles.

"The only thing bigger than our egos is the muscle between our legs," I retort.

"Oh, please!" She snorts. "Enough with the clichés, and how do you know your brothers are as well-endowed as you, anyway?"

"So, you think I'm well-endowed?"

"Forget I said that." She glances away, "Seriously, give you an inch, and you'll take a mile."

"I know my cock is wide, but to say that it will take up an entire mile is giving me too much credit."

"Ugh!" She makes a gagging sound.

"Now, that's what I'd like to hear from you when I'm choking you with my length down your throat."

"Stop it." She scowls. "Does every conversation have to begin and end with your dick?"

"Yes." I smirk.

She glowers at me, her cheeks growing red. So fucking cute.

"Aurora and Christian, you guys ready?" Nonna calls out.

Aurora straightens. She pulls away, trying to put some distance between us, and I let her. Just because I'm feeling charitable. Only so I can lull her into a sense of complacency so when I move in for the kill, she'll have no idea what hit her.

"Ready when you are," I call out to Nonna, who reaches for the sheaves of papers by her side.

21

Aurora

After Nonna handed out the lists of clues to each of the teams, Christian and I peeled off—or rather, he stalked off with the list, and I had no choice but to follow him. We found a quiet space in the study at the end of the corridor. Massimo, and later Seb, peeked in, only to be told off by Christian. The guys retreated, leaving us to examine the list of clues.

Now, Christian pulls his chair close to mine so our knees bump. I pull away, and of course, he shoots me a glance. "How long will you keep running, Flower?"

"As long as I am breathing."

"Not what you were saying earlier." He smirks.

"Can we focus on the task at hand—namely, this treasure hunt?"

"Technically, it's a Christmas-specific murder-mystery scavenger hunt," he reminds me.

"Whatever." I blow out a breath.

Can you share the list with me, please?"

He holds it up, and I lean in closer to read it.

Bring your gloves to this clue!

At least, that's what I'm told.

I hear it's very cool—

Maybe even too cold to hold.

. . .

I am your winter.
I halt; I put time on ice.
Untended, I burn.

Under the skies,
Among the trees
In a place not too far away,
though you'll have to look for it
You'll find it...

And when the sun goes behind the clouds,
And the wind blows
And the blood runs cold
You'll need it…

I read it a second time. "Okay, what does that mean?" I frown.

"Something cold," Christian says slowly. "Maybe too cold to hold?"

"That's what it says." I scowl. "And it's somewhere outside, not too far away?"

"Maybe we should step out and go in search of it?" Christian offers.

"Maybe, that's the first really good suggestion you have come up with in a long time?"

"Getting sassy, are we?" Christian wraps his fingers about my neck and pulls me so close that I can make out the individual lines fanning out from the corners of his eyes. The heat of his body surrounds me; the force of his dominance presses down on my shoulders. I try to draw in a breath, and my lungs burn.

"Getting violent, are we?" I manage to force out the words.

He peers into my features.

I lick my lips, and his gaze drops to my mouth. The air between us thrums with electricity. The hair on the back of my neck rises and my toes curl.

"If you think this is violent, then you have no idea what I am capable of, Flower." His hot breath sears my cheeks. A bead of sweat trickles down my throat and into the valley between my breasts. He follows it with his gaze, and the tension between us skyrockets further.

"I think," I clear my throat, "I think we need to leave if we have any hope of winning this scavenger hunt."

"And is that important for you?" he murmurs. "Winning?"

"It's what most people aspire to."

"But you and I are not like the others, are we?" He releases his hold on me, and I draw in a breath. Another. What the hell was that all about? Why did he look at me like he wanted to ... kiss me, hold me, ravish me? Why does every part of me want him to do that and more?

"Better dress warmly. It's going to be cold outside."

Ten minutes later, we walk across the garden at the back of the chalet. Or rather, Christian walks ahead, and I half-run to keep up with him. Of course, the asshole doesn't realize that my legs are much shorter than his, so I have to literally jog to keep up with him. Not that it would make a difference, even if he did comprehend it. He'd probably purposely walk fast so that I'd have to struggle to keep up. The wind blows again, and I shiver. I stab my hands into the pockets of my jacket and draw abreast with him. "Where are we going?"

"Searching for something that fits the description of the damn clue."

"But where would we look?"

"Where would we not look?" He gestures to the area around us, "Under the bushes? Behind tree trunks? No wait, maybe it's hidden somewhere up in the branches of one of these ancient fir trees?"

I follow his gaze to the tall trees that crowd the slope ahead of us.

"You really don't have a clue, do you?" I scowl.

"Do you?" he retorts.

"Nope," I heave out a sigh. "Surely, it can't be that difficult?"

He laughs. "Nonna came up with the clues; don't expect it to be a cakewalk."

"Not that I am underestimating her or anything, but this is a Christmas scavenger hunt. Surely, she would want us to solve the clues and find the objects that we are seeking and bring them back?"

"Doesn't mean that it's going to be easy." He begins to walk through the dense trees, and I follow.

A soft, powder-like substance drifts down in front of my eyes. "Oh..." I hold out my palm, then glance up to find snowflakes floating down. "Oh, wow, it's snowing." I pause, take in the sight, then because I can't stop myself, I open my mouth, pop out my tongue, and try to catch a flake.

A couple of them hit my lips, and I lick them off. I glance up to find him staring at me. The look in his eyes... It's hot and yearning, and yet also, strangely, shut off. Like he wants me, knows that I know that he wants me, and is not happy about it.

"Why do you dislike me?" I burst out.

He frowns. "Don't be ridiculous."

"I'm not being ridiculous." I march up to him and thrust a finger in his chest. "Since the first time you saw me, you… You've had this thing for me. It's like you can't stop noticing me, and you hate yourself for doing it. Like you want to throw me down and fuck me, but you're afraid that you'll enjoy it so much that you'll never walk away from me."

"Is that what you think?"

"It's what I know." I tip up my chin. "It's why you saved me from your brother's anger. Knowing that I'd be fully dependent on you. That you'd own me and be able to command me to do whatever you want, but you know what?"

"What?"

"I'm not the kind who gives in that easily." Turning, I race through the trees and up the slope.

22

Christian

"What the hell? Where are you going?" I call out after her, "Stop, Aurora."

She hightails it up the slope and through the trees. I take off after her just as the snow begins to come down in earnest. I swipe at the flakes that cling to my cheeks, blink away those that cling to my eyelashes. For someone who struggled to keep up with me, she's definitely hot-footing it. I increase my speed and begin to gain on her; that's when she disappears behind a particularly thick wall of shrubs. *"Cazzo!"* I push through the bushes and burst into a clearing. I race forward, my steps sinking into the snow. My foot slips on ice, and I manage to right myself. I slow down, and ahead of me, Aurora, too, loses speed. She continues to walk forward, putting distance between us.

"Where the hell do you think you're going?" I yell. "I won't stop until I get my hands on you, and when I do, I promise, I'm going to spank your ass so hard that you won't be able to sit down for days."

She holds up her middle finger, and I can't stop the chuckle that bursts from my mouth.

"If you think you can scare me, think again, asshole," she throws at me over her shoulder. "I don't answer to anyone, and certainly not you."

"The ring on your hand says otherwise."

"This one?" She half angles her body, so I have a clear view of her pulling my ring off of her finger.

Anger threads through my veins.

"Don't you fucking take that off, Flower, you hear me."

"Loud and clear." She tosses the ring up in the air once, then catches it and flings it over her head. A ray of sunshine breaks through the clouds, illuminating the yellow sapphire, which sparkles before the ring hits the snow and vanishes out of sight. The sun disappears behind the cloud, and the snow seems to thicken. There's an ominous crackling sound, and I glance down to find I'm standing on the surface of the pond. Tiny fissures seem to be expanding around me.

"Fuck!" I growl. I should have paid more attention to where we were going, and this, after Cassandra had explicitly warned us not to go onto the pond. "Aurora, don't move," I call out. The snowflakes seem to thicken, and the visibility shrinks further. I see her figure through the blizzard, the white already settling over her, lending her features a luminous glow.

"Christian," she calls out, her voice shrill, "what am I going to do?"

"I'll come to you." I take a step forward, and the ice holds. Another step and I can see that the ice is thinning. A third and I hear a crack.

She screams as she topples over; the sound cuts off when she hits the surface of the water. My heart slams into my rib-cage. At least, the water is shallow so there is no fear of her drowning. "Hold on," I yell as I inch forward slowly.

She pushes up to standing, and the water reaches up to her waist, "J-Jesus... This is freakin' c-cold." Her teeth chatter so loudly I can hear them even from this distance.

She takes a step in my direction, then stumbles and falls into the water again.

"Fuck," I swear, take a step forward, then another. The ice seems to hold, thank fuck. I push forward as quickly as I can, all the while trying my best not to crack the surface of the ice further.

By the time I reach her, she's standing again.

The wind whipping across the surface of the pond crashes into me, fuck! It has to be so much colder for her, since she's wet.

She drags herself onto the surface of the ice which creaks under her weight. "Chr-Christian, p-please help me!" Her voice trembles.

"Hold on," I call back. Adrenaline laces my blood. My breath comes in pants. I need to get to her.

I lower myself onto my stomach to distribute my weight evenly then belly crawl forward. When I am as close as I dare get to her, I swipe out my arm in her direction. She grips my hand, and I haul her toward me. The piece of ice where she was gives way, and she screams, "Christian!"

"I've got you." I hold her gaze, as I tug her forward. Simultaneously, I slide back toward the thicker ice near the edge of the pond.

Her gaze is wide, her skin pale; her lips are already turning blue. Fuck, I need to get her out into warmth before hypothermia sets in.

"Omigod, omigod, Christian"—she babbles—"d-don't let g-go of me."

"I won't." I grip her hand as I draw her forward. I rise to my feet slowly and the ice holds. Thank fuck. I draw her up, take a step back pulling her along with me. Another few steps, and she pauses. "I'm ... so ... so ... cold." She shivers.

"Just a few more steps. We are almost on firm ground," I coax. "Come on, Flower."

"I ... I c-can't," she whines. "I'm too c-cold."

"Give me your other hand," I growl.

"I ... I c-can't," she hiccups.

"Yes, you can."

"I am ... free ... z ... ing." Her lips tremble.

"I'll get you to warmth, I promise. Give me your other hand. Now!" Even before the words are out of my mouth, she raises her free hand. I grab it and haul her toward me as I move back.

My foot touches firm ground, thank fuck. I step off of the pond and onto the shore and yank her forward. She stumbles toward me, and I haul her into my arms.

A tremor grips her, and her teeth chatter. Her skin has definitely turned a shade of blue. ·

"Porca miseria." I pull off her scarf, toss it aside, then reach for her wet jacket and peel it off. She stands quietly as I push it down her shoulders and onto the ground.

When I reach for the sodden sweater she's wearing inside, she protests. "Wh-what are you d-doing?"

"Taking off your wet clothes so you don't catch hypothermia. You're a doctor; you should know that."

"Oh." Her shoulders slump. She doesn't say another word as I peel off her sweater. She's wearing a shirt inside. I shrug off my jacket which is dry—thank fuck—and drape it over her shoulders. Then snatch my hat off of my head and place it on hers.

A trembling grips her and she sneezes.

Cazzo, I need to get her to warmth right now. I grab her clothes off of the ground before I haul her up in my arms, then push forward until I reach a wall of bushes. I step through them, then pause. The snow seems to increase in intensity. A particularly big piece of ice slaps into my face, and I flinch. I hunch my body over hers, trying to protect her the best I can.

She stirs, then murmurs, "W-where are we?" She coughs and her entire body shudders. It seems to set off a bout of shivering, and she huddles closer to me.

I glance around. Which way did we come? Damn it, why wasn't I more cognizant of our surroundings? I juggle her around until I manage to pull my phone out of my jacket pocket. I try to turn it on, but of course, the battery is dead. I had been wearing a waterproof jacket, and while I had belly crawled on the frozen surface of the lake, I hadn't gotten drenched the way Theresa had. So that should't have affected the phone. Did I remember to charge the device, though? I can't remember now.

"Your phone," I ask her, "do you have it?"

"In my p-po…cket," she says through her chattering teeth.

Cazzo, I need to get us to warmth before she comes down with pneumonia. I reach for her jeans pocket, but can't find the phone. Feel my way around to the other side and pull out her phone, but it's also dead.

Fuck," I growl, "fuckin' fuck."

"Wh-what are we g-going to do?" She presses her lips, which have already turned blue.

I glance around, spot a break in the trees, and head for it.

Another burst of shivering grips her. A moan spills from her lips. "C-cold… I'm so … c-cold, Ch-christ… ian." She shudders.

I break into a run. My lungs burn, and my breath catches in my throat. Her wet clothes slap against my thigh, the cold penetrating through my skin, into my bones, and I swear, I can feel my blood freeze. I reach the break in the trees and find a path. Finally, fuck. I race up the path which winds and turns.

"Wh-where are we g-going?" she asks.

"Back to the chalets, I hope."

"Th-this isn't the w-way … we c-came." By now, her shivering is constant.

"Yeah, I figured that out a few minutes ago."

"So w-why are you s-still—"

"Running? Because it's better than freezing to death standing in place. And if there's a path, surely, it must lead somewhere?"

I continue to jog, trying to hold her as close as possible. Her wet clothes weigh me down while my boots make every step an ordeal. My thigh muscles protest and my feet are so numb I can barely manage to grip the surface of the path with my soles. My shoulders hurt; my lungs scream for a break. I slow down, all sensations in my arms having faded long ago, but I dare not put her down. I glance down to find her eyes closed, her features so pale that her eyelashes stand out in stark contrast to her leached-of-color cheeks.

Her body convulses, and I can only stare helplessly. Fuck, I won't be able to save her. She is going to die in my arms, and there is nothing I can do about it. Just like I was unable to save Xander.

By the time I had driven up, flames were leaping from Michael's car. I'd jumped out, gone over to the car, and with Seb's help, managed to pull Xander out. But he hadn't stirred. Not when we'd lowered him to the ground. Not when I'd reached for the piece of metal protruding from his chest, and Seb stopped me. He'd cautioned me to wait for the medics to arrive.

So, I'd slid down to my knees next to him, held his hand, locked my gaze on his face, and willed him to live. I had not let go when the ambulance arrived and the medics ran to him. They'd checked his vitals and declared him dead, and I still hadn't let go. I'd gripped his hand, beseeched him to open his eyes, to tell me he was okay. But he never had.

I'd refused to let go of him, and it had taken Massimo folding his arms around me and begging me to release him, for him to unwrap my fingers one by one from that of my soul brother, my twin, my life partner, my life saver... And when I'd finally released him, and they had taken him away in the ambulance, I knew that I'd never be the same again.

And now, she is going to die, and nothing can bring me back from this tragedy. I cannot live to see another day like this. If she is gone, then so am I. If she leaves me then ... I'll kill myself. I stare down at her closed eyelids; I will never let myself feel again, think again... Never let myself live. No. I will retreat from this life, from this hell on earth that I find myself in again. I will—

Her eyelids flutter. Those golden orbs stare at me. The light in them is dulled, but as I watch, something sparks deep inside. She moves her lips, but I can't hear anything. Can't understand what I'm seeing. Then she raises her hand. Her palm connects with my face, and my neck snaps back; pain shudders down my spine, and heat flushes my skin. My gut twists, and blood rushes to my groin.

I lower my head and smash my mouth to hers with such force that our teeth clash. I draw off her breath, drink of her essence, and thrust my tongue over hers. I dig my teeth into her bottom lip, and the coppery taste of her blood fills my palate. I tear my mouth from hers. My breath comes out in puffs. My chest rises and falls as I stare at her.

"Wh-what... ha-happened?" she whispers. "You l-look like you saw a g-ghost." Her teeth chatter, and I haul her even closer.

"I..." I shake my head. "Nothing. I was just..." I glance away. A ball of emotion fills my throat, and I swallow it down. I take in my surroundings, blinking back the moisture that threatens to overflow my eyes.

Something catches my eye in the distance. I peer through the snow. What the hell is it? Is that a—? I begin to walk toward it. My steps speed up. Before I realize it, I'm running again. I turn a bend in the path and come to a halt.

"Finally, fuck!" I scowl.

She turns to glance in the direction where I'm looking. "Is th-that a h-house?" she whispers.

"It's the lodge."

I break into a run toward the structure. Step up on the patio and reach the door. I push my shoulder into it, but it doesn't budge. I try again, and the wood creaks but it doesn't open.

"Cazzo," I growl. "Now what?"

"Maybe there's a k-key under a p-pot or so-something?" she mumbles.

"Surely, that only happens in movies?"

"Why d-don't y-you... At least, t-try?" Her teeth click together, a staccato rhythm that matches my racing heartbeat, and she attempts to pull her legs up, trying to hold onto what little warmth there is trapped between us.

I swivel around and notice a pot near the edge of the patio. I walk toward it, then sink down to one knee. "Can you reach for it?"

She reaches for the pot, and I lower her further until she can feel under it.

"F-found it," she cries out.

Well, whaddya know? The movies did get something right, after all.

I straighten and walk over to the door. Hands shaking, she struggles to fit the key in the lock. Finally, the key clicks into place and turns. I put my shoulder to the door, and this time, the door gives way.

I step into the darkened interior. Bluish light streams in from a window on one side. I head for the fireplace and lower her down to the carpet in front of it.

I peel off my jacket from around her, then her shirt and bra. I reach for her waistband. "I'll ... d-do it," she insists.

I watch as she tries to grip the zipper, unable to stop the quaking of her hands. Her fingers slip on the zipper once, twice. I reach over and brush her fingers aside. She protests.

"Don't be ridiculous," I mutter. "I've already seen what's inside your clothes, remember?"

I lower her zipper, peel her jeans and panties down her legs and notice she's still wearing her boots. I guide her to the couch then help her out of her boots and socks. I straighten, grab the cover off the back of the settee and wrap it around her shoulders. She shivers, then sneezes.

"Porca miseria." I scowl. "Better get the fire started." I turn to the fireplace, get to work with the kindling and matches I find next to it. Once the tinder sparks, I add the logs. Within minutes, flames lick around the edges of the wood, and the warmth builds in the space.

I spring up, walk over to where she's seated, then haul her up into my arms and deposit her on the plush rug in front of the fire. She doesn't protest, and I know I've done the right thing when she sinks down with a sigh and snuggles deeper into the cover.

I shrug off my shirt, step out of my boots, and pull off my socks, pants, and boxers.

I walk over to the bar in the corner of the living room—yes, the lodge is small, but no way, would we Sovranos have compromised on having a bar in the house —and grab a half-full bottle of whiskey and two glasses.

I walk over to her, place the bottle down on the ground, then sink down next to her.

She turns, and I don't miss how she rakes her gaze down my body. She takes in the tattoos on my chest and upper arm, then lowers her gaze to my crotch. Her lips part,and she takes in another shaky breath.

"Here…" I pour some of the liquor into a glass and offer it to her.

Her hand trembles as she reaches for it. She downs the whiskey in one gulp and bursts out coughing.

I sip mine at a slower pace, and by the time I'm done, she's placed her glass down on the ground next to her.

"How are you feeling?" I peer into her flushed features.

"St-still… c-cold." A trembling grips her. Her teeth chatter, and the sound of them clacking against each other is loud in the space. "Sorry, it's p-probably the sh-shock s-setting in," she stutters.

I place my glass next to hers, then pull her onto my lap. She doesn't protest. I cradle her and tuck her head under my chin.

"I should p-probably take this c-cover off." Her entire body quakes. "Skin … to … s-s-skin is b-be… t-t… er for g-getting w-warmed up."

She wriggles out of the spread, managing to pull it off of herself. She wraps it around my shoulders, turning so that her breasts collide with my chest.

She draws in a sharp breath, and her already erect nipples seem to cut into my chest. She glances up at me from under her eyelids. "You are n-not g-going t-to—"

"Take advantage of you?" I smirk. "Not that I'm not tempted, but trust me, my focus here is to make sure neither of us gets frostbite after that dip in the pond— which, by the way, was your fault."

"M-my f-f-fault?" She frowns. "H-how is it m-my f-fault?"

"You wandered off in a hissy fit, not looking where you were going."

"I-it wasn't a hiss-sy … f-fit." Another bout of trembling grips her. She pushes away, then turns to leave, and I yank her back. The curve of her shoulder, the dip of her waist, the swell of her butt, all fit snugly against me. I widen my legs to notch her between my thighs so that my cock nudges into the groove between her ass cheeks. My dick instantly thickens, and she stills. She shoots me a glance from under hooded eyelashes. "Is th-that… Are y-you—?"

"Only human, Flower," I growl. "I have a naked woman in my arms. I would have to be dead to not react."

She presses her palms against my chest, and I wince, "Fuck, you are cold."

"Not as c-cold as your h-heart." She sniffs. "Wh-why do you m-make m-me so m-mad?"

"Why do you insist on turning me on with everything you do?"

"I'm not d-doing anything."

"You exist, don't you?" I counter.

"So, n-now what? You b-blame me for drawing b-breath?"

I glance down at her. "Not that," I clear my throat, "never that. When I saw you disappear under the water, I thought—"

"That it was Chr-Christmas?"

I thrust my face into hers. "That I had lost you forever. That before I had a chance to tell you how I felt about you, you were gone. That I'd never be the same again. That, just as I had lost Xander, I had lost you too, and this time I wouldn't survive the pain."

23

Aurora

"Oh, Ch-Christian," I whisper, "do you m-mean that? D-do you really f-feel s-something for m-me?"

"That's the big question, isn't it?" He scowls down at me. "It's not like I want to, trust me. If I had a choice, I'd have turned my back on you and walked away the first time I saw you, but something about you," he searches my gaze, "holds me captive. And it's not only because you're good-looking."

"At least, y-you admit that y-you find m-me g-good-looking."

"Of course, I do. You're beautiful," he scowls, "but it's not about that."

"Th-then?"

"It's this goodness that I sense inside you. This need to save the world which is so intrinsic to you."

My cheeks heat. "P-please," I huff, "d-don't m-make m-me out to be a s-saint."

"But you would try the patience of a saint," he murmurs.

"N-not that you'd know the f-first thing about th-that, considering y-you are more of a s-sinner."

"It's why I intrigue you."

"You d-don't."

"Oh, please." He smirks. "Admit it. You wanted to know how it would be to bed the beast."

I raise a shoulder. "The thought m-might have crossed my m-mind. B-but you spoiled it by nego...tiating w-with m-me about the s-safety of my f-family."

"It was the quickest way to get you to agree to my condition."

"You c-could have asked," I point out.

"Would you have consented to being my fake wife?"

I look away.

"That's what I thought," he says with some satisfaction.

I stare into the flame. "N-now what?" The heat from the fire envelops me. But the man at my back is like a wall of warmth. My fingers and toes begin to hurt, and I moan, "Shit, I'm b-beginning to th-thaw out."

He reaches down and massages my hands, then moves over to rub my feet. The twinges shoot up my arms and legs. I squeeze my eyes shut and try to tamp down on the pins and needles sensations in my limbs. A trembling grips me, and I cuddle even closer to him.

Not lying; that dip in the icy pond scared me. My eyes begin to close, and as a doctor, I know it's because of the shock wearing off, but as a woman I can't refute the fact that being held in his arms brings a sense of security that blankets me. Heat from his body is like a furnace that surrounds me, driving away every last bit of cold from my bones. I yawn so widely my eyes tear.

"Guess that incident took it out of you, eh?"

He pushes the hair back from my forehead, and the gesture is so soft, so tender, that I glance at him confused.

"Christian..." I fight the waves of sleep that envelop me. "Just because you s-saved my life doesn't mean that I have forgiven y-you for what you coerced me into d-doing."

"We'll see." His lips curve in a smile. My eyes flutter shut. Something brushes my hair. Did he kiss my forehead?

I come awake slowly. Warmth, delicious warmth pours into my bloodstream. Every part of me feels toasty. I wriggle my toes and hit something hard. I dig down with my heel and encounter living, breathing flesh. I draw in a breath, and the scent of dark coffee laced with brandy, his scent, fills my lungs. My belly trembles, and my core clenches.

I try to turn, but something heavy around my waist stops me. I close my hand around it and encounter hair roughened skin. I drag my fingers up the length of his arm and brush against corded muscle. My limbs quiver. To say I am turned on right now would be an understatement. Somehow, being next to him, surrounded by him, with my arse pushed into his groin and his thickness stabbing into my hip, all I want to do is turn into him, lick up the demarcation of his pecs, slurp on his skin, taste the salt of his sweat as I wind my fingers around that hard, heavy part of him that I want to feel inside of me.

I try to turn again, and his grip tightens around me. Shit. He's awake. Of course, he's awake. As is his length, that seems to thicken and lengthen against where it is tucked between us.

I glance around us and realize I'm on a bed, which means that he moved us to the bedroom at some point. I'm facing away from him and toward another fire, in which the embers glow, keeping the room warm. A dull, bluish light streams in from the windows behind us. It must be early still. Did I sleep the night away? Did he carry me here? Of course, he must have. Clearly, I'd been out of it to not awake even then.

He pulls me closer, if that were possible, and every part of my back seems plastered to every inch of that hot, warm, hard, sculpted front. I gulp. Sweat breaks out on my brow. I dig my fingertips into his corded forearm, and a sound of agreement rumbles up his chest. My nerves seem to ignite, and all of my brain cells melt.

Oh hell, just being in the same room as him affects me, and now... When I am flush against him, with my neck supported on his bicep, I feel tiny, helpless, fragile. Prey caught in the jaws of this beast, to toy with, to break apart. To lick me up from head to toe with particular attention to the parts of me that crave his attention. An empty sensation gnaws at my core. I squeeze my thighs together to find some relief.

"Flower," he whispers, "if you wriggle any more, I'm going to come right here, and that would be very embarrassing, especially since I'd rather spill my cum inside of you."

"Oh," I squeeze my eyes shut. That was filthy—exceedingly so. My pussy throbs, like every word he spoke was addressed to that part of me.

"If I slide my fingers inside of you, will I find you wet?"

Yes.

Yes.

"No," I clear my throat, "of course, not."

"Liar." He laughs. The sound rumbles up his massive chest, sinks into my blood, arrows straight down to... You guessed it, my center.

He slides his fingers down my chest, over my belly, until his fingertips brush the strip of skin between my core and my stomach. He leaves it there, and I squirm. I try to bring my hips up, wanting, needing to feel his fingers brush against my aching pussy.

"You want me to touch you, Flower?"

Yes.

No!

I bite the inside of my cheek. My nipples pebble, my belly trembles, and my thighs feel like they have turned to jelly. "Christian," I finally plead, "please."

"Please, what?"

He grazes his fingertips against the top of my pussy lips, and moisture beads my core.

"Bloody hell," I whisper, "what are you doing to me?"

"Do you know you sound even more British when you're turned on?"

I huff. "Is that supposed to be a compliment?"

"It's certainly different. Most people relapse into the accent of their childhood in situations of high emotion. You, however, have gone the other way."

"My time in England was one of the happiest times of my life." I swallow. "I guess I wanted to cling to the British accent because it has such good memories for me."

"And you never were happy to be from a Mafia background." He brushes his lips against my temple. "Yet here you are, in the arms of a Mafioso, begging him to fuck you."

"Fuck," I squeeze my eyes shut, "fuck, fuck, fuck."

"I didn't say it to make you regretful, Flower."

"You're right, though. I spent all my life running away from the Mafia; I should have realized that your background always comes back to haunt you. That you have to face your past before you can move on."

"I'm not your past, Flower," he says in a hard voice. "I'm your present and your future."

"No," I shake my head, "I don't want that."

"Fine." He pulls his arm from under me and rolls away. The cold instantly overpowers me. I shiver, goose bumps pop on my skin, and I drag the cover up and under my chin. It's no substitute for the warmth from his hard, naked body, which had cocooned me.

I hear him pad over to the other side of the room. A door snicks shut, and I realize he's stepped into the bathroom. I swing my legs over the side, pull the cover up and over my shoulders, then walk into the living room.

I take in the comfortable sofa flanked by two chairs in front of the fire. Next to it is a side table with a basket of yarn, complete with knitting needles. Also, there is a sewing kit which is open, with satin ribbons trailing from it. Next to it is a chess set and various board games. Whoever furnished this place knew to provide various ways to amuse yourself inside.

I turn to find him walking into the living room. Still, completely naked. I rake my gaze down his sculpted chest, his concave stomach, the divots that run down each side of his belly to his groin, forming a perfect Adonis belt, and between that, his cock, which is already standing to attention. Hell, doesn't this guy believe in downtime?

He smirks, and my cheeks heat.

He walks in the direction of the back of the lodge then returns with our clothes in his arms. "Here." He hands mine over to me.

"You ran them in the wash?" I blink rapidly.

"Figured we'd need our clothes this morning, so…" His tone is casual.

"So, you woke up in the middle of the night and ran the washing machine so we could have clean clothes in the morning?"

"Your point being?" He scowls.

"Hmm," I tap my cheek, "so you don't think of doing laundry as a woman's job or something suitably chauvinistic?"

His eyes gleam. "Now that you mention it..." he drawls.

My scowl deepens, and his lips kick up.

"Take it easy, Flower, I was just kidding you. I admit, I have a housekeeper who comes in daily to do my laundry and take care of my place, but yeah, in a pinch, I can run a washing machine."

"Don't do us any favors." I raise my gaze skywards.

He chuckles, and hot damn, the sound is so masculine, so growly that it tugs at my nerve endings.

He pulls on his clothes, and yes, I want to watch those muscles flex and bend. Instead, I get dressed. Under the sheet it's challenging, but I manage. I toss aside the sheet and turn to find him smirking.

"What?"

He holds up his hands. "Can't I look at you without getting called out for it?"

"You'd never do anything as innocent as just 'looking.'" I toss my hair over my shoulder. "More like, you're already planning on how to get me out of these clothes."

He looks me up and down. "I could always ask you to undress," he drawls.

"And I could always refuse."

His grin widens. Damn him, he knows that if he orders me to take off my clothes, I'll have a hard time refusing. His gaze intensifies, and my pulse rate kicks up. The space between us seems to thicken with unspoken emotions. My belly flip-flops. Heat flushes my skin, and suddenly I feel like I have too many clothes on. Damn it, another minute or so and I'd probably strip without his asking. I tear my gaze away from him, then walk over to the window and glance out at the completely white world. The snow is still coming down in thick tufts, and visibility is less than a meter.

It's so silent, so calm.

The heat of his body curls over my back, and I stiffen.

"Beautiful, isn't it?" His voice sounds from somewhere above me. "We could be the only two people left in this world."

"Except, we're not. We'd best try to contact your family; they must be worried about us."

"I spoke to them earlier today."

"You did?" I glance at him over my shoulder.

"I woke up earlier, but you were out of it. So, I let you sleep. Checked on the status of our phones." He nods to where the devices are laid out in front of the fire. "Luckily, mine is water–resistant, and it had enough charge left that I could speak to Michael."

"What'd he say?"

"We are in the middle of a snowstorm, apparently. They haven't had so much snow in so little time in the last hundred years."

"That's what the weather guys do best: exaggerate." I sniff. "So, the next thing you're going to tell me is that we are cut off, no one can come to get us, and we can't leave because the way to get to them is treacherous?"

He blinks and looks surprised. "How did you guess?"

"I've watched enough Christmas holiday movies to know that's the most likely scenario here."

"That's what Michael told me. He also said that we should stay put here until they can send help," he adds.

"Which would be when? Tomorrow? The day after?"

"As soon as the weather clears."

"Which would be?"

"Your guess is as good as mine." He scowls. "I don't have a crystal ball and no access to news or the weather."

"A likely story." I huff. "This must be a ploy for you to keep us here. In fact," I prop my hand on my hip, "I'll bet it was you who put Nonna up to this stupid treasure hunt."

"Scavenger hunt."

"Whatever," I snap, "and it must have been you who decided to team us up together."

"That was fate," his jaw hardens, "and believe me, it's not like I was happy about it either."

"After the way you crept into my room two nights ago, you expect me to believe that?"

"Trust me, the last thing I want is to be trapped with you in an enclosed space with no means of escaping."

"Well, that's what marriage is like, so get used to it."

He frowns. "Thought that was supposed to be my dialogue, and what do you have against marriage, anyway?"

"You mean, what do I have against being a slave to a man who'll spend his day doing Mafia business and come home with blood-splattered clothes and expect me to clean them?"

"The only thing I'd expect you to clean is the cum off my dick."

My belly clenches, and my core quivers. That was filthy, like really filthy, so why am I so turned on?

"If you think I'm going to stand here and be insulted by you, then you thought wrong."

"What's insulting and what's wrong with being upfront with my expectations for our relationship?"

"Fake relationship," I correct him.

"Didn't seem that fake when you were begging me to let you come."

"Aargh!" I bunch my fists at my side. "Typical male chauvinistic behavior. But then, I'd expect no less from you."

"What, because what I said is the truth of our last interaction?"

"You drive me crazy, you know that?" I scowl at him. "First, you propose this crazy fake relationship thing because of some cock-and-bull story of how you want to fool your family into believing that you're marrying me, only so you can separate from me later and get on with your philandering ways and now, you actually seem to believe that we're in a real relationship." My breath comes out in little puffs. Blood thuds at my temples, my cheeks heat, and honestly, I feel so mad that I'm sure if I stay here a second longer, I'm going to slap him or throw myself at him and beg him to impale me with his monster cock and put me out of my misery. Or both. Preferably.

"Sod this." I race for the door.

24

Christian

"Che cazzo!" I growl, "What the hell are you doing?" A-n-d I have begun to sound like a stuck record where this woman is concerned. Why the hell does she always make me so mad that I want to throw her over my lap and spank her ass, right before I pull her up and kiss the sass out of her?

"Don't open the—"

She flings open the door, and a gust of wind blows in along with snow. The cold instantly crashes over me. The breath leaves me in a huff, and before I can take a step forward, she's gone. The door slams shut, cutting off the wind. In the silence that follows, I race for the door and fling it open. Once more, the cold slaps me in the face. The wind buffets me as I step out. My hold on the door slips and it bangs shut as I race forward. I see her figure stumbling through the snow, which already comes up to my knees, and I am six-feet-three-inches which means for Flower, it's at least thigh-high. She was wearing her boots, wasn't she? Which is more than I can say for myself.

"Minchia!" I growl as the dampness and the cold penetrate through my skin to my bone. I swear my blood freezes. My temper rises. Anger thrums at my temples. "Fuck this shit," I roar. "When I get my hands on you, Flower, I'm going to—" A gust of wind hits me in the face with such force that I stumble back. *Porca miseria!* I'm going to kill this woman, after I finally fuck her.

I lunge forward through the snow, my feet already so numb that I can't feel them. Good, it makes it that much easier to ignore them. I push through the piles of snowflakes, closing the distance between us. Not for the first time, my height works in my favor as she struggles to move through the snow, only to fall over. I double my speed, and reaching her, haul her up, then throw her up over my shoulder.

"Let me go," she yells. "Let me the fuck—" The wind buffets me again, the snow coming down so hard and fast that it seems like we're in a snow globe. I can't see my hand in front of my face. At least, I turned in the direction of the house, so I assume if I keep walking forward, I should reach it.

I take a step forward when she slams her fists into my back. The pain only slices down my back and settles in my groin. My dick twitches. If nothing else, the circulation to that part of my body is working fine. She pulls back her knee, and I have no doubt that she's going to sink her foot into my groin. I wrap my other arm around her thighs, holding her so close that she is unable to move.

"Let me the fuck go, you asshole, you—"

I throw her down in the snow.

She lays there, the snow falling over her and covering her almost completely in seconds. I fling myself on her, planking at the last second to avoid crushing her under my weight.

"You're crazy, you know that? You stupid, idiotic—"

I close my mouth over hers, drawing in her essence, sucking on her tongue as the snow covers both of us. I tear my mouth from hers, and she stares up at me. White flakes stick to her hair, to the tips of her eyelashes, to her cheeks.

Her pupils are blown, her lips parted. I stare down at her mouth as her shoulders shudder.

"*Cazzo*," I say through gritted teeth, "you always make me so mad that I lose my mind and forget where I am."

I spring up to my feet and hold out my hand. She must be really cold, for she grabs my hand. I haul her up, then sweep her up in my arms, bridal style, and push through the snow. By the time I make it to the doorway, every part of me is drenched. I can't feel my feet or my hands, or for that matter, my nose. I shoulder my way through the door and step through, letting it slam shut behind me. I head through the living room, into the bedroom, and straight to the en-suite.

I place her down next to the tub and turn on the water. Hot water instantly gushes out.

"Th-this ... p-place has hot w-water?" she says through chattering teeth.

"It's owned by the Sovranos. Of course, it has hot water."

I pull my shirt over my head and toss it aside. I'm reaching for my pants when she squeaks, "Wh-what are you doing?"

"Getting naked so I can get in the tub. Suggest you do the same, Flower." I shuck off my pants and my boxers and slide a foot inside the hot tub. My toes protest as the sensations come rushing back. "Minchia," I swear as I shift my weight to that foot, pull my other leg over, and slide down into the fast-filling tub. The warmth instantly infuses my limbs. The pins and needles feeling in my arms and legs is a testament to just how much the cold has already affected me.

I turn to find her watching me warily, shivering, her clothes dripping water onto the floor.

"Get in," I order.

She hesitates.

"I promise, I'll keep my hands off of you."

She tosses her head. "Th-that'll be the day." She reaches for her sweatshirt, pulls it off, then toes off her shoes, and pushes down her pants and socks. She straightens, clad in her bra and panties. I rake my gaze over the tops of her creamy tits, her curvy stomach, those thick, gorgeous thighs that I want wrapped around my face as she rides my mouth.

The blood drains to my groin, and I bet if I look down, I'll find my cock indulging in a little periscope action. I widen my legs, then jerk my chin in her direction. "Take that off," I command.

She scowls, seems like she is about to protest, and I click my tongue. "You don't want to be wearing snow-soaked undergarments. You'll never get completely warm that way."

She blows out a breath, then reaches behind her to unhook her bra. She pulls it off, then shoves her panties down her legs. Goose bumps cover her skin. She props her hand on her hip, thrusts her breasts out as I take in the pebbled nipples, the curve of her waist, the strip of hair that draws attention to her pussy lips. The pulse flares to life at my temples, at my wrists, even in my fucking balls. My groin hardens. I can't take my gaze off of that beautiful cunt of hers.

She walks toward me, hips swaying, tits jiggling. When she reaches the tub, she swings one leg over, then the other. For a second, I glance up at her lush figure as she stands over me. Then, the woman slowly squats, so her pussy is positioned directly over my aching, throbbing cock.

"*Cazzo,*" I growl as I grab her hips, "what the hell are you playing at?"

"I'm c-cold, so are you. I th-thought this would be the b-best way to warm ourselves up." Another shudder runs down her spine, punctuating her sentence.

"Once you start this, there's no going back, Flower."

She peers into my face. "M-maybe I don't w-want to go back. M-maybe I'm t-tired of fighting."

"Somehow, I don't believe you." Fuck me, can't believe I'm going to say this, but... "Maybe that dip in the pond, followed by your running out into the snow, has given you brain freeze?" I mutter. "Maybe you're not thinking straight."

"And here I thought y-you'd take any chance to f-fuck me." She lowers herself further until her wet core chafes my very willing cock.

"Fuck," I bite out, fighting the urge to thrust my pelvis up, wanting, needing to bury myself in that hot, tight hole of hers.

"Exactly," her breath hitches, "th-that's what I want you to do to m-me."

"You sure, Aurora?" Why the hell am I giving her a chance to back out when just a few days ago, I'd have thrown her down and rutted into her the first chance I got?

She holds my gaze for an eternity, for a second. Then she bares her teeth and pushes down onto my throbbing length.

25

Aurora

I push down on his dick, and the thick head of his cock breaches me. His grip on my hips tightens, holding me in place, so I'm unable to move. I stay poised with my slick opening enveloping the crown of his length.

A nerve throbs at his temple, and his gaze bores into me. The silence stretches, broken only by the sound of the water flowing into the tub. Then, just as I'm sure that he is going to push me away, he thrusts up, and in one smooth move, breaches me.

I throw my head back, bite down on my lower lip as the hard column of his arousal impales me. Pain pinches me deep inside, and my thighs quake. A moan bleeds from my lips, and I grip his arms and hold on. A beat, another.

"What the fuck?" he swears. "Are you? It's not possible... Tell me it's not true, Flower."

I squeeze my eyes shut. "D-don't stop," I say through gritted teeth. "Don't you d-dare stop now."

He raises me up until, once more, I'm poised with my pussy clamped around the head of his cock. Then he lowers me slowly, centimeter by centimeter, so slowly that I can feel every ridge of his thick, hard cock.

The pain recedes and is replaced by a trembling that sparks off in my lower belly. I dig my fingertips into the muscles of his forearm, then lower my chin to my chest. I keep my eyes closed for two reasons. One, because I don't want to see the inevitable question on his face and two, because all of my senses are focused on that part of him which is inside of me. His shaft swells and fills me and stretches me in a way that I have never been before.

"Flower," he murmurs, "you okay?"

Without opening my eyes, I squeeze down on his length, and a groan rips from me.

"*Cazzo!*" he growls. "What the fuck are you doing?"

I crack open my eyelids and take in the color that sears his cheeks. His eyes are half-closed, his lips parted. His nostrils flare as his gaze meets mine. "Just because you surprised me, don't think I'm going to go easy on you."

"I would be disappointed if you did," I retort. And I mean it. The part of me that has stopped fighting welcomes his possession, the force of his dominance that crashes into my chest and leaves me panting.

I bare my teeth, and he surges up. He flips me over so that I'm on my back in the tub.

He grips my legs, raises them, and hooks my knees over his shoulders.

"If you think you can control the first time I fuck you, you are sadly mistaken."

Of course, I don't. It's why I'm surprised that he has allowed me to take the lead for as long as he has. He's too macho, too dominant, too everything to not direct the proceedings.

He reaches between us, slots his cock into my slit, then with one thrust, he plunges home. Too much. Too full. If I thought that having him inside me earlier prepared me for his intrusion, then I'm sadly mistaken. He's so goddam big I swear I can feel him all the way in my throat.

"Christian," I groan, "omigod, Chris."

He pulls out of me, then breaches me again, once more hitting that part deep inside of me that I didn't know existed. I surge up, wind my arms around his neck, and push my swollen nipples into that hard chest as I strain against him.

He pulls out again, then angles his hips so when he impales me next, the ridge of his cock hits my swollen clit. Pleasure vibrates out from the contact. Goose bumps pop on my skin. He slides one hand between us and pinches my clit, and I explode.

The shivers run up my legs, up my thighs, swirl around my belly as he continues to fuck me. He rams his cock into me again and again. Each hit sends a fresh burst of sensations up my spine. My eyes roll back in my head. I dig my heels into his back and bury my teeth in my lower lip as I begin to ride the waves of pleasure that surge up my body. A flash of light crashes behind my eyes, and spots of black flicker at the edges of my eyesight.

He continues to plunge into me over and over again. His muscles bunch, his shoulders go solid. He pulls out and then comes, shooting thick ropes of cum across my chest.

My limbs tremble, and I float for a few seconds. When I open my eyes, he's looking at me. His eyebrows are furrowed, his blue gaze burning like he's trying to figure out the answer to something.

"What?" I frown. "What is it?"

"You know what." He glares at me. "When were you planning on telling me?"

"Never?" I hunch my shoulders. "It's not a big deal, okay?"

"I took your virginity, and it's not a big deal?"

"Surely, you're not going to go all caveman about some stupid piece of skin, are you?"

His jaw tics. "What game are you playing with me, Aurora? First, you resist me. Then you change your mind and decide to jump me, only for me to find out that you are a virgin?"

"Firstly, it really isn't a big deal, and secondly, you took off your clothes and told me to take off my clothes and join you in the tub, so of course, I assumed the worst. I thought that if I—"

"Took the lead; you could steer the proceedings?" he says in a hard voice.

"Something like that."

"It's difficult for you to give up control, isn't it?"

"Finally," I throw up my hands, "finally, he gets it."

He folds his arms across his chest, and his massive biceps bulge. "Get up," he says in a hard voice.

"What?" I scowl, "Why should I? I'm just getting warmed up."

"From now on, for as long as we are in this house, you will do as I say."

"What the hell?" I fold my arms around my waist. "Why should I do that?"

"Because I'm going to show you just how good it is when you give up your need to be in charge all the time."

"Says the man who can't let go of his dominance for even one second."

"That's different."

"Why? How is it different?"

"I'm a man; it's my job to be dominant. You're a woman, ergo," the asshole raises his shoulder, "of course, you derive more pleasure by being submissive. In fact, the more you are able to let go of control and allow me to take care of your needs, the more pleasure you'll derive from it."

I gape at him. "What the—" I shake my head. "I can't even..." I try to form the words, but my brain seems to have trouble piecing my thoughts together. "Do you hear yourself?" I finally sputter. "I mean, how can you say what you did with a straight face?"

"What, did I say something wrong?" He seems puzzled.

No, seriously, the bastard actually does believe every single word of what he just said.

I splash some water onto myself to clear his cum off my chest. Then I jump up, not caring that I'm naked, and step out of the bathtub. I head for where the towels are folded on a shelf. I pull out one, then begin to dry myself. My core twinges, but I ignore it.

What was I thinking, giving this man my virginity? I mean, sure, it probably had to happen sooner or later. For all that he says this is a fake relationship, I knew that sooner or later, I was going to sleep with him. I just wish I weren't such a cliché. Twenty-four and still a virgin, ha! At least I won't have to suffer through the embarrassment of that again. And to be fair, I enjoyed it. But that ... is the last time I'm sleeping with him willingly. At least, I climaxed, and it was a mighty fine orgasm, so... There, I did get something out of it. Better to quit while I'm ahead then. I wrap the towel around myself, tucking it under my arms.

"What are you doing?" His voice comes from just behind and above me.

I start. "What do you think?" I scowl. "Going in search of some clothes."

"This conversation is not over, Flower," he calls out behind me as I stalk out of the bathroom.

I walk into the bedroom and take in the simple but luxurious furnishings of the space. The bed is king-size, the sheets and pillows snowy white. So is the cover. The headboard is made out of wood and carved with intricate designs, between which are set two iron rings, one on either side. Speaking of, there's also a ring on a chain that dangles from the ceiling. The kind a gymnast would use to work out with, except there's only one of them. Is that for... It can't be, can it?

I hear his footsteps and scowl at him over my shoulder. "Is this really a lodge, or is it some kind of getaway you use for your kinky sex stuff?"

"It is a lodge." He smirks. "It's also used for kinky sex stuff."

"I assume Nonna doesn't come here then?"

"My brothers use it on the occasion that they need a getaway place."

"Are all of you Sovrano brothers into fetishes?"

"Some more than others." He looks me up and down. That's when I realize I'm still practically naked. Jeez, am I already so comfortable in his presence that I don't care I'm parading around him in the nude?

"Turn around." I snap.

"I've seen everything there is to see. He folds his arms as if ready to watch me change.

I scowl, and he raises an eyebrow. No doubt, he expects me to turn tail and return to the bathroom to change. And I'm not going to give him the satisfaction of thinking that he's unnerved me again. I turn away, then drop my towel to the floor.

I hear him exhale behind me. Good. I can't stop my lips from curving as I head for the closet and pull it open. There are no clothes… Nothing, except two bathrobes hanging from the rod. I choose the smaller of them and shrug into it. Tying it around me securely, I yank out the other one from the closet and toss it at him.

He snatches it from the air. "Not able to see me naked without wanting to throw yourself at me, I take it?" He smirks.

I resist the urge to roll my eyes. "I only gave it to you in case you felt cold. If you'd rather parade around naked—" I drag my gaze down his sculpted pecs, to where his monster cock hangs between his legs. He's not fully erect, but hell, if that length of his doesn't seem w-a-a-y too big for it to fit into where he put it earlier. My pussy spasms in recollection. Moisture laces my core. As if he's aware of what I'm thinking, his shaft begins to thicken.

"As I said," he drawls, "if you'd rather I stay without clothes, you only have to say the word, Flower." His grin widens. "So, what's it going to be?"

26

Aurora

I flip my hair over my shoulder, "You can do whatever you want; I don't care." I flounce past him, and he grabs my wrist and tugs. I fall against him and the contact of skin on skin makes my breath hitch.

"I haven't given you permission to leave."

"Excuse me?"

"You can't leave until I let you."

"Says who?"

"Says your future husband."

"No ring, remember?" I raise my left hand.

Truth be told, I can't believe that I actually threw away that ring. And I actually liked it… No, I loved it. It was beautiful. And surely, he had chosen the color of the stone because it reminded him of my eyes. Not that he had mentioned it to me, but it had to be that, right? And I had flung it away. It had to be expensive, as well…

But more than that, it had meant something to me. The fact that he had remembered to get me a ring. So what, if it was because his grandmother had pointed out that without a ring, he couldn't call me his fiancée? Still, it had been my ring. And I had discarded it.

I try to pull away, and this time, he releases me. I march past him and toward the door. I am about to step out when he calls out, "Just remember, we are only getting started."

I resist the urge to show him my finger. And I don't mean the one missing a ring. Instead, I walk out the door and to the kitchen. I open the door to the pantry and stare at the range of packaged food stocked inside. Dried pasta, cans of tinned fruit and vegetables, pancake mixes—not very common in Italy, so it must be imported from the UK?—pasta sauces, hell, there is even bread flour and a cookie dough mix. Huh. Apparently, the Sovranos believe in slumming in style.

I pull open the door of the refrigerator, and this time I'm not surprised to find the bottles of beers and wines. Also, eggs, juices, and a Christmas Pudding wrapped up in festive paper and stored on the bottom shelf. All the comforts of home and more.

When I open the freezer, I find packets of frozen vegetables, meats, and fish.

I pull out what I need, then turn and crash into a hard chest. The scent of darkness—dark coffee mixed with brandy—teases my nostrils. I try to step around him, but he moves to block my way.

"What?" I scowl. "I'm busy."

"You going to cook for us?"

"Unless you'd prefer to do it?"

"I'm good at numbers, but cooking… It's best I leave that one to you." He smirks. "Also, I loaded the washing machine with our clothes."

"Oh, that's good." I try to brush past him, but he doesn't move. "Now what?" I frown. "I'm hungry, and if we are going to be stuck here, I'd prefer to get the cooking underway so we can eat before I starve."

He steps aside, and I walk over to the kitchen counter. I place all of the items I'd pulled out and busy myself. "I hope you like omelets," I call out.

"I love omelets," he says from behind and above me. Again.

I squeal, "Jesus, can you stop creeping up on me like that?"

"Somehow, when I'm with you, I can't stop myself from following you around," he mutters with a strange expression on his face.

O-k-a-y. Did he just say that? What did he mean by that. Before I can ask, he steps back. "Why don't I set the table?" He walks around to the cabinet, pulls out the plates, and places two of them next to me. He retrieves cutlery and napkins, then returns to the island.

I find bread in the bread-box and cartons of milk on the shelves next to the stove. "Wow," I marvel, "this place is fully stocked." I turn on him. "Did you plan all this?"

"Plan what?" he asks.

"This," I wave my hand in the air, "me falling into the pond, then us stumbling across this lodge by—" I make air quotes, "'accident'?"

"Would I do that?" He widens his gaze.

"Ha!" I scoff. "I'm not going to answer that question."

"You wound me, Flower." He thumps his chest. "But to put your mind at ease, no I didn't plan any of this. I assume Nonna told the housekeeping team to keep the place ready for guests, as a precaution."

"Hmph," I flatten my lips, "not sure I believe you." I turn back to the omelets, and by the time I have plated them out, along with the toast that I remembered to pop in earlier, he's already seated. I place his plate in front of him and take my seat at the right of him.

Both of us dig in and start eating. By the time I'm halfway through my food, I'm already full. Which is normal for me. I think I'm hungry, but when I start eating, I find I'm not able to finish everything on my plate. I glance up to find he's polished off everything. I keep my fork and knife aside while I push my plate toward him. "Here, have it."

"You sure?" He frowns. "You didn't eat much."

"I can't eat too much at one sitting," I explain, "but I'll nibble at something in a few hours."

"So, you literally eat like a rabbit?" He laughs.

"Hopefully, my diet's more varied than a rabbit's." I sniff. "Go on," I nod toward my plate, "it's all yours."

He digs in and seems to inhale everything on my plate, then sits back with a sigh. "That was delicious."

"You sound surprised."

"Thought you doctors were too busy studying and interning to learn how to cook."

I tilt my head. "I did study a lot to qualify. Also, because I was away from home, I began to miss home-cooked food. Apparently, as much as I wanted to be away, the food was one thing I couldn't turn my back on."

"So, you learned to cook?"

"It's also a great stress buster." I play with my napkin, then crumple it. "When things got too hectic and I felt overwhelmed with the magnitude of what I had set out to do, I turned to cooking." I glance at him. "And you? What do you do for relieving stress?"

"You mean when I'm not killing people?"

I stare at him.

"Just kidding." He chuckles. "I haven't been involved with the enforcing side of the Mafia world for a long time. My specialty is interpreting the law; I am the Consigliere for the clans."

"But you have been involved with … killing people, in the past?"

He straightens his spine. "If you are asking me if I have killed men, then the answer is yes."

I glance away. What did I expect him to say? That he hadn't been involved with taking lives? How naive can I be?

"I am part of the Mafia, Flower," he says in a soft voice as if he's read my mind. "It's part of what I am, to take lives if needed."

"And it's part of who I am to save lives." I tip up my chin. "Guess the two of us really are on opposite sides of the spectrum." I rise to my feet, then reach over to collect his plate, but he stops me.

"There's one place where we do meet."

"You mean the sex?"

"I mean in bed. Where we can forget that we come from two very different positions in life. Where you don't have to bring the weight of your expectations, of the path you have set yourself. Where you don't need to do anything but give yourself up to me."

"You mean to submit to you, don't you?"

"What you don't realize is that the person who submits holds the power."

I snort. "A likely story."

"It's true." He laces his fingers with mine, and the gesture is so gentle, so intimate that my breath catches. I peer into his face, and one side of his lips quirks. "Think about it," he murmurs, "you give up control, you put your trust in me, and that is a big responsibility. I'm in charge of making you feel good, for pushing you so that you redefine your boundaries. The ability to cause you pain or pleasure would lay in my hands, and that's a task that I wouldn't take lightly." He rubs his thumb in small, slow circles over my wrist, and a shiver runs up my spine. "Imagine that, for the time that you have handed over control to me, you don't have to make decisions or choices; everything would be decided for you. You'd only have to do as you're told."

"That sounds like slavery."

"Or like freedom."

"Freedom?" I scoff, "You're delirious."

"You wouldn't have to think about the pros and cons or worry about the consequences of your actions or stress about whether you made the right choice or not. All that worry would be mine."

"So, what does that leave me with?" I swallow.

"The right to enjoy yourself, to focus on yourself, your pleasure, your needs." He leans in close enough for his eyelashes to brush mine. "Your wants. Everything you've always dreamed of. Your deepest desires. Your filthiest, dirtiest dreams. Everything you've wanted to try but were too afraid to ask for, and maybe things that you didn't even know you would enjoy… I would be able to fulfill those experiences for you."

27

Christian

Her breathing grows ragged, and color smears her cheeks. Her pupils dilate, and I know then that she's thinking of the kind of pleasure that I could bring to her. How I could play her body, wring out every last drop of desire from her; how I would arouse her, make her aware of her own needs, then satisfy her.

She licks her lips, and my gaze drops to her mouth. A moan wheezes from her lips, and my cock thickens. "When you come to me, and you will come to me, I promise, I will be waiting for you. Everything you desire is right there in front of your eyes. All you have to do is reach out and take it."

I release her, and she stays in the same position for a second longer. Then, suddenly realizing that she is free, she grabs my plate and straightens. She pivots on her heel and heads to the sink, and I follow her.

"Leave it," I command, and she squeaks.

"God, you have to stop scaring me like this."

"Your mind is involved somewhere else. I understand that."

"You understand nothing." She moves to the side. I approach the sink, run the water, and begin to rinse off the plates.

"What don't I understand, Flower?" I murmur, "Enlighten me."

"Everything." She grabs a dishcloth and wrings it between her fingers. "It's not that easy for me to give up control."

"Have you ever tried it before?" I ask as I pour out the dishwashing liquid. Thankfully, this place really is fully equipped with everything needed for a short stay. It's something I'll need to thank Nonna for.

She ensures everything is in working condition, not just during this getaway, but even during family gatherings which she had been at the forefront of organizing before Karma came along. She's always tried to keep the family together, even if it meant that, at times, she was heavy-handed about it. I suppose with a man as ruthless as the previous Don for her son, a daughter-in-law unable to stand up for herself, and with seven troublesome grandsons, it was the only way to get everyone to fall in line.

"Tried what?" Aurora accepts the plate from me and begins to wipe it.

"Giving up your sense of order and need to always have to steer everything your way."

"No," she admits with some reluctance, "I couldn't have gotten to where I am if I had done that."

"But you'd have had more fun if you had."

"Is that what this is all about, fun?" She places the dried plate down and reaches to take the next one from me.

"Life is about living in the moment. And that means enjoying yourself when the opportunity presents itself."

"Is that your personal motto?" she scoffs.

"It's my experience." I wash the fork, hand it to her, but when she takes it from me, I don't release it. "Life's short, Flower. It's all well and good to plan for the long-term, but what if you don't get to see it? What if something unexpected happens, and you aren't able to see the dawn tomorrow? Wouldn't you have regrets about everything that you didn't experience?"

She holds my gaze, her own troubled. "I'm a doctor, Christian. No one sees death more closely than me. But that's not an excuse to relinquish rules and live a life of excesses."

"But you could do so for a short period of time, knowing the time was going to end, couldn't you?"

"What are you getting at?" She tugs at the cutlery, and I hand it to her. She wipes it with the dishcloth, surveys it, then carefully rubs the tines again. Her every movement is restrained. She doesn't stop until she is satisfied with it. She places the fork down, then turns to find me staring at her. "What?" She frowns.

"We are stuck here until the storm lets up. No one can come here; we can't leave. We may as well as use the time wisely."

"It's a good excuse for you, isn't it?" She throws up her hands. "Just because we have nothing else to do, let's have sex."

I hand the knife I've just washed, handle first, to her. "It's as good a reason as any—" She accepts the knife, opens her mouth to protest, and I raise my hand. "And it's not just any sex. I'm talking about sweaty, down and dirty, filthy, kinky sex. The kind that will leave an imprint in between your legs sex. The kind that will ensure that you can't walk straight for days sex."

She draws in a breath. Her hand trembles, and the knife slips from her fingers. I swoop down and catch it by the handle again, then straighten and place it on the counter. "So, what do you say, Flower? Do we have a deal?"

"No." She flings down the towel, then marches past me.

I laugh. "I'll wear you down yet, Flower. You know that, right?"

"Keep trying." She raises her middle finger above her shoulder as she heads out of the kitchen.

I chuckle as I wash and dry the rest of the dishes, then put them away. After wiping down the counter, I head out of the kitchen to find her curled up with a book in front of the fire.

"What are you reading?" I murmur as I sink down on the settee next to her.

"None of your business," she retorts, then blows out a breath. "I found it on the bookshelf." She nods toward the array of books on the opposite corner of the living room.

She holds out the book, and I read the title on the cover.

"Murder for Christmas by Agatha Christie." I whistle. "That's a rather bloody book for Christmas, don't you think?"

"Somehow, murder and Christmas seem to go together." She tosses her hair over her shoulder. "Must be the fact that you are shut in an overly warm house with family you don't normally see during the rest of the year. The setting is ripe for old resentments to boil to the surface. Sounds to me like the perfect recipe for committing murder."

"Didn't see you as such a bloodthirsty person, Flower." I survey her features.

"Reading is one of the ways I relax, and I find there's nothing like a good murder-mystery to act as a stress buster."

"I can think of other ways of relieving stress." I waggle my eyebrows.

She frowns. "Can't you go for five minutes without thinking with your dick."

"Can't you go for five minutes without talking about my dick?"

She makes a sound at the back of her throat that goes straight to my groin. My cock twitches, and damn, if I don't want to throw her down, part her legs, and show her just how quickly I can relieve her stress.

She must have an inkling of what I'm thinking, for her cheeks redden. She throws the book in my direction, and I snatch it out of the air. She jumps to her feet and begins to pace. "This is useless. How long are we going to be stuck here? Isn't there any way of reaching the rest of them and asking them to speed up the rescue?"

I glance to the windows outside and notice the snow climbs halfway up the panes. "Doesn't seem like anyone is going anywhere anytime soon."

"Bet you are happy about that." She drags her fingers through her hair. "I still think you planned all of this."

"I know I'm a powerful Mafia guy, but controlling the weather is beyond even my capabilities."

"Thank god!" She throws up her hands. "At least, you admit that there is something that you can't do."

"Now, if we were talking about what I can do with my fingers," I hold them up, "or my tongue," I stick my tongue out and wiggle it suggestively, "that would be a different story."

She squeezes her thighs together. It's a subtle gesture, but I'm watching her so carefully that I catch it.

I draw in a breath, and I swear, I can detect her arousal. I toss the book onto the seat next to me and rise to my feet.

She pauses and watches me warily as I prowl over to her.

"Why don't you try to relax a little?" I drawl, "Look on this as a paid holiday."

"Not sure I can do that with the specter of our upcoming nuptials," she retorts.

"Forget about that. Forget about the fact that you're a doctor, that I'm a Mafia guy you love to hate. Forget about everything except that we are here, unable to go anywhere, and that we're attracted to each other."

She swallows, then holds up her hand. "No more corny dialogue from you now, please."

"How about I show you, instead?"

"What?" She scowls. "Please don't ask me to stop thinking and start feeling or something stupid like that."

I laugh. "Trust me, I'm as good with my words as I am with other parts of my anatomy."

She folds her arms around her waist. "This isn't going to work."

"At least, give it a chance." I bend my knees and peer into her eyes. "Can you do that for me?"

28

Aurora

Don't do it. Don't do it. Don't do it. I peer into his eyes. Take in the sparks in the depths of that blue gaze. Something hot stabs at my chest. Maybe it's because I'm tired of fighting him, or the fact that he had rescued me from the pond finally sinks in, or maybe… All this talk about his cock and sex and about giving up control finally gets to me. Either way, I can't stop myself from whispering, "Okay."

His gaze widens, then he nods. "Good."

"That's all you're going to say, good?"

"It's just the start, baby."

The use of that endearment makes my pussy throb. Shit, what the hell is wrong with me? How could I have given in to him so easily? Now he's going to think that he can take me for granted, that he can ask me to do anything, and I'll obey.

"Don't," he says in a sharp voice. "Don't do that."

"What?"

"Whatever you're thinking, don't go there."

"You have no idea what's on my mind."

He chuckles. "Oh, I have a good idea. It's written all over your face that you are going to freak out."

"I'm not going to freak out." I swallow. "I might hyperventilate a little…" I try to smile but my chin wobbles, "…but that's par for the course."

"You don't have to worry about anything from now on."

That's what I'm afraid of.

"All you have to do is trust me, Flower." He peers into my eyes. "Can you do that?"

"I…" I swallow. "I'm not sure," I reply honestly.

"I won't do anything that you don't want me to do." He frowns. "Unless, of course, I think it's good for you."

"How can you say that?" I throw up my hands, then slap his chest when he chuckles.

"You think this is a joke? All of this—you proposing this stupid arrangement which, by the way, I could have told you for free that it wouldn't work, and now suggesting we play this stupid BDSM game."

"Not a game," he presses his palm over mine and holds it to his chest, "and BDSM is not stupid. It's one way of learning to test your limits and find out what you enjoy, find out just what reserves you hold inside of yourself. Find out" he leans in close enough for our breaths to tangle, "just how many ways I can make you come."

My belly trembles. My core clenches. Moisture trickles down my thigh. I dig my heels into the ground, so I don't do something stupid … like close the remaining distance between us and throw myself at him and beg him to do with me as he wants. Gosh, why is this so difficult? Why can't I simply let go as he's asking me to? Why am I fighting myself so much?

"Shh," he tucks a strand of hair behind my ear, "don't be so hard on yourself, Flower."

"And you?" I tip up my chin. "Aren't you being too hard on yourself because of Xander's death?"

Shut up! Why did you say that? Why is it that, the moment he tries to show that there's more to him than the asshole Mafia guy persona that he likes to portray, you have to try to shut him down?

His jaw tightens. His gaze intensifies for a few seconds, then he wipes all expression from his features.

"You want to play dirty, is that it?" he says in a hard voice. "You want me to be mean to you? You prefer it when I'm uncaring, when I don't consider your feelings, and instead use you for my own pleasure? Is that what turns you on, Flower?"

Yes.

Yes.

"No," I say through a throat gone dry, "of course, not."

He peers into my eyes, then shakes his head. "You don't know what you need, do you, Flower?"

"And you do?"

He blows out a breath. "Isn't that what this entire conversation is about?"

I try to pull away from him, but he holds my hand captive against his sculpted chest. The feel of the planes under my palm, the thud-thud-thud of his heart that mirrors the pulse between my legs, the warmth of his skin that creeps into my skin, all of it confirms to me that I am here with him, in this moment. That we are alone in this house, snowed in from the world. That there is no one to judge me for what I want him to do to me. There is no one to taunt me for my wanting to give in to him. There is no one but myself, the woman who wants to experience the highs of pleasure and the lows of depravity that he has promised that he'll show me.

"Show me," I murmur. "Show me what you can do to me."

His gaze narrows. His nostrils flare, then he straightens. I pull my arm away and lock my fingers together in front of myself. He glares at me, and I shuffle my weight from foot to foot. The seconds stretch by; he doesn't look away from me. I hold his gaze until it gets too much for me. Until my skin heats, my thighs clench, my toes curl, and my skin feels too tight for the rest of me. Another second, and I am going to self-combust. "Christian…" I finally chuckle. "Wh-what are you doing?"

"Strip," he growls.

"Excuse me?" I blink. "What the hell do you mean by that?"

"Exactly what I said, Flower. You put yourself in my care. Now do as I say. Take off your bathrobe."

"But it's cold," I whine.

He lowers his voice to a hush. "Do it, Flower." All of my nerve endings seem to pop. I open my mouth to protest, but he shakes his head. "Now," he snaps. The cold air hits my shoulders, and I realize that I have untied my bathrobe. It slithers down my arms to rest around my elbows.

He sweeps his gaze down my front, where my skin is bared.

"Lower your arms," he commands.

When I do so, the bathrobe falls off to pool around my ankles.

"Hmm." He taps his cheek as he looks me up and down. He walks a slow circle around me, and I have to stop myself from glancing over my shoulder to follow his progress. Goose. bumps track across my skin as he comes to a stop in front of me.

"Stay." He stabs a finger at me. Before I can protest, he spins around and walks over to the fire. He prods at it, then adds more wood to it until it's roaring.

Heat fills the space and suffuses my skin. By the time he walks over to me, there's a thin film of sweat over my upper lip.

"Better?" he asks.

I nod, then point at his bathrobe. "Why are you still dressed?"

"Because I'm the dominant in this relationship."

I pout. "So, you get to say anything and do anything—"

"Including you."

"And I have to take it?"

"Yes." He smirks.

"What kind of a stupid relationship is that?"

"The kind that will take you to heights that you've never dreamed of."

"So you keep saying. Why can't you—"

"Shh!" He puts a finger to his lips. "No speaking."

"What?"

He shakes his head. "No speaking until I let you."

I open my mouth, then close it again. Damn it, it seems my body is keen to obey him in this too. I purse my lips, watch as he, once more, rakes his gaze down my chest until he stops at my core. He stares at my pussy for so long that my core throbs. I swear my pussy lips seem to engorge. A fat bead of moisture slides down my inner thigh. My nipples harden; my limbs grow so heavy that I'm sure I'm not going to be able to keep myself upright. My nerve-endings stretch. What the hell is he doing? Why can't he come closer and touch me instead of staring at me like I'm his last meal? Still, the silence stretches. I open my mouth to scream, and that's when he closes the distance between us. He lowers himself to his knees until his face is directly in front of my core. Finally!

He leans in until his hot breath curls over my throbbing flesh, then he swipes his tongue up my pussy lips. My knees buckle. I grip his hair to keep myself from falling.

"Part your legs," he murmurs.

I hurry to oblige.

He glances up at me as he slides one finger inside my sopping channel. I moan as he curls it inside me. Bloody hell, if this was a gynecological examination, I would have been embarrassed that I was so turned on from his finger inside me. Luckily, it's not, so I guess it's okay that I'm so slick between my folds, right? He pulls out his finger, then brings it to his mouth and sucks on it. My head spins. Hell, that is … hot. So hot. It feels more filthy, more intimate than anything he has done to me before, and honestly, I can't tell you why it feels that way when he has done filthier things to me than this.

"You taste sweet, you know that?" He smacks his lips. "Like honey and my favorite liquor, you go right to my head."

"Oh." My eyelids suddenly feel too heavy to lift up. My core clenches on itself. I already miss his touch, how he felt inside of me. Please, I plead with my eyes. Please, Christian.

A gorgeous smile splits his face. It transforms his features, making him seem even more handsome, more confident. He seems so sure of himself, so dominant, so pleased with me that my heart begins to race. The pulse pounds at my temples, at my wrists, and I hold his gaze, wanting, needing so much more.

He rises to his feet, then locks his fingers around my wrist, and leads me to a chair. He sits down, pulls me onto his lap, then grabs my book and hands it to me.

I glance up from the book to his face, then back to the book.

"Go on, read it," he murmurs.

Like that's possible when I'm seated in his lap. Not to mention that thick column between his legs makes its presence felt against my bottom.

"Go on," he places his cheek next to mine, "why don't you continue reading?"

I try to focus on the page in front of me. I even manage to get absorbed in the story. Then he pushes my hair over one shoulder and kisses my neck. A tremor runs down my spine. I try to turn, but he pinches my chin. "You focus on the reading."

Umm! Easier said than done, considering you have your hands all over me.

He licks the shell of my ear, and I can't stop the moan that bleeds from my lips.

"You like that?" he whispers. His breath coils over my cheek as he presses tiny kisses down my jaw. I lean my neck to the side to give him more access, then sigh when he buries his head in the curve of my neck. He bites down on the skin there, and my pussy instantly clenches. He slides a hand around to cup my breast. He squeezes the nipple, and moisture coats my channel. He brings his other hand around to frame my other breast, and I throw my head back against his shoulder. He covers my breasts with his big palms and massages them. OMG, I didn't realize my breasts could be so sensitive. So arousing. He pushes them together, then twists my nipples, and my entire body jerks.

"Your tits," he growls, "they're the most incredible pair I've ever seen."

"They're too big," I mutter, "the bane of my life."

"And I fucking love them. Gonna fuck your tits, Flower," he rasps. "Gonna come all over them, then lick my cum off your sweet breasts and make you come again. Gonna lavish your nipples with so much attention that you'll never forget how it feels to have me suckling on them."

Oh, god. I squeeze my eyes shut, thrust out my chest, pushing my breasts deeper into his palms. My flesh hurts. My breasts feel weighed down. If he doesn't massage them soon and tighten his grasp on them and suck on them like he's promised, I'm going to cry.

As if he hears me, he tightens his grip, kneading them with such force that a groan spills from my lips.

"These noises you make," he rumbles, "they make me want to throw you down and rut into you to show you just how much you affect me."

Yes. Please. Please. Please.

He turns my head to him and captures my mouth with his. At the same time, he releases his grip on my breast, only to drive his hand between my legs and thrust three fingers into my melting core. A scream boils up, but he swallows it down. He begins to finger fuck me in earnest—in-out-in—while he thrusts his tongue into my mouth and mirrors the action. He deepens the kiss, sucking on me, tasting me, possessing my mouth with such confidence that my limbs weaken.

I part my legs, allowing him further access, and he slips a fourth finger in. He plunges his fingers in and out of me. The squelching sound penetrates the sexual haze that has wrapped around me. Heat sears my skin as I realize just how turned on I am. I've probably dripped all over his bathrobe. I try to wriggle away, and that's when he curves his fingers, hitting that spot deep inside of me. My belly seems to fold in on itself. Sensations spiral out from his touch as he doesn't stop cramming his fat digits in and out of me. The tremors race up my legs, up my spine. I clamp my thighs together, trying to stop that headlong rush to that place where I know my pleasure lies. Even as I strain against him, curving my body as I try to reach for that hallowed space where I can finally give in to this pleasure that threatens to overpower me. He grinds his heel into my clit, and that's when I explode. Moisture rushes out from my core, and the pressure at the base of my spine shatters.

I must scream, but he absorbs the noise. He continues to plunge his fingers in and out of me as I lazily circle back to earth. He releases my mouth, and I sense him watching me as the aftershocks grip me. He finally pulls his fingers out of me. The next second, he drags his fingers across my lips. "Open," he says in a husky voice.

I open my mouth, and he feeds me his fingers. I lick them off, still not opening my eyes. He leans in, kissing me on each eyelid. I turn my face into his chest, curling into him. Allowing myself, for the first time, to drink in his scent, to revel in how he surrounds me, how his heat cocoons me. How the taste of his skin and my cum coats my tongue. Darkness tugs at me, and I give in to the sleep that pulls me under.

When I wake up, I'm alone.

29

Christian

I hadn't meant to allow her to come this quickly. I had wanted to withhold that orgasm a little longer, until she had earned it. Until I had a chance to push her boundaries a little more. Until I had made her yearn for her release so her orgasm would be even more intense. But when I had felt her sweet curved bottom against my already hard shaft, all restraint had slipped from my mind. I couldn't stop myself from touching her and squeezing those gorgeous tits. And when she had moaned and cried out, I hadn't been able to hold back any longer. I had smelled her arousal, had known that she was already halfway to coming, and that's when I had kissed her and fucked her with my fingers. She had been hot and tight, and so wet.

I hadn't stopped kissing her, thrusting my fingers in and out of her. Not until her back had bowed, her shoulders had gone rigid, and she had come.

I bring my fingers up to my mouth and suck on them. The taste of her clings to them, combined with her scent. That distinctive honeysuckle taste of hers clings to my palate and goes straight to my head. My cock thickens—of course, it does. Fuck this. Can't I go a few minutes without wanting to be inside of her?

I spring up to my feet from where I had been seated by the fire and head for the back door. As soon as I open it, the cold rushes in. I slam the door shut behind me, stomp through the piled-up snow and toward the small shed in the back. The cold sinks into my blood, and I shiver. Shit, I should have, at least, worn my coat, but I had been in such a hurry to get out of there that I had forgotten to put it on. I stalk over to the shed, pull open the door, then head for the pile of wood in the corner. I grab hold of as many as I can, then shoulder the door open—walk back to the main house. Once again, the wind slams the door behind me with a crash that reverberates around the place.

I prowl over to the fireplace, place the stack of wood next to it. Bending down on one knee, I add some of the logs to the fire.

The hair on the back of my neck rises, and I know she has entered the room. She walks over to stand next to the fire, and she's still naked. Good, at least she's still obeying my orders.

"Did you just go out into the snow?" She glances sideways at me.

I don't answer.

"I assume you had to go get the firewood. That's why you went out?"

I stare into the heart of the fire.

"And you didn't wear your coat?"

I turn to scowl at her, "Don't tell me what to do."

She sets her jaw, "So, you're a big, bad Mafia guy, but going out into the cold without a coat is not good for you."

"Aww, are you worried about me, Flower?" I smirk.

Her face tightens. "You know what, forget it. I don't know why I keep trying to have a normal conversation with you."

"My point, exactly." I rise to my feet and glance down at her. She really is so tiny; I keep forgetting that. Of course, when I am inside her, nothing matters. Nothing except that hot, tight hole of hers which had clasped around my dick and milked me with such intensity, I had been overwhelmed with pleasure. The kind that I had never experienced before…and that's saying something.

Since being celibate is not one of my strengths, I have been with enough women to know when I find something that is different. And she is different. She's unlike the others. All the more reason to find a way to keep my distance from her. I initiated this fake relationship with her. Doesn't mean I have to conceal my tastes from her, now do I?

"There is nothing normal about my proclivities, Flower," I drawl.

"Like I care."

She turns to flounce away, but I call out to her, "Stop, right there."

She pauses at once, and fuck, if I don't come right then. The fact that she obeys me without hesitation… Is she aware just how much of a turn-on that is?

"Turn around."

She hesitates, then slowly pivots to face me. The light from the fire reflects off of her features. I look her up and down, then slowly shrug out of my bathrobe.

Her lips part as I place it over the chair next to me. "Stay right there," I murmur as I walk over to the sewing kit. I run my fingers across the different colors of ribbons. Blue? No. Green? Nope… A warm, golden yellow that reflects the fire in her eyes? Yes. I pick it up then walk over to her.

I walk slowly around her, taking in her curves—the thrust of her breasts, the curve of her belly, the lushness of her hips, the slope of her inner thighs leading to the slice of paradise that I've found between her legs. She wriggles her feet and brings one arm to cover her chest; she places the other hand across the space between her thighs.

"Don't." I frown. "Don't hide."

"Easy for you to say, you're not the one being ogled at."

"Feel free to ogle me right back." I raise my arms wide, and her gaze skitters down my chest. Her pupils dilate, then she glances away.

"Uh, it's not the same thing." She shifts her weight from foot to foot.

"That's true." I drum my fingers on my thigh. "I'm not the one who needs to be taught patience."

"Patience?" She chuckles. "And you? Now I've heard everything."

"You don't believe me?"

"Nope." She firms her lips. "If you had been patient, you wouldn't have rushed into declaring our upcoming fake wedding to your entire family."

"If I hadn't been patient, I would have taken your ass, and the other holes in your body, at the same time, by now."

She flushes. "No need to be so filthy."

"Oh, I'm just getting started." I frown. "Speaking of, I don't recall giving you permission to speak."

She scowls. "Surely, you don't expect me to stay silent after everything that has happened."

"All that happened was me being nice to you."

"That was you being nice to me?" She opens and shuts her mouth. "Gesù Cristo, you really have a way with jokes, don't you?"

I pause behind he. "I never joke, Flower." I shake out the ribbon, and it makes a faint swishing sound.

She shudders. "Wh-what are you going to use that for?"

"You trust me, don't you?"

"Umm... Now that you mention it," she swallows, "I … I'm not so sure."

"Do you want me to stop? Just say the word."

She tips up her chin. and stares straight ahead. The silence stretches a beat, another, broken only by the crackling of the wood in the fireplace.

Then she nods. Thank fuck!

Something hot stabs at my chest. Something that seems curiously like gratitude. Shit, am I actually being thankful for the fact that she chose to agree to go through with what I have in store for her? Does she even know how much power she holds over me right now? If she had said no, if she had said that she wasn't interested in the experience I have in mind for her...

I'd have stepped back, but reluctantly. And I'd only have plotted to find another way to get her to agree. Yep, once I set my sights on something, I want it. No way would I have taken refusal as the final answer. Not that it's ethical to do so, but fuck that. When it comes to her, there are no holds barred. I'll do anything to possess her... Marry her... Make her mine...

And then, I'll let go of her. For why should I have these experiences when he can't? When my soul twin, the brother who meant to me more than anyone else, the one for whom I'd have given up my life itself but whom I couldn't save... The one whom I'd let down when he most needed me. When he can't find his true love, or get married, or have children, why should I?

A ripple runs down my body. I raise my hands and place the ribbon over her eyes. She stiffens, but doesn't protest when I tie the ends behind her head. My fingers tremble—from suppressed grief? From excitement? Possibly both. But I ignore it. I knot the ribbon, then move around to stand in front of her. "Nod if you feel comfortable with this, Flower."

She slowly jerks her chin.

"Good girl," I murmur as I snatch up another piece of ribbon. Walking behind her, I pull her arms behind her back and tie the ribbon about her wrists.

Goose bumps pop on her skin. Her shoulders shudder. I glance down to find her nipples hard and beaded. She squeezes her thighs together, and I know she's already aroused. I lower my face and blow gently over her ear; she shivers. I push the hair over one shoulder, and a shudder grips her. I press a kiss to the curve where her neck meets her shoulder, and a moan bleeds from her.

"Shh..." I drag my nose up her jaw to nuzzle her cheek. "Give into it, Flower. Just let me do this for you, okay?"

She draws in a breath, then the muscles of her shoulders relax.

"Good girl," I praise her again, and she bites down on her lower lip. Oh, Flower likes it when I praise her, all right. If I were to slide my fingers between her thighs, bet I'd find her even more wet. But first, I need to do the one thing that I have had in mind ever since the first time I saw her gorgeous breasts.

30

Aurora

He walks around me. I know because the heat of his body flows over me as he heads in the direction of… It has to be the side table. What's on the side table? The sewing kit and the pile of yarn. I sense him pause, then reach down. Is he picking up something? What could he possibly want from there? He already used the ribbons from the sewing kit. Surely, he's not going to pick up more of the ribbons… I… Is he? What else is there? The pile of yarn? Is he going to use the yarn? But for what?

He seems to linger there for a few seconds as if making up his mind. Then his footsteps approach. The hair on my forearms rises. He stops in front of me… Again, I know, because a cloud of heat leaps off of his body and slams into my chest. And to think he's just come in from the cold and is not even wearing a shirt. The man's a bloody furnace. The scent of him—testosterone and musk and dark coffee edged with brandy—envelops me. My toes curl.

OMG, how can he smell so hot and sexy and yummy like a Christmas pudding laced with dark chocolate? My mouth waters. That's when he leans forward. His breath sears my lips. I tremble as he grips my wrists which are still shackled behind my back and pushes them up.

"Hold them there," he murmurs, before he slides something around my back and front. He seems to wrap it around me again, then knots it in the front. He repeats the movements once more, and a third time. He's tying something under my breasts... Something that is going to push them up? Bring them even more attention? I quirk my eyebrows, and he must notice it, for he pauses.

He lowers his head and brushes his lips across my forehead. "Don't worry, baby, I'll take care of you; I promise."

And what if I like it too much when you do so? What if... I enjoy all the twisted, depraved things that you are going to do to me and never want you to let me go; what then?

He steps back, his heat recedes a little, then he picks up where he left off. He continues to loop the wool... It has to be wool, based on the slight roughness that chafes my skin every time he coils another circle under my breast. He winds his way down my waist and across my belly until he reaches my hipbones. He pauses. I sense him lower himself to his knees in front of me, for his breath shimmers across my pussy.

Jesus Christ! My belly trembles, my chest rises and falls, my knees buckle from under me, and I'd fall, except he grips my hips to hold me in place.

"Easy, Flower," he soothes me, "easy." He rubs circles with those big fingers across my skin. My heartbeat races as I draw in a breath, another. When he seems sure that I have calmed down somewhat, he presses a kiss to my belly button. He darts his tongue inside the dip in my belly, and a moan bleeds out of me. I strain against the ties that he's bound around my wrists, wanting, needing to grip his hair and tug on the thick strands to punish him for what he's doing to me. I open my mouth, wanting to say his name, but all that comes out is a whine.

"I know, baby." He licks my skin. "I want it too, but we need to hold on a little while longer."

For what? I pout, then gasp when he drags his wide tongue up my slit. Ohmigod! I throw my head back as he curls his tongue around my clit. He sucks on it, and I dig my nails into my palm. Jesus H Christ, this man is going to kill me if he keeps that up.

He raises his head, and I open my mouth to tell him off, when he taps the inside of my thigh. "Part your legs for me, Flower."

I do as he says. Honestly, I don't think I could deny him if I tried, which I admit, I am not. All of my attention drops to the throbbing pulse between my legs.

I sense him rise up on his knees. His knuckles scrape my stomach—guess he must be looping the wool into another knot there?—before he drags it down over my pussy. I gasp as he loops the string—or is it strings?—over my labia, between my pussy lips, pulling me apart, stretching me, pulling it between my legs and up the cleavage between my arse cheeks. He winds it up my spine and knots it under the yarn he's wrapped about the underside of my breasts. He tugs on it, and the movement chafes the wool across my pussy and the valley between my arse cheeks.

Sensations shoot out from the contact and coil in my lower belly. Moisture coats my channel, and I'm sure if I touched my inner thigh, I'd find my cum clinging to my skin. He swipes his fingers down the wool that runs down my spine, back between my arse cheeks, and up to my clit. He presses down, and the combination of the tension of the yarn pulling my pussy lips apart combined with the pressure on my clit makes my entire body jolt. Oh, god. Oh, god. Oh, god.

I bite down on my lower lip to stop myself from screaming with the tension that fills me, that pulls at my lower belly and stretches my nerves until I'm sure I'm going to explode.

He rises to his feet, then presses a gentle, almost chaste kiss to my lips. I sense him move away and follow him with my senses as he heads back to the side table. He returns to stand behind me. I hear a snipping sound, then he steps back.

Goose bumps dot my skin, and it's not because I'm cold. I can sense him looking me up and down before he walks back to the side table. I hear a soft thunk… Did he replace the scissors, perhaps? He returns to stand in front of me, but not close, because his heat isn't as searing as before. The silence stretches a beat, another.

A bead of sweat trails down my neck and between my breasts. I sense him move. The next instant, the wet slap of his tongue against my skin as he laps it up makes me jolt. He straightens and tucks a strand of hair behind my ear. "Would you like to see yourself, Flower?"

He brushes his lips across mine once, twice, but when I open my mouth to deepen the kiss, he steps back.

"Not yet." He chuckles as he turns me in the direction of the bedroom. He wraps his arm about my shoulder, then guides me forward. One, two… I count twenty steps as I walk forward, for I have lost all sense of direction, and this is the only way I can orient myself. He pauses, then steps behind me and places his hands on my shoulder.

"You look incredible. Your tits… They are the most gorgeous I have ever seen, and if you saw how your cunt is wet, swollen, and begging to be eaten by me…" He draws in a breath. "Speaking of, are you hungry?"

I nod.

"I think we should eat before I show you my masterpiece, don't you?"

No, you jerk. I want to see what you have done to me. I want to glimpse how I look after having been tied up by you. I want to—

He reaches around and pinches my nipple, and goose bumps pop on my skin. He cups my other breast in his palm and squeezes, and vibrations of heat sear my skin. He tweaks both nipples, yanks them with enough force that it's painful, and my pussy clenches. Oh, hell. I throw my head back so it's cradled against his shoulder. My hands are trapped between us as he continues to tweak my nipples. He plays with them, plucks on them, squeezes them, and when he finally clamps down on them, my breath catches in my throat.

A trembling grips me. The vibrations scream up from the soles of my feet to coil around my belly. My pussy clenches down, wanting, needing him between my legs. Moisture trickles down from my core, and that's when he releases my breasts. I collapse against him, breathing hard as he steps around to grip my shoulders.

"What are you doing?" I finally burst out, "Why did you stop?"

"Because we need to feed you first."

Ten minutes later, I'm seated at the kitchen table, still wearing this goddamn blindfold that prevents me from seeing anything. I can hear him moving around the kitchen, though. The sounds of the refrigerator being opened, water running, the flame being lit on the stove, then the scent of food cooking; the tangy scent of garlic and pepper makes my mouth water. "What are you making?" I ask.

"You'll see."

"Thought you don't like to cook?"

"I can make a basic cacio e pepe."

"If you untie me, I can cook for both of us." I try to flutter my eyelashes. "I promise it will be more interesting than a basic pasta."

"Nice try." He chuckles. "And a basic pasta is all I need right now. Besides, I prefer to cook and feed you."

"Really?" I bite the inside of my lips. "Is this all part of you taking care of me?"

"It is," he replies as he approaches me. I hear the thud of the plate he places on the table in front of me. Then the sound of his chair being pulled out as he takes his seat. The scent of food teases my nostrils, and he growls, "Open."

I open my mouth, and he slides the fork in between my lips. The tangy taste of pecorino, combined with the pungent flavors of herbs, teases my palate. I chew, swallow, then open my mouth for more. He feeds me another mouthful, then a third. I lick my lips then tip my chin in his direction. "Aren't you eating?"

"I will, soon."

He continues to feed me until I finally turn my head away. "I have had my fill."

"You sure?"

"Of course." I tilt my head. "Why don't you eat now?"

"Oh, trust me, I'm going to have my fill."

The sound of the fork clattering onto the plate reaches me. Then I hear the scrape of the chair on the floor as he rises to his feet, presumably to carry the plate to the sink. Then he returns to stand in front of me. He places his hands on my hips, and I gasp as he hauls me up and seats me on the table. "What are you—"

I hear the scrape of the chair again, then my legs being pulled apart as he thrusts his shoulders between them. Ah hell. "So when you said that you were going to eat, you meant—"

"I'm skipping lunch and going straight to dessert."

"Wait, don't do tha—" I wheeze as he thrusts his face into my pussy.

He sucks on my already sensitive clit. I arch my spine. He grips my thighs and pries me apart even further as he thrusts his tongue inside my melting channel.

"Omigod!" I can't stop the yell that slips from my lips as he begins to tongue fuck me. He releases my thighs, only to grab my arse cheeks and squeeze them with enough force that pain slices through me. At the same time, the thrust of his tongue in and out of my channel, along with the roughness of the wool that continues to keep my pussy lips open and bared to him, is too much for me. My eyes roll back in my head as my climax overwhelms me. It crashes over me with such force that I scream. Moisture squirts out from between my legs, and I sense him lap it up. Darkness overwhelms me. When I come to, I'm being carried in his arms.

"Where are you taking me?"

31

———————

Aurora

"Don't you want to see yourself, Flower?"

Yes.

Yes.

"No." I shake my head.

"Liar." He laughs lightly. "Admit it; you were dying of curiosity to find out how I have tied you up."

"You into Shibari or something?" I huff. "Is that why you needed to tie me up before you made me come?"

"I allowed you to come earlier too," he reminds me, "but that was before."

"Before?"

"Before I realized that I need to show you exactly what kind of a man I am."

I scowl. "I'm not sure what you mean, Christian."

Without saying anything else, he comes to a halt, I assume, in front of the mirror in the bedroom. He lowers me to my feet. My knees tremble, and he grips my shoulders to hold me in place. Then he pushes my hair to the side and leans in close enough for his breath to raise the hair on my temples. "Do you want to see yourself? Do you want to see how I see you, Flower?"

I swallow. Somehow, I know this is more significant than he is letting on. The previous times when he made me come, when he fucked me, he didn't tie me up. So, what changed that he decided to indulge himself this time around?

My mouth dries. I slowly nod, and I feel his chest rise and fall behind me. Then he loosens the knot on my blindfold, and the ribbon falls away. I blink as I adjust to the light, then take in my reflection in the mirror. Flushed cheeks, parted lips, a glow to my skin that I definitely didn't notice before, and his handiwork.

"Oh my god," I whisper. "You...you..."

"Wrapped the wool around you to accentuate your most beautiful physical asset—your breasts."

I take in how he's looped the yarn just under my bust before crisscrossing it so it frames my breasts. He's wound the yarn in a series of intricate twists, coiled it in a pattern that is complicated enough that I can't believe he did it himself, then knotted it under my cleavage. The result is that he's pushed my breasts up as if they are an offering, my brown nipples beaded, with the areolae framing them like they are a rare flower. He's drawn the yarn down to hold my pussy lips apart, baring my clit like a glistening jewel.

I can't take my gaze off it, and he must notice, for he places his cheek next to mine. "What do you think?" he murmurs.

"It's..." I try to form the words, but my brain cells seem to have short-circuited. "It should seem lewd," I finally say, "but..."

"But?"

"But the entire effect is so much more...worshipful," I whisper.

"And it is," he says in a serious tone. "It's a combination of pain and affection, of my wanting to push your pain limits by mixing torture like impact play, biting, wax, needles with the sweet comfort of being touched and held and kissed."

"Hold on..." I gulp. "Did you say torture?"

He loops his finger around the strip of yarn that parts my pussy lips and tugs. Pain slithers over my nerve endings, and heat suffuses my skin. Moisture pools between my thighs, and I can't stop the moan that bleeds from my lips.

"Exactly." He nods as if we have been communicating without words. "This is my way of offering up my time to you, so the focus is entirely on you."

"So, you've done this with others?"

"And if I have?"

"You have focused entirely on other women too?"

"Right now, my focus is entirely on you."

"You fucked me earlier," I remind him, "but you decided to tie me up only now?"

"Like I said, I felt it was time you understood what kind of a man you are dealing with."

"Which is?"

"I have proclivities, Flower."

"No kidding." I tip my chin toward my tied-up reflection.

"This is just the start, you know." He holds my gaze in the mirror. "It's only going to get rougher from here on."

"And you're trying to scare me, why?"

"So you know what you're getting into."

"Are you saying you're giving me a way out?"

He raises a shoulder. "I'm offering you a chance to let go of your inhibitions."

"And that helps me, how?"

"Have you looked at yourself in a mirror when you have stripped back the mask you wear to the world and liked what you saw?"

"Is that what this is?" I scowl back at his reflection. "Me ... unmasked?"

"It's you, as I see you."

"Which is how, exactly? As your, how do you say, your submissive?"

"As mine."

A thrill runs through my body.

"Wh-what does that mean?"

"Mine to do with as I want. Mine to hold. Mine to play with. Mine to push your limits."

"Ah…" I tilt my head. "Now I get it."

"You do?"

I nod. "I am how you strip back the mask you wear to the world." I turn to face him. "You use my body as the canvas through which you can express your deepest desires. The ones you can't even admit to yourself. You use my emotions to articulate what you are feeling, my tears to give voice to your expression, my—"

"Your pain to revel in what I cannot ever tell anyone." His lips twist.

"And what is that, Christian? What is it you cannot tell anyone else but which drives you to reach for extremes to feel something?"

His gaze widens for an instant, then all expression fades from his face. That mask I referred to before? It's back in full force. If he seemed inscrutable before, now he seems unreachable.

He steps back from me, and the cold air instantly rushes in to occupy his space. "Stay," he commands as he spins around and stalks out of the room, only to return with a pair of scissors.

"What are you—?"

He cuts through the ribbon that ties my wrists together, then snips off the yarn that runs from the wool around my breast to my pussy. The pressure on my labia ceases, and already, I miss it. He cuts through the knots he's woven under my cleavage, then up the side of the corset he's created out of the wool. The entire composition falls apart, and he snatches up the pieces as I stand in front of him absolutely naked.

But does he look at me again? Nope. He walks toward the doorway. "You can use the bed. I'll be sleeping on the couch."

32

Christian

Maledizione! It's goddamn difficult to walk when you are sporting a hard-on, and don't let anyone tell you otherwise.

With every step I take, my cock stabs into the crotch of my pants. With every step I take, the remnants of her scent cling to my skin and tease my senses. With every step I take, the sensations of how her gorgeous curves felt against my chest when I held her seem to be imprinted into my skin. The way she looked, all bound up with the wool, all knotted up into the beauty of my creation—the image is seared into my brain.

I've bound others… But no one… No other woman responded this openly, this incredibly generously. She shared all of herself with me in the little time we spent together; she didn't hide any part of herself. She was giving and trusting… Despite her hesitation to be part of what I had in mind for her, she gave herself over to me, and that's not something I expected.

Hell, I also didn't realize that it would affect me so much. Nor did I expect her to see past my words or my need to tie her up. I have to have her naked and knotted and begging to come, I have this constant need to withhold from her and see her wanting and open and needy. I need to come all over her and mark her. Fuck! I curl my fingers into fists at my sides as I stare into the fire in the living room.

I left her without any aftercare, stalked out here, and now, I can't stand to think of going back in there and attending to her, which is so wrong. But this woman… She's gotten under my skin to such an extent that if I stood there for one more second, I would have said or done something, revealing just how much I'm affected by her.

"You'll catch a cold if you don't put on your shirt." She appears next to me. "Are you sulking or something?"

"I don't sulk," I snap.

"So, are you angry about something?" she retorts.

"Should I be angry about something?" I set my jaw.

"You tell me." She walks around to stand in front of me. "One minute, I was sure you were going to fuck me. The next, you ran out of there like you were being pursued by your monsters or something."

"I don't run from anything." Which was the truth, until I met her. "You forget, I am the monster in this relationship." That last? Not a lie.

I'm the person who introduced her to the world of kink, and she took to it like a kid opening up presents on Christmas Day. She may have been hesitant at first, but the more she unraveled the layers of herself that had been locked away for so long, the more she basked in the sensations they evoked in her. Only, she isn't aware of just how much she has revealed to me… Or to herself, yet.

She peers up into my features, still naked, by the way. The logs crackle behind her, the heat from the flame turning her skin rosy. Her cheeks flush as she searches my face.

"You're not wearing clothes either," I point out.

"Thought you wanted me to be naked?"

I rub the back of my neck. "Not so sure about that anymore."

A line appears between her eyebrows. "Why, because you feel threatened by how you react to me?"

I scowl. "I'm not threatened by anything or anyone"—I look her up and down —"and definitely, not by an overweight doctor who has so many issues that she couldn't bring herself to sleep with anyone else."

She pales. The next moment my head snaps back. Pain blooms on my cheek. Before I can stop myself, I swoop down and grab her wrist. "Did you just slap me?" I growl.

"Yes," she spits out, "and unlike you, I don't hide behind lies."

"You've done it now." I bare my teeth. "How dare you raise your hand to me?"

"Oh, I'll do more than that." She tries to pull free, but I tighten my grasp on her. "Let go of me, you jerk ass, you … you imbecile, you complete wanker. I thought there was something inside you, some part of you which hadn't been corrupted by your background or the experiences you have been through. Hell, I was sure that you turned away from me because I had touched on something that was sensitive, that I had hurt you; but maybe, I was wrong." Her breath heaves. "You are beyond redemption, and immature, and have the brain of a goldfish."

"What?" I open and shut my mouth. "A goldfish?"

"No, a cockroach. A toad, actually. The kind who is poisonous, so when you lick them, you get high first but then find yourself on death's door."

"You are not making sense."

"Good, because after how you insulted me, I can't understand how I allowed myself to feel anything for you."

"You felt something for me?"

"It doesn't matter now." Her chin trembles. "After what you said earlier... I ... I don't want anything to do with you."

"Good, because I don't want anything to do with you either."

"Fine," she spits out. "You're an arrogant baboon who thinks just because his father emotionally and physically abused him, it gives you the right to get off on other people's pain. You twisted, perverted, weirdo!"

Anger thrums in my veins. My guts twist. Only when she makes a sound of protest do I realize that I have tightened my hold on her. I release her, and she stumbles back. We stare at each other for a few seconds, then I turn and stalk out of the room.

Six hours later, it's dark outside, and I've spent the last few hours working out. After 500 pushups, 500 sit-ups, and as many biceps and triceps curls using the heaviest book that I found in the bookshelf in place of weights, I lie in a heap on the sofa and pick up said book—In Search of Lost Time, a translation of a French novel about, you guessed it, the loss of time and lack of meaning in the world.

All of which I could have told you for free without having to read the book, considering time once lost never comes back, so really there's no point looking back, for the past doesn't exist. Neither does the future. And there's no meaning to events; it's all one long string of happenstance. Shit happens; deal with it.

Like I dealt with our father's physical and emotional abuse. I managed to protect Xander from the worst of it. Oh, our brothers thought that he had left us alone because we were too young. On the contrary, he'd wait for Xander and me to be left on our own before he'd corner us, then proceed to tie us up before hitting us. All in the name of disciplining us. I often begged him to let Xander go, and he'd oblige on condition—that I'd take Xander's share of the punishment. Which meant he'd hit me twice as hard, often until I blacked out.

So yeah, she's right. It doesn't take a rocket scientist to figure out where I got my need for tying up women before fucking them.

Each time I have, they've developed feelings for me, which is why I have stuck to the rule of fucking them once, then moving on.

Just like I should do with her... Correction—just like I have done with her already. I turn over on my side, toss the book aside, and sit up.

She walks out of the bedroom, dressed in her now clean pants and shirt. Which is fine. This is best, us behaving like strangers. After everything I said to her—none of which I meant—I deserve the insults she hurled my way. It was uncharitable and immature, to say the least, and I hit her where it would hurt the most.

I hunch my shoulders. Not my fucking proudest moment either. But the woman drives me crazy. Hell, snowed up in this lodge instead of celebrating our delayed Christmas with the rest of the family is crazy. Not that I had looked forward to spending time with my brothers. Every time I am with them, it only highlights the fact that Xander is gone.

I draw in a breath. He's fucking gone; he's never coming back. I dig my fingers into my hair and tug. The pain ripples down my back. Good. I deserve to feel that and more.

If I could, I would take your place. You know that, brother, don't you? I wish I had reached there just a few minutes earlier; if I had, I'd have been able to help you. But I hadn't, and I'll always blame myself for it.

The sound of dishes being clanked in the kitchen reaches me. The scent of cooking tickles my nostrils. My stomach grumbles.

Yeah, Xander is gone, and I'm still alive and hungry. My twin will never feel these basic urges again. These sensations that confirm to me that I'm alive. And fuck, if that's not messed up. Why the hell can't I will my body to shut down? To go through what he did. To feel, for one second, how it would be to not feel, to not exist. To not have to worry about feeding or clothing myself. Or wanting to be inside her again.

Why is it that I want to resist her, but I can't? Every time I see her, feel her, smell her, all I want is to fuck her one more time? Why is she everything opposite to what I want to be right now? To shut myself off and mourn. That's what I should be doing.

Instead, I've put myself in a position where I have no choice but to go through this fake marriage with her. To feel alive every time I see her. To long to possess her every time I smell her. To need to mark her as my own every time I touch her. And I, apparently, can't stop myself from hurting her.

"*Cazzo!*" I spring to my feet and head for the kitchen. I burst inside to find her standing at the island, mixing something in a bowl.

She glances up as I barrel toward her. "What are you—" she begins to say, but I push aside the bowl, then grab her by the shoulders and apply enough pressure so she bends over the counter. "What the hell, Christian?" she splutters. "What the hell is wrong with you?"

I release her shoulders, only to grab her one wrist, then the other. "This is all your fault," I rage. And I know I sound unreasonable, but fuck that. Ever since she's come into my life, everything has turned upside down. "If you hadn't helped Karma escape, then none of this would have happened."

"If I hadn't aided Karma, she and Michael would still be at loggerheads." She glowers up at me. "Which doesn't explain why the hell you're holding me down?"

"You make me crazy; you know that? Every time I think I know you, something happens that completely overturns what I think of you."

"Join the crowd." She snorts. "You're the most annoying, frustrating man I've ever met. Speaking of, you really are a bully; you know that?"

"Took you so long to figure that out?" I glance around the kitchen and spot the apron hanging over a chair. I grab it and begin to tie her wrists with it.

"Christian, what the hell?" she explodes. "I was making dinner, and you just interrupted the proceedings."

"Fuck dinner," I growl as I complete tying up her wrists. She tries to straighten, and I push my palm into the center of her back. I hold her there, then reach around to unhook the waistband of her pants.

"Stop that," she yells.

I pause with my fingers on her zipper. My chest rises and falls. I hold her gaze, and she stares back. Color smears her cheeks. Her pupils are blown, her lips parted, and her hair flows about her shoulders.

"Do you really want me to?" I drawl. "Or are you so turned on by the fact that I couldn't keep away from you, that I had to come in here as you were midway through making dinner and throw you over the island and am ready to take you now, you can barely stop your arousal from leaking down your inner thighs?"

She swallows.

"Say the word, Flower, and I'll leave right now." I release her, step back, and hold up my hands. "Do you want me to untie you and stop touching you? Do you, Aurora? Just say the word, and I'll do so."

"I.." She shakes her head. "I…" She squeezes her eyes shut. "I want you to fuck me, Christian."

The blood drains to my dick. "Open your eyes and tell me when you are looking at me."

She blows out a breath, then snaps her eyes open. "I thought you didn't like how I look."

"Cazzo!" I drag my fingers through my hair. "I was pissed off, okay. I didn't mean what I said."

"Are you sure?" She trains her gaze on me. "It didn't seem like that when you shared your real opinion about me."

"I'm sorry I hurt you." I lower my arms to my side. "I promise you I didn't mean a word of what I said earlier."

"Why should I believe you?"

I blow out a breath. "Because the opposite is true."

"What do you mean?"

"Because I love your curves. I love the heaviness of your breasts, the slight bulge of your stomach—"

She winces.

"No … no, don't be ashamed of it. It makes you so human, so womanly. It makes me want to tie you up every time I see you, so I can see your flesh criss-crossed by the marks when I take them off."

"Is that supposed to be romantic?" She half-laughs. "I don't know if you really mean it or if you are simply saying it because you want to get in my pants again."

I close the distance between us and push into the curve of her ass. She stiffens, then a shudder runs up her spine.

"Do you feel that?" I demand. "Can you see how much you turn me on? How much I want you? How crazy you make me, Flower? Every time I see you, I want to be inside you. Hell, even when I'm not with you, I want to fuck you. Every time the events of the past crowd in on me, I want to stuff myself into your hot, slick hole while I finger your ass and cram my fingers into your mouth."

"That's"—she clears her throat—"an oddly specific image."

"Not to mention that I want to take your ass."

She purses her lips. "Not that again. What is it about guys and anal, huh?"

"What isn't it about anal?" I laugh. "Don't mock it 'til you try it, Doc."

"Exactly." She blows out a breath. "As a doctor, I can tell you that, that particular part of your anatomy is not meant for that particular type of use."

"When it's someone you are obsessed with, when every curve of their body is imprinted in your mind's eye, when you can't stop thinking of their gorgeous behind, and how it'd look to have your handprints etched into the beautiful swell of their butt, then—I can assure you— that particular type of use takes on a whole new meaning." I lean in until I can place my mouth next to her ear. "And when you are tied up and aroused to fever pitch, it's even more fulfilling."

"So, you're telling me that it won't hurt?"

"I'm not saying that."

"You're not selling this to me." She huffs.

"Not trying to." I tuck a stand of hair behind her ear." Just as I hope you'll accept it when I say that I love everything about your body. But especially, your thick thighs and your gorgeous behind. I'm so turned on by you; it's why I've been pushing you away. It's why I—"

"Insulted me earlier?" She murmurs, "And by the way, I'm not sure you calling my thighs thick is supposed to be romantic."

I slide my hand down to her thigh and squeeze. "Believe me, there's nothing like having these gorgeous curves to hold onto while I take you from behind."

She bites the inside of her cheek. "I have a confession to make, as well."

"Oh?"

"When you bent me over and shoved your hand down my pants, and I was resisting you, but you didn't stop?"

I nod slowly.

"It really turned me on."

I pause, then step back. "I'm not sure what you're saying."

She straightens, then turns to face me, her hands still bound behind her back. "You said earlier that you wanted to push my limits; did you mean it?"

The hair on the back of my neck rises. "Yes." I school all emotion from my face. "Why do you ask?"

"What if I said that I liked what you did?"

"You have to be more specific than that."

"When you came tearing in here and pushed me onto my front and reached for my zipper, I thought—"

"That I'd take you by force, even if you said no?"

"This is not the only time," she confesses. "The time you barged into my home, and you were so angry with me that you ripped my dress." She shivers. "I was sure, then, that you would take me against my will."

Ah! I hold her gaze. "And it excited you, didn't it?" In a flat voice, I add, "You expected the worst of me because I'm from the Mafia. So much so, you were sure I wouldn't take no for an answer. In fact, you hoped that I wouldn't take no for an answer, because then you could have blamed the entire experience on me."

Her cheeks redden. "That's true," she admits. "In a way, it would have been easier if I had not been one of the consenting parties. Then, I wouldn't have to hate myself so much for enjoying what you do to me."

"I'm still not sure what you're getting at."

"Are you really sorry for what you said earlier?"

I nod.

"Do you want me to forgive you for what you said earlier?"

"Yes, of course. " I lower my chin to my chest. "What are you getting at, Aurora?"

"Consensual non-consent."

33

Aurora

"Gesù Cristo!" He growls, "Do you even know the meaning of what that is?"

"I know more than you realize." I firm my lips. "I may have been a virgin, but that was by choice. It wasn't because I was too insecure to fuck anyone else; it was because I didn't want to fuck anyone else."

"But you wanted me to fuck you." He scowls. "Didn't you?"

"Yes," I nod, "and it was a first. I mean, the attraction between us is, clearly, off-the-charts and not hidden from either of us. It's also why I agreed to play along with this fake marriage thing you had in mind."

"O-k-ay." His brows twist. "So, you are saying that if I want your forgiveness, I'll have to fuck you, but in a scenario that involves—"

"My being non-consensual."

"Why would you want to do that?" He frowns. "Is it because you think I'm already depraved, so why not use the scenario to live out all of your fantasies?"

"Something like that," I admit.

"Is there something else you're not telling me, Flower?" He peers into my features, and his own soften. "Did something happen that makes you want to enact this non-consensual scene?"

My heart begins to race in my chest. My mouth dries. Don't look away. Don't.

I firm my lips and hold his gaze. "As you said, we are snowed in and away from everyone else. Nobody can reach us; we can't leave either. This is the only time in my life when I don't have the responsibilities of my job. Not to mention that I'm not currently at the beck-and-call of the rest of the Mafia."

"When you become my wife—"

"Fake wife."

He scowls. "Fake wife," he corrects himself. "When you become my fake wife, you won't be a doctor to the rest of the clan anymore."

"Does Michael know that?"

"I'll make sure he does." He tilts his head. "But you were saying…"

I draw in a breath, then square my shoulders. "It's a fantasy of mine, okay? It's something I've always wanted to try out because, as you can see, it arouses me a lot. So," I flip my hair over my shoulder, "so if we are going to do this, then I want to go all the way. I want to make sure that the situation benefits me, as well. This way, I'll get something out of it too."

"Something more than the safety of your family, don't you mean?" he reminds me.

My pulse rate ratchets up, my muscles tense up, and I force myself to breathe. "Exactly," I finally say. "The safety of my family and this ... chance to live out my fantasy."

He peers into my features, and I'm sure he's going to refuse me, when he finally jerks his chin. "Okay," he nods, "you've got yourself a deal."

"Okay." The tension oozes out from my shoulders.

He reaches behind me and tugs on the apron with which he had secured my wrists. I bring my hands in front and rub my wrists together.

He glances down, and I follow his gaze to where the apron ties have indented my skin. His breathing visibly changes, and his muscles seem to tighten. I hold up my arms, and his gaze stays riveted on the marks on my wrists.

He reaches out to trace them, then cups my wrist and brings it toward him. He lowers his head and presses small kisses along the dents. I shiver. He holds both of my wrists, then turns them over to kiss the delicate skin where the pulse beats against it.

My toes curl. My pussy clenches. His tenderness is as much of a turn-on as his dominance, but in a very different way. It's like I'm seeing a completely different side of him. One that is more lost, but also more patient, more transparent… More lovable?

My head spins. I must make a noise, for he glances at me. He tugs on my wrists, and I stumble toward him.

"I really am sorry, Flower." He presses a kiss to my forehead. "I love your figure so much that it was the first thing that came to mind when I was trying to hurt you."

"With anyone else, I could have defended myself; you know." I peer up at him. "But from you, it really hurt me, Christian. You were supposed to protect me, not find out my weak points and..." The pressure behind my eyes builds. Jeez, I'm not going to cry. Not going to cry. Not after the two of us seem to have to come to some kind of understanding. But maybe it's the tension that seeps from me, leaving me shaken. A tear slides down my cheek, then another.

"Aurora," Christian says in a shocked voice, "please don't cry, please don't."

He scoops me up in his arms, and that only makes me give in completely to the emotions that are choking my throat. Shit, why the hell did I have to choose this moment to have a complete bloody breakdown? I bury my face in his chest and allow the sobs to overwhelm me.

He walks over to a kitchen chair and sinks down into it with me in his lap. He rocks me, holds me, presses kisses to my forehead, and hell, that only makes it worse. Somehow, it was so much easier to stay angry at him, to see him as my enemy, when he was all snarly and growly over-the-top alpha. This ... this more tender side of him, on top of the apology—which, honestly, I wasn't expecting, because he'd only told me what I already know, hadn't he?

I do have body image issues. It's one of the reasons I never believed that he finds me attractive. No matter that everything he's said and done since we met points to the opposite.

And the chemistry between us, well, that speaks for itself. Neither one of us is faking that. And when I was with him... I'd forgotten that I was curvy and overweight, so when he flung that in my face... It was a shock.

And maybe it's that which prompted me to ask him to play at enacting a consensual non-con scene. Somehow, the fact that he could be so cruel to me completely tore off any masks I used to shield myself from the world. Not only has he seen me naked, but he has stripped me of any sense of guilt I may have about what I want. Guess, in a strange way, he empowered me... Even though he insulted me before that.

I try to pull away from him, but he doesn't let go of me. "Please, baby." He tucks my head under his chin. "I'm so, so sorry for what I said. And honestly, the fact that I am your first, you have no idea how that makes me feel."

"How does that make you feel?" I hiccup.

"It makes me want to take care of you, to protect you, to make sure no one ever hurts you again."

"Not even you?" I peer up at him from under spiky lashes. "What if you hurt me again?"

"Then," he draws in a breath, "then you have my permission to tie me up."

Wh-a-a-t? I blink. "That ... that's huge, right?"

"It is." His lips kick up. "I'm too dominant, way too controlling—"

"You don't say."

"Too up my own ass to allow anyone to order me around—well, except for Michael, and that's only because he's my Capo and the man who brought me up more than my father did. But other than him, I'd never bend my knee for anyone else, except..."

"Except?"

"For you, Flower. Only you have that kind of power over me." He shakes his head. "And fuck, if that doesn't scare me."

"It's why you lashed out at me... Because you were ... afraid?"

"Terrified." He chuckles. "It's why I proposed the fake marriage, in the first place. Thinking if I got ahead of the curve and reduced whatever was between us to something we both knew to be playacting, then—"

"You'd be safe?"

"I hoped." He wipes the tears from under my eyes. "To be fair, I already knew, going in, that I was going to be changed. But I hoped to control the extent of the damage." His lips twist. "I should have known there was no way I was coming out of this unharmed."

"Gee, thanks." I wrinkle my nose. "You make me sound like an accident waiting to happen."

"Or something momentous." His gaze intensifies. "A collision I'll never recover from." His lips curve. "And I mean that in a good way."

I hold his gaze, and something knotted inside of me unclenches. Warmth suffuses my cheeks, and I'm the first to glance away. "Now what?" I rub my cheek against his chest—his still naked chest. The man seems to be happy to walk around half-dressed, not that I'm complaining, even though I do worry that he might catch a cold if he isn't properly dressed.

"Now, why don't we see about that dinner?"

34

Christian

She insisted that I put on my shirt, and initially, I refused. But then I sneezed, and she looked at me with a telling look, and I complied. I pulled on my shirt, then grabbed a bottle of wine from the collection at the bar before returning back to the breakfast bar in the kitchen. I poured a glass for each of us before I seating myself as she turned back to her cooking. I watched her for a few minutes, not feeling the need to say anything. She glanced at me over her shoulder and smiled.

And my heart stuttered. It confused me enough that I drained my glass of wine, then poured myself a new glass. Technically speaking, I should be the one cooking for her, but I admit, it's one of the things I'm not good at. I know, shocker, me admitting that I'm not proficient at something? But hey, even I have my limitations. Not many, but cooking is one of them. Also, it seems to calm her to have something to do. So, when she'd insisted on cooking dinner, I had not protested.

Now, I watch as she bustles around the kitchen, putting together the makings of what already smells delicious. I rise to my feet and walk over to her, "What are you cooking?" I peer over her shoulder at the pans she has on the stove.

"Pasta a la Norma," she replies. "It's made from dried pasta and frozen vegetables, but it'll have to do."

"I can't wait to eat it." I wrap my arm around her waist and pull her flush against me.

She shivers. "Don't," she protests, "I'll screw up the cooking."

"I'd rather screw you instead."

She chuckles. "Your word play is impressive."

"You are impressive."

She pauses, then turns to glance at me over her shoulder. "I am scared," she murmurs.

"Of what?"

"This truce between us is too good to last."

"We'll see." I kiss the top of her head. "You have to admit, when we fight, it gets the blood flowing too."

"It is exciting," she admits, "but that worries me even more."

"Because you like how it feels when I get you all flustered?"

"I like just being with you," she bursts out, then wrinkles up her nose. "Okay, for the record, I didn't mean to put that out there."

"For the record, I like being with you," I purse my lips, "mostly."

She scowls. "Gee, thanks."

"Just kidding." I smirk. "The only thing I like more than being with you is being inside you."

"And there he is," she raises her gaze skywards, "the arrogant, over-the-top, macho, chauvinistic—"

The pasta boils over, and she lets out a yelp. She shuts off the flame under the pan, then grabs a colander and moves to the sink. I move with her, not letting go of her as she strains the pasta.

"Why don't you do something useful," she scowls at me over her shoulder, "like set the table? Dinner will be ready very soon."

Ten minutes later, we are seated at the table. I dig my fork into the pasta and scoop up a few strands. The tangy taste of tomato, the lushness of basil, the complex taste of peppers, combined with the perfectly al dente pasta explodes on my tongue. "Hmm," I chew appreciatively, "this is good. Like really good."

"You sound surprised."

"You did say you could cook, but this is eccezionale, especially given the circumstances we are in. I can't believe these vegetables came out of the freezer."

"My nonna always said that you should be able to cook with the most basic of ingredients, else you weren't really a cook."

"Your nonna was wise."

"And your nonna is…" She blinks rapidly."A force to be reckoned with."

"That she is," I readily agree. "Our father was a terror, and our mother didn't have the strength to stand up to him when she was alive. After she died, Nonna stepped in. It's thanks to her that we were pulled away from the influence of our father and sent to study in LA, all seven of us."

"Seven?"

I nod, "Five of us brothers, as well as Sebastian and Adrian, our half-brothers."

"Half-brothers, huh?"

"I'm surprised there are only two of them. I wouldn't put it past our father to have more fruit of his loins running around the country that we are not aware of."

"You sound bitter." She places her fork on her plate. "I thought the Mafia took it as par for the course to impregnate as many women as they could."

"Maybe others do," I raise a shoulder, "but I'm old-fashioned that way. I believe in fidelity and remaining faithful to the vows of marriage."

"Oh…" She bites down on her lower lip. "That … that's refreshing to hear."

"You sound surprised." I curl my lips.

"Didn't expect to hear words like fidelity from someone like you."

"Just because I'm kinky in my sexual preferences doesn't mean I can't be loyal."

"So, if we were to marry—"

"When we marry," I correct her.

"You'd stay faithful to me?"

"Absolutely."

"Hmm…" she pauses her lips.

"You don't believe me?"

"I want to." She resumes eating. "But it's only a fake marriage, so it shouldn't matter, either way."

Anger spurts through my veins. Why should I be upset with her? I mean, I have given her no cause to believe that the upcoming nuptials are anything but the arrangement I proposed them to be, never mind the fact that I intend to stay faithful to her. And somehow, it doesn't seem wrong to want to do so. Marry her for real, I mean. Also, the thought of being with anyone else doesn't hold the kind of appeal it once did. Fuck, I really am falling for her, and I'm not sure exactly when that happened.

"Christian?" She waves a hand in front of my face. "Your pasta is getting cold."

I resume eating and don't stop until I've wiped my plate clean. When she's done as well, I carry both of our plates to the sink and begin to wash them. She walks over with the wine glasses and places them in the sink, then begins to dry the dishes I've washed.

In silence, we complete our tasks, and at my urging, we move to the living room. Going over to the bookshelf, she pulls down another book to read, then joins me on the settee. I pick up my previously abandoned copy of In Search of Lost Time and begin to read, or rather, pretend to read.

To be fair, the narrative is not too bad, and the author does talk about the role of memory in triggering recollections. Not that I need that. Some scenes are imprinted in my brain, like that of my father hitting my mother, my father trying to come after Xander, my father tying me up and hitting me and then ... Xander in the burning car. Massimo and I dragging him out, stamping out the flames from his jacket, only to find the piece of metal sticking out from his chest... Fuck!

I place the book aside, then rise to my feet. "Dance with me."

"What?" She blinks up from the book she's been reading. "What did you say?"

"Dance with me." I hold out my hand.

Her gaze widens. "You mean now?"

I stare at her steadily.

"Here?" She glances around us. "There's no music."

"We'll create our own music."

She opens her mouth, as if to protest, and I shake my head. "Humor me."

She holds my gaze for a second longer, then slowly nods. She places her book down on the side table, then rises to her feet and puts her hand in mine. I pull her close, and she giggles as she stumbles into me. I place one hand on her hip, the other holding her palm, as I lead her in a slow dance.

Outside, the wind has died down, and the only sound is the crackling of the wood in the fireplace. She rubs her cheek against my shoulder, and the scent of her fills my senses. My dick twitches, and I tighten my grip on her waist. She glances up at me, and her pupils dilate.

"This is a bad idea," she whispers.

"On the contrary." I move my feet in a basic two times four-step, and she follows.

I release my hold on her hip, twirl her around in a circle, and she laughs. "You know how to dance?"

"And more." I haul her close, continuing to move again in the basic steps.

Our gazes clash and hold. I turn her again, then dip her, and she gasps in surprise. I pull her up, her hair flowing around her shoulders. Her cheeks are flushed, golden eyes sparkling. She bites down on her lower lip, and fuck, if I don't feel the tug all the way down to the crown of my dick.

"You know what I want to do right now?"

"What?"

"I want to replace the grasp of your teeth with mine."

"So do it," she whispers as I come to a complete stop.

I lower my head at the same time she tips hers up. Our lips clash, and then I'm kissing her, biting down on her luscious lower lip, devouring her mouth as I thrust my tongue in between her lips and suck on hers. I bend my knees, grip the backs of her thighs, and lift her up. She wraps her legs around my waist, and I walk us over to the sofa. I place her on it and follow her down. She winds her arms around my neck, and I grab her wrists, forcing them up and above her head. I shackle them there as I grind the throbbing length of my column into her soft core. She moans, and the sound chafes my nerve-endings. My cock thickens further.

I sit back on my heels and take in her flushed features, her shirt gaping in the front to reveal the tops of her gorgeous breasts. "Fuck, you're beautiful," I growl, then push away to stand on my feet.

"What are you—"

"Run." I jerk my chin in the direction of the door.

"What?" She gapes.

"Run, I'll even give you a head start."

"I … I'm not sure what you're trying to do here. I—"

"Five," I begin the countdown.

"Excuse me, you're crazy if you think I'm going out in the dark."

"Four." I crack my knuckles, and the sound seems to penetrate through the thoughts in her head.

She blinks, then springs up and onto her feet. "You know what I said about us getting along earlier; you can strike that out."

"Three." I roll my shoulders as I look her up and down.

"In fact, you can forget anything I said about liking to be in your presence," she snarls.

"Two." I bare my teeth. "You're running out of time, Flower; I suggest you capitalize on the advantage I'm giving you."

"Fuck that," she yells. "I hate how you lure me into feeling comfortable with you, only to pull the rug out from under my feet. I'll never again believe a word of what you say, you, you asshole."

"One." I lunge for her.

35

Aurora

"Fuck you," I yell over my shoulder as I slide aside to evade him. I run into the hallway, turning to look behind me, then scream again when I find him right there.

"Fuck, fuck, fuck." I race into the hallway and toward the front door. Am I actually going to do this? Run out into the cold and dark again to evade him. And if I don't? He'll catch me. Hell, he's going to get his hands on me anyway, and damn, if I'm going to make it easy for him. I leap toward the front door, grab hold of the door handle with my bound hands, and twist it. That's when a heavy hand descends on my waist.

"Let me go," I yell as he snatches me up and throws me over his shoulder. "Let me the hell go." I lock my fingers together and bury my fists into his back, but he doesn't even flinch. He simply turns around and marches into the living room.

Anger thuds at my temples. I wriggle in his grasp, try to kick out, but he tightens his hold around my thighs. I raise my hands, and crash them down into his side.

His muscles tense. His shoulders go solid. Then his heavy palm connects with my butt. C-r-a-c-k.

I freeze. Not only did he catch me before I could make it out the door, but he's spanking me? Anger crowds my mind. I squirm around in his grasp and—c-r-a-c-k, c-r-a-c-k—this time he spanks me on each butt cheek, then again. The pain coils in my belly and arrows straight to my core. My pussy clenches, my toes curl, and the flicker of lust that shoots through my veins is so intense that I freeze.

He takes advantage of my temporary acquiescence and marches into the living room. He throws me down on the settee. I spring up to my feet and brush past him. I've only taken a few steps before he grabs my arm and pulls me toward him. Once more, he pushes me down onto the settee. My hair pours over my face, and I shake it back. "What the hell?" I yell. "What's wrong with you? If this is your idea of playing a game?"

"No game," he growls as he grabs the lapels of my shirt and tugs. The buttons go flying, then ping across the floor.

"What the hell! That's the only shirt I have here, asshole—" I gaze up at him in shock, anger, and damn it, also arousal. My thighs quiver, and my chest hurts with the sensations that coil against my ribcage.

He thrusts his face into mine as he pushes against my shoulders. I fall back against the settee, and he plants his hands on either side of my face. "Do you still want to run?"

"Always," I snarl back.

"Try it then, Flower." he bares his teeth, and a shiver grips me.

I raise my hands, flatten them against his chest and push, and heave, and strain, but he doesn't budge, not one inch.

"Cute." He smirks. "That all you've got for me?"

A hot sensation stabs at my chest. My vision tunnels. I bend my knee, then plant it in his groin.

His features crumple, and the breath whooshes out of him. But does he move? Nope, of course, not.

He shakes his head as if to clear it, then glares at me. He lowers his voice to a hush. "You shouldn't have done that." All of my senses pop, and my nerve endings all seem to fire at once.

"L … let me go," I whisper.

"No," he snaps.

"Please," I beg, "please don't do this."

"You knew the stakes when you entered into this relationship." His lips widen in the semblance of a smile that is not one. It's a proclamation of intent, of what he's going to do to me.

Moisture beads my core, and my throat dries. "No," I whisper.

"Yes," he says in a hard voice. A shiver runs up my spine. The pores on my skin pop. He reaches behind, grabs his shirt, and pulls it off.

I take in the tattoo of a coiled snake that covers his chest and the bicep of his left arm; it flows down to disappear under the waistband of his pants, and I know that more tattoos cover both of his thighs. I have seen them before, but not had the chance to pay such close attention to them. In between the coils are a chrysanthemum, a peacock feather, an anchor, a weeping Virgin Mary, a scorpion... I also spot 'Xander' scrawled on the right side of his chest, over his pec with the dates of what must be his birth and his death. There are more objects that I can't make out. I know the tattoos cover his back as well; all of the designs are in black ink. His entire body is a tapestry; almost every inch of his torso is covered. All except for a space over his heart. But I can't ask him about that. He straightens, grabs one wrist of mine, then the other.

My body trembles in anticipation, and hell, if that doesn't make me angry. I've only spent a few days with him, and damn, if he hasn't already trained me to enjoy his kinks. Anger jolts through me. I pull back both of my knees and plant my heels on his chest. The hard plane of his chest digs into my soles as I push.

He huffs out a breath, and his feature break into a delighted smile. "That's it, Flower," he croons. "Fight me; fight for what you want from me."

"I want you to get off of me."

"Liar." He smirks, then reaches over for the length of a satin ribbon from the sewing basket. I draw in a breath, then push against his chest with all my might. He laughs as he begins to wind the ribbon around my wrists.

The slither of the satin against my skin sends goose bumps trailing across my body. My belly shudders, my sex quivers, and moisture drips down my inner thigh. His nostrils flare, and I know the asshole has smelled my arousal.

Bloody hell. If I stay here for a second longer, I'm going to be parting my legs and inviting him to take me. And I want it. I want him to bury his thick, hard, wide cock inside me and stretch me, and yet... I don't want to give in, not yet. I will not make it easy for you, alphahole.

I grit my teeth, tighten all of my muscles, and throw everything I have behind it as I push.

He pauses, blinks, then barks out an exuberant laugh. "More." He bares his teeth. "Do that again, Flower. It makes for a hell of a massage."

"Argh," I make a sound deep in my throat as I pull up my knees, then plant my feet on his chest again and again and again.

He smirks.

I snarl and lower my feet to the ground.

"Giving up so soon?" His lips curl.

I allow my lips to curve. "Come closer," I murmur. "I have something to confess."

"You do?"

I nod. "Come on, baby, don't you want to hear what I have to say?"

His smile widens. He leans in closer, and that's when I rear up and snap my neck forward. My head connects with his nose. I hear the crunch of cartilage. The next moment blood drips down between us.

I lean back, my breath coming in pants, and glance up to find his lips twisted, nostrils flared, blood flowing down his mouth to splatter on his chest. His gaze widens as if he can't believe what I just did. Then a growl rumbles up his chest. Those blue eyes glint with intention, and something deep in their depths seems to catch fire. He seems both shocked and angry, and something more. Something very much like arousal.

"Don't—" I open my mouth. That's when he closes the distance between us and smashes his mouth to mine.

36

Aurora

The coppery tang of his blood fills my mouth. He thrusts his tongue between my lips, owning my mouth, possessing me in a way that I know I'll never get used to. He bites down on my lower lip, and pain shivers down my spine. My core clenches, and I'm aware of the flutters in my belly, how my breasts swell, how my nipples harden into pinpoints of pleasure, even as my heart races in my chest.

The combination of fear, of arousal, of being trapped, of wanting to escape, yet needing to be overpowered, grips me. My breath comes in pants, and my palms begin to sweat. That's when he plants his hips between my thighs, forcing them wide apart.

He winds his fingers around my throat, leans his weight forward, and I can't move. I'm pinned in place by his massive chest on mine, his thick column stabbing into my sensitive core, his wide fingers around my throat. I raise my bound hands, and he grabs my wrists with his free hand and forces them back.

I snarl into his face, then wriggle and writhe in his grasp, and the thickness between his legs seems to grow bigger, more insistent. A melting sensation grips my core even as anger fills my chest. I know what he's doing. I asked him to indulge my consensual non-con scene, and that's what he is doing. So why am I so angry that he's able to arouse me by doing so? He's only giving me what I asked for, so why am I so upset with him? Is it because he's able to slip into the role of someone who enjoys taking me without my consent? Is that what's bothering me. Or is it because I'm enjoying this role play too much? Is it because I'm disgusted with my own needs?

More blood drips down from where I smashed into his nose, and he licks it up.

My gaze widens. "You're an animal," I burst out.

"And it turns you on." He smirks. "Admit it; you love to see me lose control and not give you a choice. My kinks bring out that part of you you've been dying to reveal to the world, but haven't had the courage so far."

"I admit no such thing," I snarl, "you, you … jerkaloupe."

He blinks, then a chuckle bursts from his throat. "Cute," he murmurs, "but it's not going to distract me from what I want."

"And wh … what is that?"

"You." He lowers his head until his mouth is directly in front of mine. "Your lips, your breasts, your pussy, your ass… It's all mine."

"Fuck you," I spit out.

"With pleasure." He holds my gaze. "But first, I need to tie you up."

"No, no, no, goddamn you." I surge up against him, but this time he is better prepared. He applies enough pressure on my throat that darkness flickers around the edges of my sight. I black out for what feels like a few seconds, and when I awaken, I'm suspended from a hook in the ceiling in the bedroom. What the—? I glance up to find the ribbon with which my wrists have been restrained is threaded through the hook and looped around my wrists.

"You're back," he murmurs, his gaze taking in my features, the way I'm displayed.

I cough, and he reaches over, grabs a glass of wine that he has placed on the side table nearby, and takes a sip. He places the glass down, then uses his mouth to dribble the liquid against my lips. I swallow down a few mouthfuls before I turn my head away.

"Aww, don't be like that, Flower," he drawls. "I'm only trying to soothe your dry throat."

"Fuck that." I scowl. "Untie me, right now."

"But I'm just getting started." He reaches over to the side, grabs a ball of yarn, and begins to unravel it. My belly ties itself up in knots, and my thighs tremble. Jesus, I can't believe I'm getting turned on by the thought of him tying me up again. I don't want it. Don't want it.

"Don't do that again," I snap.

"What?" He doesn't glance up from his task.

"Make me black out."

"It was only a bit of breath-play," he murmurs.

"It may be nothing to you, but it scared me, okay?"

"I won't do it again"—he glances up at me—"unless it's to increase the intensity of your orgasm."

"You really are messed up in the head; you know that?"

He pauses and seems to consider my statement carefully. "I am," he acknowledges, "but so are you. Admit that you are turned on by the prospect of what I'm going to do to you, that you find being at my mercy delicious, that you can't wait to find out what surprises I have in store for you."

My belly flip-flops, and my pulse rate ratchets up. "No," I growl, "of course, I'm not."

"Liar." He tosses the ball of yarn over his shoulder, then walks around to stand behind me.

"What the hell are you—" I have an inkling of his next action a second before… W-h-a-c-k. His big palm connects with my butt.

"What the fuck?" I screech, "Don't you dare—"

"You know better than to challenge me." W-h-a-c-k.

I yell as my entire body jolts forward. Pain screeches up my spine. I almost lose my footing, and he winds his arm around my waist. I sense the heat from his body slam into my back a second before—W-h-a-c-k. W-h-a-c-k. W-h-a-c-k. W-h-a-c-k—he slaps my alternating arsecheeks, each slap more intense than the last. Each one sends a spurt of sensations that spirals down to my belly. My pussy seems to throb and swell with each one. Jesus! Even as the pain …the pain… "Ow," I howl. "Stop it, you monster."

He pauses a beat, another. "Then count down from ten, sweetheart," he growls.

"What? No, I won't last if you—"

His palm connects with my butt, and I cry out, "Stop, stop, please…"

"You're forgetting to count, baby."

"Don't baby me you, you. wanker."

"That's another five slaps."

"No," I hiccup.

"Yes," he says with conviction.

"You have lost your mind."

"Twenty slaps."

"Wh-what?" I sputter. "What the fuck is wrong with you?"

"Twenty-five, Flower." He massages my already aching arsecheeks, and pain shivers up my spine. My pussy clenches painfully at the same time, and damn him, but this is not good. This is so not good.

"Fine," I say through gritted teeth, "I'll count."

"Start now."

I hesitate.

"Now, Flower." His voice lowers to a hush, and I shiver. Shit, that mean-Dom voice of his. It's w-a-y too hot, too coercive, too everything I am coming to hate—and love—about him. Not love. Wrong word. I hate him. I hate him.

"Start counting, or should I add another five—"

"Twenty-five," I burst out, and his palm connects with my backside.

"Twenty-four, Twenty-three…"

By the time I finish the countdown, tears flow down my cheeks, my arse is on fire, my pussy hurts even though he has not touched it, and my nipples feel swollen and sore and achy even though he has come nowhere near them. Maybe that is the issue. If he would only stop massaging the pain into my arse long enough to fuck me, I could come, and we could get this over with.

I push back my hips so my butt pushes into to his big palm, and he pauses. "I know, baby," he croons. "I know how much you are empty for my dick, but sadly, I can't cram it inside you yet."

"I don't want your dick," I snap, and he spanks my ass again.

"Don't lie to me."

"Ow!" I cry out. "That hurts, you asshole!"

"Yep, time I took you there too." He slides his hand around to play with my pussy lips. "Good thing you are so wet I won't need lube; not that there is any available here."

"You wouldn't." I stare at him over my shoulder. "You … you … wouldn't do that."

He clicks his tongue. "There you go, trying to dare me again."

"I … I am not."

"So, you won't mind if I tie you up, first, hmm?" He thrusts his fingers inside my channel, and the squelching sound is a reminder of just how wet I am. It's not possible. Honestly, he hurt me, and yet my body seems to like it. What the hell is wrong with me?

He grinds his heel into my clit, and my entire body bucks. A shudder grips me, and I throw my head back and pant, then pause when he pulls his finger out of me. He walks around to stand in front of me, then holds his fingers up to my mouth. "Open," he orders.

I part my lips, and he slides his fingers inside. The taste of my cum, mixed with that darker taste of his skin fills my mouth. I dig my teeth into his finger and bite down. He laughs. I bite him hard enough to draw blood, and his gaze intensifies. The coppery tang of his blood, once again, fills my palate, and his breathing grows heavy.

My eyes widen in disbelief as I look at him. "Fuck, you like that, don't you?"

He smirks.

I scowl at him, and he chuckles. He pulls his finger out from between my lips, then points it at me. "Stay."

Like I'm going anywhere, jerk face!

He retrieves the ball of yarn, then turns back to me. He pushes my shirt out of the way, then begins to wind the wool above my breasts. He knots it, then loops it under my breast again and again. He does this until he has a framework of crisscrossing wool that encases my breasts, with only the nipples bared. He knots it a few times under my cleavage, then pulls it down to hold back each of my pussy lips. He draws it under me and up the cleavage between my ass cheeks. The chafe of the wool against my already abraded skin sends shudders of heat vibrating out from the contact. My thighs clench, my pussy spasms, and I squeeze my eyes shut.

"Oh god," I groan, "it's too much. I can't take it."

"You can." He loops the wool under the lattice he's woven under my breasts, then tugs. Pinpricks of sensation burst up my spine and flash behind my eyes. A whine bleeds from my lips. "Please, Christian, please," I moan, "please, please, please."

"Hush," he admonishes me. I hear the scrape of metal against metal as he lowers his zipper. I open my eyelids to find him glaring down at me. He grips the backs of my thighs and hauls me up. I wind my legs around him, and he's inside me. I huff as he slams into me, tugging, pulling, stretching at my channel.

"Jesus," I snarl, "did you have to be this big?"

"Did you have to be this tiny and hot and tight, and so goddamn perfect?"

I frown. Perfect. He called me perfect? "I am not—"

"Yes, you are." He pulls out, then lunges forward, and once more, crams himself into me. "You're perfect; you hear me?" He retreats, then pushes into me again with enough force that my entire body shudders. "Perfectly made. Perfect for my cock. Perfect to be fucked. Perfect to be broken. By me."

He drills into me, and I throw my head back and yell, "Oh my fucking god."

"Don't blaspheme the name of the Lord, Flower."

"What the hell?" I scowl. "So, you can say a four-letter word in the same breath as the Lord's name, and I—"

"You can't." He smirks. "Just how it is."

I open and shut my mouth, and he laughs again. "Just kidding, Flower. What do you take me for, a misogynist?" He smirks.

Among other things.

"You're hurting me," I snap.

"And you love it."

"You can't keep professing to read my thoughts."

"Want me to stop?" He raises one eyebrow. "Just say the word, and I'll pull out."

I hesitate, he begins to retreat, and that's when I dig my heels into his back. "Don't you dare," I say in a low voice. "You're already in; you may as well finish what you started."

He peers into my eyes. "I have news for you," he says in a conversational tone, "I'm not even half-way in."

"What the—"

He pulls out, then slams into me with enough impact that his balls smash into my lower arse. Ouch! He rams himself inside me, and ow, it hurts, it hurts. He's so big, so thick, so bloody massive that I swear, I can feel him in my throat. He begins to fuck me in earnest—in, out, in… Each time, his pelvic bone grinds into my clit. Pinpricks of heat vibrate out from the impact. The tension at the base of my spine spirals out. Oh, god. Oh my god, I'm going to come.

It's as if he reads my mind for that's when he pulls out.

37

Aurora

What the hell? What is he up to? He sinks to his knees in between my legs and swipes his tongue up my pussy lips. A groan bleeds from my lips. That's so hot and so damn filthy. The fact that he'd stop mid-fuck and begin to eat me out is way too much for me to process. My brain cells seem to melt, all at the same time, as I give in to his ministrations. He hauls one knee over his shoulder, spreading me further, then he thrusts his tongue inside my channel, in, out, in. He squeezes my ass cheeks, and pain bursts across my already abraded skin. My pussy instantly spasms, and a groan rumbles up his chest. He slides his fingers between my ass cheeks and brushes against my puckered hole. I draw in a breath as he bites down on my clit, and shudders grip me. My fingers tingle, and I strain against the satin ribbon, which is surprisingly resilient. Goddamit, I want to touch him, want to dig my fingers in his hair and tug on it and hold on as he continues to eat me. Tremors slide down my back, and I squeeze down on his tongue; I throw my head back, knowing I am going to slide over the edge, and that's when he withdraws. Again. What the—! I snap my eyes open to find that he's rising to his feet. He grabs my leg, wraps it around his waist, then slides his fingers to my melting core. He scoops up the moisture and smears it across my back entrance.

"N-no," I stammer, "please no."

"You don't get a say in how I take you, Flower."

My heart begins to race, my pulse slams against my wrists, and my nipples tighten, even as my stomach ties itself in knots. "You're too big," I whimper.

"You can take it."

He slides his finger inside my back hole, then adds another. I grimace, even as my hips seem to rotate of their own accord, allowing him further access.

"Good girl." He bites on my lower lip with such force that I scowl.

"What the—" I begin to protest, and that's when he replaces his fingers with his cock. His big, thick, fat cock. He notches the head of his dick against my puckered hole and pushes in.

"Ow," I burst out. "It hurts, it hurts."

"Stop complaining," he says in a mild voice. "You know you want this, Flower."

My pussy clenches down, and a knowing smile curves his lips. He slides his hand between us and pinches my clit.

"Jesus…" I inhale as he lowers his head and bites my nipple.

"Oh god," I cry out as the trembling once again overwhelms me.

That's when he slips in another inch.

Sweat beads my forehead as I bite down on my lower lip. "I can't," I murmur, "I can't."

"You can," he says in a hard voice as he plays with my pussy lips. "Let me in, Flower. Now."

He places his forehead against mine as he slides into me further. Too much. Too full. He's impaled me, and it feels like I will never be the same again. My arms and legs tremble, and I almost lose my balance.

"Fuck," he growls. "You're so hot, so tight … so everything. You are going to kill me."

He reaches above and loosens the knot around my wrists, the ribbon gives way, and he hauls me to him. He winds both of my legs around his waist, and without pulling out of me, he walks over to the bed. He lowers me onto the mattress, follows me down, and begins to drill into me.

"Jesus," I moan as he thrusts into me again and again. He grinds the heel of his hand into my clit, and with the other, he pinches my nipple. A line of fire erupts from the point of contact, and all of my nerve endings seem to sizzle at once. I try to pull away, but he has me pinned down with his cock inside me.

He pulls out, then plunges forward, and the entire bed seems to move with the action. He releases my nipple long enough to grab my wrists and position them above me. He wraps my fingers around the headboard. "Hold on," he growls. Then he tilts his hips and pumps into me, hitting a spot deep inside of me that I never knew existed.

"Christian," I yell as my entire body bucks. I arch my back, pushing my breasts into his chest. "Christian, I'm going to—"

"Come," he snaps, and I explode. The climax crashes over me as I squeeze down on his fingers and dick. I cry out, but he swallows the sound. I feel consumed by him, owned, possessed, claimed by this Mafioso, my fake husband-to-be, the man who knows my body, my fears, and my mind more intimately than anyone else.

He continues to thrust into me as the aftershocks grip me. His entire body goes solid, his muscles flex, his features take on an anguished look, and he comes with a hoarse cry. He shoots his cum inside me before he finally tears his mouth from mine. He pushes his forehead against mine and stays there as the tremors course down my body and his. He stays there holding my gaze for a beat, then another. When he pulls out, a whine slips from my lips.

I didn't like that. I didn't… Oh, who am I trying to convince? That climax was, by far, the most intense I have ever had with him. And now I feel empty and spent, and not sure what hit me. I glance down to find him shoving the cum that slips out back inside me.

Jesus, I shouldn't find that hot, but I do. How depraved am I really? On a scale of one to ten, right now, I am a hundred.

He reaches up to unwrap the ribbon from around my wrists. Then he hauls me up to a sitting position and yanks on the wool that's wrapped around me. He unwraps me slowly, like I'm a Christmas present that he's anticipated for so long that he can't wait to see what's inside; except, he's already been inside of me. He pulls off the yarn, tosses it aside, and takes a few minutes to peruse my body. Then, he throws himself down next to me. He pulls me down and tucks me close to him. "Sleep," he murmurs.

I close my eyes and drift off.

When I wake up, I'm alone in the bed. I throw off the cover he must have pulled over me before he left, roll off the bed, and pad toward the bathroom. My back hole twinges with every step. My nipples ache. My core clenches, and I'm reminded of just how empty I still feel.

I step under the shower and stand there until the water begins to run cool. Feeling more alert than I have in a long while, I dry myself with a towel, wrap it around me, and walk out to find my bathrobe laid out on the bed. Did he come here and lay it out earlier? I shrug into the bathrobe, then walk into the living room to find him on the settee. He has my shirt in his hands, and he seems to be stitching buttons onto it.

"Hold on a minute," I burst out. "Are you really—"

"Mending your shirt?" He glances up at me. "I tore off the buttons, so I'm fixing it for you."

"Wow..." I blink rapidly. "Didn't think you could sew."

"I can knit too," he murmurs as he brings the thread to his mouth and uses his teeth to cut it off. He rises to his feet, then walks over to me. "Here," he holds out the shirt, "you should be able to wear it now."

"Did you say that you can knit?"

"Remember, you asked me what I do to destress?"

"You ... knit?" I widen my gaze at him.

"I use yarn for my kink; it stands to reason that I respect it enough to learn how to use it in other ways too, right?"

"A sadist with a moral code."

"I wouldn't be a sadist if I didn't have one. After all, being a Dominant is no joke. It means being totally committed to your sub and ensuring that she lacks for nothing. And I couldn't do that if I didn't have a very strong sense of right and wrong."

"Oh..." I blink rapidly, not sure how to reply to that.

"Also, the knitting really does help me destress, not to mention, it helps me find my feminine side."

"Feminine side?" I look him up and down. "There's nothing feminine about you."

"I'll take that as a compliment." He thrusts the shirt at me, so I have no choice but to accept it. "Now, go change, so I can feed you."

Ten minutes later, we are back in the kitchen. This time I'm at the table, watching as he pulls out frozen vegetables and lasagna sheets.

"You sure you don't want me to cook?"

"I took your ass; the least I can do is cook for you."

I scowl. "Just don't go making it a habit," I mutter to myself, but of course, jerk face catches it.

"I'll take your ass when I want, how I want. And you'll deal with it."

"You don't expect me to agree to that, do you?"

"Sure, based on the way you were screaming through your orgasm earlier."

My cheeks redden. "Yeah, I climaxed; doesn't mean I have to like how I got there."

"Stop whining," he drawls. "You like the pain as much as the pleasure that accompanies it."

I bite the inside of my cheek. I know he's right, dammit. As much as the thought of anal still worries me, the way I climaxed around his dick... It was spectacular. And when he spanked me, it hurt... But hell, if it hadn't also aroused me. Does he know my body better than I do? Is that what this is about?

I lean my hip against the table. and watch as he pulls out a baking tray, then begins to layer the lasagna.

He catches me watching and winks at me. "Why don't you take a seat."

"Umm…" I redden. "No, thank you. I prefer to ah, stand."

"Is it because your ah, ass is sore?" He smirks.

"No, it's because I need the exercise."

"If you feel like you need more exercise, I could simply keep you in bed longer." My nipples tighten, and tendrils of pain vibrate out from where the shirt I pulled on slithers across the already sensitive skin. Bet that's why he mended the shirt and asked me to wear it—just so it would remind me of how he touched me and made me come earlier.

When I don't reply, his grin widens. Asshole! I take a seat, my arse protests, but actually the pain is not as bad as I expected. "There," I murmur, "happy?"

"Hmm…" His brow furrows. "Clearly, I haven't fucked you enough if you can actually sit down."

"What the—" I throw up my hands. "There's no winning with you, is there?"

"Relax." He chuckles. "I was only teasing you."

A likely story.

He turns back to his cooking. When the sauce begins to boil in the saucepan, he tastes it and makes a humming sound.

"Thought you said you prefer not to cook?"

"Doesn't mean I can't cook." He smirks over his shoulder. "Just don't expect me to do it often. And while you're at it, why don't you pour us some wine?"

All said and done, dinner is a relaxed affair… Well, except for the constant hum of sexual tension between us, which never goes away. If anything, the fact that he knows my body so intimately only turns the act of his eating and drinking the wine into one long anticipation of what's going to come next. We do the dishes together, him cleaning the dishes, me drying them. Then we retire to the living room. He pokes at the fire, and when it's roaring to his satisfaction, he picks up the book he had been reading while I choose a different one from the shelf.

"Do all you Sovranos like to read; is that why there's such an extensive collection?" I nod toward the shelves of books that occupy an entire wall.

"Another thing we all have in common," he admits. "A love for the written word. We get that from our mother. She insisted on reading us a bedtime story each night, and sometimes a different one for each of us."

"Tell me about her." I fold my legs up under me.

"She was delicate and tiny." He glances into the fire. "And she was relatively young when she had us. Looking at her, you'd find it difficult to imagine that me and my brothers had come from her."

"You loved her?"

"We all did. And our father? Well, he never did take good care of her. When he wasn't physically abusing us, he took out his frustrations on her. If only I had been old enough to do something about it. If only I could have protected her from him."

"But you guys were so young. You must have been only a child when she died."

"Old enough to know that I should have done more to help her. I was too busy trying to protect Xander from our father's emotional and physical abuse. A part of me knew, even then, that our mother was bearing the brunt of it, but I didn't do anything to help her.

"Your brothers are older than you. Surely, it fell to them to help her?"

"We all had equal responsibility toward it, and I would never pass off my burden onto them."

"Of course, you wouldn't." I lean forward. "You are strong, brave, and have an ego that would never allow anyone else to bear your burdens."

"You say that like it's a crime." He chuckles.

"Not a crime, but sometimes, it's healthy to share what's on your mind so others can try to help you."

"You mean, you want me to do the emo shit and spill my guts to you?"

"That would be a start, yes."

"You do realize that I've told you more about myself than anyone else?"

"Is that good or bad?" I hold his gaze.

"It's ... different," he concedes, "and dangerous."

"For whom?"

"For you." His lips twist. "You don't want me falling for you, Flower."

"Oh?" I swallow. "And why is that?"

"Because once I set my sights on you, I won't stop until I own you, possess you, ravish you... Until I make you mine."

Mine. Mine. Mine.

His voice echoes in my ears. After that very hot, very possessive statement, Christian rose to his feet, donned his coat and boots, and said he was going to get more wood for the fire. He ambled outside, leaving me completely shaken.

God knows why. It's not like I don't know about his caveman tendencies. Hell, since the day I met him, it was clear to me that Christian is an alpha male, and not just an ordinary alpha male. He is an ultra-controlling, ultra-protective sadist with a touch of pervert thrown into the mix. The way he enjoyed my pain and was turned on by it, then made sure he turned me on with the pleasure that followed the pain, the way he held me close after he fucked me and made me orgasm, then tucked me into his side and lulled me to sleep...

All of it is confusing, and I admit, very appealing. Wonder what that says about me, hmm? I rise to my feet and walk to the window. Outside, the world is completely white. The moonlight shimmers off of the snow, and everything appears eerily bright. It's also stopped snowing.

Which means it won't be long before we are out of here. And how will things change? Will he go back to being obnoxious? Will the parts of him that I have uncovered mean that I'll understand him better? Will the intimacy that has sprung up between us survive? Will I feel the same when he decides to go all filthy on me again and tie me up and fuck me as he did today?

My cheeks heat. Why do I enjoy it so much? I never thought of myself as a submissive, or indeed, as someone who'd enjoy kink, but the last few days have convinced me otherwise. My core trembles. I squeeze my thighs together, then press my forehead to the windowpane.

That's when a face appears in front of me.

I scream.

Christian

I've just stepped into the house and shut the backdoor when her scream rips through the house. My heart slams against my ribcage so hard that I'm sure it's going to burst out of my chest. I drop the logs I've gathered and lunge forward through the hallway into the living room. I race across the floor and reach her, just as she turns to me. Her features are pale, her green eyes dilated with fear.

"What's wrong?" I grip her shoulders. "Why did you scream?"

"The-there was..." Her chin trembles. "There was ... someone outside."

I glance past her and see nothing except the snow-covered ground and the trees in the distance; their branches bent under the weight of the snow they are carrying.

"Are you sure?"

"Y-yes!" She shudders. "He was ... right there... And when I screamed, he turned and ran."

I glance at the scene outside again, then turn to leave.

"Where are you going?" She grabs hold of my arm. "Don't go out there, please don't."

"I need to go and check who is there, Flower."

"No!" She clings to me. "Please don't leave me and go out there. Please, Christian, not now."

"I can't let whoever it is get away; if he is a threat of some kind, then I need to neutralize him."

"No, no, no!" She throws herself at my chest. "Don't leave me alone. Besides, whoever was there is long gone. And the snow has stopped. So, we should be able to return to the other's tomorrow, or they may even find us, and you can use their help to find out who was here. Please don't go out there on your own; I beg you. If something were to happen to you, I wouldn't be able to live with it, please."

I take in her features, her heightened breathing, the way she stares up anxiously at me even as she wraps her arms about my waist and presses herself so tightly against me that I can feel every single curve of her breasts, the dip of her waist, the hollow between her legs... Every luscious part of her is as if stamped into my skin.

I hesitate, and she rises up to her tiptoes and presses her lips against my throat, "Please, don't go. Please tie me up instead, and fuck me again."

A-n-d, my dick instantly thickens. Fuck. Not that I haven't been inside her so many times already, but to take her again, to tie her up for my delectation and bury myself in her sweet heat versus traipsing outside for an intruder who is likely already gone? Yeah, no contest. "Okay," I murmur.

Ten minutes later, we return to the living room. I ensured that the house was secure, and she followed me as I made the rounds. I locked the back door, then tested each of the windows in the house to make sure that they were shuttered and bolted, before locking the front door. Walking to the bar, I pour myself a glass of whiskey. "What would you like to drink?" I turn to her.

She glances around the bar, and her gaze alights on a bottle of chocolate liqueur. I reach for it, but she shakes her head. "No, I'm good. Maybe some water?"

"Nonsense, we're still in the Christmas celebratory mood; why don't you have the liqueur?" I snatch up the bottle and pour out the drink for her.

"No"—she holds up her hand—"really, I'm good."

"I've already poured it out."

"I don't want it."

"Why don't you have it, when you so clearly do want it?"

"Just because I want it doesn't mean I should have it."

"It's precisely because you want it that you should definitely have it." I hold out the glass to her.

"No, no, no." She takes a step back.

"Why not?" I frown. "It's only a glass of liqueur."

"Easy for you to say that," she scoffs.

"What's that supposed to mean?"

"You've never had to watch your weight, have you? Measure every ounce of calorie that goes inside your mouth. Then weigh yourself to see how it has affected you? You don't know how it feels to have those same calories stick to your thighs."

"Gorgeous thighs," I murmur.

Her cheeks flush. "And if you are like me, also to your boobs."

"Spectacular tits."

"Don't make fun of me."

"How many times do I have to tell you that I absolutely worship your breasts, and as for your thighs?" I place my glass on the counter, then sink down to my knees in front of her.

"What are you—" she begins to protest as I run my hands up the backs of both of her jeans-enclosed thighs, then kiss her one thigh, then the other. "I adore your thighs." I straighten, then press my face into her stomach. "I love your curves." I press small kisses up her waist as I rise to my feet. Then kiss each breast in turn before I press my lips to her throat, then her chin, until finally, I place my lips close to hers. "I completely and utterly adore the way you look, Flower, you must know that."

"And yet you said—"

"I was an ass, a complete *stronzo*, no, a *testa di cazzo*, to have said what I did. I said it in anger, and I am sorry. I am really very sorry for having upset you. I didn't mean it; I promise." I take her hands in mine, then kiss the tops of her palms. "I have never been attracted to anyone the way I am to you." I kiss the tips of her fingers. "I have never wanted to tie anyone else up the way I want to tie you; never wanted to fuck anyone as much as I want to fuck you."

"Thanks, I guess?" she mutters.

"I have never wanted to…" I swallow, "never wanted to be with anyone the way I want to be with you. When I'm not with you even for a second, I miss you."

"Oh." She blinks rapidly. "What are you trying to say, Christian?"

"That part of your charm is that you are so confident in who you are, what you are, that it's not just how you look physically, but what you are inside. Your big heart that was so moved by Karma's distress when Michael took her, that you put your life and that of your family on the line to help her escape; your selflessness which led you to train as a doctor so you could help other people. Your generosity of spirit which allows you to give yourself up to me every time I tie you up and take you, that allows you to submit—"

"I didn't submit," she protests.

"Oh, you did." I laugh.

"No, I didn't. I—"

I place my fingers over her lips. "Let me finish complimenting you, woman."

"Ah…" She purses her lips but finally subsides. Thank fuck.

"As I was saying, whether you think you submitted to me or not, your body bent to me beautifully. You had me in your power; you know that, don't you, Flower?"

"Me?" She laughs. "I had you in my power?"

"Absolutely, utterly, completely. You allowed yourself to bend to me. You showed me just how it felt to have control over you. To inflict pain on you, to watch you squirm under my ministrations. To bring you to the height of passion. To push you over the edge and see you fall apart. You addicted me to the sensation of watching you yield to me. You made me realize I've never felt this free with anyone else. You set me free, Flower, and now I'm hooked."

"You … you are?" She swallows.

I peer into her eyes. "In every sense of the word."

"I … I'm not sure what to say."

"You don't need to say anything."

She draws in a breath. "Okay."

"Okay." I curve my lips.

"That was not what I was expecting to hear."

"You and me both." I laugh, and the sound comes out uncertain. Me, the consigliere to the *Cosa Nostra*, uncertain? Me, the kinky, perverted asshole who vowed never to sleep with a woman more than once, wooing this curvy, exquisite force of nature with words? Whoa, what the hell is happening to me?

"Now what?" She licks her lips, and I lower my gaze to her mouth.

"Now," I lower my face to hers until our breaths mingle, "we make love."

38

———————

Aurora

Make love? Did the alphahole just say make love? Doesn't mean he is in love with me, though, does it?

He holds my gaze. "What do you say?" he murmurs. "Can I make love to you?"

"Wait…" I laugh. "Did you just ask my permission to make love to me?"

His brow furrows as if he's hearing himself for the first time. "I did, didn't I? Minchia!" He drags his fingers through his hair. "Well, what do you say?" He peers into my features, and for a moment, he seems almost unsure of himself. But that's not possible. Christian is way too confident, too dominant to defer to my decision.

"Do you want to fuck me?" I tip my chin up.

"I want to make love with you."

"And that's different from what we did earlier; how?"

"Want to find out?" He curls his fingers around the nape of my neck. I shiver. Damn, he may have asked me for my permission, but the strength of his personality remains unchallenged. He draws me up to my tiptoes, then just as I think that he's going to kiss me, he lowers his knees, places his other arm under my butt, and lifts me up. I wrap my legs around his waist, and he brushes his lips over mine once, twice. He nibbles on my lips, and I part them. He sweeps his tongue inside to tangle with mine, and goose bumps pop on my skin. When he is this tender, yet this overpowering, he completely slays me. I wrap my arms about his neck and press my breasts into his chest. "*Cazzo*," he swears, "those tits of yours are going to be the death of me."

He presses little kisses across my cheek and down to my throat as he walks toward the bedroom. He places me down on the bed, then throws himself down next to me. He moves up until he's resting against the headboard, then wraps his hands behind his neck. "Take off your clothes."

"And I only just put them on." I huff. "Why can't you make up your mind once and for all about what you want from me?"

"You done being bratty, babe?"

I blow out a breath, then nod.

"Good, then take off your pants."

I swing my legs over the side of the bed, then rise up to my feet and shove the zipper of my pants down. I reach for my waistband when he admonishes me. "Slowly," he growls.

I resist the urge to roll my eyes, then wriggle the pants down my hips. I step out of them, kick them aside, then reach for my panties.

"Did I ask you to touch that?"

I scowl.

He smirks, looks me up and down, then jerks his chin. "Take off your top."

I grab the hem of my top and whip it off, then throw it at him. He catches it, then buries his head in the fabric, and draws a long breath. "Jesus, you smell so good, baby."

He drops my top to the side, then surveys my chest. "Remove your bra."

I slide my hands up my back, unhook my bra, then slip them down my shoulders. I hold the bra-cups against my breasts for a second, hiding them from view.

He growls.

I lower my arms to my side, and my bra slides down to the floor.

He draws in a sharp breath and his shoulders rise and fall as he stares at my breasts. "Your tits, fuck; they are fucking perfect." He flexes his fingers as if he can't wait to cup them. My breasts seem to swell, and my nipples harden.

I bring my palms up to my breasts, and he clicks his tongue. "Did I give you permission to touch them?"

Fucker.

I glower at him. He chuckles, then jerks his chin. "You may remove your panties now."

I slide my fingers inside the waistband of my panties, then make a great production of sliding them down my legs. I step out of them, then hold them up on one finger before I throw them at him.

He snatches them up, and of course, he sniffs them.

"Ugh!" I cringe. "You are an animal."

"But I'm your animal, baby." He tosses my knickers aside, then taps his chest. "Come 'ere."

"Excuse me?"

"Ride my face, Flower."

"Wh-what?" I blink. "You mean, I should—"

"Not going to repeat myself." He glares at me. "Will you come here, or do you want me to make you?"

I hesitate.

"Come here," he snaps. "Now."

My knees seem to hit the bed of their own accord. Shit, I hate it when he makes my body obey him, even when my mind insists that I do otherwise. I scramble up the bed, swing my leg over his shoulders, then scoot up until I'm poised over his face.

He stares up at my pussy like it's the most delectable food, like it's chocolate-covered marzipan. No, more like mince-pies that he gets to see only once a year. Jesus, all this talk of Christmas is going straight to my head. Better than my hips —ha! My core clenches. Or rather my pussy.

He peers up at me from under thick eyelashes. "What did I tell you?"

"To … ah, ride your face."

"So why don't you?"

I squat over him, unsure. "Ah… I am … you know... Maybe I'm too heavy? What if I suffocate you?"

"Stop hovering there and plant your pussy on my mouth, woman."

I bite the inside of my cheek. "I … I can't."

He makes a growling sound deep in his throat, then he grabs my hips and pulls me down with such force that I lose my balance. I face-plant—um, is that right word? Hell, it's the only way to describe how I shove my pussy onto his mouth. He holds me there, then takes a long deep breath, inhaling my scent. Heat sluices through my veins.

OMG, this man... He's so carnal, so ... so real… He doesn't hesitate to show his desire to the world. He wants it; he goes after it.

And I thought I was like that too. After all, I managed to run away from the Mafia long enough to qualify as a doctor. I would have even started a life separate from the *Cosa Nostra*, if not for my father falling sick. But throughout everything, I have hidden from my desires. Hidden from doing what I might like because I've been too conscious about my size.

And here is this guy, making me ride his face, and actually seeming to like it. No, he is eating me up with such intent that there is no doubt he relishes my taste. He drags his tongue up my slit to curl it around my clit. He slurps on my core, thrusts his tongue in and out of my channel. He drags his cheeks across my inner thighs, so the days' old whiskers on his chin abrade the delicate skin.

My toes curl. I dig my fingers into his hair, trying to pull him away, even as my thighs close around his face in a bid to drag him closer. He squeezes my arse cheeks, and my entire body jolts. He slips his fingers down to play with my back hole, and my core clenches around his tongue.

A growl rumbles up his chest. He thrusts his finger inside my puckered hole at the same time as he bites down on my clit, and I explode. The climax shudders through me, sparks seem to explode behind my eyes, and I sway. Moisture gushes out of me, and he licks up my cum. Drags his rough tongue up my pussy lips and wipes me clean.

"Delicious," he rumbles. "Better than Christmas pudding."

Heat sears my cheeks, but before I can say anything, he hauls me off of him, to the side and on my back, before he settles himself between my legs. He kisses me, and I can taste myself and him, and it's so potent, yet right, that my head spins. He swipes his big hands up the backs of my thighs then hooks my knees over his shoulders.

"What are you—" Before I can complete the sentence, he's inside me.

The breath rushes out of me at the same time as he groans. He holds my gaze as his thickness throbs inside of me, stretches me, fills me up with such assurance that I know I can never have anyone else inside me again. No one can compare to him. I open my mouth at the same time that he brushes his lips over mine. "I fucking love you," he murmurs as he pushes his forehead against mine. He tilts his hips, grinds his pelvis against my clit, and electricity shoots up my spine.

"I can't..." I pant, "I can't come again."

"You can," he stares into my eyes, "and you will."

He thrusts into me with enough force that the entire bed moves. He pulls out until the crown of his fat cock is poised against my entrance, then he drills into me. My body jolts. The headboard slams against the wall. It's as if he's putting his entire body and soul into his fucking... Not that he hadn't previously; just ... this time, there's an added dimension to the way he crams his cock into me, over and over again. The skin stretches across his cheeks, a bead of sweat slides down his temple, and his blue eyes gleam with intent. He seems like a man possessed, a man intent on ensuring that he wrings every last drop of orgasm from my body.

"Come with me." He plunges into me again and hits that spot deep inside me that sends tremors shivering up my spine.

"Oh, Jesus! Oh my god!" My eyes roll back in my head.

"Look at me," he commands.

I peel my eyelids open and meet his gaze as he slams into me, burying himself so deep inside me that I swear we've melded into one.

"Come all over my cock," he orders, and the orgasm crashes over me. I scream, and when I try to swallow, my throat hurts. He thrusts into me once, twice, then his shoulders go solid. His chest muscles heave, and I know he's going to come. He begins to pull out, and I lock my ankles around him.

"I'm on the pill," I burst out. "For medical reasons," I add. "It helps regulate my cycle."

"You sure?" He hesitates.

"Yes, please." I reach down between us, circle him at the part where he's joined to me, "Come inside me, please. I want to feel you, Christian."

His gaze intensifies, then he pushes back inside of me. He closes his mouth over mine as he shoots warm gusts of cum inside of me. He slumps over me, keeping most of his weight off of me, as I run my fingers through the sweat-drenched hair on the nape of his neck. I squeeze my arms around him, urging him to lower more of his weight onto me. "I'm too heavy," he murmurs.

"No, you're not," I insist. "I can take it. I want to feel the weight of your body on mine, please."

He relaxes a little more, and his weight pins me down, and I draw in a breath. My eyelids flutter down. We stay that way for a few minutes, maybe more, then I'm dimly aware of him pulling out of me. I protest, and he gathers me close. He drags his fingers through the mess between my legs, then he rubs his fingers over my lips. I suck off the evidence of his arousal and mine as he continues to scoop up the remnants of his cum and rub it into my skin. I shiver, a part of me appalled that I'm enjoying this blatant show of his possession. Even as everything in me revels in it.

Sleep overcomes me, and when I wake, the covers are pulled over us. I'm tucked into his side, his arm under my neck, the other one around my waist. He's pinned me down with one thigh flung over my legs. I'm surrounded by him—his heat, his scent, his complete masculinity—which feeds that hunger inside of me I wasn't aware I possessed. When I awaken next, both of us are in the same position. The bluish light of dawn streams in through the window.

The pressure in my lower belly makes itself known, and I manage to extricate myself from his embrace inch by inch. He doesn't stir as I swing my legs over the side of the bed and go to the bathroom. I catch sight of my face in the mirror as I'm washing my hands. Flushed cheeks, sparkling eyes, hair mussed up in a way that hints at just what I've been up to. I feel content, and more than that, I feel excited. And alive. I can't wait for a life together with him, a life I can have if I want it. I only need to reach out and grab it.

When did everything change? When, over the last few days, did I go from hating him to … falling for him? And he loves me too. He does. I can't wait to tell him so, but first, I need to ensure that I secure the safety of him and his brothers.

I need to find a way to protect both of our families. I can't allow anything to happen to any of them. Is that even possible? I don't know, but I'm not going to give up without trying.

I step into the bedroom and pull on my clothes. With one last look at the sleeping Christian, I step out into the hallway. I pull on my socks and boots, shrug into my jacket, and tug Christian's hat over my hair. I let myself out through the back door, and the cold instantly assaults me. I shove my hands into the pockets, despite wearing gloves, and walk past the woodshed, then hesitate. Which way should I go?

I cross the snow-covered ground toward the tree line, then take the only path there is, the one that heads through the woods.

The silence wraps itself around me. There's not a breath of air, no sound from insects or birds. The pale dawn light is cut off in places by the thick overhead cover. I step in the snow, and while my boots guard me from the worst of the wetness, instantly, a chill runs up my spine. I increase my pace in a bid to keep warm, then cry out when a shadow peels off from a nearby tree.

My heart pounds in my ribcage, and my pulse rate ratchets up. I bring a shaky hand up to push the hair off of my forehead as the man comes to a stop in front of me.

39

Aurora

"Hello, Ms. Garibaldi " The man folds his massive arms across his chest. The lower portion of his face is covered in a mask. It seems to enhance the impact of those grey-blue eyes that glare at me.

"H-how did you get here?" I stutter. I had seen him peek in through the window last night, and that was when I screamed. A part of me knew then that this meeting was inevitable. I left the house knowing that he'd find me.

"You mean, the snowstorm?" He arches an eyebrow, "Turns out, this lodge isn't the only place to take shelter in. I found another cottage not very far off where I could hunker down until the snow stopped falling. Evidently, folks in these parts are trusting enough to leave the key to the front door in the most obvious of places. I didn't even have to look too hard to find it." He sounds disgusted like he'd have preferred more of a challenge.

"How did you know where I was?"

"I followed the two of you from the chalet, before the storm swept in."

My cheeks heat. "So, you saw us on the pond?"

"You mean, did I see you fall into the ice hole and watch lover boy rush to save you?" He smirks, or at least I think he does behind the mask. "I did." He raises his shoulder. "Now that we've cleared that up," he tilts his head, "what information do you have for me?"

"I… I've changed my mind."

His expression remains unchanged. "Have you, now?" he drawls.

"Y-yes." I shift my weight from foot to foot. "I can't tell you what you want to know. I can't betray Christian."

"Afraid it doesn't work like that." The wrinkles at the edges of his eyes tighten, but his eyes themselves stay dead. In the few times I've met him, I've never seen any hint of life in them. They are dark holes in a face that is otherwise so classically handsome, you'd think he were a fairy tale prince. Only this man is everyone's worst nightmare come to life. But because of the way he looks, the way he speaks with that cultured British accent, the way he is dressed in that fitted coat which emphasizes the width of his shoulders, and boots that cost more than the economy of a third world country, you'd never call him that, and that's what makes it worse.

"What do you mean?" I tip my chin up. "I agreed to share information with you then, but I'm not going to do so now."

"So, you'd risk the lives of your father and sister, for that of your fiancé?"

"Fake fiancé," I correct him out of habit, then bite my lip. Shit, he isn't my fake anything, but how the hell do I explain that when I'm not sure myself when things changed?

"I see." He nods. "So it's like that?"

"What do you mean?" I scowl. "There's nothing 'like that' about it; I've simply decided I'm not going to let you dictate what I do."

"You're in love with him; it happens." He raises a shoulder. "That's why human relationships are so messy." He slides his hand into the pocket of his coat. "It's why I prefer to keep things on a strictly business basis. It's why, if you don't tell me what you know, I'm going to put a hit out on his head."

"Don't do that," I cry out. "Please, don't hurt him."

"That's entirely up to you, if you tell me what you know about the dealings of the Sovranos."

"I... I can't..." My shoulder's slump. "I can't do that."

"Then, I don't have a choice." He raises a shoulder. "He's going to die, and you'll still owe me information."

"Don't do this. Please..." I take a step forward. "It's not like I know much anyway. The Sovranos don't discuss anything of consequence in front of me."

His lips draw up in the semblance of a smile. "You are about to marry one of their brothers. Clearly, you are in their inner circle. And you expect me to believe that you haven't heard anything?"

"You know the Mafia." I raise a shoulder. "The men don't discuss anything in front of the women."

"That may be so, but you are also their doctor. Chances are good, you have heard or seen things in passing which are bound to add up to something."

"It won't." I shake my head. "I really just focus on doing my job when they call me in as a doctor. I tend not to hear or see anything else when I'm concentrating on a patient."

He looks me up and down. "I don't have time for this." He pulls his hand out of his pocket and aims a gun at me.

"Wha … what are you doing?" My heart slams against my ribcage.

"If you're not going to help me, then I have no choice but to kill you."

"I don't understand." I take a step back. "How is killing me going to help?"

He shakes his head, ignoring my question. "Don't move, or you'll make this worse on yourself."

"What do you mean?" Shit, why did I decide to take a walk? Why didn't I stay back in the house, in that comfy bed with Christian? Better still, why haven't I told Christian about the deal I made with this stranger? Because if you had, he would hate you. And he's just professed his love for you.

No, no way could I have told him; which leaves me at the mercy of this man who's walking toward me, the gun held in his gloved hand. He reaches me and stares into my face. Something in those soulless eyes, that look of intent, laced with an indifference… Shit! This man would shoot me in a heartbeat, and he'd still go after Christian. Jesus Christ, how could I have gotten myself into this situation?

His gaze narrows. I sense him getting ready to shoot. Adrenaline laces my blood. I lunge toward him, grab his hand, shove it up just as he depresses the trigger. The sound of the gun shot echoes around the space. The bullet whizzes past me so close that the breeze raises the hair on my head.

A scream boils up. I swallow it down as I stumble back, then lunge away from him and into the forest. My ears are ringing from the gunshot fired so close to me, but I'm sure he's following me. Fuck. Fuck. Fuck.

He's going to kill me. He's going to kill me. He's going to—something thwacks into the tree trunk next to my head. Shards of wood hit my cheek, and I can't stop the scream that slips from my mouth. I increase my pace. My boot-clad feet sink into the snow, and my breath comes in pants. Sweat beads my forehead and seems to instantly freeze. Shit, this is not good. Not good, at all.

I run further into the woods. Snow slides off of a branch and falls in front of me. I swerve around it and run for a few more minutes. My heart is thumping so hard in my chest that I can barely breathe. My limbs tremble, and my thigh muscles seem to cramp. I push myself forward, but my steps seem to slow. No, no, no. I can't be tired that quickly. Just one more step; one more. I see a light through the trees and force myself to walk toward it. Apparently, I've circled around and raced toward the lodge without even realizing it. I take another step forward, then another as I head for the clearing. I try to draw in a breath, and my lungs burn. My blood is pounding so hard that I can hear it pumping in my ears.

Behind me, I sense his approach. Just one more step, please, just one more... A ball of emotion clogs my throat. Pressure builds behind my eyes, and moisture trickles down my cheek. So, this is how I'm going to die? At the hands of a mad man who is going to shoot me first, then him. No, I can't let him get to Christian. I can't.

I turn to face the man who stands not six feet from me.

"Don't kill him, please. Kill me; take my life, but not his."

He raises his gun, and I squeeze my eyes shut. Please let it be quick. Please let it not hurt... Please let him spare Christian. Oh, Christian, why didn't I tell you I love you? Why?

At least, I can warn him. If I scream again, perhaps he'll hear me and be warned. I open my mouth to do just that when a shot rings out. I scream, clamp my hands over my ears, and squeeze my eyes shut. The ringing seems to intensify, then someone grips my shoulder. I scream again and try to pull away. "Let me go, don't touch me," I yell.

"Aurora, it's me," Christian soothes. His voice sounds like he's a long distance away, although I know he's standing right beside me.

I snap my eyes open. "Christian?" My voice echoes inside of my head. I glance from side to side to find no one is there.

"He's gone," Christian murmurs. "Who was he? Did he hurt you?" He straightens, takes a step in the direction of where the other guy has gone, but I jump up and grab his arm.

"Please, don't go after him. Please don't."

He glances down to where I'm clutching at his sleeve, then back at my face, where he can, surely, see my fear. "Who was he, Aurora? Why were you talking to him?"

"He..." I swallow. "I..." I glance away. I don't want to lie to Christian, but can I afford to tell him the truth?

"What is it, Aurora?" He frowns. "You can tell me anything. You know that, right?"

Do I?

I bite the inside of my cheek and shake my head. "Christian, please don't make me." More tears run down my cheek, and I wipe them away.

"What is it?" His voice softens. "You can trust me."

Can I? What if I tell you and you end up hating me? How could I live with myself then?

"Why did you come out here, Aurora? Did you know him? Did he know that you would be meeting him? Was he waiting for you? If so, how did you communicate with him?" He wrinkles his brow, and I swear, I can see the gears clicking in his head. "The face at the window yesterday..." he muses. "That was him, wasn't it?"

I glance away, unable to meet his eyes. Shit, shit, shit, what's wrong with me? Why can't I tell him everything? Why do I feel like he's going to judge me for what I did? Why do I feel like I made a huge mistake? Because I did. Because I was so against the Mafia, I jumped at the chance of taking revenge against them. And when Christian proposed the fake marriage, my feelings only intensified. I'd made up my mind to do anything to get my freedom, including sacrificing his life, if necessary... Only, I've changed my mind. At least, I've managed to save him... This time... Which doesn't mean that monster won't come back and try to kill us again. Not to mention, he told me he'd take a hit out on Christian. OMG, what am I going to do?

I glance around the space, then back at the lodge. "We should get back inside."

Christian's gaze narrows. "What is it? What are you not telling me, Aurora? Are you worried that he will come back for us? Do you know something that I don't?" He closes the distance between us and peers into my eyes. "I can't keep you safe unless you tell me what's happening here."

"It's you I'm worried about, Christian." I swallow, "If something were to happen to you—I ... I couldn't live with myself."

"What's going to happen to me? Is that man after me? If so, why was he trying to shoot you? I'm asking you again, Aurora, tell me what you know." The skin stretches across his cheekbones, and the color seems to fade from his features.

"I ... I can't." I shake my head. "Please, Christian, you have to believe me."

"I'm not sure what to believe." He releases my hand and takes a step back. "Perhaps you're not what you seem." Sweat beads his brow. "Perhaps it was wrong of me to trust you. Perhaps there's more to you than meets the eye." He sways, then glances down. I follow his gaze to the red that stains the left side of his shirt.

"Oh my god, Christian," I cry out. "He shot you?"

I jump toward him, but he throws up a hand. "I can take care of myself."

"I'm a doctor." I push away his arm, and the very fact that he doesn't protest worries me even more. He sways again, and I grab his uninjured shoulder to steady him. "We need to get you back inside." I throw his arm over my shoulder and steady him. We begin to head back, and he seems to grow heavier with each step. By the time we reach the entrance to the lodge, I'm almost bent double by his weight.

We make it to the living room, and I lower him onto a chair. The fire must have gone out sometime in the night because the inside of the house seems almost as cold as the outside. I undo the buttons of his shirt, push it aside, and take in the wound on his shoulder. Blood bubbles out from it. "Shit, shit, shit." I race to the bathroom, grab a towel, then run back to him. I push the towel against his wound. "Hold this there." I grab his hand and place it on the towel. Once I'm convinced that he has enough of a hold on it, I grab his uninjured shoulder. "Sit up."

"What?" He scowls up at me from his slouched position.

"Sit up, so I can check the damage," I explain as I nudge my shoulder under his uninjured arm and heave. He sits up, then sways again. "Shit!" I manage to take some of his weight. I push down the sleeves of his shirt and manage to peel it off, so I can take a closer look at the wound on the shoulder… It's deep, but hopefully, it's not so deep that I can't stitch it. The bullet only grazed the flesh. The breath I wasn't aware I'm holding whooshes out. "Where's the first aid kit?" I demand.

"In the cabinet in the bathroom," he says in a low voice. His features have definitely gone even more pale in the last few minutes. Shit!

I change direction, race to the bathroom, and rummage around in the cabinet. "There!" I grab the kit, and race back to him, open the kit, and scowl. "There's nothing here that I can sew you with."

He glances at the sewing kit, then back at me.

"Oh, no. I'm not using that to stitch you up."

"Poetic justice, don't you think?" His lips curl. "Thought you'd like the opportunity to stick a needle into me."

I draw in a breath, then release him before I walk back to the bathroom and grab all the clean towels I can find. Next, I go to the kitchen, boil the kettle, and carry it and a bowl to the living room. I help him out of the remnants of his shirt, then grab the bottle of whiskey from the bar.

"You ready?"

He holds out his hand, I place the bottle of whiskey in it, and he swigs from it before handing it back to me. I pour the whiskey over the wound, and he winces. Once I'm sure that the wound is reasonably clear, I clean it with the quickly-cooling water from the kettle. I drop the blood-sodden towels into the bowl, then walk over to the side table to survey the sewing kit. Thankfully, the kit is fancy enough that I can find a curved needle and silk thread to run through the eye of the needle.

"This is going to hurt."

"I have a feeling that you've already hurt me much more than the damage you can inflict on me with a needle."

I stiffen. "It's … it's not what it seems, Christian."

"Then what is it? Explain it to me, Aurora, because from where I am, it doesn't look very good for you."

Of course, I know that. And of course, I know what it looks like. But if I tell him the truth behind why I was speaking to the man, that I knew him, had arranged to meet him, had agreed to give up the secrets of the Sovranos to him… Then, not only will he no longer be interested in marrying me, he'll kill me and my family right away. The needle almost slips from my sweaty fingers. "*Cazzo*," I swear aloud as I tighten my grip on it at the last minute. "I need to sterilize this, at least."

I thread the needle before I head to the bar and grab a bottle of vodka—it's a clearer spirit than whiskey, so hopefully, it should sterilize it. I pour some of the vodka into a glass, then drop the needle and thread in it. I pull on a pair of gloves from the first-aid kit, then fish out the needle and thread before returning to him.

"This is all wrong. I shouldn't be doing this. I'm a doctor, not a … a … savage. What if the wound gets infected?"

"I know you won't let that happen," his voice is slurred.

I glance at his face and find the shadows under his eyes are more pronounced. His features are gaunt, and when I glance down at his shoulder, I find the blood is running down his arm to pool at his feet.

"Maledizione!" I snatch up another towel, press it to this shoulder, and hold it there for a few minutes until the blood oozing out seems to slow somewhat. I throw the sodden cloth aside, then once more, clean the wound with the warm water.

I hand him two of the painkillers I find in the first aid kit. Before I can get him a glass of water, he swallows them dry.

"Go on." He jerks his chin toward his chest.

I hesitate only for a second, then begin to stitch him up.

For a few seconds, there's silence, then, "You swear in Italian when you're upset, you know that?"

"What?" I frown, trying to focus on pushing the needle through the gaping lips of the wound.

"You swear in Italian when you're under emotional stress."

"It happens," I mutter.

"And you get these cute wrinkles between your eyebrows when you are focused on something."

"Mmm-hmm."

"And your scent… You always smell of honeysuckle and crushed rose petals."

"Eh?" I glance up at him. His pupils are dilated with… Pain? Awareness? Pain, probably. It has to be painful when I stab the needle through his skin, but he hasn't jerked once. "Not long now," I mutter, then turn back to my task.

"Take your time. At least this way, you have a real reason to stay close to me."

"You're delirious," I murmur.

"Am I?" He clears his throat. "I know the only reason you've stayed with me is because I threatened your family."

I don't reply.

"If I had asked you to pose as my fake wife, you never would have agreed."

"That's true," I agree.

"But it doesn't need to be that way, you know."

"Right." Just a few more stitches to go now. I can do this.

"Just tell me what you're hiding from me, and I'll forgive you, and I promise not to hurt you or your family either."

My finger slips, the needle stabs his skin extra hard, and he winces. "I know you don't like me, but try not to kill me with that needle, okay?"

I shoot him a glance from under my eyelashes. "Don't be a baby; you can take the pain."

"But can I take the agony when I find out that you have been betraying me?"

"What?" I stare, "I … I haven't been betraying you."

"Haven't you?" He chuckles. "You're such a bad liar, Flower." He reaches up and pushes the hair off of my forehead. "But that's okay. I know how to spank the truth out of you."

"You're not going to be doing much of anything except lying on your back and recovering."

"I'd rather you be lying on your back," he smirks, "with me on top, of course."

"Of course," I say dryly as I continue with my task.

"Better still, I can lay back, as long as you practice some of your kinky doctor shit on me."

"Kinky doctor shit?" I chuckle. Drunk-with-pain Christian is a lot more fun than sober Christian. "What does kinky doctor shit involve?"

"You know"—his lips curl—"you giving me a thorough full-body examination."

"The only thing you're getting from me is a prostrate examination, buster."

He laughs.

I scowl at him. "No, don't tell me. With your perverted tastes, you'd probably enjoy that too much."

"I'd enjoy it more if I could return the favor with a breast examination, followed by a pelvic scan. You know, the kind where I get to use my dick instead of a probe."

I raise my eyebrows. "Really, you're going there?" I knot the thread one last time, then grab the scissors and cut it off.

His muscles go solid.

I raise my gaze to his face to find his eyelids shut. "You okay?"

"What do you think?" He opens his eyes and fixes me with that blue gaze. "My fiancée—"

"Fake fianceé."

"—is hiding a secret from me, and I've just been shot."

He rises to his feet and sways. I grip the arm attached to his uninjured shoulder. "We need to get you to a hospital."

"Fuck that."

"The wound can still get infected, and all I have done is patch you up temporarily, at best. Maybe I should find my way to the chalet and get help?"

"I'll be fine," he snaps. "Just help me to bed, will you?"

40

Aurora

He's not fine; he's not doing well at all. Outside, it begins to snow as I dip the cloth in cool water and place it on his fevered brow. Sweat clings to his upper lip and coats his chest. He stirs restlessly, his eyeballs moving behind closed eyelids.

I helped him to bed, where he collapsed and fell asleep almost instantly. That was two hours ago. The blood loss must have weakened him more than he'd been letting on. I managed to throw my clothes into the dryer, pull on my bathrobe, then build up the fire in the living room. It is warm inside the house, but you wouldn't be able to tell from the way he shivers under the covers that I pulled up to his neck.

There are no antibiotics in the house that I can give him, and stitching up the wound, clearly, isn't enough. The infection is mounting, damn it. I pace the floor next to the bed and watch his ragged breathing. I need to do something, but what? I chew on my fingernail. Do I dare leave him and try to find my way back to the main chalet?

He groans, and my breath catches in my chest. I've never seen him stripped of his confidence and in so much pain. Even now, lying there wounded, his big body is a massive presence that seems to suck up most of the oxygen in the room. His skin is almost as pale as the sheets he lays on, and that is not good. Oh god, he's sinking…

He's going to die. No! I squeeze my fists at my sides. Not if I have a say in this. It's my fault that he got shot, and I'm going to make sure that I save him. I turn to head off to the dryer to get my clothes when his voice stops me. "Phone," he slurs, "the phone."

"What?" I pivot and close the distance to the bed. "What are you trying to say?"

"The phone"—his eyelids flutter open, and he fixes his blue gaze on mine—"in the woodshed."

"The woodshed?"

"Phone… Call… Michael…" His eyes close.

"Christian?" I touch his shoulder, and his skin is so hot that I freeze. Shit, shit, shit. I don't even have a thermometer here to monitor his temperature, but clearly, his condition is worsening by the second. And what did he mean by 'phone'? "Is there a phone in the woodshed, Christian? Is that what you're trying to say?"

His eyes stay closed.

"Damn it." I press my fingers together. I need to find out if what he said is true. But if there is a phone, why didn't he call for help sooner? I shake my head. First things first, I need to check if what he says is true.

I head for the dryer, pull out my clothes, and slip them on. Then pull on my boots and jacket and head out of the backdoor. It's snowing again, but at least, the wind seems to have died down. I stomp through the snow and reach the woodshed. I push the door open and still.

It's warmer than I expected in here, so there definitely is some kind of temperature regulation at work. On one side, the firewood is piled up neatly, as expected. On the other side, there is a chair and a table, with a laptop computer and a phone connected to the laptop. What the hell?

So, there had been a way to keep in touch with the chalet. And Christian must have used it… For what? To let them know that we were here and safe, which is why no one had come in search of us. I had wondered about it, but then, I had been so caught up in the sexual haze he'd been spinning around me that I hadn't bothered to pursue that line of thought.

So, he has been hiding this from me all along? Why? So he could keep me here and fuck me, wear down my defenses? But to what end? I was already his captive; he could have done what he wanted with me… But did he want time alone with me? Is that why he planned this elaborate ruse?

And he had accused me of keeping a secret from him. Seems I'm not the only one. I head for the phone, pick it up, not surprised to find that it's fully charged. I try to swipe the screen, but it's locked. Of course, it is.

I march back to the lodge, tiptoe up to the bed, and place Christian's finger on the touch ID. The phone screen unlocks. I lower his arm to his chest, then look up the names in the phonebook and press Michael's number.

"Pronto?" Michael picks up on the fifth ring. "I didn't think I'd be hearing from you in a few more days, *stronzo*," he jokes.

"Michael?" I square my shoulders. "There's been an accident."

Half an hour later, I clamber onto the helicopter, which arrived within twenty minutes of that phone call. Apparently, the Sovranos don't mess around when it comes to their own. Michael had listened to me without interruption, then ordered me to stay with Christian until help arrived. Before I could ask any more questions, he had disconnected.

He's no less bossy than Christian. It seems like each Sovrano brother has an ego the size of Texas… How the hell do they manage to sit at a table and do business? Not to mention, actually get together under one roof… A feat which I now realize no one other than Nonna could have pulled off. She is the only one who seems to know how to handle these alphaholes, and when Christian finally wakes up, I'll have one very irate alphahole to deal with.

I glance down to where the paramedics have strapped him to a stretcher. They had checked his vitals as soon as they had arrived at the lodge, started an IV drip, placed an oxygen mask around his nose, and moved him to a stretcher within minutes. The trembling had set in then, once I realized that he was in good hands. And I haven't stopped shaking since.

"Here." Michael places Christian's jacket around my shoulders, then sits down next to me.

"I didn't expect you to arrive with the air-ambulance," I murmur.

"He's my brother." Michael scowls. "Of course, I was going to be there for him."

He holds out his hand.

"What?" I blink.

"The phone…" He gestures to the device that I have clutched between my fingers. "I assume that's Christian's?"

"Ah, yes." I hand the phone over, and Michael pockets it.

"How did he get shot?" he asks.

I look away, then reach over and run my fingers through Christian's sweat-dampened hair. "If I had known that he had a phone, I would have called you earlier," I say softly.

"Hmm…" Michael folds his arms over his chest. "What's going on between you two; why didn't he tell you about the phone earlier?"

"I … I don't know," I lie.

"Hmm..." He purses his lips. "And I assume you don't know anything about who shot him either?"

I glance away and bite my lower lip. No way am I letting any of them in on what my connection with the stranger is. And definitely not when Christian is unconscious. He's the only one who has been on my side since the beginning... Although, when he's awake, that might change too.

"Ever since you helped Karma to escape, I haven't trusted you. I wasn't in favor of Christian marrying you either, but he convinced me otherwise. Now, I wonder if I should have questioned the situation further. Whether I should have shot you like had been my first instinct."

I pull the jacket closer, then glance out of the window for a few seconds. "The gun... Christian had a gun he used to shoot at the other guy." I turn back to Michael. "Someone needs to find the gun; he dropped it in the snow."

He peers into my eyes, then nods. "I'm on it." He holds my gaze. "If anything happens to my brother, I won't let you live, Aurora," he says in a voice filled with menace.

A shiver runs down my spine, and I hunch my shoulder. "If anything happens to him, I don't want to live," I say in a low voice.

He scowls at me. "My brother seems to think that you can be trusted; you'd best pray that he is right."

Christian

I come awake with a start. The scent of antiseptic is so strong in my nostrils, I know I can only be in one place. I take in the glare of the fluorescent lights that bounce off of the white sheets, the white ceiling, the white tiled floor, the white walls. I try to move, and my entire body protests. My side feels numb, and my limbs feel weighted down. I raise my arm and find it's attached to something warm.

Slowly, I turn my head to find her on a chair pulled up next to the bed. Her fingers are clasped around mine, and she's curled into the back of the chair, fast asleep. Her eyelashes are dark fans against her cheekbones; dark circles shadow her eyes like she hasn't had much sleep. Her legs are pulled up under her, and I'm sure she must be uncomfortable all coiled up like that. I lower my gaze to where her slim, delicate fingers are twined with mine.

She's ringless, of course, considering she tossed the engagement ring into the snow. I don't care about the cost; I can get her another one... But the fact that she did it makes me see her in a new light. This isn't some spineless woman who would accept my dominance without questioning it... And the fact is, I like that. After the women I've met who were taken in either with my money or my notoriety—neither of which seem to have any impact on her—she's a breath of fresh air.

Clearly, she also saved my life. I glance down at the bandage covering my chest. The last I remember is her stitching me up, then helping me to bed. I must have fallen asleep right away, for I don't remember much after that. I raise my left arm and wince. But the pain isn't too bad. Maybe it's the meds or the painkillers, but while I feel like I've been put through a wringer, all said and done, I feel okay.

I glance up to find her staring at me. Her golden-brown eyes seem to burn with unsaid emotions. "Whiskey," I murmur, then clear my throat, "it's like drowning in whiskey."

"What?" She frowns.

"Your eyes"—I quirk my lips—"they are whiskey-colored, and your mouth"—I lower my gaze to her lips—"like a red rosebud in half-bloom."

"Are you feeling unwell? Do you have a fever?" She reaches over to place her palm on my forehead. "Are you still in pain?"

"No." I shake my head. "I mean it, you know. You are beautiful, Aurora."

"Stop it." Her blush deepens. "How are you feeling now?"

"I'll live." I try to sit up, then wince when my chest hurts. "How did I get here?"

"I used your phone to call Michael."

"Ah," I hold her gaze, "so you found the phone?"

"Why didn't you tell me that you had one? Why did you tell me that there was no way of calling the others?"

"Because I wanted to spend time with you. Alone."

"So, you lied to me?"

"No..." I shake my head. "It's you who lied to me. Who is he, Aurora? Who is the man who shot me?"

"I... I can't tell you." She glances away.

"A former lover, maybe? Someone you care for?"

"No," she shakes her head, "far from it. I don't really know him at all."

"Another lie?" I growl.

"I'm not lying." She tugs on her hand, and this time, I loosen my grip. She places her hands in her lap. "I really don't know him, Christian. Every time I've met him, he's worn a mask that covers the lower half of his face."

"So, you've met him more than once?"

"I'm not getting into this with you." She jumps up and begins to pace. "You're feeling better; you're going to be okay. My work here is done." She wheels around and heads for the exit.

"Where do you think you're going?"

"Out of here, away from you; you're fine now. And clearly, after what happened, you don't want anything to do with me, so…"

"You're not going anywhere."

"Says who?" She scowls at me over her shoulder.

I glare back at her, and she throws up her hands.

"Look, it's my fault you got shot, okay? I am truly sorry, but after what happened, I think it's best we stop pretending about whatever there is between us."

"Are you pretending, Flower, because I am not."

She pauses, then shakes her head. "We can't go on like this, Christian, we can't. I don't know what you want from me."

"What I want from you is to stick to the terms of our agreement."

She blinks. "You mean, after everything that happened, you still want to go ahead with the fake marriage."

"Especially because of what happened. And considering I got shot in the process, the least you can do is see through your part of the bargain, then set me free, so I can live life the way I want."

"Which is footloose and fancy-free and bedding as many women as you want?" She sets her jaw.

"If that's what I want. Although, as long as we are fake married, I'll be more discreet about who else I'm sleeping with."

"So, during the time we are fake married, you still get to sleep with others, as long as you are not caught, but I don't get to see anyone else?"

"Exactly."

Her face reddens, and this time, it's not with embarrassment. Oh, she's pissed all right, and fuck, if that doesn't turn me on.

"You know what, you can stuff your goddamn arrangement up your arse."

"Don't forget, it's not just you but your family's lives which are at risk."

"I'd like to see you come near them," she snarls.

"I'd like to see you stop me."

She balls her fists at her sides, draws in a breath, then another. "I am not going to let you get away with bullying me this time." She unclenches her fingers one by one, then draws herself up to her full height. "I'm leaving, Christian, and I don't care what you do next."

She spins around, marches over to the door of the hospital room, and opens it. She attempts to step out, but Antonio blocks her path.

"Let me go," she demands. He glances at me, and I shake my head.

"I'm sorry, Aurora, I can't," Antonio says gently. Good. If he'd been impolite to her, I'd not have hesitated to shoot him.

She turns around and stares at me. "If you think you can force me to stay, you're wrong."

"I am not forcing you to stay; I am just not letting you leave."

She squeezes her eyes shut, draws in a breath, then stomps back to the chair and sinks into it. "Fine, you are not going to let me leave. I get it."

"Do you?" I rake my gaze over her features. "Do you really understand what a precarious position you're in?"

She folds her arms across her chest, but doesn't reply.

"If you were to leave right now, Michael would hunt you down and kill you. The only reason you are still alive is because you are here and under my protection."

"Do you expect me to be grateful for being held prisoner?"

"I expect you to come clean on why you felt it necessary to crawl out of the bed where I had made love to you not hours ago and walk through the biting cold for a tryst with a man who would have killed you if I hadn't come upon you."

"I ... I ... don't expect you to understand."

"Try me, Flower."

She bites down on her lower lip, and despite the fact that I'm sedated and woozy, my cock stirs. Apparently, not even being shot at and almost dying—okay, I exaggerate; I didn't almost die, though I did feel close to it—will stop my body from reacting to her presence.

"Go on," I prompt, "tell me what's on your mind.

"I ... ah—"

The door opens abruptly, and Michael walks in. He's followed by Sebastian, Luca, and Adrian. Massimo brings up the rear. Fantastico, just what I need to top off a really shitty day.

Michael strolls over to the only other chair in the room and drops into it. Seb and Luca stalk over to stand on either side of the foot of the bed. Massimo props himself up against the wall by the door; he plants his hands in his pockets and surveys the room. Adrian strolls over to stand by the window.

I take in their relaxed stances, but am not fooled. Assholes are here for an intervention, that's for sure. The silence stretches a beat, then another. Aurora squirms around in the chair. Suddenly, as if she's not able to take it any longer, she jumps up to her feet. "I ... I think I need a breath of fresh air.

She walks toward the door when Michael's voice rings out. "Sit down, Doctor."

She reaches the door and stretches her arm out toward the handle. "Flower," I order, "come and sit down, please." Yeah, I add the please because I know exactly what buttons to push to get her to comply. I'm an asshole that way. And whether I mean it or not… Well, that doesn't really matter, does it?

Aurora pauses, her shoulders shudder as she draws in a breath, then she spins around. Her gaze clashes with mine. I jerk my chin toward her chair. She scowls, and I glare at her. She pales, then tips her chin up. She flounces over to her chair and plops into it. She glowers back at me, and my lips twitch.

Damn, the woman is sexy when she's angry. Hell, she's sexy any way. But when she's angry, her color rises, her eyes turn a darker gold, and I can't wait to throw her down and have hate sex with her.

Michael shifts in his chair. "If you two have had enough of eye-fucking each other, then perhaps we can get to the bottom of what really happened earlier?"

41

____

Christian

"What happened is none of your business." I arch an eyebrow at Michael.

"Considering I had to come in and save your ass, it's very much my business," he retorts.

"I do owe you a thanks for that," I agree, "so…" I flip him off.

Michael's expression doesn't change. "If you expect me to fuck off and leave you alone, you're mistaken." Michael leans back in his chair.

Seb folds his arms across his chest. "You'd better start talking because we are not going anywhere."

"Ditto," Luca adds.

I stare at the faces of my brothers. *Che facce da culo!* Why can't these stronzos leave me alone?

"We care about you," Massimo rumbles, "about both of you." He encompasses Aurora in his gaze.

"Do you?" She glances between them. "If that were the case, Michael here would not have threatened me earlier."

I sit up; my shoulder protests, but I ignore it. "You threatened her?" I growl in a low voice, "You threatened my fiancée?"

"Calm down," Michael orders. "All I did was have a heart-to-heart with the doctor, so we both know where we stand."

Anger thuds at my temples. "That's not cool, *fratellone*. I was unconscious and couldn't come to her defense. You knew it, and yet you chose to intimidate her?"

"It's because you were unconscious that I needed to have words with her," Michael growls. "You'd have done the same thing if you were in my place."

I open and shut my mouth. *Cazzo*, he's right, though. If our positions had been reversed, and I had found him wounded with Karma under suspicious circumstances, I'd have interrogated Karma too.

"Porca miseria." I grab my hair and tug on it. "What the hell do you want to know, Michael?"

"I want to know who shot you."

"That's my concern."

"Not when it endangers all of us. He came after you. Next, he might turn his sights on any one of us, and you know I can't let that happen."

Fuck, but he's right. I square my shoulders and ignore the drowsiness that still tugs at my conscious mind.

"I need time with my fiancée to figure out this shit," I growl.

"We're running out of time," Sebastian says in a low voice. "Whoever shot you is out there roaming free. What guarantee do we have that none of us are at risk?"

"You don't," I glance between them, "but I was the one shot, and she did save my life. For that alone, you need to go easy on her, Michael."

"Not if it was her fault that you were shot in the first place."

Aurora stiffens. The threat implicit in Michael's voice is clear for everyone to hear.

"Don't fucking intimidate her," I snap.

Michael raises his hands, "It's not my place to tell you how to run your life, but when it begins to endanger the lives of my family, I can't stay silent."

I open my mouth to protest, but Seb intervenes. "He's right, Christian, and you know it."

"Fuck," I rake my fingers through my hair. "Can you give me…us a few days to figure this out?"

"I'll give you twenty-four hours."

"Fuck that, I need a week, " I shoot back.

"Forty-eight hours, and not a day more." Michael nods.

"And you won't interfere in our wedding?"

Michael scowls, then says, "Fine." He jerks his chin. "And now, you'd better brace yourself for No—"

The door swings open, and Nonna sails in. She's dressed in an impeccable silk skirt and jacket, with what looks like a mink coat thrown over her shoulders. Karma walks in behind her, followed by Theresa and Cassandra. Karma sidles over to where Michael is sitting. Michael pulls her onto his lap, and Karma cuddles into him. Adrian watches Cassandra as she walks over to Aurora. Theresa follows her. The two women flank Aurora, who shoots them a grateful glance.

It shouldn't have to be like this. Aurora is not the traitor that Michael is making her out to be... Is she? No, she can't be. I have to believe that. She's hiding something. There's no doubt about that, but whatever it is, she must have her reasons. There's no way that she could betray me... She can't.

Nonna walks over to stand beside me. "Christian...." her chin trembles, "*nipotino mio*." She refers to me by the affectionate term for grandson before she reaches over to cup my cheek.

"Nonna," my heart softens, "I am okay, Nonna. It was just a scratch."

"You can't fault me for being worried, Christiano," she chides me. "However much you boys may grow up, you will always remain my *ciccino bello.* And after what happened to Sandro, you can't blame me for being worried about you."

"I am truly fine, Nonna." I take her hand in my mine. "See, still alive and almost ready to be discharged from the hospital."

"Oh, no, you are not going anywhere," Aurora jumps in, "not unless I confirm that you are ready to leave."

"Is that right?" I arch an eyebrow in her direction.

"You are on my turf, Mister." She firms her jaw. "And my word is law here."

Massimo chortles, Seb coughs, and Luca looks amused, while Michael and Adrian content themselves with smirks.

"What?" I scowl at the men. "Are you all taking her side on this?"

"Don't involve us in your domestic matters," Seb murmurs.

"It's good to know that there's someone taking care of you." Nonna shoots Aurora an approving glance.

"Nonna, I am completely okay."

"You don't look completely okay," she retorts.

"But I want to spend Christmas with all of you," I protest.

"That's why you got lost in the snowstorm and decided to hole up in the lodge, hmm?" She smirks. Gesù Cristo, my grandmother really is a force of nature.

My neck heats. Shit, why does Nonna have this uncanny ability to reduce me to feeling like I'm still only six?

"That was a quirk of fate," I murmur.

"Was it now?" She arches an eyebrow.

"We Sovranos are powerful, but we don't control nature, Nonnina."

She laughs, then glances between me and Aurora. "It's understandable that you wanted to spend time with your beautiful fiancée, but since you two were missing for a few nights, I guess I can assume that the deed is done—"

"Nonna," both Aurora and I burst out at the same time.

"Not that I expected the two of you to keep your hands off of each other before the wedding. Or maybe I did." She raises a shoulder. "Old woman that I am, after all, guess my expectations were unreasonable."

"Come on, Nonna, that's not fair," I murmur.

She blows out a breath. "You're right." She tilts her head. "In fact, I'm willing to forgive the two of you for your misdemeanor."

"Misdemeanor?" I exchange glances with Aurora. "Is that what it's called?"

She nods. "And I know how you can make it up to me."

"Umm... Do I want to hear this?"

She glances from me to Aurora, then back at me. Her eyes gleam. Uh-oh, I'm not sure I want to hear this right now.

The silence stretches, then Aurora finally speaks up. "What is it Nonna?" she asks in a soft voice. "How can we make it up to you?"

"By moving up the date of the wedding."

"What?" Aurora bursts out. "Now you want to move up the date of the wedding?"

"Exactly that. I thought it would be good to wait for a few weeks, but given everything that has happened, I'm convinced that it's best not to delay things anymore."

"But..." Aurora protests, "Nonna..."

"I know, a dress, but you don't have to worry about that."

"I don't?" Aurora blinks.

"I've been busy working on a dress for you and for your maids-of-honor," Karma pipes up.

"Ah ... but I am not sure—"

"I am." Nonna turns to me, "and I am sure Christian, here, will only be too willing to oblige me?"

"I hate to tell you, I told you so but... " I smirk, "I told you so."

Nonna frowns at me, and I cough. "I mean, of course, Nonna, I'll be only too pleased to oblige you."

"Don't look so pleased." She sniffs. "If you hadn't meandered off and indulged in actions of the horizontal nature, we wouldn't have had to do this."

"Gesù Cristo, Nonna." I strive for an appropriately shocked expression. "You are embarrassing all of us."

"I'm not embarrassed," Nonna arches an eyebrow, "and neither is Michael." She turns to Michael, "Are you embarrassed, Michael?"

Michael coughs. "Me, embarrassed by you? Of course, not. Nonna, you could never say or do anything to make me uncomfortable."

"Are you embarrassed, Sebastian? Luca? Massimo? Adrian?"

The men shake their heads. None of them even try to hide their smiles.

Traitors. The lot of them. I scowl around at the men, then turn to glare at Michael. His smile widens.

"In fact," Michael drawls, "I propose we should have the wedding as soon as possible."

"I agree," Seb pipes up.

"Totally," Adrian adds his voice.

"Assolutamente." Luca smirks.

"Now, that is what I call a capital idea." Massimo nods his head sagely.

"It's settled then?" Nonna rises to her feet. "Christian and Aurora are getting married in two days."

42

Aurora

I am getting married? I am getting married. Jesus, I'm getting married?

After that pronouncement, Nonna flounced out of the room, followed by the rest of the men. Karma, Cassandra, and Theresa hung around long enough to let me know that they were on my side and that they would do their best to help me with the upcoming nuptials. They also told me they would be waiting for me until I was ready to go home.

Now, it's me and Christian alone in the room.

I glance at him, knowing my apprehension is written on my face. "We can't get married," I burst out, "you know we can't."

"You heard Nonna," Christian drawls. "She's made up her mind, and once Nonna makes up her mind, nothing can change it back."

"B-but after everything that happened, surely, you agree that us getting married, even under the guise of a pretense, is a bad idea."

Christian folds his good arm behind his neck and leans back. The hospital gown stretches across his shoulders, and instead of looking ridiculous, it only emphasizes how fit, how sculpted his physique is. It should be a crime for anyone to look this good, especially when they are injured. The bandages only set off the tan of his skin, which is now a healthy color, thank god.

When he had lost blood and seemed gaunt, the bottom had dropped out of my stomach. My chest had hurt, and a pounding pressure had made itself felt behind my eyes.

I have treated patients, seen them in pain, but it's so much worse when someone you love is suffering. I'd rather it be me who is hurting; that way, I know how to deal with it. But if it's someone who you—hold on, back up. Love… Did I say love? So, yes, I have fallen in love with him along the way. I'd known it on a subconscious level, but almost losing Christian had brought home the fact. No way am I going to put his life at risk again, especially when that man is out there, still hunting him. And I'm sure getting married would draw the attention back to Christian and bring that man back for him.

"We can't do this." I clasp my fingers together. "It's too dangerous."

"Dangerous?" He murmurs, "If you mean you are in danger of being fucked twenty-four-seven once we are officially married, and on our honeymoon, then yes, that's dangerous."

My cheeks heat. "That's not what I meant, and you know it."

"No, I don't." He lowers his chin. "Why don't you come closer and explain it to me, hmm?"

"Oh, no," I shake my head, "no, no, no, I am not coming near you, especially not when you are injured and need to rest that arm."

"Is it concern for me or for yourself that's keeping you away?"

"Both," I say without hesitation. "I admit, the sex between us was good—"

"Good?" He chuckles. "Christmas decorations are good, buying presents for your family is good, but the sex, darling Flower… Our fucking is over-the-top, mind-blowing, pussy-clenching, blowing-my-load-in-seconds explosive."

"No need to be vulgar." I duck my head to avoid meeting his gaze.

"Oh, now she's shy…" He laughs. "Didn't hear you complain when I bound you up tighter than a Christmas stocking before the presents are opened—"

"Shh!" I dart a glance toward the door. "Keep your voice low."

"You ashamed of your kinky side, Flower?"

"Of course, not," I murmur, "it's just… you know… I am still getting used to—"

"How much you crave the fetish?"

"Something like that." I flip my hair over my shoulder. "Anyway, coming back to the question at hand—"

"There is no question. We are getting married. In two days. End of discussion."

I glower at him.

He yawns, then settles back into the pillows. "I do believe my meds are finally catching up with me." He shuts his eyes.

"Don't you dare fall asleep." I jump to my feet, walk over to him, and hit his shoulder, the one near where the bullet hit him.

"Ouch," he grimaces, "that's my hurt shoulder."

"I know," I firm my lips, "it was the only way to get your attention."

"Bloodthirsty too?" He smirks. "Didn't peg you for being heartless, Flower."

"But I always knew you were brutal." I swallow. "Please, Christian, I don't want to do this."

"Why not?"

"It will simply draw attention to us."

"What are you afraid of, Aurora?" He scans my features. "Tell me; I can't help you unless you do."

"I … I can't." I wish I could. I do…but if I do, you'll hate me. You'll never be able to love me , and where would that leave me? But you love him, and if you truly cared for him, you'd tell him everything so he can protect himself. And if I do, I'll never be able to see him again. And that I won't be able to bear. I can't bring myself to. I can't. I spin around and head toward the exit.

"Aurora," he calls out, "this isn't over yet. I won't stop until you reveal how you knew that man."

"So, what do you think?" Karma asks.

We returned to Palermo yesterday, and then it was a headlong rush to get everything ready for the wedding. If Karma hadn't come through on the dress, I'm not sure what I would have done.

I take in my reflection in the mirror in the bedroom of Nonna's home. It's where I had returned, and this time, Christian hadn't protested. In fact, when I told him that I was returning to Nonna's place, he agreed it was a good idea. That way, he wouldn't see me the day before the wedding, as tradition dictates. Good thing too, because I can't wait to see his face when he sees me in this dress. The cream-colored gown with golden coils of thread woven through it clings to my shoulders, embraces my breasts, and cinches in at the waist before it flows down to my toes. The long sleeves are made of lace. When I move my arm, a hint of skin peeks through the gaps in the embroidery; the recurring motif is a thick braid that loops around and in on itself before it streams down to the cuffs.

The train flows behind me and is made of sheer lace with silver and gold shot through the pattern of—you guessed it—vines.

The design is so appropriate, it seems like it was created in my mind's eye and brought to life in a manner so detailed that I can't wrap my mind around it.

"Well?" she asks again. "Hopefully, you don't hate it. I only had a few days to get it right, so…" Her voice peters out.

I turn one way, then the other, and rake my gaze over my figure in profile. The silken material clings to my curves, it flattens my belly, and emphasizes the lushness of my hips. The cut shows off my shoulders, frames my face, and the golden threads in the sleeves bring out the highlights in my hair. I take a step forward, and the skirt rustles when I walk. It slides over my thighs, reminding me of his touch. Goose bumps pop on my skin. I prop my hand on my hip, stick out a leg, and the material seems to flow and resettle over my shape, with a flash of a shapely ankle—my ankle—which is encircled by the strap of a wicked six-inch Salvatore Ferragamo shoe.

On my head, I wear a simple tiara from which the champagne and gold veil flows down my back to trail behind me. The overall effect is subtle and powerful and undeniably sexy, and yet... It's also restrained. It hints at hidden depths of complexity and poetry, all melded together in one unique silhouette; the one that enfolds me.

"Aurora," Karma probes, "you're making me nervous."

"It's..." I shake my head. The pressure builds behind my eyes, my chin trembles, and damn it, I don't want to cry I don't. "It's..." I sniffle, trying to get the words out, but they stick in my throat.

"Oh my god," Karma says in horror. "you hate it. I knew I needed more time to get it right. Damnit; we should have taken you to a boutique and allowed you to buy one of your choice. I should have—"

"Shut up." I turn on her. "Don't you dare say that."

"Um... Okay," Karma chews on her lower lip, "but I have to say that you are confusing me, Aurora."

"There's no confusion." I glance from her to Theresa, who's hovering in the background, then back to Karma. "It's clear that when you created this dress, you had a very clear idea of who I am. What I like and what my deepest, most secret desires are."

"Wow," Karma blinks rapidly, "that's good, right? That's a compliment, correct?" She shuffles her weight between her feet. "So, you like it. You do like it, right?"

"No, I don't like it—"

Her face falls.

"I LOVE it, you stupid, brilliant woman!" I close the distance between us and throw my arms around her. "It's gorgeous; it's beautiful. It's the kind of dress I had hoped for, but had always thought I'd never be able to have, and now—"

"You do." Theresa walks forward and embraces both of us. "You look absolutely breathtaking, Aurora." She sniffs. "You are a vision."

A tear runs down her cheek, and I realize that she is remembering Xander and the wedding she had hoped to have with him. "I am so sorry, Theresa." I turn to her. "This must be painful for you."

"No" she shakes her head, "I am just being sentimental. Fact is, everything I had hoped to have with Xander was a figment of my imagination."

"Are you sure he didn't feel something for you?" Karma murmurs.

"Even if he did," she swallows, "it wasn't something he was sure of. He was torn inside, and I never had the courage to approach him and talk to him about it. I was too shy, too worried about upsetting people, too conscious of how it would look if I pursued him." She hunches her shoulders. "Now, I wish I had simply cornered him and told him how I felt. It might have, at least, revealed if he had feelings for me or not. But I didn't, and now he's gone, and I'll never know." Her features crumple. "Oh, hell..." she turns away, "this is a happy occasion. I am not supposed to be bawling like this. It's your wedding, and I am spoiling it." She cries harder.

Karma and I look at each other, then as one, we move to her and hug her. "Oh, honey," I rub her back. "It's okay; let it out. I know how hard this is for you. I really do."

She weeps for a few seconds more, then finally seems to get it under control. "I am sorry," she warbles, "really, really sorry. I didn't mean to put a damper all over your wedding day."

I blink. Jesus, it really is my wedding day. It's like the last two days went by in the blink of an eye.

I had returned to Nonna's residence with Theresa and Karma. The men were told to stay away, in no uncertain terms. I've been receiving periodic updates on Christian's progress by Nonna. She assures me that he is fine and staying with Massimo. Christian and I will see each other for the first time at the ceremony, which will be held at the family church where Michael and Karma were married. A ceremony which will take place a few hours from now.

Theresa wipes her face and turns to me, "I have something for you." She moves away to pick up a bouquet from the side table, then turns and hands it to me.

I glance down at the spray of sunflowers and blue orchids. They are tied together with a champagne-colored cloth knotted into a bow at the base. "Wow," I breathe, "it's gorgeous."

"I know it's tradition for the bridegroom to give you the bouquet, but Nonna assured me that it was okay for me to make it for you." Her features soften, "The colors of the flowers reflect the colors of both of your eyes." She adds softly. "I had the design in mind from the moment I found out that the two of you were getting married. The sunflowers symbolize loyalty and adoration, and the blue orchids represent power and virility, though lord knows you two don't need help in that department."

I chuckle, still trying to wrap my head around everything. "Didn't realize you knew so much about flowers."

"I should," she says with a small laugh, "I own a flower shop."

"Not just any flower shop, you are looking at an award-winning florist here," Karma says.

"Oh wow," I turn to Theresa, "I had no idea."

"Didn't you notice that's why Nonna gifted her with the tulip bulbs during dinner at the chalet?" Karma interjects.

"Of course, guess I must have been too distracted to notice," I murmur.

"It's no big deal." Theresa flushes. "I love flowers, always have, and when you work with what you love, it doesn't feel like a job at all, you know?"

"Thank you," I glance at the flowers again, "they are beautiful, and so is the dress."

There's a knock on the door, and a familiar face peeks around the door. "Aurora," her face breaks into a smile, and she bounces into the room, "you look beautiful."

"Elena." I hold out my arms, and she races toward me, then pauses.

"Don't want to spoil your dress."

"You won't, silly." I smile. "Now, hug me."

When she still hesitates, I wrap my arm around her shoulders and kiss her cheek. "You look lovely," I murmur, "and so grown up." I step back, then notice the others watching us.

"This is my sister, Elena." I smile at them.

"Hello, Elena." Karma grins. "You look so much like your sister."

"Oh, my sister is far prettier." Elena turns to me, "I can't believe you are getting married."

"I know, right? There's so much we need to catch up on."

"I have something for you." She dips her hand into the silk purse dangling from her wrist and holds out a brooch.

"That," I swallow, "that belonged to—"

"Mother." She nods. " I thought you'd like to have it with you when you got married."

"Ah, now I have something old." I take it and pin it to my dress.

"We are not done yet," Nonna adds as she walks into the room. She's wearing a simple blue dress with blue and gold stilettos and looks every bit the regal matriarch that she is. She hugs me, then holds out a small box. I open it to find an ornate charm bracelet. I hold it up and find charms in the shape of a chrysanthemum, a peacock feather, a rope, a weeping Virgin Mary, an anchor, and a scorpion. The same symbols I had spotted among Christian's tattoos.

"Christian wanted this made for you." Nonna fastens it around my wrist. "He was very specific that he wanted you to be wearing this to the wedding."

"Right..." I run my finger along the pendants. What do they mean? Would Christian tell me if I asked him? Why is he wearing these designs on his body?

Nonna steps back and takes in the four of us. "Bellissime." She wipes a tear from her eye. "All of you look gorgeous." She turns to me, "Are you ready, Aurora?"

43

———————

Christian

I am not ready to be married, not ready at all. I slide my finger under the collar of my shirt and tug on it. "Did someone turn up the heat in here?" I mutter.

Seb laughs, "It's freezing, brother."

"Is it?" I wipe a bead of sweat that trickles down my temple. "I swear, it's like a furnace in here." At least, my shoulder doesn't hurt anymore. The wound seems to be healing quickly, though I still have a bandage around my shoulder. Nothing that the suit can't hide. Looking at me, you'd never guess that I had been shot at and bleeding a few days ago. I'm lucky Flower is a doctor; her quick action saved my life, agonizing though it had been when she stitched me up. Not that I had let on. I'd wanted her focused on the task at hand… Also, I hadn't wanted to appear like a pussy in front of her.

"You nervous, Christian?" Luca smirks.

"Vaffancolo!" *Fuck off*, I growl.

"There's still time to change your mind." Michael taps me on the shoulder, "Say the word, and I'll call this circus off."

The circus being the fact that the pews are packed with people—because Nonna had, apparently, decided to invite every single person who is anyone in the city to attend. No, let me amend that. She had also invited our associates. JJ Kane, the head of the Kane Company, and Nikolai Solonik, the new *Pakhan* of the

Bratva are here, as are the heads of the five families that constitute the *Cosa Nostra*.

She's making up for the fact that Michael's wedding had been so hurried that he had married in an empty church. There had been no time to invite guests. Lucky devil.

"Well?" He frowns at me. "What do you say? Time to end this charade?"

"You'd best not insult my bride by referring to our upcoming nuptials as that."

"It must be love," Adrian pipes up.

All of my brothers are dressed in tuxes, except Adrian, who hates formal wear. He's wearing blue jeans, but at least, he has taken the time to pull on a jacket over his white button-down, his one concession to the formality of the occasion.

"The fuck you talking about, *testa di cazzo*?" I growl.

"That's the first time I've seen you give enough of a fuck to come to someone's defense," he retorts. "As you should, *fratello*. After all, she is your soul mate, the love of your life, your wife-to-be." He nods, "Get ready for when the kids come along, and the potty training begins. Are you going to be a hands-on husband? I'd hope so; it's best for the children to bond if you are—"

I pale. "Shut the fuck up, you *pezzo di merda*."

"Someone's rather edgy," Massimo drawls. "Having second thoughts, *fratellino*?"

"No," I snap. And that much is true. Finally, my plan is bearing fruit. I simply need to go through with this wedding, then wait for a few weeks and announce to the *famiglia* that we have fallen out of love and are going to separate. See? Easy.

What's not as easy to stomach is that my bride is probably a traitor. All the more reason to go through with this sham of a wedding so I can keep her close… Only until I find out what she's up to, of course. That's the only reason I am contemplating exactly how I plan to tie her up tonight, and bring her to the edge and keep her unfulfilled until she finally reveals exactly who it was that shot me.

The wound on my shoulder healed quickly. It really had looked worse than it was. The ball of emotion that I am carrying around in my chest, though, the one that insists she can't be a traitor, even though all signs point to it… That continues to fester. I didn't sleep the last two nights, and it's not because I spent them in the hospital…

Fact is, I missed the scent of her, the taste of her, her quick wit, her rejoinders, her moans when I took her, her hitching breath when I tied her up, the marks my knots made on her skin, the feel of her soft pussy giving as I buried myself inside her. Somehow, she had grown on me in the days and nights that we had spent together, and that…is not something I had expected.

Is that why I am nervous about this ceremony? Because it feels real? It's more real than anything I have faced in my life. As real as … Xander's death. As visceral as the lack of him is. Am I trying to fill the hole in my heart with her presence? I ball my fists at my sides. No, I don't think so. There's more to it than that… I saw her, I was drawn to her, and somewhere along the way, I fell in love with her. But it doesn't matter because I can't have her. I don't deserve to be happy, not when Xander is dead. Not when he'll never experience the thrill of having a soul mate. I may love her, but so what? I'll live if I don't act on my feelings for her. All I have to do is stick to the plan, marry her, then leave her and—

"Dio mio, she's beautiful." Seb's low whistle pulls me out of my thoughts. The music in the church begins to play the traditional song that marks the arrival of the bride. I turn, and it's as if a massive hand has punched me in the gut. My heart stutters, my stomach twists itself in knots, and something hot stabs at my chest. I stare at a vision in cream lace and a champagne-colored dress standing poised at the entrance to the church.

Everyone turns at once in their pews to see the back of the church then a hush falls over the crowd. All eyes focus on the woman silhouetted just inside the doors. She stands motionless as her bridesmaids move forward. First Theresa, then Karma, followed by her younger sister Elena. They move to stand on the dais across from my groomsmen, and that's when I really see her.

She's opted to walk up the aisle on her own. With each step, she inches closer, her shapely ankles peeking out from under the skirt of her dress which flatters her figure while enhancing her voluptuousness. The silver-gold threads in her dress glimmer under the light that pours in through the stained-glass windows. The veil flows down to cover her face, and she holds her bouquet of yellow and blue flowers at her chest, framing that spectacular bosom of hers as she comes to a stop in front of me. I catch a glimpse of the bracelet I had made for her around her wrist. A fierce satisfaction courses through my veins.

She stares up at me through the veil, and my heart rate ratchets up. My pulse hammers at my temples, at my wrist, even in my fucking balls. Is this what people mean by being pussy-whipped? Perhaps it's the fact that I want to reach down, push her skirts aside, and trace her luscious pussy lips through the lace of her soaked panties, even as another part of me wants to haul her into my arms and kiss her and cherish her, and give her anything she wants.

She swallows, and her hands tremble. The bouquet slips from her fingers. I step forward but before I can reach for it, she regains her grip on it. Then she hands it over to Theresa. As she lowers her arms to her sides, a trembling grips her body. I move toward her, pinch the edge of her veil, and raise it up and over her face. Those whiskey eyes stare back at me. Her features are pale, and that makes her eyes seem even larger than usual. Her chin trembles, her lips part, and it takes everything in me not to bend down and fit my tongue between them. I hold out my palm, and she places hers in it. I tug gently, and she moves closer.

"It's going to be fine," I whisper.

She nods.

"I promise; it will all be okay."

She peers into my features, then draws in a breath. "Okay," she breathes.

"Okay." I turn to face the priest.

44

Aurora

"In the name of the Father, of the Son, and of the Holy Spirit, go in peace with Christ."

"Thanks be to God."

The voices of those congregated slice through the noise in my head. After Christian had lifted my veil and peered into my face, everything else had faded. All I could see was him. All I could smell was his masculine scent. All I could feel was the touch of his fingers as he held mine. I reveled in the warmth of his body as he pulled me forward to face the priest. Throughout the ceremony, I'd been unable to focus on the priest's words. That is, until Christian had slipped the wedding band onto my left ring finger—a simple gold band embedded with a tiny amber stone and a blue stone next to it.

Massimo hands me the ring and I slip it onto Christian's ring finger. That's when I realize this entire ceremony feels too real... More than real... It feels huge... Like, life-changing huge.

I gulp, and a trembling grips me. My muscles seem to seize up, and I turn my body, ready to run. Christian closes the distance between us and steps in front of me, effectively cutting off my escape. He notches his knuckle under my chin and raises my head.

"It's too late," he whispers. "I can't let you run now."

"I have to go," I hiss, "I can't do this."

"Yes, you can."

"No, I can't."

"It's only a kiss, Flower."

"You know that's not what I'm talking about."

He lowers his face until his breath twines with mine. "Open your mouth," he orders.

I press my lips together, and he smirks.

"No kissing allowed in church," the priest protests from behind me.

We are in Italy, and unlike Hollywood movies where the bride and groom are allowed to kiss in church, here the priests frown on it unless it's a chaste peck on the cheek. Knowing Christian, he's not going to be satisfied with that.

I am proved right when he chuckles, "Sorry, Father, but we do things my way from now on." He brushes his lips over mine once, twice. He bites down on my lower lip, I gasp, and he instantly sweeps his tongue inside my mouth. He locks his lips over mine and sucks on me, ravishes me, dances his tongue across mine, and kisses me with such intensity that my head spins. My knees buckle, and he wraps his arm around my waist and hauls me to him.

I am aware of applause breaking out, of rice being showered on us, and yet he doesn't stop kissing me. He pulls me to him, close enough that every inch of my chest seems to be plastered to his. My nipples tighten, and my breasts swell. My thighs graze his, and I am aware of his arousal stabbing into my belly. I try to pull away, but Christian holds me firmly. He deepens the kiss, and it's like he is fucking my mouth with his tongue. My head swims, a groan bleeds from me, and his lips curve. He slows the kiss until his lips are barely touching mine. Then he raises his head and peers into my flushed features.

The priest clears his throat. Christian glares at him, and he pales. He glances between us, then turns and walks off.

"At least he survived the wedding," Luca jokes. He's referring to the fact that Michael shot and killed the priest subsequent to Michael and Karma's wedding. Something I heard later from Karma. She mentioned to me that was the moment she realized the kind of man she had married. Someone for whom death was as close as life.

Me? I knew exactly what I was getting into when I agreed to spy on the Sovranos for the stranger who had approached me when I was in London. It's one of the reasons I had returned to Sicily, after all. My father's failing health had provided the timely cover for me to get a foothold in their inner circle. If it were not for the fact that I had acted on impulse to help Karma, I would have continued the arrangement without being noticed by Christian. But he had noticed me, and now, here I am.

Christian twines his fingers with mine, then turns to face the assembled crowd. He brings my hand to his mouth and kisses the fingertips, and there's a chorus of sighs from the women in the audience. This is when we should be forming a receiving line at the back of the church, but it's another tradition my bridegroom seems to have dispensed with.

Nonna walks over. She pauses in front of us, and Christian bends his head so Nonna can kiss his forehead. Her eyes glisten. "You made me very happy today," she murmurs, then turns to me and kisses me on my cheek, "and you are a beautiful bride."

"Thank you," I reply.

She turns to Christian, "Thank you for delaying your honeymoon so you can spend some time with us."

"H-honeymoon?" I choke out the word.

"Yes, darling," Christian turns to me, "I know how much you are looking forward to the two of us being alone."

I open my mouth to protest, but he shakes his head, "No, I know. It's a lot to ask you to wait for our away time, but you have been so understanding about it. You are a true Mafia bride."

Jerk. He knows that's the one thing I hate being called. It's the one thing I swore to myself I'd never be, yet here I am, standing next to my Mafioso husband, wearing his ring on my finger. I try to tug my hand out of his grasp, but he tightens his hold on me.

Nonna glances between us. "You know, I was so sure that the two of you were putting on some kind of show meant to fool me into believing that you were together, but now—"

"Now?" Christian tilts his head.

"Now," she turns to me, "seeing the happy glow on your face and the glint of possession in yours, Christian," she glances at him, "I know that it wasn't an act."

"But, Nonna—"

I begin to protest when Christian interrupts, "Aren't we going to be late for the wedding reception?"

I scowl at him and he smirks. "Bet you can't wait to have our first dance together as husband and wife, eh?"

I swallow. It's done; for better or worse, he is my husband, and I am his wife. At least, for the next thirty days. A tremor grips me, my feet and hands feel numb, all of the blood drains from my head, and I sway. Christian immediately releases my hand and puts his arm around me. He pulls me close enough that his masculine scent fills my nostrils, which only makes everything worse. Pressure builds behind my eyes, and to my horror, a tear squeezes out from the corner of my eye.

"Oh, my dear," Nonna exclaims, "the events have been too much for you. Perhaps, the two of you should skip the wedding reception and proceed directly to the honeymoon?"

"No," I burst out, "I… I'll be okay. I just need to eat something, is all."

"Haven't you eaten breakfast?" Christian scowls at me.

I glance away.

"You shouldn't starve yourself, Flower." He turns to Nonna, "Why don't you head on to the reception, and I'll feed my wife before we join you?"

Half an hour later, I glance out of the window of our bedroom. Our bedroom, in our new home that Christian purchased for us. Which happens to be adjacent to Michael and Karma's home, which Michael purchased after they married. I've shed the veil, and the dress now resembles more of a gown, something that is perfect to wear to a wedding reception, thanks to Karma's design.

There's a knock on the door, and Cassandra wheels in a trolley with dishes. She glances from me to Christian, who's kicked back on the settee. "Do you need anything else?" she asks.

"Thanks for helping out, Cassandra," Christian murmurs as he rises to his feet.

"You shouldn't be working today." I cross over to her. "You did come to the wedding, didn't you? I don't think I saw you."

"I was there, all right." She gestures to the dress she is wearing under her apron. "It was a beautiful ceremony, Aurora." She smiles at me. "You were such a radiant bride; you made me cry."

"I did?" I blink. "To be honest, I was so nervous I don't think I remember much of the ceremony."

"As long as you remember the kiss at the end, I'm not complaining," Christian jokes.

"You are coming to the reception, aren't you?" I reach for Cassandra's hand and grip it. Her fingers seem too warm… Or rather, mine are too cold.

She frowns at me. "Everything okay?" she asks in a low voice.

I open my mouth then close it. Heat singes my back, and I know Christian has come up to stand behind me. He places his hand on my shoulder, and I gulp. I force my lips to curve in a smile. "Yes, of course," I tip up my chin, "everything's good. I'm just hungry, is all. I couldn't eat this morning; too many nerves." I force myself to laugh.

She peers into my features for a few seconds more. "I'll leave you to it." She squeezes my hand one last time before she turns and walks out.

Christian guides me to a chair, and I sink into it. He pulls off the covers of the plates, then places one of them in front of me. I glance down at the pasta, and my stomach rumbles.

He pours a little wine into a glass for me, then points at my plate, "Eat."

He places the other plate in front of the other setting, then takes his seat. He begins to eat with gusto, scooping up the pasta with his fork, guiding it to his mouth, before he chews and swallows. The strong tendons of his neck flex as he drinks from the wine glass. My husband is not just handsome… He's virile and so gorgeous to look at that it hurts.

"You're not eating," he reminds me, and I turn to my food. I manage to finish half of what's on my plate before I push the remaining in his direction.

"You've barely eaten anything." He scowls.

"I've had enough."

"One more bite," he coaxes me.

"But—"

"Go on." He picks up some of the pasta with his fork and offers it to me. Holding his gaze, I open my mouth, and he feeds me. To anyone watching this scene, we'd come across as a conventional couple, with the husband so concerned about his wife's well-being that he's making sure to feed her.

Only, I know how fake all of this is. He brings another forkful to my mouth, and I turn my head. "Don't," I say through gritted teeth, "please don't fake your solicitude."

"I am truly worried about your well-being, and you know that, Flower."

"And please, can you stop calling me by that nickname?" I jump up to my feet. "Jesus, why do we have to continue with this wedding, when you know that it's my fault that you got shot." I begin to pace—back, forth, back—as I wring my hands. "I can't go on like this, Christian. Especially when you are pretending to be all nice and caring toward me."

"I am not pretending, Aurora," he says in a gentle tone. "Or, let's back up. I am not strictly pretending."

"Huh?" I turn on him, "What do you mean?"

"A part of me wants to push you against those windows, so your tits are pressed against the pane, and fuck you from behind so every time I plunge inside you, you scream so loudly that our guests will hear you."

"Oh…" I shiver; my nipples bead. "And the other part of you—"

"Knows that it's best that I wait here with my arms across my chest and hear you out, so I finally understand what it is that is bothering you so much."

"If I tell you, you'll hate me, Christian. And I couldn't bear that. Don't you understand?"

"Try me." He pours himself more wine, then tops up my glass and offers it to me.

I draw in a breath, then march over to him. I grab my glass and drain it. The alcohol hits my stomach, and I cough. "That's good wine," I sputter.

"The best," he agrees. "So, what is it that you want to tell me?"

45

Aurora

Am I doing this? Am I really gonna do this? I blow out a breath, then grip the edges of the table. "When I was in London, after I had completed my residency and started working in a hospital, I was on my way home from work one day, when…he approached me."

Christian's face doesn't change expression. His shoulders stay relaxed. He's unbuttoned his tux, and the bowtie he wore earlier is untied. His hair is slightly disheveled, and that only adds to his appeal. He looks sexy and yummy, and handsome in a way that makes me want to reach over and push away the strand of hair that has fallen over his forehead. He raises his glass and has a sip. For all purposes, he seems calm and composed, except... A nerve throbs at his temple. Shit, that's not a good sign, is it?

The silence stretches. I reach for the bottle of wine, top up my glass, and take another sip. "He asked me to spy on the Sovranos."

Christian's fingers tighten around the stem of his glass. "Go on," he says in a soft voice.

A shiver runs up my spine. "You have to understand, I didn't have a choice."

"You always have a choice."

"Not in this." I gaze into the depths of the glass. "He told me if I didn't do as he said, he'd kill me."

A wave of anger seems to roll off of his shoulders and crash into me. I gasp, then raise my glass to my mouth again. My hand trembles so hard that some of the wine spills over the side.

He reaches over, pries the glass from my grasp, and places it on the table. "Any more alcohol, and you'll be drunk."

"Sounds like a plan."

"Not for what I have in mind."

"What's that supposed to mean?"

His lips twist and he raises his glass in my direction. "What happened next?"

"I refused to help him."

"You did?"

I nod. "I was so pissed off, I told him to do his worst. So he... he warned me that if I didn't help him he'd kill my sister and father."

He glowers at me.

"Yeah," I blow out a breath, "it's the same threat that you made." I nod.

"Only, you know, I never meant it."

I narrow my gaze on him, "Didn't you?"

"Your family is part of our clan. Your father has been our family doctor for many years. I wouldn't have allowed them to be hurt."

I laugh, "And we both know, when it comes to Mafia business, everything is expendable."

"But not you."

I shake my head, "I don't believe you."

"Suffice to say that no pussy has milked my dick the way you have, so purely, on that ground, I wouldn't have hurt you or anyone close enough to cause you grief if they were hurt."

"You sure know how to romance a girl, don't you?" I say wryly.

"So, you agreed to help him?"

"I did," I concur.

"Who is he?"

"I don't know; he always wore a mask. The first time we met he made sure his face was in darkness. After that we'd always meet in a cafe and sit at different tables. I heard his voice, but never managed to get a good look at him. That day in the forest was the first time I saw him face-to-face, and even then, he had a mask on, so I couldn't really make out his features. His eyes, though," I shake my head, "they seemed familiar."

"Did they?" He frowns.

"You saw him too, didn't you, when you fired at him?"

"It was already snowing, and I was too focused on saving you to pay enough attention. Although... Come to think of it, his height and the way he moved did seem familiar ... maybe." He shakes his head. "So, you agreed to spy on us?"

I nod.

"And when your father fell ill, your coming to take his place, was that also part of the plan?"

"No," I protest, "that was a coincidence. My father really did fall sick and ask me to come and take his place."

"Hmm," he strokes his chin, "how did you get the information to this man?"

"He'd call me from a phone every other day and question me about what I saw, who I met, where each of you went..." I raise a shoulder. "It just always seemed like pointless questions."

"But I took your phone from you when I—"

"Held me under house arrest?" I swallow. "He didn't call during that time. But when I moved to Nonna's and she gave me a phone, he called me again. How he obtained the number, I can only imagine. This time, I told him I had nothing more to share, and he wasn't happy. Then, when he met me near the lodge, I told him I didn't want to help him anymore. That's when he threatened to hurt you, and I panicked. I couldn't bear it if he did anything to hurt you; you have to believe me, Christian."

"Motherfucker." Christian tightens his grip on his glass, and the stem snaps. The cup of the now empty wine glass topples onto the table, rolls over, and crashes to the floor.

I jump up to my feet, but he leans over and grabs my hand. "Sit down."

"Don't hurt me. Please don't hurt me or my family. Please, Christian, please."

He stares at me, "Do you really think that I'd harm you or anyone who you care for?"

"Yes. No. I don't know," I say honestly. "You have to admit that everything you've done so far hasn't exactly been confidence-building in that respect."

He releases the stem of the glass from his grasp, and it drops to the table with a soft thud. "Have you finished eating?" he says in a low voice.

"Y-yes." I swallow. "Why...why are you asking?"

He jerks his chin, "Get up."

"What?"

"On your feet; turn around and head to the window behind you."

"Ch-Christian," I gulp, "what are you doing?"

"You don't get to ask the questions, Flower," he snaps. "Up."

My body, once again, betrays me, for I find myself rising to my feet. I glower at him, and he circles his finger in the air, "Turn around, Flower, or I'll come over there and make you do it."

I hesitate, and he pushes back his chair. Oh, hell! I spin around, pick up the skirts of my wedding dress, and scurry over to the floor-to-ceiling window that looks down over the back garden. Beyond it, the sea stretches out into the horizon, and by all accounts, it's a magnificent view. I hear his footsteps approach and stiffen.

"Put your hands on the window."

"Christian, please," I implore him.

"Do it or else..."

I huff out a breath, then plant my hands on the window on either side of my head.

"Now, keep them there."

He kicks my legs apart, and I yelp, "Wh-what are you doing?" I turn to find him looking me up and down.

He palms my butt, and a shiver runs down my spine. "You've forgotten what it's like to be spanked by me, hmm?"

"No... No..." I shudder, half in fear of the pain that he's surely going to cause me, half in anticipation from the pain that he's surely going to cause me. Argh! How can one physical action of his elicit such contradictory reactions in me?

He bends his knee, grasps the edge of my dress, then flips it up and over my head. He slides it under each of my palms, so I'm holding it up in such a way that it hides whatever it is he's going to do to me.

A ripple of anticipation runs down my spine, and my core clenches, even as my stomach ties itself in knots. He grips my lacy panties—which I admit, I had chosen specifically, with him in mind. Hell, just because this entire wedding is supposedly fake doesn't mean I can't be nicely dressed, right? He yanks at them with such force that the fabric gives way. He tears them off of me, and I gasp. Cool air envelops my naked arse and my exposed sex.

He runs his finger down the valley between my arsecheeks, and I squeeze my eyes shut.

"Please, don't, please don't—"

Thwack. A line of fire snakes across my butt, and I scream. "Bloody hell, what the hell do you think you are—"

Thwack-thwack-thwack. He lands the slaps in quick succession on each arsecheek, and with each hit, my entire body jolts. My dress-clad breasts crash into the wall of glass, stimulating my nipples further. Thwack. His palm connects with my lower thigh with even more force.

I yell, "Jesus Christ, it hurts, you asshole."

THWACK.

It's like he's put the entire weight of his body behind it. My entire butt seems to be on fire... Wait, also my back and the backs of my thighs where the pain has spread to and—

THWACK. THWACK. THWACK.

I cry out, and tears squeeze out from the corners of my eyes. "It hurts; it bloody hurts," I yell, "you monster, you pervert, you sadistic jerk-ass."

"Now you know who you married, Flower." He massages my hurting rump, and my entire body jerks in reaction.

"Oh, god." I push my sweaty palms into the glass and groan, "Please, stop, Christian. Please, please don't..." stop.

He slides his fingers between my legs and sticks them inside my sopping wet channel. "That's not what your body is telling me, sweetheart." He brings his fingers up to my lips. "Suck," he orders, and I do. I clean off every last drop of my cum from his fingers, then bite down on his digit.

He laughs, "There you are, my little wildflower."

"Fuck off," I snarl. I'd stick my tongue out at him, but with my dress between us, he won't be able to see it anyway. He pulls his hand off of my butt, and I hear the telltale jangle of his belt, then the rasp of his zipper.

Oh, hell. Oh, hell.

He squeezes my butt, and I jump. "Stop thinking so hard," he admonishes me.

"Why the hell have you put this...this dress between us?"

"So you don't get more worried about what is to come."

"What is to come?" I stiffen. "What do you mean 'what is to come'? What are you going to do, you—"'

He thrusts forward, and in one smooth move, impales me. I gasp. Jesus, he's big. So big. So damn thick and so hard. His cock stretches my channel, fills me to the brim, and, "Oh, god." I groan, "Oh, my god."

"Christian," he growls, "I have a name, Flower."

He pulls out of me, then lunges forward with enough force that my entire body jolts. The hair on his thighs scrapes against my inner thighs, and a frisson of heat coils at the base of my spine.

"Fuck," he grumbles, "let me in, Flower."

"You are in, you wanker," I snap back.

"Not even half-way."

"What?" I blink. "No, no, no."

"The right response is 'Yes, Christian.'"

He pulls out again, then brings his palm around to my play with my pussy. He pinches my clit, and I scream. He pushes into me and slips in another inch. A groan rumbles up his chest. A whine bleeds from my lips.

I push my forehead against the cool glass as he reaches down to circle the place where his dick is buried in my pussy. "Fuck, that's hot," he grunts as he begins to drill into me. Each time he pushes into me, my entire body shudders. Each time his pelvis connects with the chafed skin of my arse, tendrils of pleasure coil in my belly. He yanks on my dress. I release it, and the dress slides down to settle around my shoulders.

He grinds his heel into my clit, even as he brings his other hand up to pinch my chin and turn it to face him. He lowers his face and presses his lips to mine, and somehow, the tenderness in his kiss is at odds with how he continues to bury himself inside of me. He slides his hand inside the bustier of my dress and pinches my nipple, and my entire body jolts.

My pussy clamps down on his dick, and a groan rumbles up his chest. He squeezes my nipple harder, and at the same time, he strums my clit, even as he tilts his hips and plunges inside of me. He hits that spot deep inside that sends tendrils of pleasure radiating out from the point of contact. The pressure at the base of my spine expands, and I cry out. He swallows the sound before he tears his lips from mine.

"Come," he growls, and I shatter. Moisture pools between my legs, and my climax washes over me. He continues to thrust inside me through the aftershocks that grip me, then with a low groan, he shoots warm gusts of cum inside me. We stay that way, his dick still inside me, his hands on me, his cheek pressed to mine.

I glance down to find people gathering in the garden below. Heaters placed at intervals warm the space. In one corner, two men I don't recognize are gathered, talking to each other. In the opposite corner, Massimo and Sebastian hold glasses in their hands. Near them, Michael and Karma are wrapped in a kiss. Clearly, the Don and his wife are still not over their honeymoon stage.

"Christian," I murmur, "the guests are assembling below."

"Hmm." He turns his head and nips the side of my neck. I shiver.

"We need to go down and meet them."

"Do we?"

"They are here for us."

"They can go fuck themselves," he growls.

"We have to make an appearance at our wedding reception," I remind him.

"I'd rather whisk you away directly to our honeymoon."

"Honeymoon?" I blink rapidly, "You really plan to take me on a honeymoon?"

"You didn't think I was going to pass up the opportunity to spend an entire week buried inside of you, did you?"

My cheeks heat, and a shiver runs down my spine.

"Cute. All of the things I have done to you, and you're still able to blush, hmm?" He pulls out of me, and I wince, already missing the feel of his thickness between my legs. His cum slithers down between my thighs as he pulls my skirts down, then turns me around to face him. I try to move past him, and he stops me, "Where are you going?" He frowns.

"Need to tidy up before we head down.

"No, you don't."

"Wh-what do you mean?" I frown.

"I want you to wear my cum between your legs. I want you to feel it stick to your inner thighs with every step you take, Flower. Every second of the time that you are walking around and talking to people, I want you to remember who you belong to."

I shudder, and my toes curl. Why do I find his words such a turn-on? Why is it that the filthier he gets, the more I am aroused? Why is it that I want to agree to do his every bidding, including wearing his cum on my pussy as a badge of possession?

"Christian," I whisper, "what are you doing to me?"

"The same thing that you are doing to me?"

He frowns down at me, a confused expression on his face.

"I wanted to be angry with you for trying to betray my family. Wanted to be furious with you for trying to think that you could get away with spying on us. But every time I try to hold onto my rage, it slips away."

"It does?" I swallow.

He nods, "All I can think of is that man training his gun on you. If anything had happened to you…" He squeezes his eyes shut. "I wouldn't have been able to live with myself. It seems you have turned me into an emo version of myself, after all."

"And that's bad?"

"It's… different," he blows out a breath, "and painful. It's like ripping off a bandage and being exposed to the elements, like removing my blindfold and seeing the colors for the first time."

"Welcome to the real world," I chuckle, "it's messy and distressing and gut-wrenching and—"

"Satisfying," he says softly. "It makes me realize how much I missed out on all these years. And I have you to thank for it."

"Or be upset with," I murmur. "Don't get your hopes too high; the world is an unforgiving place, Christian, full of surprises. You never know what you might find around the next corner."

46

Christian

Her words stay with me. What did she mean by that? Was that a warning? Or was she simply looking out for me?

I follow my wife as she walks over to speak with Theresa. We'd finally left our room and made it down to the garden to meet our guests. Yes, I bought this home for her. Yes, I am officially pussy-whipped, for I can't keep my gaze off of her. She laughs at something that Theresa says, and her face lights up. Her skin is flushed from our love-making—hold on, did I just say love-making? Yep, definitely pussy-whipped—her whiskey eyes glow, and her thick hair flows about her shoulders. Her dress clings to her curves, and only I know that she is not wearing any panties. She pushes her hair back from her face to reveal the creamy curve of her throat. I can make out the faint imprint on her skin where her shoulder meets her throat—where I had marked her. Where I had sunk my teeth into her skin as I had thrust into her from behind. As I had made her mine. Mine to possess. Mine to own, mine to pleasure and cherish and shower with every happiness.

Is it really possible that I could look forward to a future with her? To a life that would be filled with ups and downs, considering how she always stands up to me, but one where I could possibly be happy? Happy… A strange word. Not one I thought could ever feature in my vocabulary, but which seems so within reach now.

I take a step forward when she and Theresa walk toward the edge of the gathering. They are talking in earnest now. Wonder what they are discussing? Doesn't matter. I want to be with her, want her attention on me and no one else. I move toward her when something brushes against my leg. I glance down to find Karma's cat, Andy, rubbing against my pants. I stare at the beast; what the hell? Wives and kittens. Now, all that's needed is children to run around screaming, and the tableau of how much the Sovrano brothers have changed would be complete.

Michael reaches down to pluck Andy up by the scruff of his neck. He cuddles the cat—he actually places the cat on his shoulder and scratches behind the animal's ears... Because, apparently, all of us Mafiosos are quickly losing our hearts and our minds and becoming shadows of ourselves.

Michael jerks his chin in my direction. "Don't look so surprised, *fratellino*," he drawls. "It's what's in store for you too, you know."

"Hugging cats that shed on my custom-made jacket, you mean?"

"It could be worse," he offers, "you could be brushing off baby puke instead."

I pale. "I just got married. Do you mind? Can I enjoy my honeymoon, at least?"

"Enjoy the grace period." Sebastian appears next to me. "Soon you'll be caught up in the day-to-day humdrum of what a marriage is really about, and that's when the reality is going to sink in."

"You should talk; the man who's avoided relationships at all costs."

"I don't avoid them. I simply choose the ones I intend to be in."

"No pun intended." I snort. "If you call your disappearing at a certain time every week to keep your appointment with a certain someone a relationship—"

"It is," he smirks, "one in which we both know the score and don't expect anything beyond that from each other; it's a perfect relationship."

"Are we talking about Seb's mystery woman?" Massimo ambles up.

"Not so much of a mystery, apparently," Seb says wryly.

"Seb has a woman?" Luca walks up to stand next to Massimo. "Why haven't I heard of this before?"

"Perhaps, because you've been too busy with your exhibitionism?" Massimo chuckles.

"You sound jealous, *fratello*?" Luca drawls.

Massimo snorts, "The last thing I want to do is fuck women in front of the entire world."

"It's not the entire world, just those watching in the club. You should try it sometime; it does wonders for your staying strength."

"I don't need to be gawked at to perform," Massimo smirks, "and I'd rather keep my sexual proclivities to myself."

"So, you admit that you have certain proclivities?"

"I admit...nothing." Massimo grins.

"Aww, come on," Luca bumps his fist into Massimo's shoulder, "where's the fun in that? Don't act coy, brother. If you have something to share, you won't find a better audience."

"Fuck, no." Massimo raises his hands. "The last thing I want is to share my kink with my family."

"Aha," Seb rubs his hands together, "the quiet and strong Massimo admits to having kinks."

"I didn't say that," Massimo backtracks. "And why are we talking about our sexual preferences? This is supposed to be a reception to celebrate our brother's nuptials. Not exactly a place to spill our secrets."

"Damn, so you do have secrets." Michael smirks.

"As much as the next man." Massimo grimaces. "Speaking of, what are Nikolai and JJ doing at this event? Thought this was supposed to be a family gathering?"

"Considering JJ loaned us his guns, and Nikolai's timely intervention saved my life... Not to mention, they are our closest allies so," Michael shrugs, "it stands to reason they are part of our 'made' family now."

"So, you trust them?" I scowl.

"Enough to invite them to your wedding reception, yes." Michael holds my gaze. "Why? Is something worrying you?"

"What if the man who shot me was one of theirs?"

Michael drums his fingers on his chest. "Not that it's not a possibility, but given that I have promised them a big piece of business in return for their coming on as our partners, I'd say it's more improbable than not."

He places Andy down on the ground, and the cat ambles off into the bushes.

"So, who the hell else could have shot me?"

"Have you had any leads yet?"

"Just that," I hesitate, "she knew the man who shot me."

"*Cazzo!*" He growls, "So, she was behind the shooting—"

"She wasn't." I drag my fingers through my hair. "He threatened to kill her and her family if she didn't help him."

"Help him how?"

"By sharing information on us."

Michael's jaw hardens. "She shared information on us? If she did so... I am going to—"

"Relax," I grip his shoulder, "she didn't share anything with him. It's why he tracked her down and confronted her."

"I don't like this," Seb murmurs. "Why didn't she simply come to you with all this earlier?"

"Because—" I had threatened her in much the same way that the guy who shot me had. Not that I can reveal that... "Because," I draw myself up to my full height, "she didn't."

"And you are going to forgive her?" Seb scowls at me. "Not to mention, you married her."

"He loves her," Michael cuts him off. "He wants to protect her, regardless of whether she is completely loyal to him."

I glare at my older brother. I can't dispute what he said. Yet everything in me insists that she cannot betray me. Not after how she had felt in my arms. How she had responded to my ministrations, how she had stared into my eyes as I had taken her. How she had taken care of me, the fear and worry on her face when she'd seen me shot. How she'd stitched me up and saved my life...

And yet, not once, had she responded to my declaration of having fallen in love with her. It's almost as if she was too scared of saying it. Like she was sure that the stranger would attack us again.

I turn to glance in her direction and find her missing. Where the hell is she? I turn the other way, spot Karma talking to Nonna, Cassandra petting Andy; a little farther off, JJ and Nikolai are deep in conversation.

"He's married to her, that makes her one of us, but if she does something to betray us..." Michael arches his eyebrows.

"She won't." I square my shoulders. "Before that happens, I'll have gotten to the bottom of what happened at the lodge; this I promise, I—"

That's when a scream rips through the air.

47

Christian

"Aurora!" My heart slams into my rib cage. My pulse ratchets up. I race in the direction of the scream. Seb is hot on my heels, and my other brothers are behind him. I run through the bushes and burst into a clearing on the grounds of the property.

I see Aurora with her back turned to me. A man stands with his gun pointed at her; the lower half of his face is covered with a mask. It's the same man who shot me at the lodge. Theresa stands frozen in between them.

I slow down, and he turns to glance at me. That's when I notice his arm is in a sling. A fierce surge of satisfaction grips me. At least, I managed to shoot the bastard.

"Porca puttana!" Motherfucker! I curl my fingers into fists. The man glances in my direction. His blue eyes are so light, so pale, so familiar. For the first time, I take in his figure, his height, the breadth of his shoulders, the way he holds himself. He reminds me of someone, but who? I take a step forward, and he shakes his head, "I wouldn't do that if I were you."

I pause; next to me, Seb shuffles his weight from foot to foot. Massimo flanks me on my other side. Anger radiates off of him. I sense Michael, Luca, and Adrian behind me. None of them move. The tension in the air ratchets up.

Theresa draws in a shuddering breath, and the stranger jerks his gaze in her direction. He glares at her, and she pales. "D-don't hurt us," she pleads.

"Put your arms up," he growls at her.

"Excuse me?" She blinks.

"Put your arms up, or I'll shoot her." He waves his gun in Aurora's direction, and anger thuds at my temples. How dare he point a gun at her. How dare he threaten her? How dare he intimidate what's mine? My muscles tense, my stomach muscles knot, and I must make a noise, for he turns on me. "That goes for the rest of you, too; raise your hands."

I draw in a breath, then slowly do as he asks.

Next to me, Seb, then Massimo, follow suit.

"You too, Don Sovrano," he scowls at Michael, "do as I say."

I sense Michael hesitate, then he says, "I'll do as you ask; just don't hurt her."

"That's up to her husband, isn't it?"

"What the fuck do you want?" I growl. "Why are you here?"

"Not to attend your wedding," he says in a hard voice, "and it's too bad that I am going to have to make your wife a widow so soon, but—"

"No!" Aurora closes the distance between them until his gun is poised against her forehead. "Don't hurt him," she says in a low voice. "I'm the one who did not stick to my side of the bargain. I'm the one you should be punishing; not him."

"Bargain?" I stiffen.

"She didn't tell you about our bargain, eh?" The man laughs. "She didn't come clean to her new husband about how she wanted him killed."

Aurora inhales sharply. "You're lying," she says in a low voice. "Why are you lying to him?"

Around me, my brothers seem to turn to stone. Massimo's big shoulders flex. Seb curls his fingers into fists.

If I turn, I know I'll see similar reactions from the rest of my brothers too.

"What the hell is he talking about?" Michael asks in a low voice.

"Christian," she half-turns, so her face is in profile, "he's lying."

I glance between the two of them. It can't be true, can it? Aurora wouldn't want me killed. She isn't capable of such a thing. On the other hand, she does come from a Mafia background, so perhaps, there's a part of her that did want me gone? If I were in her place, wouldn't I have done something similar to protect myself?

I glare at the stranger. "I don't believe you," I say flatly.

His lips curve. "You poor devil, you... Being taken for a ride by a woman and not even being aware of it."

"Christian," she pleads, "it's not what it sounds like; you have to believe me."

"So they all say." The stranger rolls his shoulders. "Nothing changes the fact that she came to an arrangement with me."

"What did she want?" I clear my throat. Don't engage with him. He's only trying to provoke you into making a mistake. Fuck, if I don't know that, so why the hell am I encouraging him to speak? Why don't I shut him down? "What was it?" I snarl.

"Your life."

I stiffen; the anger pours off of my brothers. Their gazes hone in on her… On my wife…who has eyes only for me.

"Christian," she says in a low voice, "please, please give me a chance to explain what happened."

I want to do so. I want to tell her that it's okay. That I understand that she made a mistake. That it doesn't matter what negotiations she had made. That all of that is in the past. Now, the future, that's what I need to focus on.

"So you deny that you asked him to kill me?"

I don't dare look at her. If I do, I won't be able to go through with this. Do I want to go through with this? Why am I putting her through this? She's your wife, for fuck's sake. Can't you at least have this conversation in private? Why are you insulting her in front of everyone else?

"Do you?" I clear my throat, "Answer the question."

"I asked him to distract you. I told him I needed him to do something to get your attention off of me so I could escape from you."

I stiffen. "So you did come to an understanding with him?"

"Yes, but it's not what it seems, Christian."

"Oh?" I narrow my gaze on her. "I'm not sure I believe you, Aurora."

"What the fuck are you doing?" Massimo asks in a low voice.

"This is not the place for this conversation," Seb adds.

"Christian," Michael growls, "are you trying to get us all killed?"

No, just me. Why the hell does my heart feel like it is breaking in half. Why does my chest feel so heavy? I try to draw in a breath, and my lungs burn. "Aurora," I say through gritted teeth, "answer the fucking question, you—"

"Yes," she bursts out. "Yes, I did. What else was I supposed to do? You all but kidnapped me and held me captive and threatened to kill my family."

"I saved your life by doing that."

"Did you?" She swallows. "You're no better than…than him in what you did, and you know it."

Anger grips me; the band around my chest tightens. The blood pounds at my temples, and my vision tunnels. "You dare compare me to him?" I take a step forward, and that's when he swerves his gun in my direction.

Something… Someone moves in the shadows of the tree line beyond him. The glint of metal catches my attention. My gaze widens.

Something in my stance must alert the man in the mask because he swerves around, gun in hand, and fires.

The sound echoes through the trees, and a flock of birds takes off into the air, squawking. There's a returning c-r-a-c-k as the person in the shadow of the tree line returns fire. The stranger in the mask moves so fast that he blurs. He steps in front of Theresa, and his entire body seems to shudder. He stumbles back, raises his gun, and fires again. Then he collapses to the ground.

"Oh, my god," Theresa screams. She drops to her knees in front of the fallen stranger, even as Seb, Adrian, and Massimo race past her and in the direction of the man who had fired at us.

Aurora turns toward me; her features are pale, her eyes huge in her face. "Christian," she wrings her hands together, "Christian, I am so sorry."

I close the distance between us, then walk past her and toward the sobbing Theresa. I kneel down next to the stranger, take in the blood flowing from a wound at his temple.

I pull off his mask. My breath catches in my throat, and my head spins. My heart beats so fast in my chest that I'm sure it's going to break out of my ribcage.

"It can't be," I whisper. "No way. This is not possible."

48

Christian

Footsteps sound behind me. Michael draws abreast; he takes in the features of the man collapsed on the ground and draws in a breath.

"Che cazzo!" He breathes, "How is this possible?"

Theresa glances up between us. "He's bleeding out," she cries, "why are you not helping him? Why are you standing there and—"

She follows the direction of our gazes, takes in his features, and gasps. "No," she shakes her head, "no, no, no." She reaches out, her fingers splattered with his blood. "Xander?" she whispers. "Is that Xander?"

The man's eyeballs move behind his closed eyelids. He opens and shuts his mouth. Theresa leans in close and places her ear close to his lips.

"What is it?" she cries. "What are you trying to say?"

"I am… You are…" He lapses into silence again, and she pulls back.

"Help him!" She pulls off the scarf she has draped around her neck and pushes it into the wound on his head. "Oh, Xander, oh, my god, it's you, Xander; it's you."

"It's not Xander," Michael pulls out his phone and dials. "I saw Xander's body, and he was dead; I assure you. This… Whoever it is, is not Xander."

Xander. It's Xander. I stare into the features of a face that looks so similar to mine. The same thick dark hair as mine, that square jaw, those eyes which are now shut but which had looked so familiar; now I know why. Those shoulders, that height… No wonder, every time I had looked at him, a shiver had run down my spine. I had been looking at myself… No, someone like myself… Like Xander… It can't be Xander, can it? Is it really my twin, come back to life?

The scent of honeysuckle envelops me, then she brushes past me and races around to sink down on the other side of the fallen man. "Your jacket," she scowls up at me, "give me your jacket."

"What?" I blink. "This is not the time—"

"Fuck you," she snarls. "I have no interest in whatever twisted fantasy you are creating in your mind. I need your jacket to staunch the flow of blood."

"Oh." My neck heats. Shit, why didn't I think of that? I was staring down at the body of my twin—no, not my twin, a man who resembles my twin—and didn't even think to help him. Fuck, fuck, fuck.

I pull off my jacket, and pushing Theresa's hands out of the way, I press it against his head wound. Within seconds, the cloth is soaked in blood.

"Porca miseria," I groan, "he's losing too much blood."

"Where's the ambulance?" Theresa sobs. She leans over to cup his cheek. "Come back to me, Xander. I can't let you leave me again. I've got you back, and no way am I letting you out of my sight again. You can't leave me, you … you asshole. Don't you fucking leave me, Xan, you hear me?"

More footsteps sound, then Nonna and Karma reach us.

"What—? Who?" Nonna's voice seems to shake. And that is something. I've never seen this woman unsure, let alone this shaken. Guess that's what happens when your grandson, who you think you lost forever, seems to reappear from the grave.

"Nonna!" Karma screams. I turn to find Nonna swaying. Karma throws her arm around the woman to steady her. At the same time, Michael closes the distance between them and wraps his arm around the older woman.

"Mica," Nonna breathes, "is that … is that…"

"That's not Xander," Michael replies with hard finality.

Nonna can't take her gaze off of the fallen man; she opens and shuts her mouth, then leans heavily into Michael.

"Christian," Aurora snaps, "I need your attention here."

I turn my gaze back to her. My wife's features are composed. Any trace of the earlier conflict on her face has been replaced by a quiet confidence. She is Dr. Aurora, the woman who cannot bear to see anyone else in pain, the one who is focused on saving lives… Everyone's, except mine, apparently.

"Why?" I growl at her, "Why did you do that?"

"Really, you're doing this now?" she says without taking her gaze off of Xander's—not Xander's—the stranger's face.

"Now is as good a time as any."

"A man's life is in danger... Potentially, your twin's life."

"My twin is dead," I say through gritted teeth. "This man is not my brother."

She draws in a breath, "I was at my wit's end, Christian. I felt trapped, like I had no one to turn to."

"You could have come to me. Why didn't you tell me all of this earlier, Aurora. Don't you trust me?"

"I ... I do," she swallows, "but I was worried that if I told you about the deal I'd struck with him, you'd hate me."

"What's stopping me from hating you now?" I straighten myself to my full height. "Goddammit, Aurora, you are a doctor. You took the hippocratic oath, and you judged me for what I've done, yet you didn't think twice about asking this guy to kill me?"

She winces. "It's not like that, Christian. I told you, I didn't ask him to kill you. If anything, I asked him not to hurt you. I-I just asked him to distract you so I could escape from you."

"So, you did want to escape me?"

"I did, but not anymore." She glances away, then back at me. "At that time, though, I wasn't thinking straight when I spoke to him. I was under so much pressure, from you, from him." She shakes her head. "I just wanted a way out." She glances to the side. "Also, when I spoke to him, I hadn't fallen for you yet."

"Do you expect me to believe that?" I sneer.

"No. Yes." She glances away then back at me. "I mean, initially, of course, I agreed to marry you to protect my family, not just from him but also from you, but somewhere along the way, I developed feelings for you."

"Yet, you continued to give him information?"

"No, I didn't," she pleads. "I didn't tell him anything of consequence. I just strung him along."

"The way you strung me along by pretending to care for me?"

"No," she shakes her head, "I was—am—emotionally involved with you, Christian. I have feelings for you. I... " she closes her eyes, "I love you."

"Fuck that," I snap. "You lied to me all this time. You knowingly put the lives of my entire family at risk."

"I am so sorry." She bites down on her lower lip, and damn it, despite the fact that my twin—no, not my twin, but a man who looks like my twin—is possibly dying right now... Despite the fact that she has put my life in danger, that thanks to her, the safety of my entire clan has been compromised... Despite all of that, I can't stop my body from reacting to the inherent sexuality in that gesture.

"Fuck," I growl, "fucking fuck," just as the siren of the ambulance sounds in the distance. "This can't go on."

"What?" She glances up at me. "What do you mean?"

"You, me, this marriage—it's over."

49

Christian

I watch as the paramedics strap the stranger to the stretcher and load him into the ambulance.

One of the men turns to Aurora, "Are you going to ride with us?"

She blinks, "I—"

"I am." Theresa rushes forward. "Please, can I go with him? Please, Aurora?"

Aurora nods, and she scrambles up and into the ambulance. The door shuts behind them, and the ambulance pulls away.

"Michael, take me to the hospital," Nonna orders. "I want to be there when he wakes up."

"Of course," Michael responds.

"I am coming with the both of you," Karma adds.

The three of them head off for his car just as Massimo, Seb, and Adrian return. "We couldn't find the shooter," Massimo growls.

"Asshole took off in his car." Seb drags his fingers through his hair.

"Couldn't even get a look at his face," Adrian blows out a breath. "*Cazzo*, who the hell would break in, knowing the entire Sovrano family was here, and try to shoot at us? Unless..."

"Unless he was trying to shoot at Christian's triplet?" Michael murmurs.

"Not one of my men," JJ walks over to us, "if that's what you are thinking."

"And you know I wouldn't do that," Nikolai adds as he draws abreast. "Though, whoever did it got through your security."

Antonio approaches from the other end of the clearing; he's dragging a man by the collar. "I found him trying to escape, boss." He scowls at his pale-faced prisoner. "He confessed to opening the gates to the grounds and admitting the man who shot at us."

I close the distance to the man and glare down at him. "Is that right; did you betray us?"

"I … I'm sorry," he sputters. "I … I was stupid; he said he was a friend and wanted to play a friendly wedding prank."

"And you believed him?"

"He paid me." He glances away. "I am sorry. I know it was wrong; I know I shouldn't have done it, but—"

"But you did it anyway. What's your name?" I growl.

"Marcello," he replies. "Please, Consigliere, don't hurt me; I have a grand-mother who depends on me."

"Why is it that none of you think through the consequences before you act?"

"I … I … I am sorry," he whispers.

"That won't make up for the grief you caused us."

I glance at Massimo, who pulls out his gun. He hands it over and I press the barrel against the man's temple.

"Please don't hurt me, please don't," he whimpers.

"You should have thought of that before you betrayed us." I tighten my finger on the trigger.

"Don't, Christian." Aurora pleads with me. "Please, don't do this."

"So, it's okay for you to want to kill me, but if I want to kill someone to protect my family, that's wrong?"

"Oh my god! How many times must I tell you? I didn't want you killed," she cries out. "But that's beside the point. You don't want to kill him, either Christian."

"Don't tell me what to do."

She swallows. "I am begging you, don't."

I hesitate, then lower the gun. "Take him away," I order Antonio. "I'll deal with him later."

Antonio turns and drags the man along with him. I hold out the gun to Massimo, and he slides it back into his waistband.

I turn to her, "It's time for you to leave as well."

"What?" She opens her eyes. "No, don't say that."

"Be grateful I am letting you leave with your life."

"Christian, please, let's talk this through. You know you don't want to do this."

"A-n-d, there you go again, professing to know what I want to do." I drum my fingers on my chest.

"I do know what you want," she swallows, "I am your wife."

"A fake wife. A sham wedding." I raise my shoulder. "None of it counts for anything."

"Hold on, brother," Seb cautions me, "think this one through, will you?"

"Mind your own business, will you?"

"You just married her. Surely, it's worth the two of you taking this somewhere private where you can discuss things," Massimo adds.

"There's nothing to discuss," I drawl, "my mind is made up."

"You are already married," Adrian reminds me. "You can't just decide now that you don't want to be married."

"Watch me." I yawn.

I turn and begin to walk away from them.

For a second, there's silence, then footsteps sound behind me. "Christian, stop!" Aurora runs to catch up with me. "Please, Christian, just give me a few minutes of your time."

"Not possible." I increase my pace, so she has to jog to keep up with me.

"Don't throw away what we have built so far."

"We've built nothing of consequence. Oh, wait," I raise my forefinger, "guess we made some memories, and even that doesn't count for anything."

"You don't mean it," she gasps as tears stream down her face, "I don't believe you are as callous as you make yourself out to be."

"Better believe it." I head down the driveway to where my vehicle is parked. The same one in which I had driven her here. The one in which I had held her hand and barely been able to keep my gaze off her radiant face. In which we had laughed as I had opened the door, hauled her up in my arms bridal style, and swept her over the threshold and up the stairs to our bedroom. Our bedroom. Our home. The house I had bought for her, for us...for the future… That I can no longer see with her. Not after what she did.

I reach the car, wrench the door open on the driver's side, and slide in.

"Christian, please—"

I slam the door in her face and cut her off.

She bends forward to look in the window, her chest heaving, her hair undone from the swept-up style she had worn it in earlier. Blood taints her bodice and is splashed across her neck. My twin's—no, the stranger who looks like my twin's —blood. The one to whom I must go now and figure out who the hell he is. That is more important than... Listening to the excuses that she's, no doubt, preparing to fling in my face.

She bangs on the window, but I stare ahead. I am aware of tears flowing down her cheeks, of her saying something, but I don't want to hear it. Not now. Not when I need to figure out the truth behind the appearance of the man who looks like my twin brother. I start the ignition, then press down on the accelerator so the car leaps forward. I drive toward the gates, hitting the remote on the dash so it opens. As I pull out of the driveway, I raise my gaze to the rearview mirror. My last sight is of her...in her wedding gown...staring after me. Then, I turn the corner, and she disappears from sight.

"Fuck, fuck, fuck!" I apply the brakes and screech to a halt, then slam my fists into the steering wheel, "The fuck is wrong with me?"

Half an hour later, I park the car near the hospital where the injured stranger has been taken. I walk into the reception and am directed to the first floor. I walk down the corridor to the private room where the rest of the family is waiting.

"Christian," Nonna rises to her feet as soon as I enter the room. "Oh, god, Christian." She walks over to me, her features pale, dark circles under her eyes highlighting the crow's feet. Her chin trembles as she reaches me. "I am so glad you are here, *nipotino mio*," she murmurs.

She holds out her hand, and I grip it. Then, I wrap my arm around her shoulder and pull her close. She trembles, and for a second, I am struck by how fragile she feels. I pull back and gently peer into her face, "Is there any news?"

"No," she shakes her head.

"They took him into surgery," Michael replies from the window.

"They haven't told us anything yet." Theresa sniffs. "I asked them if he was going to be okay, but they didn't reply."

"They were too busy rushing him into the operating theater," Karma says gently.

"I know," Theresa wrings her fingers together, "and they were right to do so. I just wish someone would tell me if he's going to be okay." She squeezes her eyes shut, "He's going to be okay, isn't he?"

Karma glances at Michael, who shakes his head. She pulls the other woman close, and Theresa buries her head in Karma's shoulder.

"Where's your wife?" Nonna asks, glancing behind me. "Why isn't she with you?"

"She's not with me anymore," I state blandly.

"What do you mean 'not with you'?" Nonna searches my features. "What have you done, Christian?" she exclaims. "Did you... " she shakes her head, "Surely, you can't be that stupid, can you?"

"She had planned to have me killed, Nonna," I pull away from her, "I am going to annul the marriage."

"Annulment." She throws up her hands, "What is wrong with you young people? You get married at the drop of a hat, then think you can undo the wedding as quickly?"

"It was because of her that I got shot."

"And you deserved it," Nonna snaps.

"What?" I stare, "How can you say that?"

"Holding her captive, coercing her to marry you, leaving her no choice but to say yes—"

"She wanted to get married to me," I insist.

"Ha," she snorts, "and you know that, how?"

"I know," I set my jaw.

"You mean," she plants her hand on her hips, "all of you think you are god's gift to women. You think just because you are mafioso and carry guns, your dick is the answer to everything."

"Nonna," I gape, "what are you talking about?"

Michael glances between us. He looks like he's about to intervene, then seems to change his mind. I glare at him. Traitor. He's the one who kidnapped Karma and started this entire sequence of events rolling, and now he has the nerve to sit there and watch this shitstorm unfold?

"Porca puttana! You are being unreasonable, Nonna," I complain.

"You dare accuse me of being unreasonable when you're the one acting like a...a *coglione?"* She jabs her forefinger in my chest.

"Ow," I scowl, "that hurt."

"Good, it should." She glares at me, "You broke that poor girl's heart, no doubt, by giving her this cock-and-bull story about getting the marriage annulled, I assume."

"I—uh, haven't mentioned any such thing to her yet."

"Good," she sniffs, "then you can go back and apologize to her."

"No," I set my jaw.

"Christiano Roberto Dominico Sovrano," Nonna pulls herself up to her full height, "are you going tell your wife that you are sorry and make-up with her, or not?"

"Not," I fold my arms across my chest, "I am sorry, Nonna, but on this, I am not changing my mind."

She glowers at me, then all of the color seems to leach from her face. She puts her hand to her forehead and groans, "I... I don't think I am feeling very well."

"Nonna!" I exclaim as I step toward her.

"Don't you touch me," she scowls, "not until you have put right the mess you have created."

She turns to Michael and holds out her hand. "Mica," she trembles, "please, help me to a seat; I think my poor heart is just about going to give out after all the stress that this *stronzo* has put me through."

"Nonna," I protest, "why is it that Mica is always in your good graces, and I have to work doubly hard to get a single word of praise from you?"

"Because he's smart; he knew, when he found Karma, that he couldn't let her get away. Unlike you…" She sways again, and this time, Michael crosses over to her and wraps his arm about her shoulder. "You," she raises her nose in the air, "are clearly, completely, utterly even more stupido than I thought."

"Me? I'm stupid?" I scowl as Michael guides her to an armchair.

Karma walks to the water cooler in the corner and fetches her a glass of water.

"Thank you, dear," Nonna murmurs. "At least, I can count on the two of you to keep your head in these situations."

Karma and Michael exchange looks over her head.

"You take it easy, Nonna," Michael pats her shoulder.

"I will, once I know that Xander is going to be okay," Nonna says in a tired voice. Is she actually feeling unwell, or is the old bat acting up? My Nonna is not only smart, but she is also a consummate actress. She's been known to go to any length to get her way. But she can't be playacting now, can she? She really does look completely worn-out and about to faint.

On cue, Theresa begins to weep again, "How can he look so much like my Xan. He is Xander, isn't he?" She wails. "Please, please, tell me it is Xander and that he is going to be okay?"

"Can someone tell the girl to shut up?" Nonna glances at Karma, "Please?"

Karma straightens, then walks over to Theresa; she sits down next to her, and the two women speak in hushed whispers.

Just then, the door is pushed open and Massimo, Seb, and Luca walk in. Antonio takes his position outside the door as it swings shut.

"Where is she?" Nonna asks.

The men look at each other, then Seb jerks his chin, "After he left, she stood there in the driveway until I helped her back into the house. She packed up her things and asked me to book her on the next flight to London."

"London?" I scowl, "Why is she going back to London?"

"I doubt you have the right to ask that question after how you treated her," Massimo drawls.

I shoot him a sideways glance, then turn my attention back to Seb, "Has she already left?"

"Adrian's driving her to the airport."

"Right." I hunch my shoulders. This is good; this is exactly what I wanted. So, why does everything in my body insist that this is wrong? Why does my chest hurt; why is my stomach tied up in knots? I shuffle my feet, glance about the room to find every single person is studying me. "What?" I scowl, "What do you want me to do?"

"Go after her, you *testa di cazzo*," Seb snaps.

"Get her back, *pezza di merda*," Massimo growls.

I open my mouth to protest, and that's when the doctor walks into the waiting room.

50

———————

Christian

"How is he?" Theresa jumps to her feet and races over to him, "Is he going to be okay? Please, tell me he's going to be okay?"

The doctor glances down at her, then surveys the rest of us. His features brighten, "The operation was successful."

"Thank *Santa Maria*," Nonna raises her gaze skyward.

"But," the doctor glances around the room, "he is not yet out of danger. The bullet did not hit anything vital, but it's a serious head wound and he experienced significant blood loss. We had to induce coma to control the intracranial pressure."

"Intracranial? What does that mean?" Theresa asks.

"I mean we had to induce coma to control the pressure inside his brain."

"How long will he be this way?" Nonna enquires.

"Until the swelling in his brain goes down," the doctor replies.

"But he is going to be okay?" Theresa wrings her hands.

"It's too early to tell, signorina," the doctor says gently.

"But you just said that the operation was successful," she says in a hard voice, "so that means he is going to recover, isn't he?"

"That's definitely what we hope for," he agrees.

"Can I see him?"

The doctor shakes his head, "Not yet. Not until his condition has stabilized."

"So, what… what can I do meanwhile?"

"Pray," the doctor smiles a little, "even we surgeons believe in the power of the One above to deliver miracles. Now, if you'll excuse me." Turning, he leaves.

He is going to be okay; he has to be okay. Has to. The breath I had not been aware I was holding wheezes out. My arms and legs tremble. I walk over to the nearest chair and collapse into it.

"You okay, *fratello*?" Seb grips my shoulder.

Massimo flanks me on the other side as I bury my head in my hands.

No, I am not okay. How can I be okay when the soul-brother I thought I had lost forever seems to have resurrected from the dead? He's not my twin; he can't be my twin. I saw Xander dead and in his coffin with my own eyes. I buried him. I felt the emptiness in the space where I had always felt him. Yeah, I know woo-woo stuff…but it's the only way to explain it. It's not like we had the kind of connection where if one twin fell sick, the other also fell ill, or if one was hurt, the other felt it. It had always been more discrete. Something reserved for bigger life events.

Like when I had known that my father was going to hurt him, and I had felt Xander's fear and his utter helplessness, and I had stepped in to save him. I had taken the physical abuse, and later, the emotional abuse that my father had heaped on me. Something I have never regretted.

Or the time when Xander had been confused and in so much conflict over whether he had loved Theresa or not. He had pondered about it for days until I could literally hear him thinking, mulling it over and over in his head. And I hadn't been able to stand it and had ultimately gone to him and asked him what had been bothering him. He hadn't been completely honest with me, even then, and I had known it, but I hadn't pushed it. Maybe I should have. Maybe I should have helped him think it through and resolve his feelings. Maybe then he would still be alive. Maybe he still is alive?

No, he isn't. Xander would sooner cut off a hand than pick up a gun. The man looks a lot like Xander, but he is not Xander; he can't be. So, the question is, who is he?

"Who is he?" I ask softly.

"Who's who?" Seb enquires.

Massimo shoots me a worried look. "You okay, brother?" he rumbles as I push myself up to my feet.

"Who is he?" I ask loudly enough that the noise in the room dies down. One by one, the rest of my brothers, as well as Karma and Theresa, turn to glance at me. Everyone, except Nonna, who focuses her attention on the window.

"What are you talking about?" Michael frowns.

"Oh, she knows what I am talking about, don't you?" I focus on putting one foot in front of the other as I approach Nonna. "Tell us who he is."

"I don't know what you are talking about," she laughs.

"Oh, you know what I am talking about, all right." I pause in front of her, "You know who he is, don't you?"

"Christian," Michael warns me, "don't talk to Nonna like that."

"And why not, considering she's been keeping a secret from all of us?"

"Me?" She widens her gaze, "You think I am keeping a secret?" She glances around the crowd of assembled faces, "Do any of you think I'd really keep anything from you?"

The silence stretches, then Seb mutters, "If it served your purposes, then yes, I think you would."

The others nod.

Nonna seems taken aback, then she tightens her lips, "Good to know that's what you all actually think about me. After everything I have sacrificed for this family…" she huffs.

"I know, you have," I force my muscles to relax, "and that is exactly why I think that if it would help the family, you would have kept the presence of my triplet a secret."

"Triplet?" Luca exclaims. "Did you say, triplet?"

The others stay quiet. One look at Nonna's face, and I know I am right. "Well," I ask her, "are you going to deny it?"

She opens her mouth and shuts it, then she glances around the room once again. She looks away, then back at me. "There are reasons for what happened then," she murmurs.

I draw in a breath, "So I was right?" I ball my fists at my sides. "He is my triplet?"

"You have to understand, it was the only way to arrive at some kind of settlement within the family."

"Settlement?" I scowl, "What are you talking about?"

"Sit down, will you?" She turns to Michael, "Please, sit down and hear me out, all of you," she looks at each of my brothers in turn. "please?" She turns to me, "Give me a chance to explain."

It's exactly what my Flower had asked of me, and I had refused her. Will I do the same to Nonna now?

I turn to leave, but Seb grasps my shoulder. "Just hear her out, will you?" he murmurs.

"And why should I do that? She's hidden something so big…something life-changing, from all of us, but especially me. Do you understand what it means to realize that you had a soul-brother, a life-mirror to yours alive but having never had the chance to meet him until now?"

"I know how it is to have a brother I never knew about." He tilts his head, "I can't claim to understand how it is to have lost a twin only to find a triplet, but I know how it is to lose a brother I loved, and to find I may have a chance of gaining back another," he peers into my face, "so trust me when I say that you want to listen to this or you'll regret it forever."

I hesitate, then nod. "Okay," I pivot and face Nonna, "You have five minutes to tell me what happened, and if you hide anything from me this time—"

"I won't," she raises a hand, "I promise. Will you have a seat now?"

51

Christian

I gaze through the glass partition that separates me from my triplet. After listening to Nonna, I had walked out of the waiting room and run into the doctor who'd operated on my brother. He'd ushered me into the room adjoining the recovery room, where the man who looks very much like Xander lays on a bed.

His eyes are shut, his skin is pale, and the white sheets of the bed he lays on are a stark contrast to the darkness of his hair. I take in his features again; that familiar high forehead, the patrician nose, the square jaw... All so similar to Xander, and yet, not. For one, while Xander was more on the slender side, this man is far more bulked up. Also, something about the shape of his face is a little different. Like he's Xander, but with subtle changes woven into his features. He's Xander, but not, for my twin is dead. He's never coming back, and this...

This man will never take his place. Whoever he is... He is a stranger. One who tried to kill me... So, why the hell did he step in front of Theresa to protect her? I am not sure. I hear a sniff and turn to find her standing next to me.

"He's going to wake up," she says with quiet determination as she presses her palm into the glass partition, "he has to wake up." Her gaze burns with an inner light that borders on the verge of obsession. Uh-oh.

"Theresa." I touch her shoulder, and she blinks as if coming out of a daze. She inclines her head in my direction without taking her gaze off of the unconscious figure.

"Theresa?"

"Hmm?"

"You know he's not Xander, right?"

"What?" She whips her head around in my direction. "Of course, he is Xander; why would you say that he isn't?"

"But he isn't, Theresa," I say gently. "Xander's dead, Theresa, he—"

"Don't say that," she whispers fiercely. "Don't talk about him as if he's gone because he's not." She jerks her chin in the direction of the sleeping figure. "He's sleeping right there; can't you see?"

I blow out a breath. This is going to be so much more complicated than I had anticipated. When he wakes up—and he is going to wake up—he is going to be faced with people who want him to take Xander's place... And that is not a comfortable situation. Just having a twin and often being mistaken for him becomes tiresome very quickly. And this man, whoever he is, is no doubt going to be expected to pick up from where Xander left off. Hell, much as I see him very much as a stranger and don't want to think of him as Xander, every time I look at him, I can't help but see Xander.

I roll my shoulders. "He's not Xander, Theresa; can't you see that?"

"Yes, I can. Of course, I can." She whips her head around in my direction. "You think I'm delusional to see Xander in this...this stranger who took a bullet for me, don't you?"

"I..." I hold my hands up, "I am only saying the truth."

"The truth is that despite loving your wife and marrying her, at the first sign of conflict, you lost your balls and decided to turn your back on her."

"Now hold on," I growl, "you don't know what went on between me and Aurora."

"Oh yeah?" She tosses her hair over her shoulder. "I know that she loves you and that you adore her. When you guys are in the same room together, you can't take your gaze off of her and yet... You ran from her. You're still running from her; from the chance of finding true love, the kind that I thought I could have with Xander. And you?" She looks me up and down. "Your wife is still here, and yet you waste time over stupid semantics, and waste the opportunity you've been given. If only you were in my shoes, you'd know just how much of an ass you're being right now."

"Excuse me?" I narrow my gaze on her. "You're distraught. I understand that you're not thinking clearly."

"Oh, I am thinking much more clearly than you." She turns back to stare at the unconscious man on the bed. "I know that my only chance of happiness lies with this…this stranger. Someone who I don't know, and yet, who I feel a connection with. Someone who didn't know me, and who put his life on the line for me. Someone who has the face of the love of my life and with whom I've been given a second chance. One I don't intend to waste... Unlike you."

"What are you trying to say?" I scowl.

"What she means is, what are you still doing here, Christian?" Seb stalks over to join us.

"What do you mean?" I shoot him a sideways glance. "I'm waiting for him to recover consciousness."

"Which may not be for a while."

"So?" I shove my hands in my pockets. Gesù Cristo, does everyone in this family have it in for me, or what?

"So," he snorts, "do you want me to spell it out for you?"

"No idea what you mean." I hunch my shoulders.

"*Cazzo*, you still here, *stronzo*?" Massimo prowls over to stand behind me.

"Why does everyone keep saying that?"

"Because everyone can see the truth, except you." Luca wanders over to flank Massimo.

"The fuck is going on?" I turn to glance between my brothers. "Can't a man just get some space to do… Whatever it is I'm doing?"

"No." Michael leans his shoulder against the frame of the doorway.

"Not you too." I scowl at him. "Don't you have a Mafia empire to run or something?"

"Not when one of my brothers is lying wounded, and the other is hurting so much, he's acting like a complete *carogna*."

He uses the word that implies I'm lower than rotted meat, and anger sluices through my veins.

"Fuck off, Michael," I growl. "You may be Don, but that doesn't give you permission to interfere in my personal life."

Theresa glances between us. "I'm going to hunt down the doctor and badger him until he allows me into Xander's room to see him. If I hold his hand, I'm sure he will awaken faster; I know he will." She spins around, pushes past the men, and rushes out of the room.

"Damn," I shake my head, "that woman is sure doing an incredible job of fooling herself."

"Because she's not afraid to grab at her chance for happiness with both hands?"

"You mean fool herself into believing that man lying in there is her future, when it's more likely he's going to wake up and hate her… And all of us, probably."

"I know what Nonna said earlier must have come as a shock," Luca offers.

"Shock?" I laugh. "Which part are you talking about? The fact that the woman I thought was my mother isn't really my mother, or that Nonna and our father decided to split the three of us when we were born, so my blood mother could leave with my triplet?"

"Christian," Massimo grips my shoulder, "it doesn't make you less of our brother."

I squeeze my fingers into fists. Of course, I know that. Just because my brothers are my half-brothers does not change anything… Except that my entire life to-date has been very much a lie. "Fuck," I shake my head, "this entire conversation is doing my head in."

"I understand…" Seb's lips twist. "It hasn't been easy living with the fact that I'm not a legitimate part of the family."

"Being a legitimate son isn't all that it's cut out to be either," Luca snorts.

Silence descends on the space. The tension in the air ratchets up. I glance over to find Michael scowling at Luca.

"You chose your way to make your disapproval known to the world," Michael snaps, referring to how Luca had helped Karma escape when she had run from Michael. This was before the two had gotten back together and realized they were in love and wanted to spend their lives together. And isn't that what I want too? So why did I let go of her? Why didn't I allow myself to listen to her? To forgive her for her mistakes?

"And I am sorry for what I did. I apologized to you, didn't I?" Luca offers.

"And you were lucky I chose to look past your transgressions." Michael scowls. The two glare at each other, then Michael blows out a breath, "Not here to dwell over the past, brother."

Luca jerks his chin, "Me neither." He walks over to Michael and holds out his hand, "We good?"

Michael grips his hand. "For now." The two shake, then Luca turns toward me and both of them glare at me with twin expressions of frustration.

"What?" I lean forward on the balls of my feet. "If you guys have something to say, then you better spit it out."

Michael pushes off of the door and stalks over to me. "It's been a lot to take in, but it doesn't change the fact that you would be an idiot if you let her walk away, and if there's one thing I can say about you, Christian, you are the most level-headed man I know. Perhaps, the most rational. It's why I made you the consigliere. It's why I know you are going to the airport, and you are going to stop her."

"I am?" I glance around at the faces of my brothers. "I am."

52

———————

Aurora

Can this day get any worse? I missed the flight to London. Of course, I did. I should be en-route to my honeymoon. Instead, I'm wearing worn jeans, my old leather jacket, and clutching my suitcase, which I packed hurriedly with the clothes I had bought with my own money before I met Christian. I don't miss the material benefits of being with him. I'm definitely happy to be free and able to do what I want. Hell, it's a miracle that the Sovranos let me leave at all. After everything I had confessed to, why Christian hadn't decided to mete out my punishment in time-honored Mafia tradition, I'm not sure. Perhaps, it's because he was too occupied with finding out about the stranger who looks like Xander and shot at him?

Xander and Christian hadn't been identical twins, but there were a lot of similarities between their features. And the man who'd taken the bullet meant for Theresa... He definitely resembled Xander more than Christian. All this time, I had been talking to him, and I had never asked him to take off his mask. Not that he would have done so if I had. Hell, the few times we had met, I had been too scared to even meet his eyes. We had spoken over the phone most of the time, and his voice didn't sound anything like Christian's, that much I know.

It had been a spur-of-the-moment decision to ask his help to escape from

Christian. Seems while I had tried to leave the Mafia behind, when push came to shove, I had returned to my roots. I hadn't hesitated to ask the stranger for help.

When I had realized I was falling for Christian, I had regretted it at once, but I didn't take back my words. And later, I had hoped that he'd forgotten about it. Which is silly because, why would he? Wishful thinking aside, it doesn't forgive the fact that I never went back to him and told him that the deal was off. I had been too terrified about trying to contact the stranger. Too worried that it would draw his attention back to me and my family.

And I should have warned Christian, but then, a part of me had been so pissed off with him. With how he'd treated me, how he'd made me his captive and forced himself into my bed... No...that last... I am equally to blame for that. I wanted him. I was attracted to him, almost from the moment I laid eyes on him. I'd known he was the kind of man who could make my darker fantasies come true. I had used him the same way that he had used me. So no, I can't hold him responsible for not wanting to listen to my explanations. Fact is, when I repeated to myself what my rationale was for what I'd done, it felt weak, even to me. I hunch my shoulders as I walk over to the airline inquiries counter.

When it's my turn, I ask to be put on the next flight to London.

"That will be tomorrow," the woman behind the desk tells me.

"Tomorrow?" I blow out a breath, "Isn't there a flight that leaves later today?"

"I'm sorry; they are fully booked."

I squeeze my eyes shut and force my shoulders to relax. It's going to be okay; it's going to be okay. I will live through this. I can get through this. If I could face all of those late nights studying, then interning at the ER to become a doctor, then surely, I can get through what feels like the worst day of my life so far. I blow out a breath. Something of my helplessness must show on my face because the airline employee gestures to the side. "Perhaps, you want to take a seat and wait. Sometimes, we have last-minute cancellations, so I can waitlist you on the last flight out. It's not guaranteed, but," she raises a shoulder, "if you really want to leave—"

"Oh, I do," I nod. "I'll be happy to wait." It's not like I have anywhere else to be, after all.

I shuffle over with my luggage and take a seat.

Half an hour later, I'm back on my feet. I walk over to the counter and tell her, "I'm going to walk around the airport and stretch my legs. I'll be back soon."

She waves me off, and I haul my bag over my shoulder as I wheel my suitcase behind me. I wander over to a shop, grab a book, and look at its cover. A romance novel, of course, where the hero and heroine get their Happily Ever

After. And what about me? Can I hope to get my own HEA? Or am I going to spend the rest of my life moping over the man who broke my heart? The man who was my husband for less than a day.

I play with the ring on my hand; I should take it off, but damn, its weight feels good. It feels right. The entire ceremony had been like a dream. And the way he had looked at me when I had walked down the aisle toward him. Like I was his everything. Like I was his. Like he couldn't live without me...and I couldn't... I can't be without him.

The pressure behind my eyes builds. Don't you dare cry. Not here; not in front of everyone. Not even when you are alone. You deserve what happened; you should have worn your big girl panties and called the stranger back and told him that the deal was off. You should have confessed everything to Christian and asked for his help.

Instead, I had lost my nerve. I had acted foolishly, had closed my eyes, and tried to pretend that the entire deal with the stranger didn't exist, and that he couldn't hurt Christian... And now, I must pay the price. The tears squeeze out of the corners of my eyes. I try to wipe them away, but they keep coming. Damn it, this is not good. Don't break down, not here. Please, not like this.

My shoulders shudder. I turn my head to the side and brush my cheek over my shoulder. I place the book back on the shelf, then head out of the shop and back toward my seat near the airline desk.

That's when I hear the commotion and glance up to find a tall, broad man at the desk. His shoulders stretch his shirt in a way that sets off a shiver down my spine. I know that build, the way his biceps strain his shirt sleeves, how the edges of his dark hair brush against his collar, how he plants his hands on his hips, thrusts his chin forward, and takes an aggressive stance.

I edge closer in time to hear him ask, "Are you sure that you haven't seen her? She's tiny, comes only to the level of my chest, has thick dark hair that falls in clouds about her shoulders. She has a gorgeous face, high cheekbones, the most delectable lips you have ever seen on a woman, and whiskey-colored eyes."

Is that me he's describing? Is that how he sees me? Does he really think my lips are delectable? I stare at the back of his beautiful head. What the hell is Christian doing here anyway?

"When she's angry, you can see the golden sparks in their depths, and they resemble pools of champagne then." Christian's voice softens. "I'm trying to find out if she was on the flight to London."

"I'm sorry, sir. I don't know who you're talking about," the woman replies, "and even if I did, I wouldn't be able to give out that kind of information."

"Are you sure you haven't seen her?"

"I'm sorry, sir, but I really have no idea who you are referring to."

"Please, are you sure that you can't help me? This is a life and death situation. She's my wife, you see, and she left before I could hear what she has to say, and now I may never be able to forgive myself."

The woman at the airline counter gives a long-suffering sigh. "Have you tried calling her phone?"

"Her phone?"

"Yes, sir. Surely, she has a phone, and you could call her to find out if she did make the flight?"

He seems to consider that, then pulls out his phone. "Thank you," he murmurs, then turns in my direction.

My heart begins to race. My pulse ratchets up. I should move toward him, tell him I'm here. Instead, I spin around and head back the way I came, just as my phone begins to vibrate in my handbag. Shit, I took my phone with me... Well, of course I did. It's the only means of communication I have at the moment. I pull out the phone, stare at the name on the screen, which reads Alphahole.

It continues to vibrate, and I stare at it while continuing to walk away from him. I stumble into someone else's luggage, and the phone drops to the ground. Shit, shit, shit.

I bend to pick up the phone, just as it stops vibrating. I pick it up, then jump when it begins to vibrate again. I stare at the screen, then drop the phone back in my handbag. I head toward the opposite side of the airport to the counter. I'm not sure where I'm going, but it doesn't matter. As long as I can get away from him, that's all that matters. Please, please don't let him notice me.

My phone starts vibrating again, and I ignore it. Yes, it's my fault that I'm in this situation. But he's also to blame. He couldn't give me a few minutes and hear what I had to say. He didn't even give me a chance to apologize before he took off in his car, telling me our marriage was over. Jerk. He didn't even turn to glance at me before he got into his big ass Ferrari and pulled away, literally leaving me eating his dust.

The phone continues to vibrate, damn it. I pull it out of my handbag, only it slips from my hand and falls to the floor. "Goddamn!" I bend to pick it up as a pair of custom-made Italian loafers comes into my line of sight. Oh, shit. I raise my gaze up the pair of legs in fitted slacks that mold to powerful thighs, and between them a tented crotch. No, no, no, don't look there; not now, not when you're trying to escape him. I grab my phone, straighten, then turn and begin to walk away.

"Aurora," he calls after me, "stop."

53

Aurora

Is he crazy? Of course, I'm not going to stop. The last thing I want is to see him, after that very public humiliation when he left me.

I increase my speed, and his footsteps keep pace. Oh, hell. He is going to catch up with me, and that's not what I want. I drag my suitcase behind me as I begin to run. His footsteps pound behind me and seem to get closer. My bag slides down my arm, and I yank it up and over my shoulder.

"Aurora, please wait; please give me a chance to explain myself."

Isn't that what I asked him, almost word-for-word? I should feel vindicated that I'm giving him some of the same treatment he gave me, so why does it all feel wrong? I dart down the corridor, swerving around a man with a suitcase, then past a family with the children engrossed on their tablets.

"Aurora! Flower, please stop!"

His voice sounds too close. Damn it, he's going to catch up with me, and I … I'm not ready to face him yet. Where can I hide? Where can I conceal myself so he won't find me? I glance around, and there… I spot the sign for the ladies' room, shoulder open the door, burst inside. I pause in front of the row of sinks, my breath coming in pants. I slap my handbag on the counter as a woman finishes washing her hands. She shoots me a curious look before she brushes past me and out the door. The door snicks shut, only to open again. Heavy footsteps sound, and I whip my head around to find Christian poised inside the doorway.

"Get out," I snarl. "This is the ladies' room."

He glances around the space to make sure it's empty, then turns and locks the door.

"Hey," I gape at him, "what the hell do you think you're doing?"

He merely walks over to stand behind me. I take in his reflection behind me in the mirror.

His hair is mussed up. Flecks of blood dot the front of his shirt. Other than that, he looks the same. Tall, broad, sex oozing from every pore. Damn it, it's not fair that at the end of this gone-to-shit day, I feel tired and faded while he still looks hot. And so damn edible. His chest rises and falls; his gaze narrows as he holds mine in the mirror. Those blue eyes grow cold as he glares at me. A shiver runs down my spine. Damn it, I'm not supposed to find him so hot when he's clearly pissed at me.

He folds his arms across his chest, and his biceps flex and stretch the fabric. The buttons of his shirt barely seem to be able to contain his muscled chest.

The silence stretches, and the tension in the air seems to rise with every second. I hold his gaze for a beat, another, then flick my eyes in the direction of the doorway.

"Don't even think about it," he says in a hard voice.

A ripple of anticipation shimmers over my skin. My nerve endings pop. Every last cell in my body seems to be alive and waiting, waiting for him to do something. For him to punish me for what I did. For him to show me who I belong to. For him to tell me he has forgiven me. That he has come for me because he loves me. Because he can't live without me.

"You defied me," he says in a casual tone. Oh god, that is not good. When he gets so quiet and tries to come across as unthreatening, that's when I know he's really angry with me.

I tip my chin up and force myself to meet his gaze again in the mirror. "I fail to see how you drew that conclusion, considering you're the one who told me to leave."

"And you conveniently didn't get on the previous flight out, I see."

"What's that supposed to mean?"

"You wanted me to come in search of you, to chase you through the airport, and corner you and—"

"And—?"

"And," his lips kick up, "fuck you, of course."

"How dare you," I say in a low voice. "You have some ego if you think that I missed my flight on purpose."

"Didn't you?" His smile widens. "Perhaps, it was your subconscious mind that wanted you to stay in the airport, so there was more of a chance for me to find you?"

"Fuck you," I spit out at him, and the asshole laughs.

"Good to see you haven't lost your spark, Flower."

"No thanks to you." I set my jaw. "After that stunt you pulled back at the house, I'm not sure what you want from me."

"Would you believe me if I said I was sorry?"

"You have a funny way of showing it."

"I admit that my ego gets in the way sometimes."

"Sometimes?" I snort. "And I'm still not hearing the apology, by the way."

"What if I show it to you instead?"

I bite the inside of my cheek. "Show it to me?" I narrow my gaze. "What do you mean?"

"My actions always speak louder than my words, Flower; surely, you know that by now?" He closes the distance between us, and the heat of his body envelops me.

"Stay ba-back."

My voice trembles; damn it. I shouldn't let him intimidate me like this.

"Stay away from me," I say in a firmer voice, "don't touch me."

"You don't tell me what to do. Have you forgotten that?"

"I may have let you dominate me in the bedroom, but that's where it stops."

"Is that right?" He chuckles, and the sound chafes across my skin. My belly flutters, my scalp tingles, and every part of me seems to be tuned into him. I watch as he steps closer, until his chest is flush with my back, his thighs cradle my hips, and that thick hardness between his legs pushes against my arse.

A shudder grips me, and I grip the edge of the sink even tighter.

He slides his hand around to cup my pussy through the fabric of my jeans.

"Oh, god," I squeeze my eyes shut, "oh, my fucking god!'

"Open your eyes," he commands, and I snap my eyelids open. I meet his gaze once again, and his eyes... They are burning into me with such intensity that goose bumps pop on my skin.

He pushes the hair at the nape of my neck to the side. I shiver. He bends, and without taking his gaze off of mine, he presses his lips to the curve where my shoulder meets my neck. It's so sweet, so not like the Christian I know that a moan bleeds from my lips. He digs his teeth into my skin, and I yelp. My pussy clenches. My toes curl. He drags his tongue across the bruised skin, and moisture beads my core.

"Christian, please," I whisper. "Please..." I want to tell him to stop, but I can't seem to form the words. He lowers the zipper on my jeans, then slips his fingers under my panties. He brushes across my swollen clit, and a whine bubbles up my throat.

"Fuck," he growls, "you are so wet, Flower." He peruses my features in the mirror as he shoves his fingers inside of me. My pussy clamps down instantly on his fingers, and his gaze seems to intensify. He moves his fingers in and out of me, and my entire body bucks. I throw my head back against his shoulder, even as a part of me wishes that I could resist him. But I can't. God help me, but I tried; all I have to do is see him, scent him, feel his skin against mine, and all thought seems to drain from my head. Damn it, I cannot give in to him like this, not after the way he treated me.

"Christian," I burst out, "don't. Please, don't."

He pauses. "You want me to stop?"

I squeeze my eyes shut, then nod.

"Look me in the eyes and tell me that you want me to leave, and I will."

I draw in a breath, force my eyelids open, then meet his gaze in the mirror. My entire body seems to flush with the intensity of his regard.

"Tell me," he insists, "tell me you don't want me."

"I do," I whisper.

"Then why are you resisting what's between us?"

"You told me you loved me. Yet the first time someone tells you about a mistake I committed, you turn your back on me publicly. You believed him over me." I hunch my shoulders. "And to some extent I deserve it, Christian. After all, I never did come clean to you about the details of what my deal with him was." I shake my head. "We are not good together, you and I."

"We are," he says with vehemence, "we bloody well are."

"You chose to believe the worst of me, Christian," I remind him. "As soon as he told you what I had done, you found me guilty without giving me a chance to explain my actions."

"I am sorry about that," he admits. "I went against my instincts. I knew there was a reason for what you did. I knew that I was to blame as much as you, and still..."

"How do you think that makes me feel?"

"I'm sorry," he murmurs.

"Are you?"

"I told you I'd show you how much I regret my actions."

"By fucking me?"

"By making love to you." He curls his fingers inside of me, and my hips push back and into the thick column between his legs.

"That's ... the problem," I gasp, "it's too easy for you to distract me. You only have to touch me, and I seem to forget everything wrong that you did to me."

"I don't see the problem with that." His lips kick up.

"You don't understand what I'm trying to say," I snarl. "I want to be away from you long enough to clear my head, so I know exactly what I want."

"You want me, Flower, you know that."

"I know I want what you do to my body, but what about the rest of me?"

"The rest of you?"

"What about what my heart wants?"

"What does it want?"

"I don't know, okay?" I cry. "I thought I might have fallen in love with you, but after the stunt you pulled earlier, I ... I am not sure."

"Ah," he hesitates, "so, you're telling me that you don't love me?"

"No, that's not what I'm saying." I huff. "I am just saying that I need time to think things through, okay?"

He stares at me a second longer, then he pulls out his fingers. He brings them up to his mouth and sucks my cum off of them. The heat flushes my cheeks. No matter how many times I've seen him do that, I'll never get used to the raw eroticism in his gestures.

He steps back, and cool air rushes between us. Damn it, how can I already miss him? And why did I stop him from taking me one last time? Something to stay with me in the days to follow as I figure out what I really want.

"Okay," he jerks his chin, "you got it, Flower. I'll stay away from you if that's what you want."

"That's what I want." I watch as he backs away from me.

"Fine." He hesitates, then pivots on his heel, heads to the door, and unlocks it.

"Wait," I call after him, and he turns; the look on his face is so hopeful, so unlike anything I have ever seen on his features before that I swallow, my guts twist, and I push away the ball of emotion that clogs my chest. "My family," I force out the words, "you promise not to harm them?"

He draws in a breath, seems like he's about to say something else, then nods, "I promise."

"And when your brother wakes up?"

"Brother?"

"He looks so much like you that I assume there is a family connection?"

"Family..." He shakes his head. "He's my triplet."

"Triplet?" I blink. "So you, Xander, and this stranger...?"

He nods. "Triplets." He drags his fingers through his hair. "Something my parents and Nonna knew, but none of them saw fit to tell us about his existence."

"Oh, wow," I bite the inside of my cheek, "that... that must have come as a shock, I imagine?"

"You can't make this shit up." His features grow hard. "I'm not sure if I can forgive Nonna for this."

"I'm sure she had her reasons."

"No doubt," he snorts, "but it resulted in our brother turning against us. For so many years, we were unaware of his existence, and now I wonder if it's too late to make amends for their actions."

"I bet Nonna feels it worse than you. Can't you forgive her for what she did?" Like how you forgave me and came after me?

"Do you want me to forgive her?"

I hold his gaze, then nod. "Yes," I whisper, "yes, I want you to forgive her."

"Done." He peers into my features for a second longer. "Take care, Flower."

He unlocks the door and walks out.

I stare after him.

So, he left me? He actually left me, just like that? I had asked him to, and he had agreed, which, in itself, is unusual. But he did it. He pushed his own needs aside and gave in to what I want. Whoa! I shake my head, then open the tap and hold my hands under the water. I spot the ring on my left hand. My wedding ring. I should have given it back to him. After all, this entire marriage is a sham, isn't it? I rush to the door, yank it open, and call out, "Wait, Christian."

He pauses not five feet from the door, but doesn't turn. I walk over to stand in front of him, then pull off the ring and hand it over.

He glances at the ring in my hand, then up at my face. "What's this?"

"It's yours," I murmur, "you should take it back."

"It's yours," he growls, "You should keep it."

"But… it doesn't feel right."

"I gave it to you; it belongs to you." He brushes past me. "Keep it or toss it; do whatever you think is right, Flower."

54

———————

Christian

How dare she try to return her wedding ring to me? How dare she think everything that happened between us is a sham? I should have known things were going to get messy the moment I set eyes on her. I should have walked away from her, but did I? Of course, not. Instead, I had appointed myself as her protector. I only have myself to blame for the predicament I'm in now.

I slam down the half-empty glass of whiskey on the bar in the living room. The thud resounds through my head, and I wince. Clearly, trying to get drunk is not doing any favors for the headache that has gathered behind my eyes. Well, fuck that. It's the least I can do to drown out the thoughts that insist on crowding in on me.

She owes me her life, and how does she repay me? By asking me to leave... And what had I done? I had obliged her. Is that a sign of weakness? Have I become so pussy-whipped that I allowed her to dictate my actions?

I stare at the remnants of the amber liquid in the bottle. Golden and brown with sparks where the light from above hits the surface of the whiskey. Gleaming and complex and layered... Just like her.

She is the love of my life, and I let her get away. She is the only thing that makes sense in this bizarre twisted mess my life has become, and I allowed her to leave. I had turned and walked away from her again.

Why hadn't I listened to her when she had tried to explain things to me at the house? Why had I been so quick to believe the worst of her?

I bring the glass of whiskey to my lips and chug down the rest of the contents. The alcohol burns its way down my gullet and explodes in my stomach. I can't feel my hands and feet, which means I'm doing something right. Something that will, hopefully, shut down the regrets that pinch my chest, the heaviness that coils around my heart and squeezes until I'm sure that I'll never feel the same way again.

Someone raps on the door to the living room before barging in. "Knock, knock, motherfucker."

Seb's annoying voice cuts through the thoughts in my head.

"Lost your way?" I pour more whiskey into my glass, then some more, topping it up almost to the brim.

He whistles. "You sure you've had enough? There's a little more room in the glass if you want to pour more into it."

"Ha, ha," I scoff, then survey the glass. "You may have a point there." I add to the glass until some of the amber liquid sloshes over the side. "Therrre," I slur, "is that betterrr?"

"I think you need to stop drinking, to be honest."

"Aww, come on, are you going to become all responsible and boring like our *fratellone*?" I lean down to the bar and slurp from the overfull glass. To be fair, I'm over the whiskey already, especially since my head is spinning, and I am currently seeing two of Seb. But I don't tell him that. Asshole would only bore me with another sermon, no doubt, about my shortcomings—of which I have many, as the events of the last day have shown.

"On the other hand, perhaps I should join you, eh?"

"Now that is a capital idea, brother." I reach for the bottle, but he stops me.

"I have a better idea." He slides another glass toward me, then reaches for mine.

I scowl. "What are you doing?"

"I don't know if I can share your pain, but perhaps, I can share your drink?" He tugs on the glass, and when I release my hold on it, he pours almost half of my drink into his. A good portion ends up on the bar.

"I know what you're doing." I chuckle.

"Oh, yeah?"

"You're trying to stop me from getting drunk, aren't you?"

"I think that ship has sailed," he laughs, "but yes, I'm trying to save you from alcohol poisoning."

"I don't need your… your…" I squint at him, "your…"

"Sympathy?"

"Exactly." I take another sip of the whiskey. "I don't need your symp… sympa…"

"Sympathy," he prompts.

"What-fucking-ever," I place my glass on the counter then stand up. The room tilts. Oops, wrong move. I grab the edge of the counter and steady myself. "What the fuck are you doing here anyway?"

"Michael was worried about you, so I decided to come by and take a look at what you were up to."

"And the rest of the family is—"

"Taking turns keeping Theresa company at your triplet's bedside. He's still unconscious, by the way," Seb murmurs, "thank you, for asking."

"Hey," I scowl, "you don't get to do that; you don't get to guilt trip me for mourning the end of my marriage before it even started."

"And who's fault is that?" He drawls, "I'm not the one who took off—"

"—leaving her behind. Yes, yes, I know. I'm guilty, so sue me."

"I think she's roasting your ass enough, and deservedly." Seb chuckles. "It's good to see you crawl, brother."

"Fuck off," I jerk my chin toward the doorway. "No, seriously, get the fuck out of my house, Sebastian."

"Ah, apparently you were right to come here," Massimo prowls through the door, "and you were right that he's probably crying into his drink like a pussy."

"Hey," I spin around and almost topple over. Oops, wrong move again. Apparently, that's all I'm good for right now, not being able to take a step without tripping over my own two feet. "Get the fuck out." I straighten, lean an elbow against the bar, miss it and crash into one of the barstools. I hit the floor on my ass and sprawl out. Well, on the flip side, at least my head has some kind of support now, which is fucking helpful.

Massimo's face hovers in my line of sight. "You okay down there, *fratellino*, or do you need some help getting up?"

"Nope, not needed." I fold my hands over my chest. "I'm good; class dismissed."

"Did he just say what I think he said—?"

"He did," Seb replies. "Asshole thinks drinking himself into a stupor is the way forward."

"And I thought he was brighter than that."

"Apparently not," Seb snorts.

"Hey," I protest, "I'm still here you, *stronzos*." Or at least, that's what I think I say, but all that comes out is a choking sound.

"You say something, oh, enlightened one?" Massimo smirks, then holds out his hand, "Come on, let's get you to your bed, shall we?"

. . .

I open my eyes and groan. My tongue feels too big for my mouth, I try to swallow, and my throat hurts. I sit up, and the headache behind my eyes increases in intensity. Shit, I'm never drinking again. Never.

I notice the glass of water and the two pills next to it. Who placed it there? Massimo? Seb? Doesn't matter. I down them, drain the glass of water, and stumble to the bathroom. By the time I'm done with the hot shower and am dressed, I feel a little better. I follow the scent of toast and bacon to the kitchen. I head inside and find Massimo and Seb at the breakfast nook with Cassandra serving them breakfast. She sets a plate of food down for me, then moves away.

"What are you doing here?" I frown at her.

"Michael insisted I take over the cooking until you are back on your feet."

"I'm not incapacitated, or has everyone forgotten that?"

"Hey," Massimo growls, "we're worried about you, okay? Deal with it."

I blow out a breath. "I'm sorry, Cass." I roll my shoulders. "I'm not at my best right now."

"It's understandable." She places an espresso in front of me. "Did you speak to her yesterday?"

"What do you think?" My stomach churns at the sight of the food. I push away the plate and reach for the espresso. "I met her at the airport, and she asked me to leave; end of story."

"Is it?" Seb places his phone on the table. "Did you ask her to forgive you?"

I drain my espresso, then place the cup back in its saucer. "Of course, I did. Why else would I have gone there?"

The two men exchange a glance.

"What?" I scowl. "I assume you two *teste di cazzo* have something to say?"

"Does he always have such a sunny disposition first thing in the morning?" Massimo muses.

"He always was a rude motherfucker," Seb confirms.

"Think we should tussle him to the ground and sit on him until he sees sense?" Massimo looks me up and down.

"He's taller than either of us, but if we take him together, I'm sure we can overpower him."

"Not that it would make any difference; he'd probably still be pigheaded about this entire issue."

"He's an ass," Seb agrees.

"Hey," I fold my arms across my chest, "stop talking about me like I'm not here."

"Stop acting like you don't have a brain in your head," Massimo shoots back.

"What?" I growl, "What the hell are you two talking about?"

"Clearly, your idea of asking for forgiveness is very different from what was needed to actually get her to forgive you."

"You've lost me." I drag my fingers through my hair. "I went to her, tracked her down, told her I was sorry, repeatedly."

"But did you actually mean it?" Seb narrows his gaze on me. "Did you convey just how much of an asshole you've been with every fiber of your being for every moment that you've known her?"

Heat sears my neck. I glance at him, then away.

"That's what I thought."

"What makes you two such experts on relationships anyway?" I snap.

"And n-o-w he's angry with us." Seb shakes his head. "He thinks he can distract us from our mission."

"Mission?"

"We're here to make you see reason," Massimo drawls.

"Reason?" I pull the plate of food toward me and begin to eat. "What reason?"

"Look, you were born a grump-face, are shit company, and really, the only times we have been able to tolerate you is when you have been with her."

"What?" I stop with my fork halfway to my mouth.

"She made you a better person, asshole." Seb snorts. "I can't believe I'm saying this, by the way." He looks a little shocked with himself. "I sound like I picked the dialogue from a romance film."

"You mean a rom-com," Massimo corrects him.

"How the hell do you know what a rom-com is?" I stare at him.

"It's an informed guess," he raises a shoulder, "and don't try to steer us off course."

"You guys are the ones taking this entire conversation off course by talking about emo shit." I finish the mouthful on my fork and go in for another. "This food is really good, by the way," I compliment Cassandra.

"You really are trying to change the topic, aren't you?" She folds her arms across her chest.

"Hey, I was just complimenting you on the food," I protest.

"Definitely trying to change the topic." Seb nods. "What do you say, Massimo? Do you think he's strong enough to hear the truth from us, or is he too much of a pussy?"

"Who are you calling a pussy?" I snap.

"You, little brother." Massimo smirks.

I drop my fork on the plate with a clatter. "Fuck this." I rise to my feet, and the two men stand up with me.

"Sit down." Seb scowls.

"Fuck off." I turn to leave, and Massimo steps in my way.

"Sit down, *fratellino*, you need to hear this before you leave."

"The fuck, you guys?" I roll my shoulders. "If it's a fight you're spoiling for..."

"I'd happily kick your ass." Massimo laughs.

"You wish," I interrupt him. "Why are you two being so persistent, anyway?"

"Because we care, you *pezzo di merda*," Seb says in a soft tone. "Just sit down and listen to us, okay, and we promise, we won't bother you again."

Behind us, Cassandra stops what she's doing and comes to stand next to me. "Please, Christian," she pleads, "Aurora is someone I care about, and I'd hate to see the two of you lose this chance at a future together."

I open my mouth to protest, then shut it. "Fine," I sit down, "say what you're dying to get off your chests." I glower at my brothers.

Massimo and Seb glance at each other, then both sit down.

"Go to her," Massimo says without preamble. "Apologize again. Properly, this time."

I rub the back of my neck. "She asked me to stay away from her."

"And you listened to her?" Seb's gaze widens.

"What choice did I have?" I shift around in my seat. "She was pissed at me, and it felt like the least I could do was honor her wishes."

"Oh, so now you decide to pay attention to what she wants, eh?" Seb snorts. "All this time, you ensured you got your way, to the point that you humiliated her in front of everyone else, and now, when you should be doing your best to smooth over the damage you've done, you take the easy way out and walk away from her, again?"

"It wasn't easy," I mumble. "What the hell else should I have done?"

"Are you sure you want to hear it from us?" Massimo smirks.

"It's not like you've given me much of a choice," I roll my shoulders, "so why don't you say your piece?"

"Throw yourself at her mercy and ask her for forgiveness."

55

———————

A week later

Aurora

"That's mending nicely, now." I replace the dressing on the man who accidentally cut himself with a knife and was brought in by his wife. "You should be discharged within the day."

"Oh, that's good news." He smiles at his wife, who throws her arm around him and hugs him.

"Thank you, Doctor," she says. "I can't wait to take him home and fuss over him."

I step back and let the couple have their moment. "I'll, ah, go talk to the nurse in charge to make sure they have discharge orders."

I dawdle a second longer as the couple kisses. At least someone is in love and happy about it. I play with the ring on my finger as I walk toward the common room used by the doctors. It's been a long shift, and I'm exhausted, but it feels good to finally be doing my job.

Fact is, I had missed it when I returned to Sicily. I'm very lucky I was able to return to my role as a doctor at the same hospital where I had previously worked in London. They had been so strapped for doctors that they had welcomed me back with open arms, and I had started working right away. Truth be told, it's the only reason I have been able to stay sane. I had put on my scrubs walked into the ER and had felt instantly at home.

In fact, I've been so busy that I haven't had a moment to think, and that's been a blessing.

I also managed to find an apartment to rent within twenty-four hours, which honestly, in London, is nothing short of a miracle.

There was just enough money in my bank account to pay the deposit for the rent. All in all, I settled back into my former life like I hadn't left at all. And I admit, it feels good... To be independent again. To earn my living and not be depending on someone else... Not that Christian ever made me lack for anything. The man made sure all of my needs were looked after... And I do mean, all of my needs. He satisfied me in every way, indulged even my darkest desires—the ones I dared not share with anyone else. Somehow, with him, I didn't hesitate. He'd already been so filthy in his proclivities that it seemed natural to open up that part of myself to him.

And maybe that helped heal something inside of me. Maybe, I needed his particular brand of assertiveness, his dominance that allowed me to give myself up to him, trust him, and trust my body to him.

Oh, I had also been angry with him, and it was wrong that he'd held me captive... And that he'd seduced me... Only, it wasn't something I hadn't wanted.

I craved his particular brand of filthiness. I wanted him to fuck me, to not give me a choice and take me, so I wouldn't feel so bad about being attracted to him.

And this ... this thing between us, this connection, it's more than physical. Don't get me wrong. The physical was definitely the start of it, but the more I got to know him, the more I realized that beneath that hard exterior is a man who cares for his family, who had stood up to his father to save his younger brother, and who was devastated by the loss of his twin; not to mention, the shock of finding out he has a triplet.

And he had come after me. And I had left. And he had let me.

I haven't heard from him since he walked away from me at the airport. Half an hour later, as I waited for the next flight out, Adrian had turned up. He said that Christian wanted their private jet to take me to London. I had just started to refuse when the woman at the airline counter told me there were no cancellations on the later flight either. So I was stuck.

I'd refused when Adrian asked me if I preferred to spend the night at the airport. And the thought of trying to find a hotel room for the night and trying to get on a flight the next day felt like too much.

Ultimately, I agreed to fly on the private jet, and before I knew it, I was at Heathrow airport and making my way to the taxi stand, joining the ranks of normal folks who work for a living; as opposed to being involved in illegal businesses and playing with people's lives like the Sovranos and the rest of the Mafia clan does.

This is what I wanted, right? To be away from the Mafia, to chart my own future, to lead an ordinary life where I am a doctor by day and alone by night? No, no, no… I'm not going to think about that. I'm fine, I'm happy… Okay, maybe not happy, but I'm content with what I have—my freedom, my autonomy, my independence… Yes, yes, yes, if I repeat that often enough, I might even begin to believe it.

I shrug out of my white coat, stuff it inside my locker, then grab my handbag and head out of the hospital. I take the tube home, step inside, and that's when my phone rings.

Cassandra's name pops up on the screen.

"Hello?" I answer the video call and Cass's face appears.

"Hey, you." Cass smiles. "Have you been avoiding me?"

"Umm..." My neck heats. Truth is, I have been avoiding her calls, but only because talking to her reminds me too much of Christian.

"Hey," she frowns at me, "it's understandable if you don't want to talk to me. It must bring back too many memories."

"Yeah…" I blow out a breath as I walk into the kitchen. "I just wanted a little space, so I could put everything that happened into perspective, you know?"

"How are you holding up?"

I balance the phone against the microwave, then grab a bottle of wine from the refrigerator. I pour myself a glass and hold it out to Cass. "Cheers."

She laughs and holds up her own glass of wine. "Saluti, babe."

I sip from the glass and savor the woodsy taste of the wine. It's no match to the dark taste of his skin, of course, but it'll have to do.

"How's everything there?" I finally ask.

"He's not doing that great."

"Who?" I scowl. "And that's not what I asked."

"You know who I'm talking about," she murmurs, "and you know that's what you meant, so why don't we drop the pretense?"

"I really don't want to talk about him."

"But I do."

"If that's why you called—"

I go to depress the stop button on the phone, but she calls out, "Wait, Aurora, I won't talk about him, okay?"

I shake my head. "Not that it makes me feel any better to hear you say that." I pick up the phone and head back into the living room. "I'm not sure what I want anymore."

"Do you want him?"

"What kind of a question is that?"

"Well, do you?"

"Of course, I do." I huff.

"So why aren't you with him?"

"After what he did? After how he publicly humiliated me?"

"You wanted him to forgive you for the mistake you made when you made a deal with his brother."

"I did that because I felt trapped, okay. I didn't mean it."

"Maybe he didn't mean it either? Maybe he loved you so much that the thought of you having betrayed him was too much for him," she scans my features, "and then he did come after you at the airport, didn't he?"

"Whose side are you on?"

"Yours, babe, always."

"So why are you defending him? Is it because he's part of the Mafia and because you owe them?"

"Yes, I owe the Sovranos my life, but that's not why I am saying it. Hell, I'm the first to say that you should never tolerate their machismo behavior."

"Yet you work for them," I point out.

"And I make sure that they never take me for granted. I hold my own against each of them, and don't tell me that you haven't noticed."

"They do respect you," I say slowly. "I see that. Even Nonna treats you with deference."

"I had my fair share of run-ins with each of them, including Nonna, when I first started as Michael's housekeeper."

"And how did that work out?"

"Hell, I threatened to quit, and Michael allowed me to leave. But then he and the rest of them found out just how good I was at my job." She snorts. "Turns out, finding someone who enjoys housekeeping, does it well, and knows how to be discreet with what they see is a tall order."

"One which you fill with great excellence."

"It's why Michael told me to also manage Christian's home."

"Oh, yeah?" I snort. "Don't tell me he hasn't found someone else to fill his bed and cook his food and clean his house by now?"

"The man is a mess, Aurora."

I don't care. I don't care. I glance away, and Cass sighs.

"All I'll say is that he misses you, and he regrets what he did to you. You wanted him to listen to you and forgive you; can't you do the same for him?"

I bite down on my lower lip. "I want to… Honestly. A part of me knows that I'm being unreasonable, but somehow, I can't bring myself to forgive him completely."

"Make him grovel."

"What?"

"Make him beg for your forgiveness, make him be properly ingratiating, make him… I don't know, make him apologize profusely, enough to soothe your ego, so it becomes easy to forgive him."

"Maybe you have a point."

"I know that I have a point."

"You can be persistent, can't you?"

"You can thank me later." She glances off-screen. "I think the deliveries are here. I have to go."

"Wait." I scowl. "How do I make him grovel?"

She rolls her eyes. "You're the brilliant doctor. I'm sure you can think up a plan. I really have to go now."

"Wait, you—" She disconnects the call.

That's when the doorbell rings.

56

Christian

She opens the door, phone in hand, then stills. "Y-you?" She stutters. "What are you doing here?"

"Would you believe that I was in the neighborhood and decided to stop by?" I cringe. Really? Is that the best you can do?

"Well, then you can leave the same way you came." She begins to shut the door, and I plant my foot in the doorway.

"Wait!" I protest. "Please, I came all this way just to talk to you."

"I don't want to talk to you." She pushes the door into my foot.

I grimace. "Just give me a few minutes of your time, okay?"

"That's what I asked you, but did you listen? No, you did not; you simply got into your stupid Ferrari and drove away."

"Hey," I protest, "hate me if you want, but don't insult my Ferrari."

"Really?" She stares. "That's what you want to say to me?"

"What?" I shake my head, partially to clear it because her scent is driving me crazy, and partially because I really need to get my act together. "No, of course, not. I came to … to…" Shit, why is this so hard? "Can I come inside, please?" I ask.

Her gaze widens; she stares at me with surprise written large on her features.

"I know, I'm being polite and shit." I rub the back of my neck. "I'm trying, okay?" I peer into her face. "Please, can I come in and talk to you? I promise, I won't take too much of your time. Unless you'd rather I do this out here, where all of your neighbors will hear..."

She hesitates, then nods.

Thank fuck. If she refused me, would I have pushed my way inside? Well, we'll never know now, will we?

She spins around and walks inside. I follow her into the living room. She places her phone on the coffee table, then crosses over to stand on the opposite side of the room.

I take in the bookcase, half-filled with books, the sofa, the colorful curtains, the rugs on the floor. It's a place that feels like home. "It's nice," I tell her. "You seem comfortable here."

"I am," she tips up her chin, "but you didn't come here to comment about my taste in interior decorating, did you?"

A-n-d there you are, my little spitfire, my Flower. This is why I can't stay away from you, because you're the only one who feels like home to me.

Shit, why did it take me so long to realize the truth? She not only feels like home, she is my home. It's why I haven't been able to stay away from her from the moment I laid eyes on her. It's why I keep returning to her.

After Massimo and Seb had that talk with me, I was pissed off at myself. Enough to leave on my secret mission, while the rest of my brothers took turns watching over my triplet, who is still in an induced coma.

They give me regular updates on his condition, which remains unchanged. They also tell me Theresa refuses to leave his side. As for Nonna, she comes to the hospital and sits with Theresa as often as she can.

I still haven't completely forgiven my grandmother for the secrets she kept, but if she finds it difficult to face the man whose very existence she kept hidden from us, she's not showing it.

I haven't been there to see him. I can't bring myself to go. Hell, tackling one emotional entanglement in my life at a time is, apparently, all the mind space I have. I've handled more than my share of stress within the Mafia business, but tackling something so personal? Yeah, it's a completely different sensation. I walk over to where she's standing, and she stiffens. I pause in front of her, then lower myself to my knees.

"What ... what are you doing?" she gasps.

"I'm sorry." I lower my chin to my chest. "I am truly sorry for what I said and did. All of it. From the beginning. I shouldn't have threatened you to get what I wanted. I shouldn't have put you in that position. But mostly, I shouldn't have doubted you. I should have waited and allowed you to explain. I'm sorry I shut you down in front of everyone else. I'm so sorry that I walked away from you. I'll never forgive myself for that."

Her chin trembles. "You hurt me so much, Christian," she says in a low voice. "You broke my heart."

"And I feel terrible for doing it. As long as I live, I'll never forgive myself for what I did to you. I deserve your hate. I deserve for you to loathe me, to be angry with me. If you never want to see me again after this, I'll understand."

"It's not like I'm not at fault. I should have come to you; I realize that now. It's just, I found it difficult to trust you then."

"And now?"

"Now I'm not sure anymore." She glances away from me.

"You said you loved me."

"So did you."

"I still do."

"And I… I'm not sure what I feel for you anymore." She wrings her fingers together, and I see the flash of platinum on her left hand.

"You're still wearing your wedding ring."

"Eh?" She holds up the fingers of her left hand, then glances down at mine. "So are you."

I slide my fingers into my pocket then pull out a ring.

She glances at it, and her gaze widens. "Is that…" She blinks rapidly. "It can't be; is it—?"

"Your engagement ring."

"How did you find it?"

"I looked for it."

"When? How?" She opens and shuts her mouth. "I threw it into the snow."

"I went back there. After I returned from seeing you at the airport, my brothers gave me grief. They told me how wrong I was to have treated you like that in front of everyone."

"They did?"

"They also said that if I didn't go after you, they'd never forgive me."

"Oh…" She swallows. "Is that why you came, because they asked you to?"

"I came because," my voice cracks, and I draw in a breath. Why is this so hard? I shake my head to clear it. "I came because I love you and can't live without you. And I wanted to show you just how much it means to me that you forgive me. So, I went back to the lodge, and I scoured the snow and the grounds—"

"But that's acres and acres of space."

"Yeah…" I blow out a breath. "I don't recommend doing it."

"Jesus, Christian." She folds her arms around her waist. "How many days did you—"

"Days and nights." I twist my lips. "It took me a week to find it."

"A week?" She lowers her arms to her side. "You were looking for it all this time?"

"I almost gave up." I chuckle. "At one point, I was cold and wet, and my fingers had almost frozen off, but then I knew that if I came here without it… Without the symbol of what it means to me to be forgiven, without putting in the penance for what I did… I knew, without it, you wouldn't forgive me."

She scowls. "You sound very sure of yourself that I'll take you back now."

"Won't you?" I arch an eyebrow. Damn it, and I was doing so well up until now. But the moment she challenged me, that dominant part of me surged to the fore. This groveling thing… Clearly, I need more lessons to get it right. I hold out my palm. "You're going to forgive me, Aurora; you know you want to."

She opens her mouth, then nods. "I want to, Christian, but I'm not going to."

What the fuck? I glare at her. "You're not going to forgive me?"

"Unless…"

"Unless?"

"Unless you allow me to tie you up."

57

———————

Aurora

"Tie me up?" He rises to his feet. "You want to tie me up?"

"You tied me up," I point out.

"That was different.'

"Oh, yeah?" I tip my chin up. "How is that?"

"I'm the dominant in this relationship; you're forgetting that, Flower."

"No, I'm not. It's because you are the aggressor that I am asking for this."

He glowers at me. "You know what it means if I allow myself to be tied up by you?"

"That you trust me?" I say softly. "That you're ready to strip yourself of all ego and put yourself in my hands to allow me to do with you as I want?"

"Which, I admit, is not a bad scenario at all," he murmurs.

"So, you'll let me—"

"Yes," his massive chest rises and falls, "I'll let you tie me up if it means you'll forgive me."

"You will?" Jesus, he'll actually do that? He'll actually swallow his ego and his machismo and that dominance that drips from every pore in his body and allow me to have him at my mercy? A pulse throbs to life between my legs, my pussy clenches, moisture laces my core, and honestly, I don't know why, but the thought of having this big brute of a man tied up and in my power is so freakin' hot.

"On one condition."

A-n-d, there it is, alphahole's ego always means he has to have the last word.

"I didn't think this was a negotiation." I pout.

"Oh, I'm always negotiating, Flower." He smirks. "You know that."

"And if I don't want to?"

"I think you'd enjoy it more if you did..." His smile widens. "Go on; you know you want to find out what I want in return."

"Hmm…" I hunch my shoulders. Am I actually going to give in to this ploy of his? Am I going to fall for this, the oldest trick in the book? Don't agree to it; don't agree to it. I jerk my chin. "What do you want in return?"

"For you to wear my ring."

"I'm already wearing your ring." I hold up my left hand with the wedding band on it.

"You know which one I mean." He pinches my engagement ring between his thumb and forefinger. "Wear it for me," he murmurs, "please, Flower."

And fuck, I can't refuse him when he asks me in that soft voice of his. Goddamn him. I hold out my hand, and he closes the distance between us and slides it onto my left ring finger. I take in how the two rings complement each other. I angle my fingers, and the light from the window bounces off of the golden stone in the center. The tiny diamonds sparkle, and my vision blurs for a second. I blink away the moisture in my eyes, then pull my hand back from his.

"You got what you wanted," I whisper. "Are you happy now?"

"I'll be happy when you take me back."

"So, you'll let me tie you up now?"

He holds out his wrists. "If that's what you want..."

"I want," I lick my suddenly dry lips, "to have you at my mercy."

His gaze intensifies, and a flush stains his cheeks. "Do it," he orders.

I almost laugh. He can't stop himself from ordering me around, can he?

"Wait here." I spin around and head for the bedroom, only to hear his footsteps behind me. I scowl at him over my shoulder. "Thought I told you to wait?"

"Not good at following orders, Flower."

I toss my hair as I reach into the bottom drawer of my dresser and pull out a length of satin-covered rope.

"Well, now," he murmurs, "you've been planning for this, I see."

"Maybe I have." I jerk my chin in the direction of the bed. "Lie down."

He seems like he is about to refuse, but finally, he nods. He prowls over and sprawls out on my bed. It's a queen-sized mattress, and the man seems to take up every inch of space on it. He spreads his legs, and his pants stretch across his thighs. The fabric at his crotch tents; the throbbing in my core intensifies further. Damn it, I haven't even touched him, and already, I'm so turned on.

"You still plan on tying me up?" he drawls.

"What?" I raise my gaze to his face.

His lips curve in a smile that lights up his features. "It's okay if you are admiring certain parts of my anatomy."

"Go to hell."

"Only if you'll come with me."

I snort. "Only you would say that and think it's romantic."

"If I'm with you, baby, it's always romantic."

A hot sensation stabs at my chest. Why does he have to be so charming? It makes it so difficult for me to maintain my distance from him. I flounce over, then clamber onto the bed and into the 'V' between his legs. He holds his wrists out, and I loop the rope around them. I knot it once, twice, then loop it again.

The heat of his body embraces me, and his scent intensifies. I'm very conscious of how he doesn't take his gaze off of my face as I complete my task.

"Stop staring," I mutter.

"Does it make you uncomfortable?"

No, it actually is insanely hot, but I'm not going to tell him that. When I'm certain that his wrists are secure, I push his wrists up and over his head. Which means I have to lean over him. My breasts brush his chest. The neckline of my shirt gapes. I glance down to find his gaze transfixed on my cleavage.

"Nothing you haven't seen before." The words are out before I can stop myself.

"You're wrong," he mutters. "I've missed the feel of your breasts in my palm. I've missed squeezing them, massaging them, then pinching your nipples until you cry out. I've missed sucking on them, and playing with them, and tweaking them until I bring you to orgasm."

"You've never brought me to orgasm by playing with my nipples," I scoff.

"Untie me, and I'll show you."

"Ha," I snort, "if you think I'm going to fall for that, you're wrong."

"Oh, well," he smirks, "it was worth a try, and for the record, I'd wager I can bring you to climax by touching your nipples and no other part of you."

"We'll see." I secure his wrists to the headboard, then sit back on my heels. His gaze is locked on my face as I take in the sculpted muscles of his triceps, the cut of his shoulders, the chiseled planes of his chest which strain his shirt. A bead of sweat slides down his throat.

"Take it off," he orders.

"What?"

"Take off my shirt."

I reach for his buttons, begin to undo them, then stop. "Nice try," I pull back my hands, "but you don't get to dictate what I do next."

"Okay." He smirks. The sneaky bastard smirks, knowing he's already made me do exactly that. On the other hand, I really do want to see those glorious pecs of his in all their naked glory. So, I reach down and begin to undo the buttons of his shirt.

He chuckles, and the sound rumbles up his throat.

"Stop gloating." I scowl.

He firms his lips at once. "Whatever you say."

"Are you making fun of me?" I push his shirt aside to reveal the expanse of cut planes. *Santa Rosalia*, he's even more ripped than I remember him to be. Each individual muscle of his chest stands out in relief. Each plane and dip as if carved out of granite. I shove the shirt down his arms—or rather, up his arms, since his hands are over his head—and take in the scar on his bicep. I trace the marks made by the stitches I put in him. It was the best I could do with the tools I had then, but I still regret spoiling the perfection of his skin.

"I marked you," I murmur. I trail my fingers down his chest then pause. "Wha ... what's that?" I whisper as I trace the letters he's tattooed onto the space over his heart. It's the only part of his chest that was left untouched by his tattoos, and now he's filled that in too with my name. "When did you get this done?"

"Before I found your ring."

"It ... it's..." I take in the bright yellow and blue colors he used to fill in the letters of my name. It stands out among his other tattoos which are all in black, "...beautiful." I sigh.

"And now, I will forever carry it on my body. You're a part of me, Flower, whether you like it or not."

I drag my fingers down the grooves between the planes of his chest, and he hisses.

"When you left me, it was like a part of me had walked out with you. I felt like I had hit the rock bottom that exists below the rock bottom."

I glance up at him. "That was almost poetic."

"Seems you inspire even someone like me to express myself in verse. You.. make me feel things I never have before. You make me feel like I'm alive for the first time. You fill gaps in my life that I didn't even know needed filling. Like experiencing the first warm, sunny day after a really long and shitty winter, except it goes on for longer."

I chuckle. "You really are pulling out the stops, aren't you?" I flatten my palm against his abs, and the muscles ripple in response. It's like touching a powerful beast and finding out every part of his anatomy is responsive and sensitive and so reactive to every contact.

My throat closes, and my mouth seems to dry up. I slide my palm down his concave stomach, and my fingertips brush his waistband.

A growl rumbles up his chest.

I glance up to find his gaze hooded, and his skin is more flushed than usual.

"You make me feel like I'm lost in the right direction. You just feel right to me, so right that I want to haul you to me and never let you go. In fact, if you untie me I'll bury my cock inside you and pleasure you until you come over and over again."

My toes curl, my thighs clench, and a bead of sweat trickles down the valley between my breasts.

"Untie me, and I'll show just how much I want you," he murmurs.

"You never give up, do you?" I cup the length of him through the crotch of his pants, and another growl rumbles up his chest.

My belly trembles, even as a sensation of power fills me. So this is what it feels like to be in control. To have another person at your mercy. This is how it feels to know that you can do whatever you want to him, and he has no choice but to bear it and enjoy it… Even if it feels painful in the moment.

I lower the zipper on his pants, then tug down on his waistband. He raises his hips, and I shove his pants down, along with his briefs. His cock springs free, thick and fat and so gorgeous... The head swollen purple, with a bead of precum lacing the slit. I fist his shaft, and he jerks his pelvis up and toward me.

"Fucking hell," he growls. "What do you think you're doing?"

I lick my lips, unable to take my gaze off of his length, then I bend and take him in my mouth.

58

———————

Christian

She wraps her mouth around my cock, and my entire body goes solid. I can't shift my gaze away from how my shaft disappears between her lips as she curls her tongue around the head of my dick. A groan rips from me. She continues to suck on my cock, taking it down her throat, and my muscles bunch. My groin hardens. All the blood in my body seems to rush to where she's licking up the side of my shaft. She pulls out until the head is poised between her lips, then pushes forward to take me down her throat again. She hollows out her cheeks, and I feel the suction all the way to my throat.

"Fuck me..." I strain at my restraint, wanting to grip her hair and tug, then wrap my fingers around her throat to feel my length down her throat.

"Aurora," I groan, "you're killing me."

She hums, and the vibrations travel up the length of my dick. My balls harden, and almost as if she senses it, she cups her hand around them and squeezes.

"*Cazzo!*" I growl, "When I get my hands on you, I'm going to teach you a lesson for playing with me."

She massages my balls even as she pulls back, then pushes down on my length over and over. She sucks and licks and kneads, and my thighs go solid. My chest rises and falls, my breath catching in my throat. Fuck, if this woman isn't sucking my soul through my cock. She bobs her head and continues to suck me off, and the pressure at the base of my spine coils tighter. I tug at the ropes that tie me down as she raises her gaze to mine. She stares up at me from under her thick eyelashes as she continues to slurp on my shaft. She squeezes on my balls, takes me down her throat, then gags. Saliva dribbles down her chin, but she doesn't stop. The pressure in my groin tightens until I can barely breathe. I grit my teeth, then watch as she increases the pace of sucking on my dick.

The orgasm threatens and I groan, "Fuck, I'm going to come."

She pulls her mouth off of my cock and rises to her feet on the bed. She shoves down her jeans and panties, kicks them aside, then straddles me. Lining me up with her entrance, she sinks down onto me.

Both of us groan in unison.

"Jesus," she pants, "you're so damn big."

"All the better to fill you up with, Flower." I jerk my chin, "Come 'ere."

"What do you mean?"

"Bring your face close to mine, so I can kiss you."

She bites down on her lower lip, and my cock jerks inside of her. She gasps, then giggles. "Gosh, I had no idea how responsive you actually are."

"Come closer, and I'll show just how responsive I can be to your needs."

"Umm," she pretends to think, "no thanks."

She rises up, then impales herself on my shaft again, and a tremor grips me. A moan bleeds from her lips. She holds onto my waist and begins to ride me in earnest. Each time she sinks down onto me, the heat, the softness, the way her pussy clamps down on me... The sensations consume me. The next time she pushes down, I thrust up and into her.

"Oh," she gasps, her gaze wide, "you're not supposed to do that."

"Fuck that," I growl, "take off your shirt."

"What?"

"Take. Off. Your. Shirt. Aurora. Right now."

She swallows, then begins to unbutton her shirt. She takes it off and flings it aside.

"And now, your bra."

She looks like she is about to refuse me, and I snap, "Do it, Flower."

She draws in a breath, then reaches behind her to unhook her bra. It falls off, revealing those glorious tits.

"Come here," I growl.

"No." She shakes her head.

"Your breasts are swollen and tender, and you want me to squeeze them and suck on them, Aurora."

"I ... I do?"

"Yes," I insist, "come on; give in to the need, and let me bite down on them and relieve the pressure you feel in them.

She pushes her breasts together, making a valley between them, and I almost lose it.

"Come here," I lower my voice to a hush, "and let me lick them and suckle on them, baby girl."

She swallows, then leans over, so those gorgeous tits are suspended in front of me. I reach up and fasten my mouth around one nipple and suck.

She moans, throws her head back, and pushes her breast into my mouth. I nibble and suck and bite down, and her pussy spasms around my cock.

My balls draw up, and I know I'm not far off. I release her nipple only to fasten onto the other one and slurp on it. I drag my tongue around the swollen flesh, and she throws her head back.

"Oh god, Christian, that feels so good, so … so hot." Color suffuses her cheeks as I thrust up and into her, again and again and again. She squeezes down on my cock, and I know that she's not far.

The next time I propel into her, her entire body jolts. She gasps, pinches her features together, and I growl, "Come with me, Flower."

Her spine arches, and she screams as her climax grips her. She collapses on me as I push into her once-twice-thrice until I empty myself inside of her. I continue to thrust up a few more times, then tug on my ropes again, wanting to hold her. Goddamn it. I scissor my legs around her and flip her over.

She raises her heavy eyelids and stares up at me. "You're not supposed to be able to do that."

"There's enough slack on the rope," I point out. "Also, you can't tell me what to do, remember?"

She blows out a breath. "How can I forget?"

I press my forehead to hers. "You unravel me. You know that, don't you?"

Her breath hitches, and that golden gaze of hers widens. She parts her lips, and I place my mouth on hers. I share her breath as I touch my lips to hers. I hold her gaze, both our eyes still open.

"Are you real?" I murmur.

Her lips curve up. "Why do you ask that?"

"I sometimes wonder if you're a figment of my imagination. Is that why you're so perfect for me in every way?"

"I'm not perfect." She grows serious. "If I were, I would have told you about asking for his help to escape you—something I'll always regret."

"And I'll never forgive myself for turning my back on you, so we're even."

She thrusts her breasts up and into my chest, and I feel myself grow hard inside her.

"Again?" She blinks. "Didn't think you had enough stamina to go another round so soon."

"You casting aspersions on my staying power?"

"Well, you are older than me." She blinks. "How old are you, again?"

"I'm thirty-three."

"I'm twenty-four."

"And clearly, a genius, which is why you qualified so quickly as a doctor."

She chuckles. "Let's just say, I was determined to get through my exams with excellent grades, and as quickly as possible. It's another reason why, when I met you, I was still inexperienced."

"Thank fuck." I lunge forward, and she gasps.

"God, I'll never get used to your size."

"Keep talking, Flower," I smirk, "it does wonders for my ego."

"Like you need that?"

"All I need is you—your voice, your scent, your wide-eyed innocence when you look at me with those big golden eyes."

"I'm not that innocent." She tips up her chin. "After all, I did want you to tie me up and ravish me, more than anything, I wanted you to do all of those filthy things that you hinted you were capable of." She swallows. "I found it so erotic, and I couldn't understand where those thoughts were coming from."

"It's not shameful to want to explore your sexuality and boundaries." I bump my nose with hers. "It's because you were honest with yourself, because you let me push your limits, that we made it this far."

She peers into my eyes,=. "You won't leave me again, will you?"

"Never." I kiss her lips. "How can I, when everything I want is right here in front of me?"

59

A day later

Karma

I bend over the ceramic bowl of the commode and throw up the breakfast that I've just eaten. I puke until there's nothing left, then manage to flush away the disgusting mess before I sink back onto the floor. I push my head back into the wall.

Holy shit, this is the third morning in a row this has happened. Combined with my tender breasts, and the period that I've missed, that tells me that I'm probably pregnant. I stay there for a few more seconds as I will my head to stop spinning. I close my eyes, take in a breath, then another. A few more breaths, and I feel slightly better. I push up to my feet, and my knees don't buckle under me. Score!

I walk over to the sink, rinse out my mouth, and splash some water on my face and wrists. By the time I leave the room, I feel much better. I walk over to my studio, which is just down the hallway from me, and push open the door. Andy glances up from his cat cave bed in the corner of the room. He stares at me as I cross over to where I have been sketching my latest creation. It's for a bride in London.

Since the day I sold my first creations in Camden Market, the orders have been flooding in. They are growing at such a fast rate, I have had to both hike up my prices and turn down a few because I couldn't meet the demand.

Michael suggests it's time I expand. He's offered to build me a separate studio on the grounds surrounding the house. Then, I can hire a couple of seamstresses to help me.

I've thought about it and decided that's not right for me at this time.

The Karma label is my first baby, and I want to keep the creativity, the quality, and the attention to detail that it has come to embody as consistent as possible. Which means, I need to be hands-on, for now. Maybe later on down the line, I might think of expanding and getting help. For now, I'd rather work on it myself.

It's a good thing Michael has been away on business the last few days, or my morning sickness would have sent him into a tizzy. For now, though, it feels right that I can hold onto this part of me—this feeling, this sensation of being a mother again—to myself. I flatten my palm against my stomach as I stare at the finished design on the drafting board.

I pull off the paper and carefully place it aside. Just need a little break before I begin translating that into fabric. Meanwhile, I pick up a pencil and begin to draw. This one is different. This one is unlike the designs I have created so far. Something softer, more fragile, smaller in size…

A Peter Pan collar, simple long sleeves, a slight gathering at the waist, opening at the back, so it's easy to put on and pull off. I step back and glance at what I have drawn. It's a bodysuit for a baby … a newborn. Tears prick the backs of my eyes, and I wipe them away. Shit, I'm not even, like, fully pregnant—is that even a concept? I mean, I just found out I'm pregnant, and already, the pregnancy hormones seem to be taking effect.

If Michael were here, he'd probably just wrap me in fluff, scoop me up, place me on the bed, and order me not to move until the baby is born. I scowl at the drawing. Not likely.

I intend to work until my last week. I intend to continue to design and sew and ensure that all the orders I have taken are fulfilled with Karma originals. No bride who orders a dress from me is going to be empty-handed. No, siree. I only need to convince my husband of that.

Speaking of…. I place my pencil on the table. There's a much bigger discussion I need to broach with my husband. I wince. I've been putting it off for so long, and now, I really need to tell him. And if I don't…

No. I shake my head. I can't do this to him. It's bad enough I haven't brought it up with him so far. He deserves to know. It's his right to know.

The sound of footsteps reaches me a second before the edgy scent of testosterone—musky, like leather with a hint of woodsmoke—envelops me. I draw in the fragrance of his aftershave, like fresh snow on earth. The cold rush of a winter's wind, followed by the snap and crackle of a fireplace. The images flow over me just before his arms wrap around me. Goose bumps pop on my skin, and my core trembles. I turn around, tip-up my chin, and meet those brilliant blue eyes. Warmth flares in their depths, and silver flashes riddled with sparks of gold. The look he only wears when he is around me, as I have learned.

"Don," I murmur, "I wasn't expecting you back until tomorrow."

"I missed you, Beauty." His dark voice flows over me, coils in my chest, and sinks into my blood. A cascade of warmth flares out from my core to my extremities. My toes curl. I bite down on my lower lip, and he lowers his gaze to my mouth. "I missed my wife." He tilts his head and replaces my teeth with his own. He tugs on my lip, and my pussy clenches. Moisture beads my center, and my stomach flip-flops. My pulse ratchets up. Sweat beads my forehead, and I tear my mouth from his. I tip up my chin and watch him watch me with a curious gaze.

"Everything all right, baby?" He frowns as he pushes the hair back from my face. He pauses with his palm on my forehead. "Your skin is clammy." The lines in his forehead deepen. He peers into my face, no doubt, taking in my sudden pallor. My stomach ties itself in knots, the wave of sickness pushing up against my breastbone, my throat. Turning, I race to the bathroom.

I throw up into the toilet bowl. Michael comes up behind me and holds back my hair as I proceed to empty what little is left in my stomach—namely, bile—then dry heave. Finally, when my stomach stops roiling, I slump back against the wall.

He flushes the disgusting remains, then wets a towel and wipes my mouth with it.

"Thank you," I say gratefully. He throws the towel aside, wets another one, and holds it to my forehead.

The coolness from the cloth sinks into my skin, and I sigh.

"Better?"

"I am now that you're here with me." I reach for his hand and twine my fingers with his.

He peers into my eyes. "Are you—?

"Pregnant?" I bite the inside of my cheek. "I think so."

"You haven't checked?"

"I was waiting for you to return."

"I'm sorry I had to take off on such short notice. I'd have preferred to be here, especially with Christian's triplet still in a coma."

"It's understandable," I murmur. "It's been nearly two weeks since he was shot."

"And we still don't have a lead on who did this." He pulls me up to my feet, then scoops me up in his arms. I cuddle into his chest. There's nowhere else I feel as I do, here with him, in our home. Not that I have been spending much time at home recently either. With Christian leaving for London to track down Aurora, and Michael and Seb leaving to take care of business, it left me and Cassandra, along with Nonna, Massimo, Luca, and Adrian, to take turns being with Theresa.

The woman is stubborn. She refuses to leave his side. It had taken a lot of persuasion, but she finally agreed to head back once a day to shower and change her clothes before returning to keep her vigil.

The doctors moved him into a suite in the hospital which resembles a hotel suite, except for the medical equipment, that is.

It's a brighter, more cheerful room, and at least, there is an extra bed that Theresa can use. Of course, her preferred spot is in the chair near the bed, holding his hand. She also speaks to him and reads to him, and the doctors say that's good. It helps to keep his subconscious engaged and gives him a reason to return.

"How is he?" Michael places me down on the bed, then sits down next to me. "I haven't been to the hospital yet. I came here directly from the airport."

"He's the same," I murmur. "It's difficult to see him and not think of Xander. Of course, if Theresa has her way, he'll wake up and think of himself as Xander." I laugh.

He blows out a breath. "It's not healthy, the fact that she has her hopes pegged on his waking up and for the two of them to then have a chance at a real relationship, unlike what she had with Xander."

"It seems cruel to destroy her expectations." I raise a shoulder. "Also, he did step in front of her and take a bullet for her, so that must mean something."

"Perhaps…" Michael doesn't sound convinced.

"Perhaps, he did it out of instinct?" I offer. "Perhaps, it's that same instinct which will have him look for a relationship with her?"

"Hmm," Michael's lips firm. "And Christian? Is he back?"

"They are returning tomorrow. I'm glad you convinced him and Aurora to stay in London and take a few days for themselves."

"He wanted me to call him if there was any change in his triplet's condition. But … I get the sense that he is also dreading meeting his triplet when he wakes up."

"We still have no idea about who he is, do we?"

"I had my contact at the police station run his prints through the database, but we found nothing."

"Nothing?" I blink.

"Whoever he is, he's managed to cover his tracks well."

"Or it could mean that he is innocent?"

"Maybe." He cups my cheek. "When do you want to take the test?"

I draw in a breath. "Now."

"You sure? We can wait until you feel stronger."

"I feel much better now that you're here." And it's true.

As long as Michael is with me, I can face anything. Only question is, what will his reaction be when I tell him about the potential consequences of my pregnancy?

60

Christian

Earlier today, I spoke with Michael on the phone, and he told me that my triplet is stable but still unconscious.

I felt guilty about staying away when my family needs me, but Michael convinced me that it was just as important for me to woo my wife and bring her back home. I had hesitated and he was insistent that I take as much time as needed to consolidate my relationship with Aurora. He promised that he'd call me if anything changed in my triplet's condition, and that's when I finally relented.

We spent an idyllic weekend in Aurora's apartment, after which she went back to work, returning exhausted every day. Seeing her in her natural habitat, taking in just how much effort she put into her role as a doctor, has put things in a new light. Oh, I knew she was clever and that she was a good doctor, but I had never appreciated just how much of herself she puts into building up her career... To be fair, it's more than a career; it's a calling. And it feels wrong to ask her to give it up and move back to Palermo with me.

So, I haven't. Instead, I've focused on the now, and the time I have with her. I've made sure that there was food to eat—yes, I did order it in— when she got back and ensured that she got a good night's sleep. After I fucked her, of course.

That's how we passed most of the week, and now it's Friday, and I'm scheduled to fly home tomorrow.

The doorbell rings, and I let in the caterers. They get to work laying the table, complete with cutlery, candles, and wine glasses. They place the prosecco in the bucket and leave. Just in time, for a few minutes later, Aurora walks in.

She takes one look at the table and pauses. "Wow," she breathes, "what are you celebrating?" She kicks off her boots, takes off her coat and drops it, along with her bag, on the sofa in the living room. She walks over to the table and raises the lid of one of the dishes. The tangy scent of spaghetti fills the space. "Oh, yum." She reaches for a fork, and I click my tongue.

"Now, now, don't be naughty, my Flower."

"But I'm hungry," she whines. "I'll take only a bite; I promise." She dips her fork into the food, scoops up some of the strands, and brings it to her mouth.

"Oh my god," she groans, "this is so good. Did you have it catered from a Michelin-starred restaurant?"

"Even better." I smirk. "I had Zia Anita's Cucina make it special for us."

"Zia Anita?" She blinks. "You have an aunt who lives here?"

"She's actually my cousin's husband's sister's uncle's wife."

"Huh?" She scowls. "Isn't your cousin's husband's sister's uncle the same as your cousin's husband's uncle?"

My grin widens, and she frowns. "You're kidding me, right?"

"Almost." I laugh. "She really is a distant relation who moved to London thirty years ago and now runs one of the most authentic Sicilian restaurants in all of London."

"Right…" She licks her lips. "Well, whoever she is, her spaghetti rocks."

"I'll be sure to tell her that." I walk over, then scoop up some of the sauce from the corner of her lips and bring it to my mouth. "Hmm…" I survey her features. "You're right; it really is delicious."

Her pupils dilate, and by god, I'm sure I can smell the ripe scent of her arousal. I wrap my fingers around her wrist, then bring the fork to my mouth. I swirl my tongue around the tines, and a whine spills from her lips.

"Not fair," she whispers, "you're seducing me."

"Was under the impression that it was the other way around. You're seducing me, baby."

"Me?" She glances down at her scrubs, then back at me. "I'm hardly dressed for seduction."

"You could wear a sack, and the moment I take in your curves—which, by the way, no cloth can ever hide from me—I'm a goner."

She laughs. "Sometimes, I don't know if I should believe you or not."

"Oh, believe me, baby." I ease the fork from her fingers, drop it on the table, then bring her palm to my crotch. "See what you do to me?"

Her breath hitches. She massages the evidence of my arousal, and fuck, if my dick doesn't thicken further.

"And here I was, trying to make sure everything is perfect today."

"Everything is perfect." She squeezes the column between my legs, and my groin hardens. My balls ache, and hell, if it isn't tempting to throw her onto the table and fuck her senseless, but that won't do.

"It's our last night together," I whisper. "I want it to be a night to remember."

"Oh," her features seem to crumple, "that's right." She pulls away from me, but I don't release her. She glances away, and her chin trembles.

"Hey," I wrap my arm around her and bring her closer, trapping her hand on my crotch between us. "Don't be upset, Flower. You know I'll come back to you as soon as possible."

"It won't be soon enough." She shakes her head. "You've not even left, and I already miss you." She presses her lips together as if she regrets her outburst.

"I miss you already, as well," I admit. I press a kiss to her forehead, then to the tip of her nose. "I have no idea how I'm going to live without you, but I need to get back; my family needs me."

"I know." she bites down on her lower lip.

"Fuck," I groan, "don't do that. You're not allowed to do that. Only I can bite down on your lip, Flower." I lick her mouth, and as soon as she releases the hold on her lip, I close my teeth around it. I tug, and she trembles. I lick the abraded flesh, and a moan squeezes past her lips.

"Christian," she moans, "please fuck me."

I release her mouth and press my forehead to hers. "I intend to, but not yet."

"But why?" She massages my throbbing length through my pants. "It's not like you don't want to."

"Of course, I do," I confess, "but I promised myself I'd make sure we have at least one civilized meal together before I make love to you."

"Make love to me, now." She tips up her chin. "Please?"

"As soon as we finish dinner." I frame her face. "I need to make sure you are well fed and taken care of. Otherwise, between the demands of your job and my demands on your body, I'm going to wear you down."

She holds my gaze for a second, then nods. "Okay," she jerks her head, "I'll take a quick shower."

I have the candles lit, the music playing softly over the speakers—which I had specially-ordered a few days ago. I admit, I have consumed a couple of glasses of whiskey to curb my nervousness—why the hell am I nervous anyway?—by the time she returns.

I take in the simple pale pink dress that covers her from shoulder to knee and which shows off her curves, and the blood drains to my groin. She walks over to me in her six-inch heels, which show off her legs to advantage, and all I can think of is that I want them wrapped around my waist while I take her right here.

"You know what?" I glance down at her. "Fuck what I said earlier; let's forget about dinner."

Just then, her stomach rumbles, and I can't stop my chuckle.

"Guess you should feed me first, after all?" She laughs as she takes her seat.

I pop the prosecco, pour the sparkling liquid into her glass, then into my own. I fold into my seat next to her and hold up my flute. "To us?"

"To us." She smiles and sips from the bubbles. "Mmm," she licks her lips, "is this also Sicilian?"

"You bet." I take another sip, relishing the fizz of the bubbles on my tongue.

"Didn't think Sicily was famous for its prosecco."

"This comes from one of our vineyards."

"Your vineyards?"

"We own them in Sicily. Also, in Argentina, Australia, and in the Napa Valley. In fact, we have had some interest from a UK-based investor, and we may be collaborating with them to grow the business."

"Ah," she takes another sip, "you mean, grow the legal aspect of your business?"

"Exactly." I take in her features. "You're really good at piecing things together to get a glimpse of the big picture, aren't you?"

"Thanks." She laughs. "You forget, I grew up in the lap of the Mafia; I know how you guys think."

"How we guys think."

"What?" She blinks rapidly.

I place my glass down, then reach for her left palm and turn it up. "How we guys think." I drag my thumb across her engagement and wedding rings. "You are one of us, Aurora; you always have been. You have the Mafia in your blood."

"I know," she whispers. "I ran from it for so long, and apparently, I was running to you all this time."

I link my fingers with her. "I know it's wrong of me to ask you this, and these last few days, I've come to appreciate just how good you are at what you do... Clearly, your patients need you, and it's so very wrong of me to ask this of you, but—"

"Yes."

"What?"

"I said yes."

"You mean..." I stare at her. "You mean..." I don't stutter. I never do. But seriously, this woman, she's pulled the rug from under my feet. "You mean—"

"I'll come with you." She smirks. "That's what you were going to ask me, right?"

I nod, unable to process what I'm hearing.

"So you'll—"

"Leave my job and come to Palermo and be the medic for all of you undeserving Sovranos and your clan? Yes."

A hot sensation stabs at my chest. "But being here, living your life, finding your identity, all of it is—"

"It's important," she nods, "but so are you."

"I could commute." I hold her gaze. "I'd spend alternate weeks here in London."

"But you are the consigliere," she points out. "I know that means you are not just their lawyer but often help to act as a liaison on the Don's behalf too."

"One of my brothers would have to step up a little more. I'd find a way to manage."

"But being away from the *famiglia* would put you at risk, wouldn't it?"

"I'd make sure to up my security presence, and that'd go for you too."

"You mean, instead of the two guards you have following me, you'd have four?"

"You noticed?" I laugh. "Of course, you did; in fact, I had made a bet with myself that you would."

"Yeah," she glances down at our joined fingers, "as you said, I grew up with the Mafia; it's in my blood. Like it or not, I picked up on the signs to look for when it comes to having someone tailing me. I also know that you have, at least, ten of them surrounding my apartment building, and that both of my neighbors have been replaced by your people who've moved in."

"Jesus, woman," I chuckle, "is there anything that slips past you?"

"I didn't realize the man who threatened me was related to you." She lowers her chin to her chest. "If only I had come to you first with it, I—"

"Shh," I reach forward and rub my thumb across her mouth, "don't waste your breath on it."

"But I asked him to distract you, Christian. How could I have done that, knowing he could use my words against me? Knowing he could have easily decided to hurt you anyway? How could you forgive me for that?"

"Because," I hold her gaze, "it's what I would have done if I were in your position, and if I had been under so much pressure. Because I'm equally to blame. After all, I didn't think twice before believing him, despite my every instinct screaming that he was lying. Because"—I lean in close enough for our eyelashes to tangle—"we both have Mafia blood in us. It's in our DNA, and try as we might, we can't get away from it. Because you hadn't yet fallen in love with me, and what you did tells me that you can look after yourself when you are in a tight spot; it reassures me that you can take care of yourself. What you did shows that you were born to be a mob wife."

She winces.

"I meant that as a compliment."

"What's scary is that I understand what you mean, even though I wish I didn't." She draws in a breath.

"And most of all, because that part of our life is done, we're starting afresh, remember?"

"Yeah," she nods, "it's why I want to come back to Palermo with you, Christian."

"But your job—"

"They'll miss me, but they understand. Also, they have agreed that I can consult with them, so—"

"That's wonderful news." I grip her hand between mine. "I don't want you to feel like you are being pushed into this decision. Or that you are compromising more than I am in this relationship."

She stares.

"What?" I quirk an eyebrow. "What's wrong?"

"Are you the same macho, misogynistic Christian who implied that cooking was a woman's job and that a man's role is to take care of her?"

"Hey, I still think so."

She tries to pull her hand from my grasp, and I laugh. "Just kidding. But no, seriously, I admit I have been an ass sometimes."

"Sometimes?"

"Okay, many times. I have been a jerk, a complete … what do the Brits say—a wanker," I quirk my lips, "but somewhere along the way, this fiery doctor wore me down and made me see the error of my ways."

She sniffs. "Now you're making me cry." She half-smiles. "Also, don't stop talking; it's good for my ego."

I throw back my head and guffaw. "Woman, you're one of the few people who can go toe-to-toe with me, you know that?"

"I enjoy it, though." She places her hand on mine. "I find it exhilarating when you challenge me and push my limits, in bed and outside. It's an adrenaline rush to stand up to you, take you on, knowing I can't possibly win, and then when I do"—she shakes her head—"I can never figure out if you let me win or if it was—"

"It's you." I bring both of her hands to my mouth and kiss the backs of her palms. "You worm your way under my skin and figure out just what my failings are, and you take advantage of them, and you get your way. And you know what?"

"What?"

"I love you even more for it."

61

***

Epilogue

Aurora

The next day, we fly back to Palermo on the Sovranos' private jet. Even though I have grown up with the Mafia, I'm still not used to the Sovranos' lifestyle. Christian held my hand all the way through on the flight, and even now, as we walk into the elevator of the hospital where his triplet is, he doesn't let go. I glance up at him and recognize the slight tic at the edge of his jaw. A telltale sign that he is on edge. I squeeze his hand, and he glances down at me. "You okay?"

"I should be asking you that." I peer up into his face. "You're still not used to the idea that you have a triplet, are you?"

"No." He rubs the back of his neck. "A part of me insists that Xander can't be replaced, while another part of me is ecstatic that there is a chance to recapture some of the relationship I had with him. And that only makes me feel guilty." He blows out a breath. "I don't think I'll ever get over the fact that he's not here. That he won't be able to live life and experience what it is to have found a soul mate, a woman who is mine, who is so tuned in to me that she sometimes reads my thoughts before I have said them aloud."

A warm sensation fills my chest. This past week, when we were on our own, even though I had to go to work, and had even been called into the ER twice in the evenings, we still had time to get to know each other. Away from the pressures of his job, when he's had a chance to let down his guard, Christian can be incredibly charming, attentive, not to mention panty-meltingly sexy, whether he's dressed in sweats or in jeans, or like now, wearing his tailor-made suit.

He filled my little apartment with his presence, uncomplainingly shared my queen-sized bed, which was too small for his frame, and made sure I was always fed and taken care of when I returned home tired from the day's work. It's like he was trying to show me that he really wants this relationship to work, and that he respects me, loves me and wants to spend his life with me.

"I love you," I burst out.

His lip quirks. "I love you too." He dips his head and captures my lips in a kiss that is so deep, so hard, that I can feel it all the way to my toes.

The elevator dings, but we don't stop kissing each other. He pulls me up to my tiptoes, molds my body to his, and thoroughly kisses me.

Someone clears his throat, but I don't pull away. I tip up my chin, tilt my head, and open my mouth even more, so he thrusts his tongue in between my lips. A groan rumbles up his chest, and my nipples tighten. Moisture slides down between my thighs and—

"You guys coming out or what?" an amused voice calls out.

I pull away, and Christian reluctantly releases me. He turns, and I glance around him to find Adrian holding the doors of the elevator open. There's a grin on his face as he glances between us. "Good to see the two of you are back on speaking terms."

"Not that good to see your ugly mug," Christian retorts before shooting me an amused glance. Still holding my hand, he steps out of the elevator, and I follow him.

Adrian flanks me as we walk past the guards posted at intervals along the corridor. I peek into the rooms as we pass and find they are all empty.

"We had to empty the floor for security reasons," Adrian informs me.

Of course, the man who shot at Christian's triplet is still out there, so it makes sense to be careful. But still, the scale of power that the Sovranos wield hits me all over again. We reach the doorway to the room where Christian's triplet is, and he pauses.

Adrian steps back, and I turn to Christian. "You ready?"

He draws in a breath, then pushes the door open. We walk inside the room— no, it's a suite, actually.

Karma looks up from her book, then jumps up and rushes over to me. "Oh, you're here." She throws her arms around me, and I hug her back. "I missed you," she cries out.

"Me too." I squeeze her shoulders, then step back. Massimo pushes away from the window and prowls over to us. He and Christian do that half-hug men often do, then Massimo slaps his back. "Welcome back, *fratello*, we missed you."

"You mean you missed having someone who can take you on in a fight?" Christian snorts.

"A week away, and you have forgotten how I thrashed your sorry ass the last time." Massimo laughs, then sobers. "But seriously, it's good that you are here; we need the family together right now." He turns to me. "I should say 'thank you' for coming back with our brother and making him happy."

My cheeks heat. "I…" I shake my head, not sure how to react. "I'm glad we could return together."

"So am I." Christian pulls me close and kisses the top of my head. "How's—" he jerks his chin toward the door to the inner room.

As a doctor, I've been to some nice hospital rooms, but this particular suite is more like an apartment within the hospital, with its own living room where the family can wait while Christian's triplet is in the adjoining room.

There's also a second door that now opens. Seb enters the living room. "There's no change in his condition." He walks over to sit down in a chair. "Except for the fact that we seem to have temporarily moved our working space to the hospital." He gestures to the room he's just entered from. Before the door shuts, I get a glimpse of tables with laptops. Behind one is Luca; he nods in our direction. In the far corner of the room, Michael stands near the window, speaking on the phone.

"The deals with both the Kane Company and the Bratva are coming into play, and our overall level of business transactions has gone up," Massimo explains.

"There's also the question of what we want to do with Xander's paintings—" Seb starts, but Christian cuts him off.

"It's too early to talk about that," he growls. "For fuck's sake, my brother has been just over a month, and you are already talking about disposing of his paintings."

"Or not," Massimo butts in, "which is why we wanted to talk to you. We discussed maybe setting up a foundation, but—"

Christian shoots him a glance. "Not now, Massimo, okay? Not until our triplet wakes up."

Massimo and Seb exchange a glance, then Seb nods. "Whatever you feel is right, brother."

Just then, the door to the inner room opens, and Nonna walks out. She spots Christian and pauses, then seems to steel herself before walking over to us.

"Christian," she pauses in front of him, "I'm so glad you are back, *nipotino mio*."

The two of them stare at each other. Something unspoken seems to pass between them. Then Christian steps forward and hugs her.

Nonna's features crumple, and she buries her face in his shoulder. "I'm so sorry I didn't tell you about the existence of your triplet," she murmurs. "You deserved to know, but I kept it from you. It was the deal we made with your mother."

"My mother," Christian pauses, "is she—?"

"She died a few years ago," Nonna replies.

Christian steps back. "How did you find out?"

"When news of her death reached me, I paid people to try to track down your brother, but he seemed to have disappeared."

"Until the day he appeared," Christian says softly.

"When your mother fell pregnant, your father was not only married, but he'd also just brought Seb and Adrian into the family after their mother had died. Your mother gave birth to triplets, and by then, she'd realized what kind of a man your father was. She wanted to leave with all three of you, but your father refused. But your mother came from a powerful mafia family as well; not the *Cosa Nostra* but the *Camorra*. They weren't happy about what she'd done, but she was one of theirs, so they negotiated a deal with your father. Your mother could leave with one of the three, and we'd keep the other two children. Also," she glances away, "there was an exchange of assets, as you can imagine, assets which helped your father's reach grow further."

Christian squeezes his eyes shut.

"I wanted to stop him, but you have to understand, I didn't hold that kind of power. If I had gone against your father, he would have disowned me, and that would have meant that I couldn't have been around to protect the rest of you from him."

"So, you stayed?" Christian says in a low voice.

"I stayed, and your brother was taken by your mother. I kept tabs on them, right until the time he turned eighteen and left home."

"Who knows what he's gone through." Christian drags his fingers through his hair. "What made him turn on us? Why did he threaten Aurora? Why did he agree to kill me, knowing I was his brother?"

Suddenly, a scream sounds from the inside room where his triplet is. Christian stiffens, then races for the door.

To find out what happens next, read Mafia Crown **HERE**

Get this exclusive epilogue in which Christian reveals the meaning of his tattoos.

Read an excerpt from Mafia Crown

Theresa

"Who are you?" His blue gaze bores into me. Considering he's been unconscious for two weeks, he shouldn't seem this alert. But nothing about this man has been predictable from the moment I laid eyes on him.

"Don't you remember? You stepped in front of me; you took a bullet for me." Shit, hadn't meant to blurt it out like that, honestly, but it's the only thing I have been able to think of for the time that I have sat here staring at him.

"Bullet?" He tilts his head then winces.

"Your temple," I gesture to the bandage around his head, "the bullet hit your temple. You lost a lot of blood and they had to put you in an induced coma so that you could heal faster."

The expression on his face doesn't change. If he's surprised, he doesn't show it. He raises his gaze back to mine, then glances around the room, before staring at the glass of water on the side table.

"Oh, are you thirsty?"

He doesn't reply. Simply looks at me again.

Of course, he's thirsty, what an insane thing to ask. His gaze tracks me as I reach his bedside. I raise the glass of water and hold it out. He stares from my face, to the glass of water, then back at me.

"Oh, right." I lower the glass until the edge of the straw stuck inside it brushes his mouth. He parts his lips and sips from the straw. The tendons of his throat moves as he swallows.

Awareness prickles up my spine. I've stared at him so closely over the past couple of weeks that I know every ridge of his face, every crease at the edges of his eyes, the jut of his nose, the strong square jaw of his, the way his lower lip is pouty and fat and almost too feminine for the rest of his face, the way his long lashes brush across his cheekbones, the width of his shoulders which strain against the hospital gown they'd draped on him, the tan of his skin, still dark, even after all this time in the hospital, hinting at his bloodline. A bloodline that I know well, considering I had been in love with his triplet before he'd died. A man I'd had crushed on since I had been a child. A man who is now gone, never to return and instead… this man, with the face of my past love had appeared out of the blue to take his place. It has to be a sign, surely, that his path and mine have crossed. Xander is dead but this guy is alive. And he saved me from the bullet. Surely, there is no logical reason he'd do that… Not unless he'd felt pulled toward me, even though neither of us knew each other. Of course, I know who he is now, but the intensity with which he's watching me indicates he has no clue about how we are connected.

When he slumps against the pillow, I place the glass back on the bedside.

"Uh, I think I need to call the doctor," I shift forward in my chair before rising.

"The doctor?"

I nod, "You've been in a coma for two weeks."

He frowns.

"Basically, since you got shot, you've been out. We, uh, had to rush you to the hospital—"

"We?" His scowl deepens.

"We, as in me—even though I was on the verge of a nervous breakdown, seeing as I was covered in your blood—and your brothers and—"

"Brothers?" His gaze intensifies. "Did you say my brothers?" he says with slow deliberation.

"Yes," I nod. Surely, it's okay to tell him about his brothers, right? I mean, he does know about them, doesn't he? Or else, why would he have sought them out and intruded on the gathering at Christian and Aurora's place?

His eyebrows knit. A wary gaze in his eyes.

Unless he doesn't really know about their existence, or that of his triplets, or the fact that one of them is dead. Oh, crap. I swallow. Maybe I shouldn't have spoken to him and called the doctor instead. Surely, it isn't good for him to get all worked up, and that's exactly what I am doing right now.

"Umm," I take a step back, "I think it's best I get the doctor."

I turn to leave, then gasp when he grabs my wrist. Electricity travels out from the point of contact. I glance down at where the darkness of his fingers contrasts with the paleness of my skin. It's as if I am the one who's been unwell, considering my pallor.

"For someone who's been unconscious for a few weeks, you seem to have retained most of your strength," I mutter.

"No doctor," he rasps. I glance up to find his face is definitely a few shades paler than earlier.

"You are in a hospital and you've just emerged from a coma. I really do need to call the doctor."

"No," sweat beads his forehead, "no doctor." He glances between my eyes. "Please," he seems to force the word out, "no doctor."

"Look, I am not sure why you are having such a panicked reaction to the idea of a doctor checking you out, but they saved your life. If it weren't for them, you might be dead."

There's still no response from him. His hold on my arm seems to tighten. Jesus, this man must have been in peak physical condition if he's this strong emerging from a coma. To be fair, he had moved so quickly when he'd stepped in front of me that I hadn't even realized what was happening. Not until I'd heard that sickening thwack of the bullet piercing through his flesh and then... I swallow. Then, a part of me had known how close to death I had been. As he had stumbled back, I had known he'd stepped in front of me to protect me. I had jumped forward to try to catch his fall and had half collapsed under the weight of his body before sinking to my knees with him sprawled across my lap. And even then, I had not known who he really was, until Christian had taken off the stranger's mask and I had seen Xander's face, as if resurrected from the dead. My heart begins to race in my chest as I take in the features of the man on the bed. Even now, I can't believe just how similar the two of them look.

Christian and Xander were twins, but they hadn't been identical. But this man, he resembles Xander so much, it makes my chest hurt just looking at him.

"Okay," I nod, "no doctor…for now, but someone is going to come and check in on you eventually."

He doesn't reply, doesn't let go of my arm either. "Who are you?" he asks again. "Do I know you? Have we met?"

"Not until you stepped in front of me and took the bullet."

He winces.

"Does it hurt?" I glance at the bandage around his head, "Damn, I knew I shouldn't have agreed not to call the doctor. Look, I don't want anything to happen to you, okay? They need to come and check you and out and make sure that you are okay and—"

"I'm okay," he rasps.

"You don't look okay." I take in his features, which have definitely gone paler in the last few seconds. "You look like you are about to lose consciousness again, and that's not good, that's really not good, I—"

"Will you calm the fuck down, woman," he growls.

"Excuse me?" I stare, "What did you say?"

He blows out a breath, "I am fine. I don't need you making a fuss over me."

My chest rises and falls. I'd been waiting for him to wake up all these days. I had practically chained myself to the bed and kept vigil and prayed that he'd open his eye and now that he has... He tells me to fuck off?

"Let go of me," I say through gritted teeth.

"Not until you tell me how the hell I came to be in this hospital room."

"That's what I have been trying to explain, if you'd put your paranoia aside for one moment and listen to me."

"Paranoia?" He scowls, "What the fuck gave you that idea, anyway?"

I glance down at where his fingers are still curled around my wrist, and his grasp tightens.

"You're my insurance," he says in a hard voice. "I am not letting you go until I understand what kind of a situation I am in."

"You're in a hospital and I should have called a doctor who's going to be pissed that I didn't at the first sign of your waking up, that's the kind of situation you are in," I scold. "Now, will you let go of me, please?"

"Why are they keeping me here? Who are these brothers you spoke about?"

"You don't remember? And for the record, as I have already explained, no-one is keeping you here. You were shot, so they brought you to the hospital—'

"Who's they?"

"The paramedics who your brother Michael called?"

"Michael?" He frowns, "And he is...

"Your oldest brother."

"How many brothers do I have, anyway?"

"Um...five? No, there's four, actually."

"Which is it, four or five?"

"Four," I nod my head. "Xander, your triplet—"

"Hold on, did you say triplet?"

Oops, I hadn't meant to reveal that yet, but he'd have eventually learned about it, one way or the other, right? So, it's okay for me to tell him that he has a triplet. I mean, he must have known, considering he turned up at Christian and Aurora's wedding, right?

"Umm, yea...and then, you have two half-brothers, so including you, that makes it seven brothers again."

"Again?" He scowls, "What do you mean by that?"

"Xander is...you know—"

"No, I don't know." Sweat beads his forehead and his grasp on my arm loosens. "What happened to Xander?"

"He's... uh... " Damn, it's not easy to break the news to him, and especially when he's only just woken up from a coma. Speaking of, how the hell could he be so lucid so soon? "It's best you hear about it once you recover completely."

"Tell me...now," he begins to slur. "Tell me..." his eyelids flutter, "I... in-insist." He releases me and slumps back against the pillows. His features go slack. I hesitate, watch as his breathing deepens. Best to call the doctor now, before he wakes up again and insists that he doesn't want anyone to examine him.

I turn to leave, and that's when the window of the hospital room shatters. The glass pieces scatter across the floor as a man jumps into the room.

To find out what happens next, read Mafia Crown **HERE**

Start the Series with Mafia KING, Michael & Karma's story **HERE**

Read an excerpt from mafia king

Karma

"Morn came and went—and came, and brought no day..."

Tears prick the backs of my eyes. Goddamn Byron. His words creep up on me when I am at my weakest. Not that I am a poetry addict, by any measure, but words are my jam. The one consolation I have is that, when everything else in the world is wrong, I can turn to them, and they'll be there, friendly, steady, waiting with open arms.

And this particular poem had laced my blood, crawled into my gut when I'd first read it. Darkness had folded within me like an insidious snake, that raises its head when I least expect it. Like now, when I look out on the still sleeping city of London, from the grassy slope of Waterlow Park.

Somewhere out there, the Mafia is hunting me, apparently. It's why my sister Summer and her new husband Sinclair Sterling had insisted that I have my own security detail. I had agreed...only to appease them...then given my bodyguard the slip this morning. I had decided to come running here because it's not a place I'd normally go... Not so early in the morning, anyway. They won't think to look for me here. At least, not for a while longer.

I purse my lips, close my eyes. Silence. The rustle of the wind between the leaves. The faint tinkle of the water from the nearby spring.

I could be the last person on this planet, alone, unsung, bound for the grave.

Ugh! Stop. Right there. I drag the back of my hand across my nose. Try it again, focus, get the words out, one after the other, like the steps of my sorry life.

"Morn came and went—and came, and... and..." My voice breaks. "Bloody asinine hell." I dig my fingers into the grass and grab a handful and fling it out. Again. From the top.

"Morn came and went—and came, and—"

"...brought no day."

A gravelly voice completes my sentence.

I whip my head around. His silhouette fills my line of sight. He's sitting on the same knoll as me, yet I have to crane my neck back to see his profile. The sun is at his back, so I can't make out his features. Can't see his eyes... Can only take in his dark hair, combed back by a ruthless hand that brooked no measure.

My throat dries.

Thick dark hair, shot through with grey at the temples. He wears his age like a badge. I don't know why, but I know his years have not been easy. That he's seen more, indulged in more, reveled in the consequences of his actions, however extreme they might have been. He's not a normal, everyday person, this man. Not a nine-to-fiver, not someone who lives an average life. Definitely not a man who returns home to his wife and home at the end of the day. He is...different, unique, evil... Monstrous. Yes, he is a beast, one who sports the face of a man but who harbors the kind of darkness inside that speaks to me. I gulp.

His face boasts a hooked nose, a thin upper lip, a fleshy lower lip. One that hints at hidden desires, Heat. Lust. The sensuous scrape of that whiskered jaw over my innermost places. Across my inner thigh, reaching toward that core of me that throbs, clenches, melts to feel the stab of his tongue, the thrust of his hardness as he impales me, takes me, makes me his. Goosebumps pop on my skin.

I drag my gaze away from his mouth down to the scar that slashes across his throat. A cold sensation coils in my chest. What or who had hurt him in such a cruel fashion?

"Of this their desolation; and all hearts
Were chill'd into a selfish prayer for light…"

He continues in that rasping guttural tone. Is it the wound that caused that scar that makes his voice so…gravelly… So deep…so…so, hot?

Sweat beads my palms and the hairs on my nape rise. "Who are you?"

He stares ahead as his lips move,

"Forests were set on fire—but hour by hour
They fell and faded—and the crackling trunks
Extinguish'd with a crash—and all was black."

I swallow, moisture gathers in my core. How can I be wet by the mere cadence of this stranger's voice?

I spring up to my feet.

"Sit down," he commands.

His voice is unhurried, lazy even, his spine erect. The cut of his black jacket stretches across the width of his massive shoulders. His hair… I was mistaken—there are threads of dark gold woven between the darkness that pours down to brush the nape of his neck. A strand of hair falls over his brow. As I watch, he raises his hand and brushes it away. Somehow, the gesture lends an air of vulnerability to him. Something so at odds with the rest of his persona that, surely, I am mistaken?

My scalp itches. I take in a breath and my lungs burn. This man… He's sucked up all the oxygen in this open space as if he owns it, the master of all he surveys. The master of me. My death. My life. A shiver ladders along my spine. *Get away, get away now, while you still can.*

I angle my body, ready to spring away from him.

"I won't ask again."

Ask. Command. Force me to do as he wants. He'll have me on my back, bent over, on my side, on my knees, over him, under him. He'll surround me, overwhelm me, pin me down with the force of his personality. His charisma, his larger-than-life essence will crush everything else out of me and I… I'll love it.

"No."

"Yes."

A fact. A statement of intent, spoken aloud. So true. So real. Too real. Too much. Too fast. All of my nightmares…my dreams come to life. Everything I've wanted is here in front of me. I'll die a thousand deaths before he'll be done with me... And then? Will I be reborn? For him. For me. For myself.

I live, first and foremost, to be the woman I was...am meant to be.

"You want to run?"

No.

No.

I nod my head.

He turns his, and all the breath leaves my lungs. Blue eyes—cerulean, dark like the morning skies, deep like the nighttime...hidden corners, secrets that I don't dare uncover. He'll destroy me, have my heart, and break it so casually.

My throat burns and a boiling sensation squeezes my chest.

"Go then, my beauty, fly. You have until I count to five. If I catch you, you are mine."

"If you don't?"

"Then I'll come after you, stalk your every living moment, possess your nightmares, and steal you away in the dead of night, and then..."

I draw in a shuddering breath as liquid heat drips from between my legs. "Then?" I whisper.

"Then, I'll ensure you'll never belong to anyone else, you'll never see the light of day again, for your every breath, your every waking second, your thoughts, your actions...and all your words, every single last one, will belong to me." He peels back his lips, and his teeth glint in the first rays of the morning light. "Only me." He straightens to his feet and rises, and rises.

This man... He is massive. A monster who always gets his way. My guts churn. My toes curl. Something primeval inside of me insists I hold my own. I cannot give in to him. Cannot let him win whatever this is. I need to stake my ground, in some form. *Say something. Anything. Show him you're not afraid of this.*

"Why?" I tilt my head back, all the way back. "Why are you doing this?"

He tilts his head, his ears almost canine in the way they are silhouetted against his profile.

"Is it because you can? Is it a...a," I blink, "a debt of some kind?"

He stills.

"My father, this is about how he betrayed the Mafia, right? You're one of them?"

"Lucky guess." His lips twist, "It is about your father, and how he promised you to me. He reneged on his promise, and now, I am here to collect."

"No." I swallow... *No, no, no.*

"Yes." His jaw hardens.

All expression is wiped clean of his face, and I know then, that he speaks the truth. It's always about the past. My sorry shambles of a past... Why does it always catch up with me? *You can run, but you can never hide.*

"Tick-tock, Beauty." He angles his body and his shoulders shut out the sight of the sun, the dawn skies, the horizon, the city in the distance, the rustle of the grass, the trees, the rustle of the leaves. All of it fades and leaves just me and him. Us. *Run.*

"Five." He jerks his chin, straightens the cuffs of his sleeves.

My knees wobble.

"Four."

My pulse rate spikes. I should go. Leave. But my feet are planted in this earth. This piece of land where we first met. What am I, but a speck in the larger scheme of things? To be hurt. To be forgotten. To be taken without an ounce of retribution. To be punished...by him.

"Three." He thrusts out his chest, widens his stance, every muscle in his body relaxed. "Two."

I swallow. The pulse beats at my temples. My blood thrums.

"One."

To find out what happens next read Mafia King **HERE**

Read Summer & Sinclair Sterling's story **HERE** in The Billionaire's Fake Wife

Read an excerpt from Summer & Sinclair's story

Summer

"Slap, slap, kiss, kiss."

"Huh?" I stare up at the bartender.

"Aka, there's a thin line between love and hate." He shakes out the crimson liquid into my glass.

"Nah." I snort. "Why would she allow him to control her, and after he insulted her?"

"It's the chemistry between them." He lowers his head, "You have to admit that when the man is arrogant and the woman resists, it's a challenge to both of them, to see who blinks first, huh?"

"Why?" I wave my hand in the air, "Because they hate each other?"

"Because," he chuckles, "the girl in school whose braids I pulled and teased mercilessly, is the one who I—"

"Proposed to?" I huff.

His face lights up. "You get it now?"

Yeah. No. A headache begins to pound at my temples. This crash course in pop psychology is not why I came to my favorite bar in Islington, to meet my best friend, who is—I glance at the face of my phone—thirty minutes late.

I inhale the drink, and his eyebrows rise.

"What?" I glower up at the bartender. "I can barely taste the alcohol. Besides, it's free drinks at happy hour for women, right?"

"Which ends in precisely" he holds up five fingers, "minutes."

"Oh! Yay!" I mock fist pump. "Time enough for one more, at least."

A hiccough swells my throat and I swallow it back, nod.

One has to do what one has to do... when everything else in the world is going to shit.

A hot sensation stabs behind my eyes; my chest tightens. Is this what people call growing up?

The bartender tips his mixing flask, strains out a fresh batch of the ruby red liquid onto the glass in front of me.

"Salut." I nod my thanks, then toss it back. It hits my stomach and tendrils of fire crawl up my spine, I cough.

My head spins. Warmth sears my chest, spreads to my extremities. I can't feel my fingers or toes. Good. Almost there. "Top me up."

"You sure?"

"Yes." I square my shoulders and reach for the drink.

"No. She's had enough."

"What the—?" I pivot on the bar stool.

Indigo eyes bore into me.

Fathomless. Black at the bottom, the intensity in their depths grips me. He swoops out his arm, grabs the glass and holds it up. Thick fingers dwarf the glass. Tapered at the edges. The nails short and buff. *All the better to grab you with.* I gulp.

"Like what you see?"

I flush, peer up into his face.

Hard cheekbones, hollows under them, and a tiny scar that slashes at his left eyebrow. *How did he get that?* Not that I care. My gaze slides to his mouth. Thin upper lip, a lower lip that is full and cushioned. Pouty with a hint of bad boy. *Oh!* My toes curl. My thighs clench.

The corner of his mouth kicks up. *Asshole.*

Bet he thinks life is one big smug-fest. I glower, reach for my glass, and he holds it up and out of my reach.

I scowl, "Gimme that."

He shakes his head.

"That's my drink."

"Not anymore." He shoves my glass at the bartender. "Water for her. Get me a whiskey, neat."

I splutter, then reach for my drink again. The barstool tips, in his direction. This is when I fall against him, and my breasts slam into his hard chest, sculpted planes with layers upon layers of muscle that ripple and writhe as he turns aside, flattens himself against the bar. The floor rises up to meet me.

What the actual hell?

I twist my torso at the last second and my butt connects with the surface. *Ow!*

The breath rushes out of me. My hair swirls around my face. I scrabble for purchase, and my knee connects with his leg.

"Watch it." He steps around, stands in front of me.

"You stepped aside?" I splutter. "You let me fall?"

"Hmph."

I tilt my chin back, all the way back, look up the expanse of muscled thigh that stretches the silken material of his suit. *What is he wearing? Could any suit fit a man with such precision?* Hand crafted on Saville Row, no doubt. I glance at the bulge that tents the fabric between his legs. *Oh!* I blink.

Look away, look away. I hold out my arm. He'll help me up at least, won't he?

He glances at my palm, then turns away. *No, he didn't do that, no way.*

A glass of amber liquid appears in front of him. He lifts the tumbler to his sculpted mouth.

His throat moves, strong tendons flexing. He tilts his head back, and the column of his neck moves as he swallows. Dark hair covers his chin—it's a discordant chord in that clean-cut profile, I shiver. He would scrape that rough skin down my core. He'd mark my inner thigh, lick my core, thrust his tongue inside my melting channel and drink from my pussy. *Oh! God.* Goosebumps rise on my skin.

No one has the right to look this beautiful, this achingly gorgeous. Too magnificent for his own good. Anger coils in my chest.

"Arrogant wanker."

"I'll take that under advisement."

"You're a jerk, you know that?"

He presses his lips together. The grooves on either side of his mouth deepen. Jesus, clearly the man has never laughed a single day in his life. Bet that stick up his arse is uncomfortable. I chuckle.

He runs his gaze down my features, my chest, down to my toes, then yawns.

The hell! I will not let him provoke me. Will not. "Like what you see?" I jut out my chin.

"Sorry, you're not my type." He slides a hand into the pocket of those perfectly cut pants, stretching it across that heavy bulge.

Heat curls low in my belly.

Not fair, that he could afford a wardrobe that clearly shouts his status and what amounts to the economy of a small third-world country. A hot feeling stabs in my chest.

He reeks of privilege, of taking his status in life for granted.

While I've had to fight every inch of the way. Hell, I am still battling to hold onto the last of my equilibrium.

"Last chance—" I wiggle my fingers, from where I am sprawled out on the floor at his feet, "—to redeem yourself..."

"You have me there." He places the glass on the counter, then bends and holds out his hand. The hint of discolored steel at his wrist catches my attention. Huh?

He wears a cheap-ass watch?

That's got to bring down the net worth of his presence by more than 1000% percent. Weird.

I reach up and he straightens.

I lurch back.

"Oops, I changed my mind." His lips curl.

A hot burning sensation claws at my stomach. I am not a violent person, honestly. But Smirky Pants here, he needs to be taught a lesson.

I swipe out my legs, kicking his out from under him.

Sinclair

My knees give way, and I hurtle toward the ground.

What the—? I twist around, thrust out my arms. My palms hit the floor. The impact jostles up my elbows. I firm my biceps and come to a halt planked above her.

A huffing sound fills my ear.

I turn to find my whippet, Max, panting with his mouth open. I scowl and he flattens his ears.

All of my businesses are dog-friendly. Before you draw conclusions about me being the caring sort or some such shit—it attracts footfall.

Max scrutinizes the girl, then glances at me. *Huh?* He hates women, but not her, apparently.

I straighten and my nose grazes hers.

My arms are on either side of her head. Her chest heaves. The fabric of her dress stretches across her gorgeous breasts. My fingers tingle; my palms ache to cup those tits, squeeze those hard nipples outlined against the—hold on, what is she wearing? A tunic shirt in a sparkly pink... and are those shoulder pads she has on?

I glance up, and a squeak escapes her lips.

Pink hair surrounds her face. *Pink? Who dyes their hair that color past the age of eighteen?*

I stare at her face. *How old is she?* Un-furrowed forehead, dark eyelashes that flutter against pale cheeks. Tiny nose, and that mouth—luscious, tempting. A whiff of her scent, cherries and caramel, assails my senses. My mouth waters. *What the hell?*

She opens her eyes and our eyelashes brush. Her gaze widens. Green, like the leaves of the evergreens, flickers of gold sparkling in their depths. "What?" She glowers. "You're demonstrating the plank position?"

"Actually," I lower my weight onto her, the ridge of my hardness thrusting into the softness between her legs, "I was thinking of something else, altogether."

She gulps and her pupils dilate. *Ah, so she feels it, too?*

I drop my head toward her, closer, closer.

Color floods the creamy expanse of her neck. Her eyelids flutter down. She tilts her chin up.

I push up and off of her.

"That… Sweetheart, is an emphatic 'no thank you' to whatever you are offering."

Her eyelids spring open and pink stains her cheeks. Adorable. Such a range of emotions across those gorgeous features in a few seconds? What else is hidden under that exquisite exterior of hers?

She scrambles up, eyes blazing.

Ah! The little bird is trying to spread her wings? My dick twitches. My groin hardens, *Why does her anger turn me on so, huh?*

She steps forward, thrusts a finger in my chest.

My heart begins to thud.

She peers up from under those hooded eyelashes. "Wake up and taste the wasabi, asshole."

"What does that even mean?"

She makes a sound deep in her throat. My dick twitches. My pulse speeds up.

She pivots, grabs a half-full beer mug sitting on the bar counter.

I growl, "Oh, no, you don't."

She turns, swings it at me. The smell of hops envelops the space.

I stare down at the beer-splattered shirt, the lapels of my camel colored jacket deepening to a dull brown. Anger squeezes my guts.

I fist my fingers at my side, broaden my stance.

She snickers.

I tip my chin up. "You're going to regret that."

The smile fades from her face. "Umm." She places the now empty mug on the bar.

I take a step forward and she skitters back. "It's only clothes." She gulps, "They'll wash."

I glare at her and she swallows, wiggles her fingers in the air, "I should have known that you wouldn't have a sense of humor."

I thrust out my jaw, "That's a ten-thousand-pound suit you destroyed."

She blanches, then straightens her shoulders, "Must have been some hot date you were trying to impress, huh?"

"Actually," I flick some of the offending liquid from my lapels, "it's you I was after."

"Me?" She frowns.

"We need to speak."

She glances toward the bartender who's on the other side of the bar. "I don't know you." She chews on her lower lip, biting off some of the hot pink. How would she look, with that pouty mouth fastened on my cock?

The blood rushes to my groin so quickly that my head spins. My pulse rate ratchets up. Focus, focus on the task you came here for.

"This will take only a few seconds." I take a step forward.

She moves aside.

I frown, "You want to hear this, I promise."

"Go to hell." She pivots and darts forward.

I let her go, a step, another, because... I can? Besides it's fun to create the illusion of freedom first; makes the hunt so much more entertaining, huh?

I swoop forward, loop an arm around her waist, and yank her toward me.

She yelps. "Release me."

Good thing the bar is not yet full. It's too early for the usual officegoers to stop by. And the staff...? Well they are well aware of who cuts their paychecks.

I spin her around and against the bar, then release her. "You will listen to me."

She swallows; she glances left to right.

Not letting you go yet, little Bird. I move into her space, crowd her.

She tips her chin up. "Whatever you're selling, I'm not interested."

I allow my lips to curl, "You don't fool me."

A flush steals up her throat, sears her cheeks. So tiny, so innocent. Such a good little liar. I narrow my gaze, "Every action has its consequences."

"Are you daft?" She blinks.

"This pretense of yours?" I thrust my face into hers, "It's not working."

She blinks, then color suffuses her cheeks, "You're certifiably mad—"

"Getting tired of your insults."

"It's true, everything I said." She scrapes back the hair from her face.

Her fingernails are painted... You guessed it, pink.

"And here's something else. You are a selfish, egotistical jackass."

I smirk. "You're beginning to repeat your insults and I haven't even kissed you yet."

"Don't you dare." She gulps.

I tilt my head, "Is that a challenge?"

"It's a..." she scans the crowded space, then turns to me. Her lips firm, "...a warning. You're delusional, you jackass." She inhales a deep breath, "Your ego is bigger than the size of a black hole." She snickers, "Bet it's to compensate for your lack of balls."

A-n-d, that's it. I've had enough of her mouth that threatens to never stop spewing words. How many insults can one tiny woman hurl my way? Answer: too many to count.

"You—"

I lower my chin, touch my lips to hers.

Heat, sweetness, the honey of her essence explodes on my palate. My dick twitches. I tilt my head, deepen the kiss, reaching for that something more... more... of whatever scent she's wearing on her skin, infused with that breath of hers that crowds my senses, rushes down my spine. My groin hardens; my cock lengthens. I thrust my tongue between those infuriating lips.

She makes a sound deep in her throat and my heart begins to pound.

So innocent, yet so crafty. Beautiful and feisty. The kind of complication I don't need in my life.

I prefer the straight and narrow. Gray and black, that's how I choose to define my world. She, with her flashes of color—pink hair and lips that threaten to drive me to the edge of distraction—is exactly what I hate.

Give me a female who has her priorities set in life. To pleasure me, get me off, then walk away before her emotions engage. Yeah. That's what I prefer.

Not this... this bundle of craziness who flings her arms around my shoulders, thrusts her breasts up and into my chest, tips up her chin, opens her mouth, and invites me to take and take.

Does she have no self-preservation? Does she think I am going to fall for her wide-eyed appeal? She has another think coming.

I tear my mouth away and she protests.

She twines her leg with mine, pushes up her hips, so that melting softness between her thighs cradles my aching hardness.

I glare into her face and she holds my gaze.

Trains her green eyes on me. Her cheeks flush a bright red. Her lips fall open and a moan bleeds into the air. The blood rushes to my dick, which instantly thickens. *Fuck.*

Time to put distance between myself and the situation.

It's how I prefer to manage things. Stay in control, always. Cut out anything that threatens to impinge on my equilibrium. Shut it down or buy them off. Reduce it to a transaction. That I understand.

The power of money, to be able to buy and sell—numbers, logic. That's what's worked for me so far.

"How much?"

Her forehead furrows.

"Whatever it is, I can afford it."

Her jaw slackens. "You think… you—"

"A million?"

"What?"

"Pounds, dollars… You name the currency, and it will be in your account."

Her jaw slackens, "You're offering me money?"

"For your time, and for you to fall in line with my plan."

She reddens, "You think I am for sale?"

"Everyone is."

"Not me."

Here we go again. "Is that a challenge?"

Color fades from her face, "Get away from me."

"Are you shy, is that what this is?" I frown. "You can write your price down on a piece of paper if you prefer," I glance up, notice the bartender watching us. I jerk my chin toward the napkins. He grabs one, then offers it to her.

She glowers at him, "Did you buy him too?"

"What do you think?"

She glances around, "I think everyone here is ignoring us."

"It's what I'd expect."

"Why is that?"

I wave the tissue in front of her face, "Why do you think?"

"You own the place?"

"As I am going to own you."

She sets her jaw, "Let me leave and you won't regret this."

A chuckle bubbles up. I swallow it away. This is no laughing matter. I never smile during a transaction. Especially not when I am negotiating a new acquisition. And that's all she is. The final piece in the puzzle I am building.

"No one threatens me."

"You're right."

"Huh?"

"I'd rather act on my instinct."

Her lips twist, her gaze narrows. All of my senses scream a warning.

No, she wouldn't, no way—pain slices through my middle and sparks explode behind my eyes.

*T*O FIND OUT WHAT HAPPENS NEXT READ *S*UMMER *& S*INCLAIR *S*TERLING'S STORY **HERE**

*R*EAD ABOUT THE SEVEN IN THE *B*IG BAD *B*ILLIONAIRES SERIES

US

UK

*O*THER COUNTRIES

*C*LAIM YOUR **FREE** CONTEMPORARY ROMANCE BOXSET **HERE**

*C*LAIM YOUR **FREE** PARANORMAL ROMANCE BOXSET **HERE**

*W*ANT TO BE THE FIRST TO FIND OUT ABOUT *L. S*TEELE'S NEW RELEASES? *J*OIN HER NEWSLETTER **HERE**

*F*OLLOW *L. S*TEELE ON **AMAZON**

*F*OLLOW *L. S*TEELE ON **B**OOK**B**UB

*F*OLLOW *L. S*TEELE ON **G**OODREADS

*F*OLLOW *L. S*TEELE ON **F**ACEBOOK

*F*OLLOW *L. S*TEELE ON **I**NSTAGRAM

*J*OIN *L. S*TEELE'S SECRET **F**ACEBOOK *R*EADER *G*ROUP

*F*OR MORE BOOKS BY *L. S*TEELE CLICK **HERE**

*A*NSWER TO THE QUESTION AT THE FRONT OF THE BOOK: *I*N THE *D*ICTIONARY

FREE BOOK

How to scan a QR code?
1. Open the camera app on your phone or tablet.
2. Point the camera at the QR code.

3. Tap the banner that appears on your phone or tablet.
4. Follow the instructions on the screen to finish signing in.

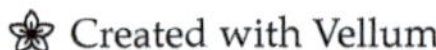 Created with Vellum